GUILT TRIP

VICKY DODDS BOOK 5

ED JAMES

This is a work of fiction. Names, characters, businesses, places, events and incidents are either the products of the author's imagination or used in a fictitious manner. Any resemblance to actual persons, living or dead, or actual events is purely coincidental.

DAY 1

Sunday

1

He stretches out against the bus stop, pushing his back until it clicks.

There.

Makes him grunt. He swears he can hear the echoes in the quiet street, darkening in the winter chill. No movement, just boxy ex-council houses and satellite dishes. Cars too expensive for this part of Dundee, the ice on the windscreens twinkling under the sodium-yellow streetlights. A missing cat poster is plastered on the Perspex shelter, another pair of them wrapped around the nearest lamppost.

How could *he* live here?

Him of all people?

Scratch that – how could *anyone* bring themselves to live here?

His watch says half three and there's still no sign of him.

Street's getting dark and it's still deadly silent.

Almost.

Just the background thump leaking from somewhere. He

can't place the source. An hour he's been here and neither the beat nor the tempo's changed. Just that constant thud. Maybe someone's making the music.

Kids these days...

A flash of lights at the end of the street traces across the Toyotas, Fords and Vauxhalls. An old Audi rattles across the icy tarmac, then stops a few feet away from him. A faster bass drum tattoo leaks out of the windows, droning bagpipes playing ten times faster than physically possible. Tartan techno, they call it. Got to love it, eh?

He pushes himself flat against the bus shelter, pulling his coat tight.

White reverse lights flash on, haloing in the frosted Perspex. The engine whirs and the car swims back into a reverse park. A phlegmatic cough and the engine dies.

Then *he* gets out of the car.

Gavin Mason. Tall and dark. Good looking for Dundee, but still far from being a film star. Hair coiffed at the front, shaved at the sides. Puffer jacket and black trousers, beige Timberlands like it's still 1998. He burps into his fist, the air misting around him, locks his car – no remote locking – and gets a flash of lights for his trouble. That slow gait of his, wandering up the path at the side of the house, head tilted to the side like he's sleepwalking. He stops and looks around, his eyes thin slits, his face glowing from his phone's backlight, then he unlocks the door and disappears inside his little box. The bottom left of a four-flat block, two storeys, pebble-dashed breeze blocks.

Gavin's coffin.

He puts his hands in his deep pockets and touches the hammer. The handle's cold, even through the gloves.

Five.

Four.

Three.

Two.

One.

He gets up and slopes off down the street towards the house.

A woman walks towards him, hunched over, wearing a duffel coat. Wispy beard on her chin, her mouth twisted. 'Excuse me, son?'

He flashes her a kind smile. 'Sorry, I'm running late.'

Her face wrinkles. 'Just wondering if you've seen my cat.' She taps another poster on another lamppost. Even her fingers have liver spots. 'Have you seen Whispa?'

'Sorry.' He shrugs, holding up his gloved hands. 'Don't live here. Just visiting a mate.'

'Aye, okay.' She trudges off up the street and opens a garden gate with a screech. Seconds later, she's inside her own box, a mirror image of Gavin's.

No movement inside his house. Good.

He crosses the road and creeps up the drive. No noise, no music. No Nirvana, Slipknot, Muse. Just silence. Can't even hear that bloody bass drum from over here.

The toilet flushes inside.

He touches the hammer in his coat, checking it's accessible, then knocks on the door, three times, rasping his knuckles.

An engine rumbles behind him.

A taxi.

Shit.

And *she* gets out. Emma. Blonde hair mostly hidden by a parka hood. Barely as tall as the door she exits from.

He slips over the wall into the back garden and crouches low, holding his breath, keeping an eye on the flat.

His back is bloody killing him.

Shitting hell. What's *she* doing here?

'Thanks!' She hauls up her tight jeans, then sets off up the drive, boot heels clicking.

The door bursts open and Gavin peers out. Looks around, then he spots Emma.

She winks at him, a sly grin on her face. 'Hello, you.'

Gavin thumbs back at the door. 'How did you do that?'

'Do what?' She wraps her arms around him, smothering him in a deep kiss.

He loosens his grip on the hammer.

Gavin's hand crawls over Emma's jeans, then slithers under the surface like a worm. She slaps his hand, then pushes him inside, tearing her coat's zip down.

The door slams, the sound rattling around the street. Still quiet, though he can hear the sodding thud of that bloody bass drum. Seems even faster now, but that just might be his own heartbeat.

They didn't care who saw them, did they?

Means they don't care what happens to them.

He's got to wait this out, though, so he settles into a crouch. And he really needs to click his sodding back again.

BLOODY HELL, it's cold. His breath's freezing in the air. Bitter wind biting at his neck. Can't even feel his back now.

He checks the watch and it's half five. Two hours he's been here. Two. Hours. Dark now.

Shite almighty.

A thin sliver of streetlight crawls over the frosted back lawn.

'Whispa!' That old dear's out on the street again, doing her hunched-over shuffle. Hopeful eyes scanning the street. 'Whispa! Here, boy!'

Doesn't see him.

Can't see him.

Gavin's lights are on. Bedroom and hall.

He grabs his ankles and pushes up until his spine cracks.

THERE WE GO.

Another taxi crawls up the street and pulls up onto the pavement with a honk of the horn.

The flat door rattles open and Emma steps out, her coat zipped up. 'We can't, Gav. Not now. Okay?'

The sweet smell of dope leeches out of the flat. Strong stuff, too. Typical of him. So bloody typical.

'We need to tell him.' Gavin's voice, deep, all vowels. 'This isn't fair.'

'Who said it's got to be fair?' Emma shrugs and reaches over to peck him on the cheek, then caresses it. 'I'll see you tomorrow, okay?'

'Wish you could stay.' Gavin steps out, topless, just wearing jeans, low enough to see his bald hips. Wispy coils of hair on his chest, a dragon tattoo snaking up his right arm. He kisses her, wrapping his bare arms around her, the dragon swallowing her up, then he breaks off and pats her on the bum. 'I love you.'

'I know.' Emma sashays down the path and skips into the taxi. It trundles off, and Emma's waving, mouthing "I love you" back. Then it's gone at the end of the street.

Gavin's standing there, arms wrapped around his body,

sucking on his joint, shaking his head. Then he trudges back over to the door.

And he's on him, battering the hammer off his skull.

The dull edge bounces off his temple with a sickening crunch.

He wraps his free arm around Gavin's throat, hand over his mouth.

The joint drops onto the path, scattering out sparks. It flickers out.

Gavin's scratching at his arm, tugging at his wrist, his nails digging into the leather. He manages to get in another hit from a bastard of an angle and Gavin goes down.

He pulls him inside, a dead weight, his naked back squeaking on the lino, then he nudges the door shut.

Quiet in here. That empty sound.

The seats are those old-style ones, all hard wood and rounded, like they should be on a veranda in the Wild West. The place is like a boy's bedroom. Video game posters on two walls, rock bands on the others.

He gets out the hammer again and sucks in a deep breath.

This is the hard part.

Gavin's blinking, looking at him. Blood running down his face from both wounds..

He lifts the hammer, his gloved hands tight around the handle.

Shit. Can he really do this? Hitting him a couple of times is totally different from ending his life.

Gavin pushes backwards, eyes wide.

He swings out with the hammer. A wet crack. Blood oozes down Gavin's forehead. Then another blow, in the same place. Crack.

He hits him again and again and again and again and again.

Ten.

Twenty.

Forty-five.

Sixty.

Holy shit.

Gavin's dead eyes stare through him.

His breathing's out of control, his heart thudding.

He reaches over and feels for a pulse through the glove.

Gavin's definitely dead.

He tosses the hammer on the floor and slumps back against the units, sucking in gasps of air, tears stinging his cheeks.

Christ. That was way harder than he expected. He shuts his eyes and lets the release course through him.

He reaches into his pocket and fumbles the plastic bag. It floats down to the floor. His hands aren't working properly.

He's absolutely covered. Blood and gore all over his clothes. He went a bit overboard there, but after what Gavin's done… He deserves worse. Way worse.

He strips down and chucks the trackies and T-shirt in, then pads through to Gavin's bathroom, stark bollock naked, save for the socks. Shower over the bath, but at least it's an electric and not an old tap job. Not the first time he's had to shower like this, probably not the last either, but the little bar of soap he brought is cutting through everything. The plughole's a red mess. He showers until the soap's all gone and the water is draining away clear and the bits of blood and brain aren't in his hair.

He gets out and dries off using a dirty towel, but leaves the shower running at full heat, a neat forensic countermeasure. He takes the towel through to the bedroom.

He can't look at the bed. The unmade bed. The unmade bed that stinks of sex. He just can't.

He kicks off the soaking socks, wrapping them in the towel.

Old black 501s and a white SUGARMAN T-shirt are on top of the chair. Perfect, though SUGARMAN went shit after his second album. Too gangsta. One of those big outdoors coats someone from Oasis would wear is hanging up. He takes the clothes back through to the kitchen and puts his own clothes and towel into the bag, stuffing the hammer in deep. They'll be burnt and that'll be chucked in the Tay within the hour. He steps back into his shoes and he's ready to leave.

DON'T LOOK AT THE BODY.

Wait.

Gavin's keys...

There, on the table by the door. The four Audi rings, interlinked, the leather tattered and worn. Gloves back on and he pockets them, opposite side from the weapons.

One last check. He's left nothing. No traces, nothing that can come back to him.

He sucks in the thick air, heavy with dope and the acrid tang of that soap. Getting quite damp in there now.

Definitely nothing left behind, no forensics traces.

Didn't touch the door and gloves anyway. Stepped over the floor. Gloves on to attack Gavin with the hammer. Socks to walk through. Showered with socks on. Clothes and towel in the bag. Dressed in Gavin's clothes.

Sorted.

He leaves through the door and walks on like he lives here, his head freezing in the cold air, stepping down the path.

He stops dead at the end.

Blue lights flashing, heading this way.

Christ.

He's been so careful. Hasn't he?

He races over to Gavin's car and unlocks the door. Drops the keys. Shit! He picks them up, opens it and gets in, then slumps back in the seat. His back crunches and he almost shouts.

The squad car passes him and double parks a few doors down.

He tracks their movement in the wing mirror. The officers get out. Both men, both big. Staring up and down the street.

The first officer limps across the road and frowns up at Gavin's flat, nostrils twitching. The second points down the street and shouts something. The first one nods and they shuffle off, the second speaking into his radio.

The music.

They're here for the bloody music.

Someone's called to complain about the bloody music.

Thank God for that din.

He breathes out and twists the key in the ignition and gets a throaty growl from the engine.

Perfect.

2

Vicky trotted down the last few steps, keeping a hand on the rail, then trudged across the chessboard hallway. The light was on the blink, a Morse code pattern flashing across the ancient tiles. The door shut in her face.

Fantastic.

She opened it and stepped out into the freezing night.

Up ahead, Jamie was shivering. 'Mum, I'm freezing.'

Cheeky wee sod.

His glasses caught the streetlights, his attention locked on his phone, held side-on like a camera. Recording a video, *again*. And he wouldn't take a telling. On that or wearing just a Day-Glo orange hoodie in this temperature. And his hair was soaking wet from his swimming event. He was looking more and more like his father every day, but his hair was way too long, swooping down over his eyes.

'Jamie, wait!' Vicky charged after him onto the pavement

and grabbed his hand. Traffic thrummed past. A bus hissed as it pulled in at the stop.

He stood on the pavement edge, staring into his mobile again. 'What?'

'This is a busy road and you're staring at that phone all the time.' Vicky joined him at the edge, stepping between the parked cars, grabbing his hand and shifting his head left and right like when Bella was little. 'Dad and Bells are at home, waiting for us. Fish suppers tonight.'

While Vicky wasn't his mother, it felt like he was her son. Especially now things were on the way to being formalised, with that glinting ring on her finger. She plipped her car, the lights flashing across the road. 'Come on.' A long gap in the traffic, so she grabbed her son's hand and pulled him across the road towards the car.

Bella was at that age where she didn't want to even be seen with her mum, let alone holding hands with her in public. Jamie, though, was always doing it, maybe because of who he'd lost.

Vicky twisted the key in the ignition and hauled her belt on while Jamie got in. 'Let's get you home.'

Jamie buckled in and the engine caught.

Vicky's mobile rang.

'Perfect...' She reached into her jacket for her mobile and checked the display:

Forrester calling...

What the hell did he want?

'Jamie, I've got to take this, okay?'

He didn't even nod, just kept his focus on his phone.

She answered it and put it to her right ear, so Jamie would only hear half of the chat. 'Hey, sir.'

'Doddsy.' Forrester let out a deep breath. 'You still in the station?'

'No, I finished up half an hour ago. Paperwork's all in your inbox.' She looked over at Jamie. 'Had to collect Jamie from his swimming competition. Rob's collecting Bells from a sleepover and—'

'Aye, spare me the details.' Forrester sighed down the line. 'Need you to do me a wee favour.'

Those favours were never small and never got repaid. 'What's up?'

'Got a lad in Craigie who's supposed to call in every day at six. It's ten past and he hasn't called.'

Vicky got that sour taste in her mouth. She knew precisely where this was going. 'You want me to visit, right?'

'Well, I'd ask Mac, but he's busy. And it's on your way home. Lad's probably not charged his mobile or fallen asleep. You know how it is.'

And Vicky was the idiot who answered the call on a Sunday night.

Cars fizzed past, barely slowing for the roundabout.

She massaged her temple – she really needed to get home. Get Jamie home. That fish supper had her name on it.

She looked over at her son, his phone screen as bright as a torch. 'Give me the details.'

'A witness protection deal. Lad lives on his own. Name of Gavin Mason.'

'Left up ahead.'

Vicky slowed at a set of traffic lights, opposite a boarded-up pub, the For Sale sign swaying in the wind. She leaned over to switch the heating up a few notches, then rubbed her hands together and glanced over at Jamie. At least having him on navigation duties stopped him filming.

Gavin Mason...

The name meant nothing to her. Nobody's relative, either. Well, not on the father's side. Witness protection job could mean a name change, though.

'Mum. It's green.'

Vicky put the car in gear and drove on, veering left onto Craigie Road. Low-slung boxy council houses, three or four satellite dishes on each one, opposite a medium-rise blocks of flats, all with a Soviet style. Parked cars on both sides thinned the road like fur on arteries. Two bus stops sat almost exactly opposite each other, surrounded by trees, their arthritic branches dusted with frost.

Vicky pulled into a parking bay in front of the address. She'd visited so many houses and flats in this area over the years that she could find any number blindfold.

A block of four flats, two on each floor. Small gardens in front, bigger ones out the back. No signs of life inside any of them.

On the pavement, a fat man lurched from step to step, arm outstretched as his equally fat Labrador hauled him along.

Jamie unclipped his seatbelt and cracked his knuckles.

'Where do you think you're going?'

'Come on, Mum!'

'Stay here and keep the door locked. No ifs, no buts.'

Jamie folded his arms, hiding the pout he'd inherited from his father. 'Can't *believe* this.'

'Stay here or you'll lose your mobile for a week. Okay?' Vicky got out of the car and the wind whipped her coat open. She zipped it up and slipped on a pair of gloves, then locked the car and walked towards Gavin Mason's flat, cold air knifing into her lungs.

She hated being hard on Jamie, but the way their particular family dynamic worked with her and Rob swapping bad-cop roles for the other's kid seemed to be working. Slightly.

Window-rattling music blasted out from a house a few doors over, a fast heartbeat of bass and clattering drums, the kind of racket kids overdosed to.

Whoever had stuck the stone cladding on the bottom right flat hadn't told the other three, all still covered in magnolia harling. At least it seemed to be magnolia under the street lighting. A patch of bare earth instead of a front garden, a low wall at the back. Darkness behind, probably a disused drying green, the weeds getting a winter breather.

No music, no smells.

Vicky opened the gate and walked up the drive, frosted over and slippery. *Gavin Mason* was stencilled on a plastic rectangle just below a panel of frosted glass lit up from inside. She knocked and stepped back.

A roach sat on the ground; the bitter tang of dope hung on the air.

Still no reply. No movement inside.

Aye, she was getting a bad feeling about this.

But this was Forrester's thing. She just had to check on him. So he wasn't in, that wasn't her problem. Just had to report back.

Aye...

Keep telling yourself that...

She flipped the letter box and peered through. Couldn't see anything. A strong whiff of dope smoke from inside. Damp air too. 'Hello? Anybody home?' She waited. Still nothing, so she knocked again. Nothing. She tried the handle and the door slid open. 'Mr Mason? It's the police.'

The smell of stale pizza hung under the sweet-sweat whiff of cannabis. Skunk. Not a casual smoker.

Vicky entered. 'Gavin?'

Kitchen-living room. The walls were a dirty off-white. Threadbare red carpet, more bare patch than threads. Scabby brown two-seater settee. Huge wall-mounted TV. Framed posters on the wall – footballers, golfers and a couple of bands she'd never heard of. Not a million miles from Jamie's bedroom walls, just missing the giant robots with even bigger guns and swords.

Whatever this guy had done, who he was in protection from, it clearly hadn't paid off for him.

A closed laptop dominated the coffee table. Glowing with blue and purple lights. A gaming laptop. Huge thing like Jamie kept pestering them for his Christmas. Next to it was a wallet, a smartphone and a heaped-up ashtray.

Vicky opened the wallet and found Gavin Mason's driver's license.

Mid-twenties. Short dark hair, stern look at the camera.

Well, some people would leave their wallet behind, but nobody that age would leave their mobile behind.

A signed Rangers shirt took pride of place in the middle of the wall, next to some lemon-yellow units with a fake-oak counter. A rusty smell like... blood.

'Shit, shit, shit.'

Gavin Mason lay on his back, a dark puddle on the laminate where his head should be, shaped like a speech balloon.

3

'The ambulance is two minutes away. Over.'

Not that Gavin Mason needed it now.

Vicky's skin tightened all over her body. Her ears hummed like a fridge. 'Perfect, thanks.' She dragged her gaze from that sightless stare. In a painting, the eyes followed you around, watching you. With a corpse, they looked right through you, as if you didn't exist. Instinct made her want to reach out and lower the eyelids. But she didn't. 'What about local support?'

'Just ahead of the ambulance. Should be with you any minute.'

'Okay.' Vicky turned around and walked over to the door. Her foot slid out from under her and she went down, face hitting the lino, her cheek bearing the brunt of it.

Her phone scattered across the damp floor.

She pushed up to all fours. The floor was wet. So wet in here – sounded like the shower was on. Her pride hurt a lot more than her face. Still, at least nobody had been around to see her fall like that. She almost saw the funny side in it.

'Hello? Ma'am?'

Vicky reached over for her mobile and picked it up. 'Hi, I need to hang up now.' She cut the call and sat up, rubbing at her cheek. It'd probably bruise.

'Mum, are you okay?' Jamie stood in the threshold, mouth open.

'Get out!' Vicky got up and charged over.

He was strong, peering into the flat. 'Holy shit, is that Gavin Mason?' His eyes widened and he threw up onto the path.

Shit, shit, shit.

Vicky grabbed his arm and dragged him back along the path towards the car. 'Jamie, are you okay?'

He shut up and let her take over. 'Was he dead?'

'He was. I'm sorry you saw that.' The street music was still thumping away. 'I told you to stay in the car.'

'You were *ages*, Mum. I got worried about you. Then I started doing some video and I saw you fall over.'

'This is a crime scene.' Vicky led Jamie towards the car. 'I need you to stay here.'

Jamie slouched out onto the pavement then over to the car and let himself into the back. Wasn't going to sit in the front next to her, was he?

The gate banged in the wind.

Vicky closed it, then took out her mobile and dialled.

'Hey, are you still at that house?' Rob's voice was almost a shout.

Set Vicky's nerves even more on edge. 'Rob, something's happened. Jamie's okay, I just need you to come here. I'll text you the address.'

The line crackled. 'We're coming. I'll bring Bella.'

'Thanks, Rob.'

'You okay?'

'I'm fine.' Vicky loosened her collar. Even in the bitter cold, sweat prickled her neck. 'Listen, I need to go. Sorry. And thank you for being you.'

'Always, Vicky. Always.' The lined clicked dead.

Vicky dialled Forrester's number.

Answered straight away. Someone was shouting in the background and loud cheers swelled up. No doubt at the rugby club. 'Have you got a hold of him yet?'

The street was now choked with vehicles – panda cars, a couple of ambulances, the crime scene van, the pathologist's four-by-four. Uniformed plod guarded the area outside the cordon, hands tucked inside the stab vests over high-visibility yellow jackets.

The crime scene manager shivered by the path, armed with a clipboard and a pencil moustache.

Vicky sat in the driver's seat, gripping the wheel like a throat.

Detective Sergeant Euan MacDonald was in the passenger seat. Long overcoat, dark suit. Scribbling in his notebook but kept glancing up at Vicky. 'Let me get this straight. You *don't* know the deceased?'

'Never heard of him until tonight when Forrester called.'

From the back seat: 'His name's Gavin Mason.'

Vicky turned. 'Jamie, DS MacDonald was talking to me. We don't—'

'But he's dead!'

Vicky fixed him with a long stare. '*Jamie*.'

'He—'

'Shhh.'

MacDonald cleared his throat. 'So neither of you know him?'

'We've been over this.' Fire burnt up Vicky's neck. 'Forrester asked me to check up on him. Door was open, dead body lying there. That's it.'

'Mum, was he murdered?'

MacDonald swallowed. 'So Jamie saw the...'

'Followed me inside, even though I *told* him to stay in the car.'

'I've got it on video.' Jamie held up his mobile, playing jerky footage of him walking up to the house, then showed Vicky inside, standing next to the corpse. Then falling on her face. 'See?'

Vicky snatched the mobile out of his hand. 'What the hell?'

'Hey! That's my phone!'

'This is... You've filmed a dead body.'

Silence while MacDonald scribbled and Jamie pouted.

Vicky couldn't believe he'd done that. 'Have you shared this with anyone?'

'No, Mum.' Jamie folded his arms around him. 'Can I have my phone back?'

'Not for a bit.' She flicked through the open apps. Instagram, TikTok, Snapchat, WhatsApp. 'Doesn't look like he's shared this video.'

'Good.' MacDonald tapped his pen off the notebook. 'So you definitely haven't heard of this guy before tonight?'

'Euan, I've told you, no. What is this?'

'Just doing my job, boss.' MacDonald swivelled round to Jamie. 'What about you? Name mean anything?'

'I'm being quiet.'

Vicky rolled her eyes. '*Jamie.*'

He huffed out a breath. 'I've never heard of him, no.'

MacDonald wrote that down, then peered over the top of the seat at Jamie. 'Must've been pretty upsetting what you saw in there, eh?'

'It's kind of cool, really.' Jamie shrugged. 'Kayden's going to be well revved when I show him at school tomorrow.' He shot a glare at Vicky. '*After* I get my phone back.'

MacDonald turned all the way around, knees on the seat. 'Need a sample of your DNA, Jamie. That okay?'

He frowned. 'What for?'

'Well, you were sick outside the house, so we need to eliminate you from the crime scene to help us find the baddie who did this. Your mum here's already on the system, so we need to get you on there too.'

Jamie was nodding fast now. First time in years he'd been interested in something that wasn't made by Samsung or Sony. 'Will it hurt?'

'Just need to take you to the station and a CSI will pop a cotton bud in your mouth. You won't feel a thing.'

'Will it be Uncle Andrew? He's a CSI, isn't he?'

MacDonald winked at him. 'Aye, it probably will be. And you can tell Kayden all about that too.'

'Cool as. Will you take my statement then?'

'Sure thing. Come on, then.' MacDonald got out and leaned against the car, waiting.

Jamie was still in the back. 'When will I get my phone back, Mum?'

'I'll try and get it to you tonight, okay? Promise.'

'Friends don't break promises, remember?' The back door clicked open and Jamie got out, chatting with MacDonald as they walked away.

'Jamie!' Rob was about twenty feet away, storming along the pavement, dragging Bella along behind him. He wore a track-suit, bright white shoes shining like his bald head.

Bella was all dolled up – thick winter jacket, stone-washed jeans tucked into Ugg boots. Her hair's designer windswept look was exaggerated by gusts of the real thing. Ten going on twenty-five.

Vicky got out of the car and sloped towards them. 'Rob.'

He grabbed her in a hug. 'Are you okay? What happened? Where is he?'

'I'm fine. He's fine.' Vicky broke off and took a step back, then ran a hand through Bella's hair, though she wasn't that far off her own height. 'He's off to have a DNA swab.'

'What, why?'

She jabbed her thumb in the direction of the van. 'Um, Jamie entered the crime scene.'

'A *crime* scene?' Rob took a deep breath. 'Vicky…'

'There's a body in the house. I didn't know that when we got here. He was filming me because, well, he films everything, and I fell over.'

'Right. Well, it'll give him something else to bring up in therapy when he's older.'

'Dad!' Jamie wandered over with MacDonald, doing his best to slouch against the wind.

Rob ran over and put his arms around his boy. 'You okay?'

'I'm well revved.' Jamie pulled back and beamed at MacDonald. 'I'm part of a murder investigation! Euan said I had to wait until you got here before he takes my statement. And I've got to give a DNA swab!'

MacDonald smiled at Rob. 'DS Euan MacDonald.' He held out a hand. 'Colleague of your... eh, of Vicky's.'

Rob puffed his chest out, eyes narrowed. 'She's my fiancée.'

'Congrats. Had one of them myself once.' MacDonald gave Vicky some side eye. 'Need to ask your son some questions about what happened down at the station. That all right?'

'Jamie, go with DS MacDonald here and I'll join you in a bit.' Rob folded his arms. 'I need a minute with your mother.'

'We'll go sit in my car, out of the wind.' MacDonald led Jamie away.

Once they were out of earshot, Rob grimaced. 'Is that him?' His voice was low.

Vicky looked at Bella, who had her headphones on and was dancing away, oblivious to anything. 'Aye, it is. Listen, I'm sorry this has happened. This shouldn't have happened. And I'm sorry it did. I... I didn't have a choice. It was supposed to be... I'm sorry.'

'We'll chat later.'

'Of course.'

Rob waved over to MacDonald's car, where Jamie was waving his hands as he talked. 'Right now, our son needs me over there.' He held out a hand. 'Come on, Bella.'

Vicky could only watch as her family walked away from her.

She had no idea what to do. She was the DI, sure, but was this her case? Wasn't even on duty. She checked her watch.

'What the bloody hell happened here, Doddsy?' Forrester

was standing a few feet away, hands on hips, scowling. His legs and arms seemed too long for his jeans and jacket. He ran a hand through his silver hair. 'It's definitely him?'

'No idea, sir.' Vicky breathed out. 'I'm just doing you a favour.' She shook her head. 'Jamie got into the crime scene.'

'Oh, Christ. Seriously?'

'He's with Euan. And his dad.'

Forrester caught Rob's eye and both men waved. 'How long had he been dead?'

'Hard to say for sure, but hours rather than days.'

'Right, right.'

Vicky waited for him to look at her. 'Who is Gavin Mason?'

'That's on a need-to-know basis.'

'That ship's sailed so far away it's dropped off the edge of the disc, sir. Whoever he—'

'Vicky, even I don't know the full story, okay? He got caught up in some shady shite down in London and Essex. Bad boy, I think. I'll get the full details when I get back to the office. But it's a Serious Crime case, hooks up with the Met's Major Investigations and Essex police's equivalent.' Forrester snorted in the direction of the house. 'Looks like she's done, though.' He held a hand aloft and got a nod of acknowledgement from a suited figure lumbering down the path, clutching a medical bag, silhouetted by the arc lamps in the bare-earth garden. 'Dr Arbuthnott, I presume?'

She signed out of the crime scene and joined them by the side of the road, mumbling something into her face mask.

Forrester gestured at her mouth.

Arbuthnott lowered the hood of her crime scene suit and tugged her mask to the side. 'Sorry, these have become a daily habit, haven't they?' She glanced back at the house. 'Just saying, Inspector, that Mr Mason was killed sometime very recently. I'd suggest the fatality occurred around about, mmm, five o'clock, according to my calculations. Give or take, but likely take. A blunt trauma to the cranium. *Several* blunt traumas.'

Forrester glowered at her. 'Somebody whacked him about the head. Murder weapon?'

'Probably a hammer of some sorts, judging by the shape. No sign of it, though.' Arbuthnott started to walk away. 'Now, the body's ready to take away. Tomorrow morning's mostly free if you need it fast-tracked.'

Forrester gave her a thumbs-up. 'Consider that request already in your inbox.'

Arbuthnott nodded and headed off towards her car. 'Catch you later.'

Vicky saw Gavin Mason's dead eyes staring at her. She blinked it away.

Forrester gave his watch a scowl. 'Right, let me—'

MacDonald appeared, scowling. 'Statement's done and dusted.' He thumbed backwards, where Rob was helping Jamie and Bella into the back of his car. 'Considine's done some digging. Victim's next of kin is his mother, name of Doreen Mason. Lives in Broughty Ferry. No information on the father.'

Vicky started over to Rob's car. 'See you tomorrow, sir.'

Forrester was staring into his mobile, oblivious. 'Sorry?'

'Said, I'll see you tomorrow.'

Forrester stood up tall, pocketing his phone. 'Sorry, need you to head round there now with Euan. Speak to her, see what you can get while we sort this mess out.'

'And I'm not on duty, sir.'

'Neither is he. Neither am I.' Forrester narrowed his eyes at Vicky. 'This is a murder case, so consider yourself on duty, alright?'

Aye, she didn't have a choice. 'Can you get someone to process Jamie, then?'

4

Vicky leaned back in her seat and focused on the road ahead. Eastern Dundee blazed past, rows of post-war council houses and tall blocks of flats, now giving way to the gentle curve of Victorian terracing, with grander houses set back from the road, harking back to Dundee's days as a mill town, when Broughty Ferry had money at the expense of brutal labour in India and the mills of Dundee. She turned a corner, following MacDonald into Mrs Mason's street. A long row of bungalows with a cracking view down to the Tay and Broughty Castle, all lit up.

She parked behind MacDonald and opposite a Škoda kitted out with the familiar Battenberg livery of yellow and blue checks, 'POLICE' stencilled in bright orange along the side. As she got out, a door opened a couple of houses along.

A uniformed police officer started walking down the drive, limping slightly. 'Can I help you?' Closer up, he seemed about fifteen, acne pocking his forehead and cheeks, a cluster of chronic spots on his chin.

'DS MacDonald. You got a name?'

'PC Billy Dewar. Sorry.' He seemed the type to apologise for his very existence. He glanced at the warrant card and compared it with Vicky's face. 'And you are...?'

Couldn't read, either. 'DI Vicky Dodds. Left my card at home so you'll just have to take my word for it.'

'No worries. Been expecting a couple of detectives.' Dewar's shoulders slumped. 'I drew the short straw. First death message. You guys done many?'

'Sure have.' MacDonald winced. 'Doesn't get any easier.'

'I can imagine. Glad I did it, though. Lads at the station think I'm a bit of a muppet 'cos I look about twelve.' Dewar paused, probably hoping for one of them to contradict him. Neither did. 'Not for me to judge, but Johnny Gilmour's the one who—'

'Look, another time, if you don't mind.' MacDonald put a hand on his shoulder and steered him back along the pavement. 'How did Mrs Mason take the news?'

'Okay, I suppose. A bit flat, like she hasn't taken it in yet?' Dewar stopped mid-stride, his face scrunching up as he thought about the question. 'She was in a pretty bad way till Emma arrived. That's her son's missus. The other one, that is. The son who's still alive. Douglas. Got here about ten minutes ago. His missus, I mean. Not the son.' He pointed at a baby-blue Fiat 500 across the street. 'That's hers there. Hybrid one, like. More of a petrol engine guy myself, but you've got to save the environment and the range on those is getting better and better, isn't it?'

MacDonald smiled. 'And where is he?'

'Who?'

'The other son.'

Dewar shrugged. 'No idea, sorry.'

Vicky held out a hand. 'Let's get this over with, then.'

'Okay.' Dewar leaned his weight on his right leg and winced. 'Sorry about the slow-going here. Girlfriend dropped a car battery on my foot this morning.'

MacDonald focused on Vicky. His face was even shinier than usual. 'Have to ask. What was your girlfriend doing with a car battery?'

'Fancies herself as a mechanic.' Dewar crunched up the pebbled driveway, passing the paved garden, just one flowerbed left, a clutch of shrubs and plants huddling together in the wind. 'We were trying to get her dad's old Capri started. Classic, but he rides the clutch like a—' He blushed at Vicky. 'So Jen replaced the battery. Got it working, after a fashion, but not without certain casualties.' He opened the front door and hobbled inside. Daft bastard shouldn't even be on duty. He paused outside an oak door a few feet along the hallway. 'They're in here.' He knocked once and let himself in.

Vicky led MacDonald through.

The sitting room was about three metres square. Too much furniture squeezed into the small space – two sofas, an armchair and a dining table. An electric fire blasted away, both bars burning orange. TV news played in the background, the volume muted, warfare footage from a desert somewhere.

The uniformed officer, perched on a stool in the corner, was a barrel of a man. Mug of tea in one hand, half-eaten Tunnock's teacake in the other. Had to be PC Gilmour, Dewar's partner. The kind of guy who'd let the injured man walk outside while he tucked into a biscuit. Or a cake. Still, it seemed like he'd bitten into the foil.

Vicky quickly put names to the other faces.

Mrs Mason shivered in the armchair nearest the fire, her white hair thick and curly, eyes puffy and red. She was wrapped up in a baggy woollen jumper, blanket folded over her legs, grey knitted slippers poking out beneath.

Emma Mason sat next to her. Mid-twenties, pretty face with a boy-ish frame. Light-red hair cropped and messy. Long-sleeved cardigan with huge buttons. Black jeans, black ankle boots with heels you could lose an eye on.

MacDonald stepped past Dewar into the middle of the room. 'DS Euan MacDonald. I work for the Dundee Major Investigation Team. My colleague here is DI Vicky Dodds.'

Colleague, not boss. Aye, spot who was still smarting about not getting the promotion.

'We're very sorry for your loss.' Vicky left a space, watched their reaction.

Emma dabbed at her eyes.

Doreen Mason rubbed at her upper arms, staring into the fire. 'These laddies said my boy's dead.' She looked up. 'Is it true?'

'I'm afraid it is.' Vicky stepped over and hunkered down in front of her, looking her in the eye. 'We believe someone murdered him.'

Her hand covered her mouth, the pink-painted nails chipped in a few places. 'Who?'

'We don't know that yet.'

'But... why? Why would someone kill my wee laddie?'

'We don't know that either, Mrs Mason.'

'Doreen. Call me Doreen. Mrs Mason makes me sound like an old wifie. Would you like some tea? It's very rude not to offer you some tea.'

'I know these are very difficult circumstances, but we'd like to ask you a few questions about Gavin, if you feel up to it.'

'Aye, sure.' Doreen pushed her blankets off her legs. 'I'll just go and put the...' She slung her arms around PC Dewar and cried into his chest.

Vicky stood up.

Emma got up too, resting her hand on her mother-in-law's arm. 'I'll make sure they get a cuppa, Doreen. Okay?'

Doreen nodded, kept her focus on her lap.

Dewar mouthed, 'Help!'

Vicky followed Emma and MacDonald into the kitchen. Dark-green units, granite worktop, silver appliances, everything spotless.

Emma sat on a stool by the breakfast bar, hand going to her stomach. She caught Vicky's gaze. 'You didn't actually want a cup of tea, did you?'

Vicky leaned against the Belfast sink in the window. 'Did you and Gavin get along, Mrs Mason?'

'Call *me* Emma, please. Two Mrs Masons could get confusing.' She rubbed at her nose. 'Gav's a nice guy. Could have a much worse brother-in-law.' She grimaced, a tear beading in her eye. 'Can't believe he's dead...'

MacDonald joined Emma at the breakfast bar and flipped open his notebook. 'When was the last time you saw him?'

'Thursday. Well, I think it was Thursday.' Emma stared into space. 'Aye, Thursday. Gav came round to pick Doug up at about half seven. They were going for a couple of pints in town, but Doug was late home from work, as usual, so I had a coffee with Gav while he waited.'

'Doug's your husband, right?'

'Right. Gav's brother.'

'You didn't go with them?'

'Didn't want to crash. Brothers, you know?'

'And how did Gavin seem?'

'The usual, I suppose.' Emma shrugged. 'He takes each day as it comes. Nothing ever fazes him.'

'You didn't notice anything unusual in his behaviour?'

'Not really. We weren't close.'

Vicky leaned back against the sink and raised her eyebrows at MacDonald. He ignored her, so she jumped in. 'Not really? Was there something?'

'No. Nothing. We talked about TV shows. Finally got him watching *Squid Game*. And he loved it.'

Vicky ignored MacDonald's glare. 'Did he mention having an argument with anyone? Nobody who might've wanted to harm him?'

Emma sniffed and plucked a handkerchief from a pocket in her cardigan. 'I told you. I don't know Gav that well. Sorry.' She blew her nose. 'He's a nice guy and everything. We get on okay. But he's just my brother-in-law.'

MacDonald smiled at Emma. 'You know if Gavin was seeing anyone?'

'Usually had a girl on the scene. Never anyone serious.'

'Any idea who's "on the scene" at the moment?'

'No one I know of. Doug might.'

Vicky frowned at her. 'Where is your husband?'

Emma fiddled with a chain on her neck. 'He's away at a conference.' She cleared her throat. 'Supposed to be there until Tuesday.'

'But I take it he knows?'

Emma sunk into the stool. 'Not been able to get hold of him yet.'

'Where is this conference? We can send a car to him.'

'It's down in Edinburgh.'

MacDonald scribbled in his notebook. 'Where does Gavin work?'

'In a bar on the Perth Road. The Worried Fishmonger.'

Vicky knew its predecessor from her time in uniform. Used to be a rough dive bar, always a fight breaking out. At lunchtime. And usually over a drug deal, which finally got it shut down and allowed some hipsters to buy it. She pushed away from the sink. 'Did Gavin ever mention any trouble with regulars or anything?'

A tear slid down Emma's cheek. 'Not to me.'

'No customers he'd had an argument with?'

'Look, I keep telling you. I don't know.' Emma wiped at the tear. 'Doug might know.' She grimaced, her face scrunching up. 'But you could, you know, visit the pub?'

5

Thick traffic on the Perth Road on a Sunday night, waves of it heading towards the centre.

Up ahead, MacDonald parked behind a blue Citroën and turned off the engine.

Vicky did the same. She let her seatbelt ride up and took a look around.

The Worried Fishmonger was trapped under scaffolding three floors high. Open-mesh sheeting flapped in the breeze above. No roofers on a Sunday, just an 'Open for business!' sign.

Two hipsters stood outside, sucking on vape sticks, shivering, their long beards obscuring the slogans on their T-shirts. Their beards were surely on a competition for the curliest in Britain.

Vicky got out of the car and barged between them.

Hardly anyone had taken notice of the sign as the place was empty. Dance music played over the speakers, slow and chilled. Seats and tables on three levels, one above and one below this. The walls had been stripped back to stonework, rough patches of brick breaking out all over. Citrusy beer fumes hung on the air like smoke used to, back when it was an under-age drinking den.

A long bar led down the side, anonymous beer taps without names or logos, just a number. A chalkboard on the wall gave the key – brewery, name, alcohol strength, tasting notes like it was wine. Everything tasted like grapefruit or orange peel or liquorice. One was called Lilt and the tasting note said: 'tastes like Lilt'.

A barman stroked a tablet screen. Maybe he was searching online for a new hairstyle because his perm was going to take a long time to come back into fashion. Even the hipsters weren't touching it. Bushy moustache, nose that had got all the growth hormones meant for the rest of him. He looked up and grinned at MacDonald, ignoring Vicky. 'What can I get you, pal?'

'Police.' MacDonald flipped open his warrant card. 'Need to speak to the manager?'

'Sorry, what's this about?'

'Gavin Mason.'

A squeal of laughter. 'What's that gadgie done now?'

'We just need to speak to his boss. They in?'

'That's me, aye. What can I do you for?'

Vicky scanned around the pub. 'Anywhere private we can do this?'

'Like that, eh?' The wee man walked out from behind the counter, his navy and green kilt flapping as he marched over to a room at the side, back stiff and straight. Either he was ex-military or his piles were playing up. He opened the door and led them into a little box crammed with filing cabinets. A grimy window overlooked the street at the back, another into the kitchen, where a giant in chef's clothes watched football on the TV while some burgers fried in front of him.

'Name's Kenneth Grove. Call me Kenny.' The wee man sat behind a glass desk and tucked his fingers into his stripy yellow-and-pink tank top. Dark pouches under his eyes. 'So. Gavin? What's he done?'

MacDonald lowered himself onto a chair on the near side of the desk, smiling as he took out his notebook. 'Works here, aye?'

'Aye. Lazy bas— guy.'

'He in today?'

'Gavin went home early. Is he all right?'

'What does he do here?'

'Pulls pints, takes orders for burgers. Not exactly rocket science, is it?' Kenny crossed his arms, rubbed his fingers up and down his unimpressive biceps. 'Decent worker, to be honest, if a bit lazy.' He scowled at the clock as if that could make a dead man turn up for a shift. 'Well liked.' Then he frowned, clearly catching on. 'Come on, what's this about?'

'We found his body this evening.'

'Aw, man alive.' Kenny slumped forward, his elbows cracking off the desk. 'Fuckity fuck.' He rubbed at his face. 'No way, man. No fucking way.'

MacDonald was staring at the floor. 'How's he seemed recently?'

'You know that prick.' Kenny rubbed tears from his face and looked up at the ceiling. 'Aye, maybe you don't. Prick's on an even keel all the time, never up nor down, eh?'

'Anybody here with a grudge against him?'

'Not that I can think of. Shite, I'm going to have to get onto the agency first thing tomorrow.' Kenny started stroking his arms again. 'Ah, fuckity fuck.'

'When I was in uniform, I was in here all the time. A bit rowdy on a Tuesday morning, if you catch my drift.' Vicky pushed away from the patch of wall she was leaning against. 'You ever get any trouble in here, Mr Grove?'

'Not since the old place shut.' Kenny rubbed at his nose. Like he was gearing up for another line. 'Had to keep it closed for six months to get rid of the old crowd. Bunch of jakey bastards.' He waved up at the ceiling. 'Wish we'd waited until those arseholes upstairs decided to renovate all those flats, you know? No end of hassle, man.'

MacDonald flashed him a smile, like he understood the irritation. 'Gavin never had to bar anyone, nothing like that?'

'Our punters are students. Fridays and Saturdays are busy with weekend warriors, but it's not like the old days. The heid-the-baws are all at home, getting tanked up on supermarket booze. And thank fuck for that.'

'How'd Gavin get on with your other staff?'

Another shrug from Kenny. 'Helpful, like. Friendly. Got a good team here, you know?'

Aye. This guy didn't know Gavin from Adam.

'Why'd he go home today?'

'Said he had the 'flu. Must be what's keeping everyone away, aye?'

'Must be.' MacDonald got to his feet, snapping his notebook shut. Clearly thought the same. 'Mind if we speak to your staff?'

'Ach, it's just...' Kenny shrugged. 'Who am I bloody kidding? There's nobody in tonight. Dirty Mike in the kitchen.'

'Dirty Mike?'

'Clean freak. Always spraying his surfaces. Only Monika in the bar. That's Monika with a "k", mind.'

'Mind if we speak to her?'

'Aye, sure. Fill your boots.' Kenny almost toppled the table over as he rounded it, then led back to the bar. 'Monika, you mind helping these two?'

The hipsters from outside returned just then, settling on a pair of stools not far away from the bar. Their schooner glasses were just below halfway. An invitation to get your drink spiked. If there'd been anyone here to do the spiking.

A barmaid walked back over. Dark hair, a permanent scowl on her face. 'Sure.' She wore a green waistcoat and cleaned some glasses, staring into space. Very dark eyes, used to the pits of boredom. Pin-straight nose, brown shoulder-length hair. Barely registered their presence. 'What's up?'

A bell rang somewhere. 'Just a wee minute.' Kenny sloped off up the stairs, carrying a pair of burgers, wooden spikes through the rolls like astronauts claiming the moon.

'Police. DS MacDonald.' He held up his warrant card. 'You Monika? With a "k"?'

'That's me. How can I help?' Sounded like she had cotton wool stuck up her nose. 'Flu or all the staff in here were doing lines in the toilets. Vicky could buy either.

MacDonald put his warrant card away. 'See Gavin Mason today?'

Monika blew air through her lips. 'No, but next time I see him, I'll kill him.'

'Aye?'

'Shouldn't have said that, should I?' She held up her hands. The black-painted nails matched her eyes. 'I didn't mean it. Just that I was on the early shift and him wimping out with bloody man 'flu meant I had to cover. Supposed to be away this weekend, but instead I'm stuck with Dirty Mike and Handsy Kenny.' She blew more air up her face, like she was trying to dislodge the fringe. 'Lucky we're not busy. Place is a disaster while all the work's going on.' She draped a towel over her shoulder. 'Why do you want to speak to him, anyway?'

'Need to—'

'Wait a minute.' Her eyes widened. Her gaze shifted from Vicky to MacDonald and back again. 'You're detectives.' She put her hand over her mouth. 'What's he done?'

Vicky glanced at MacDonald. 'Look, we just need to ask you about him. Friends, enemies, that kind of thing.'

Monika folded her arms and looked past Vicky. 'Be with you in a minute, mate.' She sighed, eyes darting between Vicky and MacDonald. 'Gav's a good guy. Friendly, hardworking. Always ready to swap a shift, despite what I just said.'

MacDonald flashed his understanding smile again, seemed to get some positive reaction from it. 'When was the last time you saw him?'

'Friday night? Both of us did a double shift. Place was stowed out, mind. Didn't get a chance to be bored with Kenny's rancid chat.' She nibbled at her lip. 'Is this about dealing?'

The roach outside his house.

Vicky jolted upright. 'Should it be?'

'Hardly...'

Vicky frowned at her. 'He likes a smoke, though, aye?'

'Who doesn't?' Monika smoothed off the edge of a thumbnail with her finger. 'It's just... He caught some guy selling coke in the gents a few weeks back.'

Vicky got in before MacDonald. 'Your boss didn't mention it.'

'Not likely to.' Monika switched her scowl to the stairs. 'He told Gavin not to report it in case we lost our license.'

MacDonald was noting it down. 'Gavin ever bar anybody?'

'Hardly.' Monika shook out the towel and dug it deep into a pint glass. 'Place used to be a dive, but it's different now. Don't even show the football, you know?'

'Thanks for your time.' Vicky smiled at Monika. 'Look, if there's anything—'

'Wait a sec.' Monika clicked her tongue a few times. 'There's a girl been in a few times, chatting to Gavin while we work. Afternoons mostly, like around two o'clock? Kept herself to herself. Just deals with Gav, only comes in when he's on. Doesn't *drink* drink but has a coffee.'

'How would you describe her?'

'Young, twenties maybe. Wee ginger lassie.'

Emma?

The plot thickened...

MacDonald gave her a knowing smile. 'Ever tease Gavin about her?'

'Obviously.' Monika laughed. 'Didn't deny it, either. Didn't say anything, mind.' Her face brightened. 'Kenny's noticed it, though, which means it must be *blatant*.'

Vicky leaned in. 'You get her name?'

'Never spoke to her. They shut up when I'm near.'

'Do you know Gavin's sister-in-law, Emma?'

'Should I?'

'This woman's never been in any other time?'

'Well. A few Fridays back? With this older guy.'

'Her father?'

'Not *that* much older. Thirties, probably. Good ten years older than her, mind.'

'Okay, thanks.' MacDonald snapped his notebook shut and slotted it into his suit pocket.

'Are you pair going to tell me why you're here?'

MacDonald ran a hand over the back of his head. 'Gavin Mason was murdered.'

Monika's shoulders sagged. 'God, I'm going to throw up.'

And she did. All over the bar.

6

Vicky pulled up at the lights at the end of the Perth Road. MacDonald's blue BMW in the lane for straight ahead. A grey Honda sat between them, indicating right.

An estate agents' window had boards filled with houses she couldn't afford. Not that she wanted to move. Odd feeling happy.

She shut her eyes and rubbed her thumbs into her eye sockets.

A picture was starting to form.

Gavin Mason having an affair with his sister-in-law.

Gave them a logical suspect. His brother.

Vicky had seen it time and time again.

Aye, hopefully it was going to be one of those cases that practically solved themselves and she could get back home to her family to see if there was any lasting trauma to Jamie.

She got out her mobile and dialled Forrester. Bounced to

voicemail. 'Sir, I need a chat about the victim. Give me a ring back.'

What the hell was going on with the traffic lights?

She dialled another number.

Answered immediately. 'Where are you, boss?' DC Stephen Considine's long, slow drawl, with that tinge of Doric that anyone from Forfar clung to.

'Are you still at the victim's home?'

'Aye, making sure the CSIs don't make too much of an arse of things.' She could picture him standing up a bit taller, like he was a proper cop and everything.

If there was ever anyone making an arse of things... 'Okay, is DCI Forrester still there?'

'Back at the station, why?'

'Okay, thanks.' Vicky killed the call. Bell Street was over the road, the brutalist Lego boxes sitting near the courthouse.

Sure enough, the light was on in Forrester's office.

THE OPEN-PLAN OFFICE wasn't busy, just a couple of the night shift setting up the Incident Room. Not a lot anyone could do now until the morning, but that hadn't stopped Forrester, his muffled voice booming through the closed door.

Probably blaming Vicky for Jamie ending up in some murdered guy's kitchen.

Superb.

MacDonald headed for the office like a moth to a flame. Or a fly to dogshit.

Vicky followed him over, but the door was already open.

Forrester was leaning back in his chair, eyes closed, a telephone headset clamped to his skull like he was working in a call centre.

Vicky smiled at MacDonald. 'Euan, can you give me a minute with him?'

'Sure thing.' He trudged off, shoulders slouched like Jamie after losing PlayStation privileges.

Vicky stepped into the office and pulled the door shut behind her. 'Sir, I need a word?'

Forrester opened his eyes. 'Just a sec, Simon.' He reached forward and jabbed a key on his mobile. 'What's up?'

'Who're you speaking to, sir?'

'More of this need-to-know stuff, Doddsy. DCI and above.' Forrester sighed. 'On with someone from the Met who worked a case which we think might tie into Gavin Mason's history, but everyone's playing silly buggers with what they can and can't share so God knows. But it's the reason we have to check on him every day.' He paused, then sighed. 'But you've got that smug expression that usually means you think you've cracked it?'

'Right.' Vicky took a seat. 'Just finished at his work. The barmaid thinks Gavin was seeing a woman, who came in a couple of times. Thing is, she matches the description of his sister-in-law.'

'This Emma lassie?'

'Correct. Mid-twenties. Ginger hair. Small.'

'Right, so this punk kills his brother 'cos he was bonking his wife?' Forrester nodded along like he was listening to smooth jazz. And he liked the sound of it too. 'Open and Shut' by Miles Davis. Cole Porter's 'A Good Statistic'. Then his monobrow seized up. 'And you want to go in all guns blazing and ask her?'

'You know me too well, sir.'

'Okay, so here's the issue.' Forrester tapped his headset. 'We're digging into this need-to-know secret squirrel shite as a possible motive. Far as I can tell, Emma isn't involved in any of that. Now, I still don't know what the hell he's done, but I'd give a kidney to have this be a simple case. So please do the doings.'

'Right, I'll go and speak to her now, then.'

'No, that's what I mean by doing the doings. Build up a picture of Gavin and Emma's movements over the last few days. See if it's her, then you can interrogate her.'

And Vicky knew just the right person to help.

7

Vicky sucked in a deep breath, then looked around the office. A window in the corner rattled against the wind, rain streaking the glass. An improvement from the frost, at least. Someone sat in front of it, head lowered, typing at a laptop.

Vicky headed over. 'Evening, Jenny. Shouldn't you be back in your coffin by now?'

'Ha bloody ha.' Jenny Morgan pushed her chair back. She wore a black shirt under a black-coloured jumper, sleeves rolled up to the elbows. Her skin was pale like porcelain. Hard to remember Jenny hadn't been born in a blue crime scene suit. She unpicked her earbuds and tucked her violent-raspberry hair behind her ears. 'Forrester asked you to get an update from me, right?'

Vicky held up her hands. 'Don't kill the messenger.'

'I wish you were just a messenger.' Jenny snorted. 'I'm thinking of organ grinders and monkeys here. And isn't it "shoot the messenger"?'

'Relax, Jenny. It's Vicky. I'm your friend.' She rested against the edge of the desk. 'Get it all out of your system. The quicker you stop moaning about how much of an arse Forrester is or I am, the quicker you can get back to work.'

Jenny didn't say anything, just silently fumed.

Vicky looked around the forensics office space. 'Thought you'd be out at his flat.'

'Trying to avoid crime scenes just now. Spent twelve hours at one last week out in Arbroath. Proper three-cigar job.'

'You what?'

'How we measure the stink. The number of cigars you need to cover it. One is eye-watering. Two is eye-stinging. And three, my eyeballs were on fire.' Jenny blinked like she could still feel it. 'Anyway, unlike your lot, my guys don't need supervision, so they're working his flat.'

'You got an update?'

'Forensically difficult. Someone had a shower, presumably your killer. Would've been completely covered in blood and brains, so it's a good way to clean yourself up. But they'd left it on. No traces left in there, but the whole flat was like a sauna.' Jenny clicked her fingers. 'No, not a sauna. A steam room. Aye.'

'And that's bad, why?'

'Because… It'll make Arbuthnott's assessment of his time of death tough. Everything in there is soaked, so forget about useful prints. DNA traces are going to be hard to isolate.'

'Shit.'

'Aye, shit. Normally, his DNA would still be in the drain trap, so we could get in there and extract it. But him leaving it running has flushed the line. Sorry, I mean them leaving it running.'

'And he's washing away his guilt.'

'Well, quite. Meanwhile, I'm looking through Gavin's laptop.'

'Getting anything useful?'

Jenny hammered her laptop's keyboard. Her slim computer sat next to a super-sized machine which took up most of the space on the desk, the rest of it filled with boxes of cables. 'This is the image of Gavin's beast, but I'm not getting much off it. Guy liked his games and his porn. Question: who downloads porn rather than streaming it nowadays?'

Vicky didn't have an answer for that.

'Perverts, that's who. People into seriously dark shit.'

'Like child abuse?'

Jenny nodded. 'Exactly. But also people into extreme stuff too.'

'Was he into it?'

'Nope. It all seems pretty vanilla. Well, as vanilla as "stepsister cheerleader gang bang" could ever be.'

Vicky smirked. 'Any messages between him and an Emma Mason?'

'Wife?'

'Sister-in-law.' Vicky raised a hand. 'Not stepsister.'

'Still, it's very saucy.' Jenny picked up a transparent evidence bag containing a phone, marked 'Gavin Mason'. 'This is going to be a long night.' She attached the mobile to her laptop, then hit keys with what seemed enough force to crack the keyboard and the desk underneath. Rows of text started filling the screen and she sat back, chewing her nails. 'He's deleted them off both his laptop and phone, so I need to get the originals from the network.'

And that wasn't at all suspicious...

'That going to take long?'

'Few minutes.'

'Okay.' Vicky tossed a bagged mobile onto the desk. 'Wondering if you can do anything with this?'

Jenny stared at it like it was unexploded munitions. 'Gavin Mason's?'

'My son's.' Vicky poked at the bag. 'He's never off the bloody thing.' She sighed. 'And he videoed me at the crime scene.'

'That was him? Thought it was Considine's kid?'

'He's got a kid?'

'No, but when you hear that some cop's let their kid into a crime scene, it's the kind of daftness I'd expect from him.'

'Can you delete that so it can't come back to bite me on the arse?'

Jenny picked up the mobile and started fiddling with it. 'Let's have a wee look.'

'Surprised to see you in on a Sunday, Jenny.'

'Three-line whip. What David Forrester wants, David Forrester gets.' Jenny sifted through a set of connectors and attached one to the base of Jamie's phone. 'If you must know, I was out with my sister at the DCA.'

'I didn't ask.'

'Saw a pretty terrible film, then spent an *hour* watching her flirt with a completely unsuitable man.'

'How do you know he was unsuitable?'

'His boyfriend arrived.'

Vicky laughed. 'Ah.'

'It's not funny, Vicky. I left her in the lurch to come here. She was in tears. Absolutely devastated.'

A blush crept over Vicky's face like cheap makeup. 'Sorry.'

'After what she's been through…' Jenny pointed at the

mobile, her face blank. 'Take it you've already looked through your boy's texts?'

'Not the sort of thing I'd do.'

'What, because his phone's locked and you don't know the passcode?'

'No, Jenny. I know it. It's because I respect my son's privacy.'

She hit a few keys. 'There. Now it's unlocked.'

'How the hell did you do that?'

'Three years at magic school.' Jenny slashed a make-believe wand in the air.

'I hope that was a benevolent spell.' Vicky glanced over at the office. 'Any chance you can make Forrester disappear?'

'Arseholeum destructus is year four, sadly.'

'Pity.' Vicky folded her arms. The desk edge was digging into the back of her leg. 'Well, I'm still not looking at Jamie's messages.'

'Your restraint's admirable.' She ran a finger down the screen. 'Jamie's a popular lad. Might want to avert your gaze, Vicks. Chances are that at least one of these is going to contain one or more boobs.'

Vicky squinted at the tiny screen. Couldn't follow what she was doing. 'Jamie's not interested in that.'

'What's wrong with him?'

'He's *ten*.'

'Oh. Right.' Jenny pointed at the screen. 'That's the video there.' She opened the file and her fingers tapped across the screen. 'Done.' She passed Jamie's mobile back.

'You didn't watch it.'

'Nope. Respecting your privacy.'

'Mine?'

'Heard you went arse over tit. Now it never happened.'

'Thanks, Jenny.'

'Never a problem. Need you to sign for it, but you can give your soon-to-be stepson his phone back.'

'Cheers.' Vicky pocketed it, then twisted her chair around and leaned in close. 'And sorry about your sister.'

'She'll get over it.' Jenny flicked to the other screen. 'Christ, these texts are taking forever.' She leaned forward. 'Ho-chee-mama.'

'What is it?'

'Well, your brother's just finished with the bedroom. Looks like Gavin had sex today.'

'There's a condom?'

'Nope. Whoever he was ploughing rode bareback.'

'Jesus, Jenny.'

'Sorry. I forget you're such a prude. Anyway, we've got semen and vaginal mucus there.'

'Can you—'

'But it'll be tough to get the forensics off it because of the steam. We'll try.' Jenny sat back and folded her arms. 'You got an idea of who the fa—' She coughed. 'Who the mucus belongs to?'

'Emma Mason.'

'The sexy sister-in-law. Got you.'

'I've been trying to build up a picture of Gavin's relationship with Emma. Texts and calls are the obvious starting points.'

'And you want something tangible, right?' Jenny clicked her fingers. 'Car.' She switched to another screen. 'Bollocks.' She reached for her mobile, tapped the screen and put it to her ear. 'Andrew, have you found the victim's car yet?' She bit her bottom lip. 'Okay, the insurance documents will do.' She pulled the mobile away and sighed. 'Your brother is *still* hard work even after you had that chat with him.'

'Well, he won't speak to me.'

'Wow.' Jenny put the phone back to her ear. 'Just the plates, aye.' She cradled it against her shoulder and typed on her laptop. 'Just running that now... Audi A4, right?' She sat bolt upright. 'What do you mean?'

Vicky crouched low. 'What's up?'

'The car's not there.'

'Do you know where it is?'

Jenny put her mobile down on the desk and shifted to the Automatic Number Plate Recognition system. 'Bingo. That's it. Purple, I'd say.'

The screen was filled with a view of the road down by the Tay, just past the Discovery, on the way out of town.

Vicky squinted at the Audi. 'That's Gavin Mason's car?'

'Aye, two hours ago. And he wasn't driving it on account of being very dead at the time. If you can find who was driving...?'

'Got it.' Vicky screwed up her eyes. 'But it could be in Edinburgh or Glasgow by now.'

'That's the thing.' Jenny beamed. 'There's another camera half a mile down that road. It didn't get triggered.'

'Wait, so they're at Tesco?'

Jenny nodded. 'Or the big Ashworth's.'

8

Vicky turned right and eased into the road towards the supermarkets. Right was Tesco, left was Ashworth's. She took the left and a shiver ran up her spine, puckering her arms with goosebumps.

'You okay there?' Jenny was in the passenger seat, eyebrow raised. 'Look like you've seen a ghost.'

'Last time I was here, a girl died and a colleague lost his mind and his job.'

'Before my time, right?'

'Nope, you were here.'

The Audi was on its own, sitting as far from the nearest cones of light as it could get.

'Pretty cold killing someone, then going shopping.'

'Don't disagree.' Vicky spotted a grey Subaru over to the side and pulled up next to it and wound down both front windows.

It might be dark outside, but Considine's red hair glowed.

His window wound down and that Movember moustache made him look like a bank manager. 'Boss.'

MacDonald sat in his BMW on the other side, window already down. 'What's the plan here?'

'Box the car in, then get Jenny's forensics guys to start doing their thing.'

'Good to me.' MacDonald waved over the way. 'Got eyes on it. Not quite old enough to be considered a classic, but it's still in the realm of high-end boy racer's vehicle.'

Considine pumped his fists. 'Ready?'

'Sure thing.' Vicky set off first, getting behind the car and parking at right angles to it.

Inside, a head bobbed up and twisted round, a red dot glowing.

Vicky stuck her car in neutral. 'What the hell?'

The Audi shot off.

Considine's and MacDonald's cars were still approaching as the Audi careered past them. Both spun around and set off after it in a squeal of burnt rubber.

Vicky stuck the car in gear and tried the accelerator. Got a nice throb. She floored it, the wheels spinning as she tore after the Audi.

'Who the hell is that?' Jenny was grabbing the oh-shit handle above the door, clinging on as Vicky took the road back to Riverside Drive.

The Audi jumped the red lights, heading right towards Perth.

MacDonald followed it through, but Considine stayed back.

Vicky blared her horn, trying to spark him into action. 'Jesus Christ! Move!'

Jenny put her phone to her ear. 'Stephen, can you shift it?'

His lights came on. Daft sod had stalled it.

Vicky swung out into the oncoming lane to round Considine, then took the turn with a percussive blast of her horn, then following behind MacDonald and the Audi, just a pair of brake lights in the distance, going under the Tay Bridge. A train was coming from Fife, the icy white lights floating in the darkness.

Vicky shifted down to second and the engine roared. Doing seventy in a forty, rumble strips digging into the car, small thuds every second. Darkness to the left, the Tay swallowing up the light.

And still they accelerated away from her.

She hit it heavy, got to eighty, her engine screaming as she slalomed under the bridge just as the train rattled over them.

Up ahead, the Audi cut in front of a Range Rover. Brake lights flashed in the black night. A horn blared. MacDonald. Another blasted in reply, held for a few seconds.

Vicky joined in, jabbing her horn a few times and flashing her lights, then breathed out through her nostrils as she powered past the stationary Range Rover.

The driver shouted something, his open mouth like a hole in an old paper bag.

Jenny gave him a little wave and the old guy held up his middle finger. 'Stupid bastard.'

Vicky glanced towards the passenger seat, the backlight from Jenny's mobile casting a pale glow across her face. Ahead, red lights raced off away from them, still heading towards Perth.

Vicky rounded three cars and onto the straight, her foot pulsing hard between gear changes. Blood pumping in her ears. She pulled out and shot past two Sunday drivers, then weaved around another bend and the gentle curve passing the city's tiny airport. The train line rose on the right. Could almost make out the crash barrier at the edge. Behind it, Dundee rose into the night sky, lit up like a birthday cake.

The Audi sat at a roundabout, wedged between the two lanes. Looked like the engine was still running, exhaust pluming around it.

MacDonald's car was in the middle of the roundabout, on its roof.

'Shit, shit, shit.' Vicky hit the brakes.

The Audi roared towards them, lights off, the four linked rings caught in Vicky's headlights.

She yanked the wheel to the left, trying to drag the car towards the old dump.

The Audi jerked in the same direction.

Vicky's car crunched against the barrier, sparks flaring, the shoulder grinding off the metal. She hauled the wheel back round.

Horns blared. Brakes squealed.

Something crunched behind Jenny. Vicky flew forward, the seatbelt biting her shoulder. The car jolted around, spinning out onto the road and stopping with a thud, facing the way they'd come.

Vicky's head banged against the steering wheel and she got a face full of airbag.

Stalled, the dashboard flashing.

Vicky's breathing came thick and hard. Everything looked black and white. Bleached, saturated.

'You okay?'

Jenny stared at her, eyes empty, mouth open.

The Audi's bonnet was crumpled up like yesterday's newspaper. No sign of the driver.

Considine's Subaru whizzed past her, his expression tight and focused, then pulled up behind it.

'I need to move.' Vicky stepped out onto the grass verge and reached into the door pocket for her torch. Reassuringly heavy. Could certainly do some damage with it. 'Can you see to Mac, Jenny?'

The words seemed to snap her into focus. 'On it.'

The fog tasted metallic. Peals of smoke burst out of it.

Bloody Audi was on fire.

Vicky jogged over and tried the door.

A young man was inside, one hand smacking the wheel, the other tugging at the handle. Smoke was building up inside. He mouthed, 'Help!'

Vicky motioned for him to sit back but he didn't seem to understand. She rounded the front of the car and smashed the passenger window's glass. She reached in and tried to grab the guy, but the bloody *seat* was on fire.

Smoke belched out. Cars buzzed past like flies in summer.

Shit.

Back around and she tugged at the door handle.

It caught and the guy spilled out onto the tarmac.

Vicky grabbed his wrist and snapped on her handcuffs. She helped him to his feet and got him away from the car, leading him back towards hers. 'What's your name?'

He said nothing.

'I'm a police officer. DI Vicky Dodds. What's your name?'

'Not telling you nothing.' He collapsed to his knees, propping himself up on her crumpled bonnet.

'Are you okay, sir?'

'Dropped my fucking joint!' He reeked of smoke and deodorant. Clutched a can of Mr Right in his hand, Luxury Leather flavour. Stupid bastard had turned Gavin's car into a Molotov cocktail.

The Audi erupted into flame, blasting them with heat.

Vicky shielded herself. Yep, there went any evidence. She focused on the driver. The killer. 'What did you—'

'Help!' Considine was over by MacDonald's car. 'I think he's dead!'

9

The corridor had that boiled-cabbage tang you always got in hospitals, but all Vicky could smell was the mixture of smoke and deodorant still clinging to her.

Dr Alison Rankine stood in the corridor, hand on her hip, brow furrowed. 'You're fine. No concussion.' She looked up at Vicky and tugged on her long ponytail, barely taming the dark-brown fizz. 'As for DS MacDonald... Let me think.' And she did, staring down at the floor.

Vicky caught Considine's gaze and he winced.

'Mac's a good guy, boss.'

'Indeed.'

But the truth was that Euan MacDonald was an acquired taste. One Vicky used to have, but one she had seen through.

Still, whatever he'd done, nobody deserved to die like that.

She hadn't even seen it. Stupid prick had raced off, solo, caught up with Gavin Mason's Audi and must've tried the Hollywood trick, taking it out by sideswiping it.

Always the hero.

The cheese pasta that passed for Sunday lunch churned in Vicky's stomach. A bitter aftertaste like sour wine.

Dr Rankine clenched her jaw. 'Both legs are broken and I think we're looking at a severe spinal injury. His skull's fractured too.'

'But he'll live?'

'It's touch and go whether he pulls through, I have to say.' Rankine gave as kind a smile as anyone could. 'He'll be going into surgery as soon as Mr Campbell arrives, but we're prepping him just now. Whatever it takes, we'll do it.'

'Thank you.'

'Are you close?'

'He works for me.' Vicky smiled. 'I've got two sergeants. DS Wood just went off on maternity leave on Friday, so I'm down to none now.'

Rankine winked at Considine. 'Might be your lucky day, Stephen.'

He nodded earnestly. 'Not the time to discuss this.'

But Vicky knew as soon as he could, Considine would be on it like an over-sugared child wanting some tat at the fair. She focused on Rankine. 'What about the other driver?'

'Well, you rescued him just in time, by the sounds of it.' Rankine started off down the corridor. 'And you're asking if you can speak to him, right?'

'Is he able to?'

Rankine puffed up her cheeks. 'He can. Nothing wrong with him except some bruising. He's just not talking.'

'One of those types?'

'Indeed. But I suppose if you steal a car and drive like an arsehole, then you're going to know every trick, right?' She stopped outside a door guarded by a big lump in uniform. 'My sister was in a crash on that stretch of road, so please prosecute him for this.'

'We'll try our best.' Vicky smiled at her, then entered the hospital room.

Dark and silent, just a single bulb above the bed.

Considine joined her in the room, staying by the door, like he expected him to run again.

Vicky took the seat next to the bed. 'You want to give us your name?'

'No.'

'You might not want to, but are you going to?'

'No.'

'Should've brought some grapes, but I don't think you'd enjoy them unless they were fermented and fortified.'

'Eh?'

'She's saying you drink Buckfast, Iain.' Considine stepped into the room. 'Been a while.'

The guy frowned. 'The fuck are you, dickhead?'

Considine grinned wide. 'That's no way to greet an old friend.'

'Mate, you're going to have to stop flirting with me here.'

'Flirting, that's good.' Considine crossed his arms across his chest. 'I arrested you for pickpocketing in the Wellgate Centre five years ago.'

'Bud, you must have made a mistake.'

'Saying you're not Iain Paton?'

Nostrils flared. Fists clenching around the bedsheet. 'That was bullshit and you know it.'

'Iain, you spent four and a half years at Her Majesty's Pleasure. Swiping wallets was just part of it. All the other stuff you'd been doing. Stealing designer gear off clotheslines. Nicking tellies from delivery vans. And then holding on to it all. And that was a treasure trove of evidence we found in your lockup. Mind Beth Carmichael?'

Paton shook his head.

'You stole her handbag. Only photo she had of her mother in her purse, so it was really nice to be able to reunite her with that. Little bit of justice.'

Paton shrugged. Fingers twitching.

'Would've thought you'd be trying to stay clean.'

'Was.'

'But you nicked a car.'

'This is bullshit.'

Considine laughed. 'Is it, aye? Because it seemed very much to me like you stole a car.'

'Did nothing.'

'We found you in it, Iain. Only reason you're not halfway to Glasgow in it is you tried to ram DS MacDonald off the road and made an arse of it.'

'Didn't.'

'He's in surgery now. Unlikely to survive. If you're a lucky boy, you'll get manslaughter. But I think it'll be murder.'

'Fuck off.'

'So you're denying being at Ashworth's?'

'No. I was there. I didn't steal the motor.'

'I don't believe you.'

'I'm telling you the truth.'

'Where did you get the car?'

'I didn't.'

'See, we've got a situation where someone's broken into a house, killed someone and—'

'Woah, woah!' Paton held up his fingers, dyed nicotine yellow. '*Killed* someone?'

'And stole their car.' Considine narrowed his eyes. 'Next thing we know, you're in the motor at the supermarket.'

'I was shopping for my gran.'

'Sounds likely.'

'I'm serious. She loses her shit if I don't go to Ashworth's. She only likes their ready-made custard, practically lives off the bloody stuff.'

Considine laughed. 'You're a creative guy. Should've taken up storytelling while you were inside because this is golden. Could've written one of those tell-all memoirs or done ghost-writing for someone.' He looked at Vicky, mischief twinkling in his eyes. 'This boy, eh?'

'Dude, I'm serious. I had sixteen cartons of custard, thirty-six eggs and three loaves of Scottish plain in the boot. She's going to lose her mind. I had to get down to Ashworth's, then back up to the Hilltown. On foot. Or it's like three buses. And that lot weighs a *ton*. Handles dig into your hands.' Paton pressed his clenched fist onto his thigh, gentle and frustrated more than angry. 'Spotted the car there, sitting down the street from her house. Keys in the ignition, engine running. So I took it. I was going to drop it back the morn's morn.'

'Aye, sure, I believe you.' Considine paused. 'Thousands wouldn't.' He bellowed with laughter, like he'd just invented the phrase. 'Come on, just admit it. You killed him.'

'Killed who?'

'Gavin Mason.'

'Never heard of him.'

'He's the car owner.'

'Right. Sorry. Never heard of the guy. Shame he's dead, like.'

'And because of you, the car's a burnt-out wreck.' Considine paused again. 'See, if it *wasn't* you who killed Gavin, then we would've been able to prove it by finding some other fabrics and DNA traces in there.'

Stretching things a lot, but Paton seemed to believe Considine. 'I swear, I didn't kill anyone. Just found it there. And, aye, there was a rolled-up joint sitting there. Been a while since I've had a cheeky wee smoke, so I thought I might as well. After I'd got the old dear's messages. Wee treat for myself.'

That's what he'd been doing when they got there. Sparking up a doobie, as Vicky's dad would say.

Or at least, it was his story and he was sticking to it. And they didn't have a shred of evidence against it. A charred boot full of eggs, bread and custard.

'Sure your parole officer will be happy to learn that.' Vicky stood up. 'Come on, constable, let's continue this tomorrow. Maybe Mr Paton will have a change of heart.'

'Listen to me. I just found that car. I swear.'

'Okay, well, you better hope the CCTV backs that up.'

Paton swallowed, his gaze shooting between them. 'It will. Promise.'

'Then that's all you need to worry about.' Vicky gave him one last smile, then left the room. She fished out her phone and found Forrester's number.

Considine joined her out there. He spotted her mobile and got his own out, always trying to look the part. 'Well done. Think we'll get him for that.'

'I doubt it.' Vicky sighed. 'Can you get hold of the CCTV? Jenny Morgan should have access to it.'

'Will do, Sarge. Aye.'

'Stephen, I'm not a sergeant anymore.'

'Oh. Right. Aye. Sorry.'

'It's okay. You did a good job in there.' Vicky hit dial and put the mobile to her ear.

'Would you put in a word with your boss about me—'

'Now's not the time, Stephen.' And he was the last cop she'd recommend.

The uniform was smirking at the line. Considine's reputation obviously preceded him among the rank and file.

Forrester answered. 'How's Mac?'

'Not good. At all. We'll know more in the morning.'

'Okay. And have you got our guy?'

'He's here.' Vicky glanced into the room. 'Considine got him speaking.'

'*Considine* did?'

'Wonders will never cease, eh? Says he just took the car from outside. Engine running. Found a joint in there, hence it going on fire.'

'You believe him?'

'Considine's going to get to the bottom of it for me.' Vicky locked eyes with him, eyes wide.

'You know he's doing the nicey-nice with that doctor, right?'

Vicky frowned as she stepped away. 'Rankine?'

'Aye.'

Rankine's curt suggestion of Considine for the acting sergeant role made a bit more sense now. 'Doing the nicey-nice?'

'What would you call it?'

'Seeing? Going out with? Being involved with?'

'Well, whatever. What happened with Mac?'

'Typical him. He raced ahead of us, got there first and... I didn't see what happened. But I think if it wasn't for Mac, Iain Paton would've got away.'

'Paton? Man alive...'

'You know him?'

'Daft wee sod. So daft even Considine managed to do him.'

'I don't think Paton's our killer.'

'Me neither. Well.' The line went silent.

'Anyway, sir, I was going to—'

'Vicky, I need you to come with me. Doug Mason's just got home.'

10

No squad cars, just a quiet back street. Post-war nothingness, filled with houses that weren't grand or aspirational. Bungalows, pretty much all with extensions upstairs. Most with some on the sides, too, filling up the gardens with even more house.

Vicky got out into the bitter cold.

The drone of the Kingsway in the near distance. Loud television playing from across the road.

Forrester got out of his car and stretched, eyes narrow. 'Doddsy.'

'Sir.'

'Mac…' That was all he had.

Vicky patted his arm. 'He's in the best hands, sir.'

'Aye, aye. Going to need a sergeant, even in an acting capacity. I've put feelers out.'

'Not Considine, please.'

'Hardly.' Forrester looked over at a house and sighed. 'Right, anyway. Are they having an affair?'

'Hard to say. All the texts between Emma and Gavin were deleted. Jenny's trying to get them restored. It's a push-button thing, but somebody at the network needs to push it. And it's a Sunday night, so it's a skeleton staff.'

'Let's keep on that, but I want to get a feel for the lad myself.' Forrester raced over the road.

Vicky had to jog to catch him. 'What's going on with that call you've been on?'

'It's a long story… Let's just say… There's a bit more to this than meets the eye.'

'Sir, if there's—'

'It could be nothing and I need to keep the circle tight on this. Usually I'd tell you, but I've been explicitly told not to mention it to anyone.'

'Nice to feel included.'

'It's not like that…' Forrester stepped up the drive, past an estate Golf then a little Fiat, then hit the button and waited.

Not for long.

A figure misted the glass, then started rattling the lock. Emma Mason opened the door and peered out, a smile flickering over her lips, but it slipped when she saw Vicky. 'Oh.'

Forrester gave her a flash of warrant card, on autopilot. 'Mrs Mason, we understand your husband's home?'

'Aye, in you come.' Emma held the door for them.

Vicky stood uncomfortably in the hall while she shut the door and redid all the locks. 'Is Mrs Mason okay?'

'She's fine, aye.' Emma winced. 'Well, not fine. But… Mrs Houston's with her. Next-door neighbour. Old friend of hers. Just wandered in. Like she does.' She seemed to shake herself off. 'Through here.' She led along a spartan hallway with no personalisation. Bare white walls, immaculately painted, but no pictures, through to the back of the house.

The kitchen was like a showroom. Granite worktop, banana-yellow cupboards. Fancy cooker. Chunky American fridge.

Doug Mason was standing by the sink, staring out across a garden lit up in the night. Didn't seem much older than his brother, same dark hair. Dressed in chinos and a zip-up jumper. He turned around to them and looked exhausted – when his eyes closed, they were like hardboiled eggs. 'Hi.' He crossed the room and stood behind Emma. He placed his arm around her chest, resting his hand on her shoulder, and kissed the top of her head.

Vicky compared Doug with the body of his brother lying on the kitchen laminate. Similar build, though he might be a couple of inches taller. 'You have my deepest sympathies, Mr Mason.'

Doug sat next to his wife and cradled her hand. 'I don't...' He sniffed back a tear, then straightened up and rubbed his face. 'Christ.'

'This isn't easy, sir.' Forrester took the seat opposite at the kitchen table. Vicky sat next to him, making it feel like an interview. 'You can take as much time as you need.'

'But you want to ask me questions, right?' A steely glint in Doug's eye, his cheek twitching. 'I mean... well, of course you do. And I want to help. Any way I can. Come on. Let's do this. Right bloody now.'

Emma tightened her grip on his hand. 'They won't tell me what happened, Doug.'

She was making out like they were keeping something back from them.

'Someone murdered Gavin in his home.'

'How?'

Vicky glanced at Forrester, got a nod, but Doug was avoiding eye contact. 'He suffered inflicted head trauma from a blunt instrument and died of his injuries.'

Doug stared up at the ceiling. 'I just... Just...' He ran his hand over his mouth. 'I went for a drink with Gavin on Thursday night. Asked him to come to this conference with me. I played Muirfield this morning. Gavin would've loved it. The seventeenth alone...' He squeezed his eyes with his fingers. 'He'd still be alive if he'd come with me.' His voice was tiny.

Emma twisted round. 'Doug, you can't think like that.'

He let go of her hand. 'Tell me it's not true.'

Emma's forehead creased tight.

Vicky cleared her throat. 'You were at a conference in Edinburgh?'

'Just got back.' Doug pressed a finger to his temple. 'When Emma called... I grabbed my bag and bombed it home.' A heavy sigh. 'You'll have to speak to the traffic cops for me. I might've broken the speed limit a few times.'

'Where was it?'

'The Neshington Grange, I think it's called. Just outside Edinburgh.'

Vicky noted it down. 'Did Gavin give a reason for not coming with you?'

'Couldn't take the time off work. And he's skint. I was going to pay for it, but he's... My brother's a proud man, put it that way.' He sniffed. 'Was.'

Forrester ran a hand through his hair. 'Mr Mason, can you think of any reason for someone to do this to your brother?'

'He's well liked.' Doug shrugged. 'Loves his music and his

beer and his golf. Generally keeps himself to himself.' He broke off, but he didn't seem intent on filling the gap.

Emma folded her arms low across her tummy. 'This is going to put your mum back on her meds.'

Vicky caught Doug's snarl. Not happy with her. 'I hope Mrs Mason isn't unwell.'

'She's struggled with depression for years.' Doug clenched his jaw. 'Been that way since Dad died.' He let out a breath. 'Gav was fifteen, I was eighteen. Hit him harder than me.'

'Do you have any other close family?'

'Depends on what you mean by close. We have an uncle, Mum's brother. Lives in Canada. Haven't seen him since Dad's funeral.' Another shrug. 'That's it. Far as I know.'

'What about friends?'

'Just a few mutual golfing buddies.'

'Gavin never talk about them?'

'I don't know anybody he socialises with. We mainly spoke about Mum. And golf and football. He had a season ticket at Tannadice, but gave it up a few years back.' Doug splayed his hands across his lap. 'Now, I'd like to go round to my mother's, if that's okay?'

'Just a few more questions.' Forrester held a smile. 'Tell me about this conference.'

Doug smiled, scratching the back of his neck. 'I think the title is "The Next Ten Years in Domestic Heating". Not exactly stimulating, but... We need to do it.' He rubbed at his eyes, then blinked hard a few times. 'It started on Friday, runs until tomorrow evening. I was on a panel at twelve o'clock today, discussing solar batteries.'

Vicky gave a smile. 'Sounds high-tech.'

'Hardly. They're just what you'd get in an electric car,

mounted on the wall to store renewable energy from solar panels or a turbine, if you're lucky.'

'Sounds very eco-friendly.'

'Just trying to make the world a better place.'

'So you own a firm?'

'Well, I'm a partner but that sounds grander than it is. Truth is, I'm just a spreadsheet monkey. An accountant, which is as dull as you'd imagine. Duller, probably.'

'Can I ask where you were after your panel?'

'Why?'

'We've been trying to get hold of you.'

'Right. Sure.' Doug shut his eyes. 'I was in the hotel bar, chatting away. Networking, as they say. Is this when Gavin was killed?'

'We think it was around five o'clock, give or take.'

'Christ, and I was in the *bar*...'

'Were you drinking, sir?'

'I don't drink. Never have.'

'But Gavin did, right?'

'Like a fish.' Doug stared at his hands. 'I gave up after university. Gavin dropped out because of his boozing, and he kept on drinking. Never stopped. Which is why I didn't like him working in a pub.'

'We visited his work this evening. He ever talk about any problems there?'

'Never talked about work. Couldn't even tell you who his boss is. Same with his colleagues.'

Forrester sat back in his chair. 'One of them mentioned that Gavin was seeing someone. A woman.'

Emma frowned at Vicky, her head tilted to the side. Didn't

say anything. That look, though. She now knew they knew. Or suspected.

Doug shrugged. 'Never mentioned anything to me. Sorry.'

'And would he have?'

'Like I said, Gavin and I talked about football and golf. He didn't talk about drinking or shagging, and I didn't talk to him about accountancy or solar panels.' Doug reached over to the sideboard and handed Vicky a business card. Thick. Embossed. Expensive. 'If there's anything I can help with, call me. Day or night.' He got to his feet and smiled. 'Now, can I go and see my mother?'

FORRESTER STOPPED outside his car and watched Doug Mason's Golf slalom past, going way too fast for a residential street. 'What's your take on him?'

Vicky shrugged. 'No idea, sir.' She yawned into her fist. 'Seems like a grieving brother.'

'But?'

'But it's possible said brother was at it with his wife.'

'You think there's anything in it?'

'Not sure. She jumped when I mentioned it. Could be coincidence.'

'I'll coincidence you.' Forrester looked around the street. 'But you're right. Could just be Emma and Gavin were the very best of friends.'

'I'll get on to Jenny. See how she's getting on building up the picture of their life.'

'Appreciate it.' Forrester leaned in close and lowered his

voice. 'Right, I've got a complaint from forensics for you letting Jamie into the crime scene.'

'From Jenny?'

'No, from your brother.'

Cheeky bastard.

'It won't go anywhere.' Forrester straightened his back and smiled. 'Now, get home and catch some kip. Morning briefing's at seven sharp.'

11

Vicky pulled up in front of the house and got out. Nudged her door shut behind her. Had to check it was properly locked.

A quiet back street at the edge of Carnoustie. The lights all off. Bare cherry trees swayed in the breeze outside. The smell of fresh rain, though it had finally stopped.

Rob stood at the front door, arms folded. 'Welcome home. You okay?'

Vicky started up the path towards the house. 'Rob, I'm so, so sorry about what happened.'

Jamie was lurking inside the door, using his father as a shield. Kid's thumbs didn't know what to do without his mobile. 'Mum.' Eyes scanning around. 'You got my phone?'

Rob patted his son's shoulder. 'You need to get to bed.'

Vicky crouched in front of him. 'How you doing?'

'Alright.' A teenage shrug, despite his age. Then a grunt. 'Got my phone?'

Vicky reached into her pocket for the mobile and held it out. 'Here you—'

'Sweet!' Jamie snatched it from her grip, then darted inside, prodding and poking at the screen.

Vicky stood up tall again. 'A whole generation of kids staring at glass and plastic, living their lives on TikTok and Instagram and Snapchat.' She peered into the kitchen as she kicked off her shoes and saw their two greyhounds sleeping back-to-back on matching beds. Jamie leaned against the living room window, lost in his mobile. 'How's he been?'

Rob pulled the door shut and eased Vicky's coat off. 'Neither up nor down.'

She let out a sigh, all she could manage. 'I'm sorry. It was just supposed to be—'

'Mum!' Jamie was in the doorway, hands in the air in a 'What the hell?' gesture, his mobile in his left hand. 'Where's the video?'

'That was a crime scene, Jamie.' Vicky smoothed down his hair, catching a tuft between her thumb and middle finger. 'You shouldn't have—'

'Dad!' Jamie jumped down the steps and stabbed a finger into his dad's chest. Barely came up to his armpits. 'She deleted it!'

Rob couched down to his height and held him by the shoulders. 'Wee man. It's okay.'

'She took that video off my phone.'

'You shouldn't have been there, Jamie. And you definitely shouldn't have filmed it.'

Jamie's mouth hung open. He choked. Started to cry. Turned his head to the side.

Vicky stood back, heart pounding. She leaned in and held him.

Jamie collapsed into it.

She whispered, 'Is everything okay?'

More blubbing. Face reddening. 'You don't know how hard it is.'

'At school?'

Jamie nodded.

Rob got back down to Jamie's level. 'Try me, champ. What's going on?'

Jamie cowered there, shaking. 'It's hell, Dad. That video... It was *so* blaze. Everyone would be, like... Everyone would've been all over it.'

'All over you?'

Jamie nodded again.

Rob brushed away some of his tears. 'You want to talk about it?'

'What's the point? She's deleted it!'

'I meant about school.'

Jamie huffed. 'Bella's so popular and...'

'You can talk to us, Jamie.'

'Can't talk to you two about *anything* without it exploding in my face.'

'Like what?'

Jamie shook his head, scowling. 'Nothing.'

'Look, this is serious, okay? If you're getting bullied, you can talk to either of us about it. Please.'

'Whatever.' Another shrug.

'Just promise me you'll talk to us, okay?'

'Okay.'

'Thank you.' Vicky leaned in and hugged her son, pulling him tight, feeling the muscles in her face tighten.

Jamie ducked down, shielding his head, then pushed away and ran through the house.

Vicky watched him go, unable to move, unable to go after him.

Rob rubbed her arm, then pulled her into a hug. 'How are you doing?'

'Shite.' Vicky let herself be consumed by it. 'How anyone's supposed to be a cop and have a family life...'

'We do okay, don't we?'

'I suppose.' She let out a long, slow sigh. Becoming a habit. 'It's the kids who suffer, Rob. Me and Andrew bore the brunt of Dad always being on shift. I worry what I'm doing to Bella and Jamie.'

'Hey.' Rob broke off so he could stare into her eyes. 'You're being a great mum to a boy who lost his birth mother. You're his mum now. Okay? Kids are difficult, alright? And I should know. I've been a teacher since I was twenty-two.' A short crack of laughter. 'Kids are sometimes tough, sometimes fragile, but they all go through this stuff.'

'Rob, Jamie's *ten* and he's being bullied.'

'I know. I'll have a word with his headteacher. A quiet word. See if she can do anything about it.'

'It's hard for him, Rob. He's a quiet boy. And that's a loud school.'

'Aye, Bella fits in there. She's the *spirited* one.'

'You can say mouthy, like her mother.'

Rob laughed. 'Not my words to use. But you're not usually clumsy. Maybe she gets that from you as well.'

She grabbed his hand and squeezed it tight. 'Thank you.'

'What for?'

'Just being you, Rob. That's it.'

'I'm nobody's saint.' He laughed. 'But I imagine you haven't eaten?'

DAY 2

Monday

12

'Maybe I'll sue you, Vicky. Abuse of process or something. Maybe show your wee boy some more of my video games. What was his name again? Jam—ugh!'

Vicky impaled him right through the genitals.

He stared at her for a few seconds before he screamed, loud and high. He collapsed back against the bench and blood trickled all over his pale jeans, soaking them a deep red.

Vicky had gone too far. He was bleeding out. She'd hit the femoral artery.

Shit.

What had she done?

Sharon stepped between them, pinching his neck. 'He'll be dead within a minute.'

'You saw that?'

Sharon nodded.

'I didn't do that just because he was a child molester. He was coming after my children next.'

'You need to be quick.' Sharon gestured at the knife still in Vicky's hands, dripping with blood. 'Right now, you need to cover this up as an accidental death. You need to prove it was a fight to the death. You acted in self-defence.'

Vicky took one look at the knife and knew she had no choice here. That bastard had poked the bear. She turned the blade around and stabbed herself in the abdomen.

Vicky jerked awake, the knife wound in her stomach feeling raw, like it had just been sliced open. In the darkness, she touched her skin, but just felt the wound, all healed over. No blood, no stains.

Except for the ones on her conscience.

She reached over for her mobile, the charging cable dangling. 05:17. She'd never get back to sleep now. Her alarm was due in thirteen minutes, anyway. She unplugged her phone, got up and sneaked through to the kitchen, where she tapped out a message:

Had the same nightmare again

She filled the kettle and put it on to boil. Her yawn felt like it might swallow her whole.

Her phone buzzed on the counter. A text from Sharon McNeill:

Morning, early bird. Want a chat?

The kettle rattled to a boil. Vicky reached into the cupboard for a mug and a tea bag, then filled it with hot water.

Did she want to?

No.

The fewer people were even aware of their continuing friendship almost two years after the incident the better.

She hit dial.

Answered straight away. 'Hey, Vicky. You can't sleep either?'

'No. And you know why.'

'Right, aye. Tell me you haven't told anyone.'

'Not a soul.'

'Good. Keep it that way.'

'Why are you up, Sharon?'

'Had a friend staying with me. Had to be up and out early.'

'Right, right. The kind of friend that's at risk of breaking your bed?'

'No comment.' Sharon laughed. 'Anyway, if you want to talk, I'm here for you. Okay?'

'Thanks for the offer, but I'll keep my peace.'

'Are you getting flashbacks?'

Vicky felt herself scowl. 'Why?'

'Well, if you are, it could be PTSD. One of my old DCs suffered from it. Ex-squaddie, good cop who was rendered bloody useless by it. He hid it from me. Don't hide it from people, Vicky.'

'I'm not.' Her heart was racing. 'But how do I talk about what happened?'

'Nothing happened, other than someone trying to kill you and threatening your kids. You turned the tables and he died as a result. Him or you, Vicky. It's really, really tough to take a life but, trust me, he'd have had no remorse over your death.'

The words rattled around her head like ball bearings.

She was right. Of course she was right. Still, it didn't make it any easier to deal with.

'I've got to get to work, Sharon. Shitloads on.'

'Okay, but the offer stands, alright?'

'Maybe I'll come and stay with you.'

'That would be brilliant.'

'As long as I get to meet this friend.'

'Oh, aye. Have a good day, Vicky.'

'See you around.' Vicky put the mobile down again and used a spoon to mash the teabag against the side of the mug.

Aye, she really did need to talk about it.

13

Rain hammered at the incident room windows, drumming like Bella at the kit she'd got for Christmas, surprisingly still in use. Rivers snaked on the dark glass, twisting into new patterns as it slithered down.

On the back wall, a handful of crime scene photos were pinned to a length of corkboard.

A photo of a man wearing a white T-shirt with SUGARMAN written in black, clutching a pint of lager, his shades propped up on his forehead, pushing up a nest of black hair, the blue-grey sea behind him, dotted with sandstone rocks.

Gavin Mason.

Other photos were less kind, showing him with his head stoved in, dead eyes staring through the camera lens.

Forrester moved in front on them, his gaze landing on each officer, one by one. 'Dr Arbuthnott's team have processed the blood toxicology early for once. He was full of alcohol, cannabis and cocaine.' He looked around the room. 'I'll be attending the post-mortem this morning. Until my return, DI Dodds is in charge. Any questions?'

Vicky perched against a desk, one of a series arranged to form a broken rectangle.

Another ten officers sat on or hovered next to the others. The windowless room already smelled of coffee, bacon and armpits.

Considine raised a hand, already eliciting a glare from Forrester. 'Just wondering if you've got an update on Mac's condition, sir.'

'Right.' Forrester cleared his throat. 'Well, the good news is his op was a success. Bad news... They've had to induce a coma. A lot of internal bleeding. Until that's stopped, well, your guess is as good as mine. I'll keep you all posted. Okay?'

Considine still had his hand up. 'Any word on who'll replace him?'

'Now's not the time, Constable.' Forrester scanned the room, his focus seeming to linger that bit longer on Vicky as it swept past. 'Oh, and we've cleared Iain Paton of Gavin Mason's murder. He was with his mother and three aunts at the time of death in a cafe in the Hilltown. He stole that car, sure, but he didn't kill Gavin Mason. We will do him for what he did to DS MacDonald.'

Why did the cast-iron alibis only ever complicate things?

Forrester clapped his hands together. 'Okay, team. We will catch this killer. Get out there and do your stuff. Dismissed.' He left the room.

Vicky slouched back against the desk. Usual empty platitudes. Nothing of substance, just vague hope. She yawned and took a sip of tea. Tasted funny, and not just that the sour milk was only good for making scones.

'Doddsy, need a word.' Forrester beckoned her over to his office.

Vicky stood up and pushed through the dispersing crowd through the door.

And came face to face with all six foot four inches and twenty-odd stone of DS Luke Shepherd. Hairy fists were balled at the end of his jacket, his shaved head sitting on top of a massive neck. His boxer's nose pointed off at forty-five degrees, broken several times. Cauliflower ears, like unpopped corn under the skin. 'Morning, Vicky.' He walked past her and shut the door, then leaned back against it, blocking any further entry. Or exit. 'Have a seat, boss.'

Vicky sat, trying to put as much distance between herself and Shepherd as possible. The walls were bare, a large crack running down the middle of one, a little squiggle at the bottom. A whiteboard on wheels was filled with the statuses of current cases but missed anything on Gavin Mason. 'Boss?'

Forrester sat behind his desk. 'Luke's here on secondment from Edinburgh to cover for Mac as your DS until I get a more permanent solution.'

Vicky rocked back in the chair, her skin crawling tight, like someone was pinning it back.

It was possible Forrester didn't know the truth, but Vicky did.

DS Luke Shepherd of Edinburgh's Major Investigation Team was really DCI Luke Shepherd of Police Scotland's Professional Standards and Ethics unit.

The Complaints.

The nasty bastards who investigated nastier bastards. Dirty cops. Bent cops.

Cops who'd killed a serial child abuser before they could face trial, after they threatened her children.

Shit.

Shit, shit, shit.

Vicky had to act like she owned the place, so she walked over and shook Shepherd's hand. 'Been a while, Luke.'

'May, wasn't it?' Shepherd wasn't letting go of her hand. 'You seem tired, Vicky.'

'Didn't get much sleep last night.'

'Just last night?'

'Been that way for a while.' She sighed. 'Never get promoted past sergeant, then.'

Shepherd narrowed his eyes at her, then bellowed with laughter. 'Not something that's likely.'

'Right, come on.' Forrester took a drink of tea. 'There're a few things we need to discuss that's not for the wider audience.' He pushed his mug away from him, like it'd said something to him. 'For starters, I've been kneeling down to pray that this is as simple as it appears, that it's a vanilla murder case. That Doug Mason caught his brother at it with his wife, then saw red and murdered him. Or it was a cold-blooded variation on that theme.'

'Praying doesn't usually solve police investigations.' Shepherd pushed away from the door, lumbering across the office like a prop forward across the Murrayfield turf. 'And Douglas was in Edinburgh at the time of death, wasn't he?'

Vicky gave a flick of eyebrows. 'I'm sure after this morning you can appreciate that driving between Edinburgh and Dundee isn't exactly driving across America or from here to Greece.'

Shepherd laughed. 'So you think Doug drove back from

Edinburgh, killed his brother, then drove back there, only to drive here again?'

'Something like that's entirely possible.' Forrester locked eyes with Vicky. 'Luke, I've asked your new boss here to focus on that possibility, first and foremost.'

Shepherd rested his bulk against the chair opposite Vicky, blocking out the overhead light like a solar eclipse. 'But?'

Forrester thought it over, his lips chewing like he was still munching his bacon roll, then crunched back in the chair. 'Here's where it gets all need to know.' He flicked his wrist at Vicky. 'Make sure that's shut, please. And nobody's lurking. Like Considine, for instance.'

'Sure.' Vicky checked the handle and, sure enough, Considine was hanging around outside. She waved him off until he actually paid attention and buggered off, then turned back around. 'Clear now.'

'Okay.' Forrester huffed out a deep breath. 'The call I was stuck on last night was with Cathryn Soutar and some senior officers in the Met. The whole reason we found Gavin Mason's body is he's got an arrangement to call in every day at six. Now, he is allowed to arrange time where he won't do it, say going to the pictures, and he has missed it before. Once, he was out on the piss in the Ferry. Another time, on the golf course without mobile reception. Few others too. But the point is, we found him each time. And when someone with that kind of arrangement turns up murdered, well, it ruffles feathers.'

'What's the connection between Gavin and London?'

'Well, here's the thing. He lived in Hackney for a while. Sort of east London but north, if you know it. Anyway, turns out that *both* brothers were involved with an Albanian people trafficking gang.'

'Shit. Albanians?'

'Aye. Nothing against them as people, but the gangs operating out of that country are among the worst in the world. Brutal, vicious. A few years back, a murder case opened things up and they busted it right open. The Mason brothers not so much turned Queen's evidence as became very, very strong informants. Backed it all up, took down the whole operation. Both relocated back to Dundee. And both need to call in at six every day, without fail.'

'Did Doug call in yesterday?'

'He didn't either. Phone was off for a few hours, said the battery ran out. When he called in, he was at that hotel in Edinburgh.'

'Convenient.' Vicky tried to process it, but nothing slotted into place. 'So they're both wanted men?'

'Right, aye. Potentially. While this gang are nasty bastards, they're not under any immediate threat according to the lads I was on with. Simon and Howard spent years prosecuting them. Doug was doing money laundering for them through a couple of businesses, whereas Gavin helped them get people onshore, driving lorries from the continent through ferry terminals with twenty people in the back. That kind of deal.'

Vicky tried to process it. The secrets people hid. 'But they're not under new identities?'

'No. Both rejected it. And, hard as I tried to stop it, the Met are sending a *liaison* on the first flight from Heathrow to Edinburgh, who should be here soon. Unless I can get someone to mine the M90, that is...'

Shepherd was frowning now. 'So you want DI Dodds and I to progress this case on two fronts?'

'No, Luke. The *case* is progressing on two fronts. The

London lot are focusing on it being a gang-related hit. We're to focus on the prospect this is a vanilla murder. Doug offing his brother for doing the nicey-nice with his missus.' Forrester stared right at Vicky. 'How about you take Luke through the case as it stands. Might be something we've both missed.'

14

Vicky pulled onto Gavin Mason's street, shrouded in morning mist, the streetlights barely making any impact. Still too early for even a glimmer of sun. Be another half an hour before it bothered to pitch up. She parked the squad car next to the crime scene van and killed the engine.

The nearest lamppost was covered in missing cat posters, some poor wee wretch called Whispa. Surely that H was redundant?

Over the other side of the road, a couple walked a Westie, all three of them hunched against the cold.

Two young lads shivered by the bus stop, jackets pulled up to their chins, woolly hats on their heads, the kind small kids used to wear but now everyone did.

The bus waddled down the road, its exhaust plume hissing out behind, looking solid in the air.

Crime scene tape flapped in the breeze outside Gavin's home. Flashlights fizzed inside. A suited figure stood outside, with the shape of Vicky's brother. She wanted to go over and see how he was doing. Long way back from being bedridden to combing a house for forensic traces, but he'd made it. Then again, he wasn't speaking to her.

Over the road, Shepherd was sitting in a sleek Tesla, talking on a call to someone. Probably Forrester. Possibly his bosses back in Edinburgh.

Vicky would kill to know who he was talking to and why Forrester had brought Shepherd here.

Of all people.

Her skin crawled. That surely meant only one thing – she was being investigated.

But how?

How did they know?

Vicky leaned back. Sharon hadn't blabbed, as she was as guilty, so who was it?

Was it Forrester just suspecting her? Did they have anything on her?

And why now? Almost eighteen months on.

Vicky had been in Edinburgh earlier in the year for a case, which was how she found out the truth about Shepherd. Surely then would've been the right time?

It didn't stack up. None of it did.

Vicky felt a throb of fear in her neck but tried to swallow it down. She got out into the freezing morning.

Considine was waiting around, coughing into his fist. 'Just saying, what's their motivation?'

'What do you mean?' PC Dewar's partner sucked on a cigarette, downwind of him. 'When they shine the Batlight into the sky, all the Gotham beat cops down tools while Batman goes and does their job for them.'

'Aye, exactly. But it's called the Batsignal, not the Batlight.' Considine laughed. 'Anyway, settle an argument for me. What's the best Keanu film?'

'*John Wick*.'

'*Speed*.'

'Come on, guys, it's clearly *Point*—'

'Constable.' Vicky gave Considine a nod. 'You busy?'

'Sarge. Sorry, boss.' Considine coughed, sounding like a lung had come up. 'This isn't shifting itself, I tell you.'

Vicky leaned back against the pool car. 'It's not covid, is it?'

'Better not be.' Considine snarled. 'Had it twice already and it'll be next year before I get my bloody booster.'

Dewar stamped out his cigarette. 'Caught it off Forrester both times, didn't you?'

'Must've done, aye. Senior officers don't need to self-isolate, do they?' Considine rolled his eyes. 'They're all immune or they're superheroes.' He focused on Vicky. 'What brings you here, boss?'

'I keep telling you that it's fine to call me Vicky.' She smiled at Dewar. 'Morning, gang. You lot getting anything?'

'Only managed one today so far.' Considine pointed over at an ex-council house. 'Another useless bugger who didn't see anything while someone was hammered to death next door.'

'What's your coverage?'

'Twenty percent, give or take.'

'Stephen, you need to up that significantly.'

'Can't do anything if nobody's in.'

'Find them.' Vicky took in the street. Every door seemed to have a separate pairing of officers, but nobody was talking to anyone.

Forrester's car pulled up and he got outup, then skittered

around the front to open the passenger door, like he was driving the Queen.

A haunted-looking man got out. Silver hair cut short. Big, muscular, his navy suit pulling tight. Puffy eyes scanned the vicinity. Guy looked like he'd been trying to get into the Guinness Book of Records for the longest stretch awake.

Aye, Vicky knew how that felt.

Forrester pointed over at Vicky and her gaggle of cops. 'You want to meet my team?'

The guy smirked. Presumably the Met's liaison, though Vicky didn't recognise him. 'Only if they know who's killed the guy.' London accent, delivered with an arrogant sneer. 'Let's get this over with.'

Forrester was giving Vicky a 'see what I have to deal with?' look. He looked back to his mate, but he had already slid off inside Gavin's home. 'Hoy! Derek! You've got to suit up, you bugger!' He raced off after him. 'Jesus Christ!'

Not just his sneer that was arrogant. Acting like a TV cop at a crime scene.

PC Dewar limped off away from them. 'Excuse me, sir, do you live here?'

Shepherd was out of his car now, rubbing his gloved hands together. 'DS Luke Shepherd.'

'Oh, right.'

Shepherd focused on his foot. 'You okay there, son?'

Dewar hobbled after him. 'I'm fine, aye.'

Vicky stopped at the end and squinted at him. 'That limp, though? Sure you should still be on duty?'

'I'm fine, aye.' Dewar hauled his gammy leg behind him. 'Should see the foot, by the way. More purple than your average Prince album. Almost lost a toenail this morning.'

Vicky turned to Considine. 'Don't let us stop you. And it's clearly *The Matrix*.'

'Nah, way too much expositional dialogue.' Then Considine's eyebrows flashed up. 'Come on.' He led up the next-door path.

Dewar sloped behind him, inching up the path. 'Swear this is getting worse, man.' He joined Considine at the door, resting against the surround, grunting and groaning. 'Any chance we can get our piece after this?'

'We've only been at it an hour.'

'Starving, though.'

Considine thumped the door. 'Had a Maccy D's breakfast myself.'

Dewar grunted. 'Hate it when people call it that.'

Shepherd laughed. 'That lad shouldn't be on duty.'

'Hard agree.' Vicky stared deep into his eyes, like she could get the truth that way. 'You want to see the crime scene?'

'Suppose we'd better.' But Shepherd was focusing on Considine and Dewar.

The house door opened and a woman stood there. Peering out, hauling a duffel coat around her shoulders like a cape, her lips twitching. 'Aye, son?'

Considine held up his warrant card. 'Police, madam, we're—'

'Have you got him?'

'Got who?'

'My Whispa!' She reached over to a sideboard and grabbed a sheet of paper.

Vicky didn't even have to see it or be anywhere near. The missing cat.

'I'm afraid it's not—'

'What? You've got him?'

Dewar smiled at her. 'We're here about an incident the other night. You might've seen police officers in the area?'

'This about the Mason laddie next door? Heard all about it. I'm Flossie, by the way. So you've not got Whispa?'

'I'm afraid not, madam.' Dewar hadn't given up yet. 'We were wondering if you'd seen anything or anybody in the area last night?'

'Son, my wee cat's missing. If you've not seen him, then I need to get on with it, so can you leave me alone?'

'Just anyone you might've seen between the hours of three and seven o'clock last night?'

'Son, I'm about to go out again and knock on the doors. Cats get stuck in garages and everything. Can't trust the little buggers!'

Shepherd folded his arms across his chest, smiling at Vicky. 'Makes you reminisce, doesn't it?'

'What, dealing with the great unwashed?'

'Oh, aye. Come on, we'll let them get on with it.' Vicky gave Considine a nod, then led Shepherd away.

'I did see young Gavin and his girlfriend, mind.'

Vicky stopped dead, then turned and darted up the path. 'What did you say? A girlfriend?'

'Aye, pretty wee lassie. Younger than him. Saw them last night when I was out looking for Whispa in the wind and frost. Gavin's lassie went up to his door. Seen her come out about an hour later.' Flossie barked out a laugh. 'No prizes for guessing what they were up to in there!'

'Can you describe her?'

'Mid-twenties. Really pretty. Small, sort of ginger. Aye, ginger. Used to have to dye it in my day!'

In other words, Emma Mason.

15

The bench is cold and wet, soaking into his thighs. The rain's teeming down. What he wouldn't give for a nice dry day. His back's giving him twinges like it's going to seize up soon.

Another glance at his watch, then behind him.

Where is she?

He checks the watch. Ten past eight. Still time for her to show.

The river thunders below, swollen by the rain. Just about make out the white foam in the murky depths.

Same as every day at this time, a tall man jogs along, his husky padding along next to him.

She's usually here by now. Why break the pattern?

He leans back on the bench and takes in the surroundings, running through it all over again. Pitch black below, just the constant hiss of the river as it ebbs and flows. He knows every inch of the way. The walkways, the bridges, the old railway tunnel at the far end.

Why has she broken the pattern now? The twentieth day of following her, knowing her movements better than she does. Better than anyone in her life does. Why break the chain?

Is she away on holiday? Christ, that'd be typical.

No, he'd know.

Wouldn't he?

Movement to the left, behind. 'Come on, Benji.'

He puts his hands into his pockets, touching cold metal, then takes them back out and stands up.

Benji's collar chinks in the morning gloom.

But it's not her.

Her dog, yes. But not her. Not the purposeful stride, just an aimless saunter. A face full of hate and disgust.

He hides in the trees, soaking his feet.

She stops to bend down, knee on the wet tarmac as she rubs the dog's back and gets a groan back. 'Come on.' She stares into the bare woods with cold eyes. No expression on her face.

Has she seen him?

He doesn't know.

He runs along here most mornings and usually bumps into Benji with Morgan... Not her.

She gets to her feet, then starts off down the path again, feet splashing in the deep puddles.

Bitter disappointment runs through him again.

Where the hell was she?

Why break the chain?

He runs in the opposite direction and hits the long straight, leading to the short path back, then takes the shortcut up the back.

And that's when he spots her.

Standing alone outside her house.

16

Vicky held her door and smiled at Dewar. 'Look, just take the statement from her and make sure it gets to the admin officer at Bell Street, okay?'

'Oh, aye.' Dewar gave a salute. His thrill at being involved in a detective case looked genuine. He limped back towards Flossie's house, not quite a spring in his step, but less of a slide.

What a guy. Vicky got in and started the car, the engine's grunt masking her sigh.

Her mobile blasted out.

Forrester calling...

She set off after Shepherd's mid-life crisis and put it on speaker. 'Sir, what's up?'

'Doddsy.' Sounded like Forrester was outside somewhere. 'You know you're a DI, right? Means you don't need my approval to do anything.'

'No, I know that. I'm heading there now, but I wanted to run it past you.' Vicky turned onto Craigie Road and followed the flow of traffic back into the city. 'Take it your pal arrived early.'

'Aye. I was expecting him to fly and take a couple of hours getting from Edinburgh, but no. He drove up overnight, would you believe?'

'Believe anything, sir. Listen, we've got the victim's sister-in-law leaving his house around the time of his death. Spotted there by an old wifie out searching for her missing moggie. In and out within an hour. Add in the description of the woman who sat with Gavin in the pub. Oh, and Jenny's lot found semen and vaginal mucus on the bed. Doesn't take a genius to work out what they were doing in there.'

'Discussing remodelling his house, probably.' Forrester hissed. 'Right, so you're taking the word of a daft old woman who's lost her cat?'

'I'll ignore the misogyny in that and remind you that old ladies have a habit of knowing who's doing what in their neighbourhood.' Vicky joined the queue of traffic heading to the Ferry. 'That's their whole life. Twitching the curtains, watching the cars coming and going. She's been out hunting for her cat, so she's going to be even more vigilant than usual.'

'Right, so you honestly think Doug found out his brother's been bumping uglies with his wife?'

The lights changed and Vicky set off, passing tall tenements on the left, a stone wall on the right guarding the posh houses. 'Two plus two, sir. And bumping uglies is an improvement on doing the nicey-nice.'

'But two plus two doesn't always make four.'

'This just makes the case even stronger. I'm speaking to her now.'

Forrester clicked his tongue a few times. 'Right, fine, you've got my approval. Speak to her nicely, okay? Just a wee chat, see what she says. Okay?'

The flats on the left gave way to Victorian mansions, the white limbs of conservatories filling most of the gardens. 'What about the husband?'

'Have a word with him too. Him being in Edinburgh's a bit of a fly in the ointment over your little theory. Phone being off is a red flag, mind. Just... keep it friendly, alright?'

'Always do. See you later.' Vicky killed the call, then pulled into Doug and Emma's street. Only a few miles from Gavin's ex-council flat, but a world away. They obviously paid a lot for the silence and privacy, but how much of that was legitimate money?

Shepherd was already out of his car, waiting. He was massive, like a bear on the prowl.

Vicky got out and followed him up the drive. Both cars there, dappled with rain, which wasn't showing any signs of easing off. 'Forrester's comfortable with us speaking to them.'

Shepherd stood by the door, waiting. 'You know you're a DI and can do what you see fit, right?'

'That's what Forrester said. I do know that but, given the sensitivity around this, I—'

The door rattled open and Emma peered out. Still in her dressing gown. Green stripes on white cotton, pulled tight around her. 'What's happened?'

Vicky flashed a smile. 'Need another word with you, Mrs Mason.'

Emma fiddled with the gown's belt. 'Doug's not here.'

'It's you we need to speak to.'

'Oh. Okay.' Emma opened the door wide and let them inside. 'Through on the right.'

Vicky followed Shepherd into the living room. A whisky glass sat on the table, next to the bottle of Dunpender, a giant label keen to show it was the centenary edition. A special occasion. A mostly full wine glass kept them company. Typical grieving drinks.

'DS Luke Shepherd.' He stayed standing near the window, keeping a look out along the street. 'Mind if I ask where your husband is, Mrs Mason?'

Emma perched on the sofa, next to Vicky. 'He went out for a run. Said he needed to clear his head.' She pulled the glasses together, seeming to gag at the wine. 'We were at his mother's until about two this morning. Doug couldn't sleep. And he likes to run when he feels like this.'

Shepherd was nodding. 'And could you sleep?'

Emma tugged at her hair. 'Excuse me?'

'Did you sleep well last night?'

'Not really. Kept lying there, needing to go to the toilet.' She picked up the whisky bottle, neck-first like she was going to brain someone with it, then stuffed it onto a shelf on the unit behind the sofa. A couple of other single malts kept it company, even more expensive ones if Vicky's knowledge of her dad's collection was anything to go by. Emma collapsed back into the chair, arms folded, legs kinked, knees together. 'Can I get you a tea? Coffee?'

'We won't keep you.' Vicky peeled off a few pages of her notebook. 'Just got a few questions about your movements last night?'

'We went over this yesterday, didn't we?'

Vicky shut her notebook with a thud. 'We didn't actually. Odd, that.'

Emma's gaze shot between them. 'What's going on here?'

'Where were you last night between, say, three o'clock and the time the police officers visited here? Half seven, was it?'

Emma nibbled her lips. 'You think I'm involved in... in this?'

'What would "this" be?'

'Gavin's murder!'

Vicky raised her hands to placate her. 'We just need to establish a timeline. That's all.'

'A timeline?' Emma tugged at her dressing gown again, like she couldn't get it closed tightly enough. 'Well, I met some pals in town for dinner. Rebecca and Alison. Went to that Spanish place near the Rep. Can't remember the name. Café something. Does tapas.'

'What time would this be?'

'Met at four. We went to the Old Bank Bar for a drink first. Had that, then we sat down for dinner. Think I got a cab home about seven?'

'And before that?'

'I was at the gym. Two hours on the treadmill. Came back here to get changed.' She nibbled at her thumbnail. 'I don't like it when Doug's away. It... It unsettles me. I like routine.'

Vicky spent a few seconds scribbling it down, longer than necessary.

Shepherd cleared his throat. 'You weren't at Gavin's flat, were you?'

'What? No!'

Shepherd stepped away from the window. 'Mrs Mason, why are you lying to us?'

'I'm not lying!' Emma was leaning forward, hands on her bare knees. 'I wasn't *there*. Why would I?'

'Well, we've got ourselves a liar.' Shepherd grimaced. 'I hate it when we spend all this time going door-to-door, asking innocent people who saw what, jogging their memories only for them to remember something. Something like you turning up at Gavin's flat just after half past three yesterday.'

'I was with my pals!'

'We'll check with the Old Bank Bar. And we'll check with the tapas bar.'

Emma's gaze shifted between the two cops. Looking for one to trust, to get her out of this hole.

The front door rattled shut. A voice boomed in the hallway. 'It's helped me, it'll help your mum.' Doug, out of breath.

'I'm off school today, so I could call back later?' A girl's voice. Sounded like she was outside.

'Come on, Morgan, let me just get it now.' Loud footsteps, then Doug stood in the doorway, wearing running gear. Soaked through, dripping all over the floor. Shoes caked in mud. His focus swept between them. 'What's going on?'

'Mr Mason.' Vicky straightened up and shifted around to see outside. Sure enough, there was a young woman standing on the doorstep. Blonde hair tied back, black running gear splashed with lime and pink. Young. Very young. 'Sorry, we can come back later.'

'No, it's fine. Bumped into Morgan on my run. I promised her mum a pill that's helped with my back.' Doug raised his hands. 'Non-prescription painkillers. The pain's not gone away, so I thought I might as well help her now.'

Vicky smiled at him. 'Well, we're just asking some follow-up questions, so we can wait.'

'I know where they are.' Emma collected both glasses and charged out of the room, like she was going to bolt for it.

Doug stepped into the room, water dripping onto the floorboards, and shut the door behind him. He huffed as he folded his arms, his smartwatch tight around his wrist. His face was lobster red, like he'd run a marathon. 'What questions are you asking her? Is it about Gavin's death?'

The kitchen tap hissed, then Emma was at the door, handing a box to the girl. Just having a wee chat.

Vicky leaned back against the window and folded her own arms, echoing Doug's body language. 'Just a few questions, sir. That's all.'

'Like I said last night, I was away at the time of his death.'

'You missed your scheduled call.'

'Mobile died, aye. Feel stupid about that.' Doug swept his hair back, a spray of rainwater flicking out across the wall. 'Do you want me to give you the hotel's name again?'

'We've got it noted, sir. We'll check with them in due course.'

'Now we're getting down to it.' Doug ran his hands though his hair again, sending a mist up into the air. 'You think I somehow magicked myself back here to kill my own brother? Why? Why would I do that?'

'All we're doing is trying to identify the last person to see your brother alive.'

Doug screwed up his eyes at Vicky. 'Well it wasn't my wife.'

The lady doth protest too much…

Vicky checked her notebook again and jabbed the pen against the paper. 'We need to establish a clear and accurate timeline for the events leading up to your brother's death, Mr Mason. It's very simple. Standard practice.'

'That's all you're doing, is it?' Doug scowled. 'Not trying to twist this so that my wife's involved in Gavin's death?'

'Is she?'

Doug made to speak but stopped himself. He looked

around the room, at Shepherd, at Vicky, then back to Shepherd. 'Why the hell would she be? There's absolutely no reason for my wife to want anything bad to happen to Gavin. None.'

'Then that's what we'll find, then.'

'Of course you will, but you're wasting your time. I'd rather you caught who'd killed him.'

Vicky narrowed her eyes at him. 'How's your mother?'

'I've...' Doug pinched his nose. 'I've not seen her since last night.' He slicked his hair to the side, flattening it. 'I'm worried about her.'

'And yet you find time to go out for a run today?'

'There's a family liaison officer with her.'

'A police officer's a bit different to a family member. Her only son.'

'Well, I need to get changed and head around there, so unless you want to torment Emma again, do you mind leaving us to it?'

'Thanks for your time.' Vicky got to her feet. 'We'll show ourselves out.' She led Shepherd out into the tipping rain, then down the path. 'Well?'

'Definitely two people with something to hide.' He stopped at the end of the drive and looked back at the house. Doug Mason was twitching the curtains in their living room. 'Whether that's anything to do with Gavin's death? No idea.'

'Thing is, Luke, we've got a few hours where Doug could've done anything. Assuming he was in Edinburgh at that time.'

'But from what David Forrester told me, we know some numpty took Gavin Mason's car from outside his house to visit a supermarket. Doors open, engine running. I want to know who left it like that.'

17

Vicky leaned back in her seat and stretched out her arms. She closed her eyes and listened to the percussive rattle of Jenny's fingers attacking the keyboard.

Forrester's voice boomed out of the office. Getting louder. No idea what had lit the fuse now.

Shepherd was outside in the car park, talking on his phone.

Making a habit of that.

Vicky checked her messages, but nothing from Sharon. Maybe this was all in her mind. She was guilty, sure, but what choice did she have? Let those animals get at Bella or Jamie? No way.

'Am I boring you?' Jenny was giving her some side eye.

'Sorry.' Vicky pocketed her mobile, took one last look at Shepherd, then leaned forward to give the pretence of her full attention. 'What have you got?'

'Who said I've got anything?'

'You usually stop to get some attention when you've done something.'

Jenny smirked. 'Ten points to Gryffindor, then.'

'Come on, you're clearly Slytherin. You got anything on Gavin's car?'

'Nope, but I've got your killer's vehicle.'

Vicky jolted forward. 'What are you talking about?'

'Like I said yesterday, magic school.' Jenny tapped her nose. 'But this is something I conjured up.'

Onscreen, Gavin's Audi was parked outside the supermarket. Sure enough, Iain Paton was inside it

Jenny wound it backwards. 'Watch this.'

The car door opened, then a van blocked the view. When it moved, the Audi's exhaust was pluming in the cold.

'So Paton's story checks out?'

'Right. But what's more…' Jenny tapped the screen. 'Now.'

A car pulled across the front of it.

'No other car ten minutes either side of it.' Jenny froze it and took it back. 'A Toyota Corolla.'

'Have you got the plates?'

'Nope.'

'Can you at least follow that car?' Vicky waved at Shepherd. 'Luke!' That got his attention. She beckoned him over.

Jenny's eyes went wide. 'Christ, Luke, you just get uglier.'

'Jennifer Morgan.' Shepherd stood up tall and held out his hand. 'How the devil are you?'

'Working for the police. How can anyone enjoy that?'

'It has its moments.' Shepherd stood there, hands stuffed deep in his pockets. 'You getting anywhere?'

'Sort of.' Vicky looked up. 'Who were you on the phone to?'

'Why do you want to know?'

'Because I'm your boss and if it's not to do with this case, I want to know why you're taking personal calls during a murder investigation.'

'Sorry.' He raised his hands. 'I was asking that Considine lad to head into town and check out this alibi of hers. Prove it's bollocks and not some daft copper's hunch. Seems like a good cop.'

'Seriously?'

'Isn't he?'

Vicky rolled her eyes. If Shepherd was who the Complaints were sending after her, she had this in the bag. 'When did it get to Dundee?'

Jenny wound back the video to 15:22, the arrival of the Toyota. Again, it was angled so they couldn't see through the windscreen. Then the same trick as the departure, waiting for a passing van to exit the car. But she had the number plates in full view. 'Bingo!' Her screen was filled with rows of data. Vicky knew it well – ANPR hits. 'That trail leads from Dundee to the Forth Bridge. Just over ninety minutes.'

'What about after the bridge?'

'No hits on the way into Edinburgh, but there are ways and means to avoid the ANPR system there, if you know what you're doing.'

'That's not Doug Mason's own car, though. He drives a VW Golf.' Vicky looked at Jenny. 'Can you dig into who owns it?'

'On it.' Jenny started tapping away. For once, she wasn't arguing about having to do police work. This was important stuff and she was about ten times faster than any of Vicky's guys.

Shepherd leaned between them. 'So, ten minutes or so after

Gavin was killed, Gavin's car arrives at this supermarket. So he swaps over to this Toyota, then drives off?'

Jenny tapped her screen, which was showing rows of data. 'It's a hire car.' She scrolled through the fields. 'Twenty-four-hour booking, done online. Dropped off on Corstorphine Road in Edinburgh. Nobody to collect it, either. Instructions to leave it at the yard.'

Vicky leaned forward to check the name fields. 'Colin Scott?'

'I doubt it's our killer's real name.' Shepherd was working at the adjacent machine. 'Quite a few Colin Scotts on the PNC, but none match that address.' He clicked a few times. 'Aye, it's a PO box in Dundee.'

'Which isn't exactly answering anything.' Jenny scowled at her, eyes narrow. 'I'll try and trace the account, but don't expect anything.' She sat back and slapped the keyboard. 'Ah, you bugger. The email used to set it up is a burner.'

'How do you know?'

'Pumpmail is notorious. Russian bots use it all the time.'

'How was it paid for?'

'Credit card.'

Vicky had a tingle of excitement in her chest. 'Can you track the cardholder?'

'I can.' Jenny tapped her keyboard again. 'But it was reported stolen this morning. In Redding, California.'

Shepherd leaned forward and cleared his throat. 'Okay, so that's showing signs of organisation and competence, right? Getting hold of an American credit card to pay for a Scottish car hire. What about earlier today?'

'That Corolla travelled from Edinburgh to Dundee just after two. Straight up the M90 then A90, no stopping. Lose it in central Dundee. Just about to check with the hire company, but I don't think that car made any other trips that day.'

Shepherd stared at Vicky. 'What's your theory?'

Vicky didn't have to think too hard about it. 'Doug Mason's down there for the weekend. Gives him a plausible alibi. He's cuckolded, angry. Hires a car, drives back to Dundee, kills his adulterous brother, then drives back to Edinburgh to maintain his cover. Then heads back home, as if nothing had happened.'

'Seem a bit of a stretch to me.' Shepherd pointed at the screen, showing the Toyota. 'That's a professional, not someone attending a conference. Same with getting a stolen credit card to pay for a car hire.'

'Luke, Doug Mason was involved in a people trafficking organisation. That means he's a professional.'

'A professional accountant.'

'That's all we know about him on that front. Could have other skills.'

'I see your point, but until we know about them, it's just guesswork.'

Vicky smiled at Jenny. 'Can you get hold of any of your old colleagues in Edinburgh and pick up the car before it's cleaned? Assuming it's—'

'No dice. Still not returned.'

'Shit. They know where it is?'

'Well, your guess is as good as mine. Probably back in Edinburgh, I'd say. Could be elsewhere, though.'

'Can you speak to them, please?'

Jenny laughed. 'Must've missed that meeting where this became my job.'

'Come on.' Vicky folded her arms. 'You owe me.'

'Fine.' A teenager huff.

Shepherd jangled his keys in his pocket. 'So, what's the plan?'

'Right now, this is one of those cases where it's equally possible it's either scenario.'

'So, a hitman killed Gavin for Doug, or Doug the hitman killed Gavin?'

'Might be something else we just can't see, but I think we need to focus on those two as likely.' Vicky took a deep breath. 'First, Emma has lied to us. Told us she was with some friends when we know she was with Gavin. It's likely she was intimate with him, but there could still be an innocent explanation. But she was there. Had been a few times, so I'm tended to go with the guilty one.'

'And if it was innocent, why not tell us the truth?' Shepherd grunted. 'Listen, Emma's a good few years younger than Doug. I'm not being sexist here, but—'

'Oh cool.' Jenny rolled her eyes. 'When people say that, they're definitely not going to sound like an arsehole.'

'I'm just trying to get into his head. Classic trophy wife for a businessman with prospects. Emma didn't have a job, which meant a lot of time on her hands that no amount of treadmill could fill. She just got bored. Liked Gavin, or it could be he just paid her some attention.'

'That's honestly how you see it?'

'Not the first time it's happened. Won't be the last, either.'

'Still, Doug driving back from Edinburgh to kill his brother? Seems a bit far-fetched to me.'

Vicky pointed at the screen. 'We've possibly got someone swapping from Gavin's car to a hire job, then driving to Edinburgh just after the time of the murder. ANPR hits all the way up and back.'

'But we don't know who was driving.' Shepherd looked up. 'As much as I *love* doing that drive loads of times in a day, I think we should head down to Edinburgh. The conference is still on. Ask a few questions. See if Doug's story holds true. Or if it falls apart.'

18

'This it here?' Shepherd hit the brakes and squealed into a large car park. Edgy blues music pounded out of the speakers, just one guy and a guitar but it sounded like an army waging war on Vicky's hearing. He wedged the car between two silver taxis, the hulking German minivans that golfers loved. 'This is definitely it?'

'Look, I don't know.' Vicky passed the map to Shepherd. 'I lost track when we came off the A90. You're an Edinburgh cop so you tell me.'

'Why didn't you say?'

Vicky hit the power button on the stereo. Did nothing. She held it down and the warped blues stopped. 'Because of that din.'

'Trust me, the only music you need is Blind Bob Bollocks.'

'Bollocks? That's a real name?'

'Blind Bob *Horrocks*.'

'I think I'm Dead Vicky Dodds.'

'Heathen.' Shepherd opened his door and got out.

Vicky rubbed at her ears, trying to get some sensation back, then got out into the freezing lunchtime air. Despite being further south, Edinburgh always felt about ten degrees colder than Dundee. Bright sunshine blared above some trees, just skirting the bare branches, blown about by the severe breeze.

The Neshington Grange was halfway up a hill and had glorious views across the expanse of the city towards more hills in the distance. Bigger ones, blocking any view south. Across the road was a thin woodland, the kind of place dog walkers found bodies.

The hotel itself was a Sixties building that seemed to have received a sizeable upgrade every subsequent decade, with a load of construction work going on now to add the 2020s to the collection. The hotel's cream stone glowed in the sun like a baked Alaska.

Cigarette smoke wafted over the car from the entrance. Shepherd sucked it in, eyes closing like a junkie shooting up. 'Feel the air.' He buttoned up his coat, digging into his flabby neck. 'That's bracing, isn't it?' He glared at his mobile, fierce as the wind, then stabbed his sausage fingers on the screen and put it to his head. 'Stephen? It's Luke.' He grimaced. 'Luke Shepherd. DS Luke Shepherd. Aye, me. How you getting on with validating Emma's story?'

Vicky leaned against Shepherd's car, her dry fingers soaking up the dots of rain on the roof. The questions burned in her gut like her hunger.

Shepherd joined her, still speaking into his phone. 'Okay, please congratulate PC Dewar on finding Whispa the cat, but I really need you to corroborate Emma's story with the bar and restaurant. Cheers, son.' He pocketed his mobile and unlocked the car, clicking his tongue on his teeth. 'Considine's spoken to Emma Mason's pals, who have backed up her story.'

'They would, I suppose. But Considine's not checked the restaurant, has he?'

Shepherd winced. 'Not yet. Still, we'll get positive press from Dewar finding the missing cat.'

'Well, that's good news, but... Considine... Bloody hell. We've driven down to Edinburgh in that time. What the hell has he been doing?'

'His job?'

'Luke, he's absolutely useless, though. And I've been stuck with him for years.' Vicky stared at him again, teeth grinding. 'Let's get this over with, I suppose.' She set off across the tarmac, trying to avoid the battlefield of puddles, wrapping her arms tight around herself.

'It's not *that* cold, is it?' Shepherd caught up with her.

'I hate it down here.' Vicky sped up, trying to get some heat into her legs, some sensation back into her feet. 'It's like we're in the Arctic, but we've gone south.' She tried to wrestle the hotel door open. 'Went to university in Aberdeen and I swear it was warmer up there.' Had to give it a good tug. Still wouldn't budge.

Shepherd pushed the door open with one blow. 'The only thing below absolute zero is Aberdeen in January.'

'Try February.' Vicky followed him inside. The heating could melt sand and turn it into glass. Must be at least twenty-five degrees in there. She unbuttoned her coat, doing the traditional Scottish winter dance. Sweat puckered the back of her shirt already.

Shepherd was at the reception, grinning at the teenager

behind the counter. He flashed his warrant card, quick enough that the kid couldn't get a proper look. 'Manager around, son?'

Vicky had to admire the way he used the word 'son' like others would fire a pistol. She stayed back and took in the place.

An atrium area, square and large, like you only really saw in New York films. Steps led down to a slightly lower seating area where a bunch of well-to-do pensioners perched on sofas at right angles, two factions who seemingly refused to speak to each other. Hats and scarves, flashes of Burberry in their jacket lining.

A waiter poured out coffees for them, one arm behind his back. Smelled like good stuff, dark and strong.

Peals of laughter came from somewhere, echoing and distant. Signs for conferences pointed towards the Banks, MacBride and Guthrie Suites, each with their own ornate entrances, gold doors folded back shut. The source of the laughter was on the right – must be lunch, one of those affairs where you clip a wine glass to your plate. Eat so much at the buffet that you want to sleep all afternoon. Drink so much orange juice or wine that you need to pee all afternoon.

Whether it was from the conference Doug Mason had attended was another matter.

A couple of businessmen in three-piece suits walked back this way, talking into mobiles while their eyes scanned the room, always hunting for the next deal or networking opportunity that might lead to that deal.

'Vicky.' Shepherd was beckoning her over, like she was a pet dog.

A middle-aged woman leaned against the counter next to him, one leg kicked up behind her. Suit jacket and navy tartan skirt. Eye makeup like a hungover panda. 'Okay, well I have only now received your warrant, Sergeant. The fax was on the blink but it's all fine now.' She smiled at him. 'We had yet another black fax protest.'

Shepherd laughed. 'A what?'

'Our parent company in the US isn't very popular with a certain demographic of far-right lunatics.' The manager held up a page, completely black. 'So they send us these. Clogs up machines across the country. And we run out of ink in minutes.' She waved a page around. 'Just so happens your fax was in amongst it all. But really, who sends faxes these days?'

'Police Scotland does, sadly. Right, so you're going to play ball, aye?'

'Least I could do after you've driven all this way.' She winked at Shepherd. Probably had a thing for big rugby types. She tucked her hair behind her ear and flicked through a sheaf of papers. 'Anyway, this is everything you've requested.' She laid them out on the counter, smoothing out the paper. 'Okay, so a Douglas Mason checked in on Saturday morning at 11.06.' She pressed down another page. 'And he checked out at 21.34 last night.'

Shepherd took the pages from her and scanned down, like he was looking for any gaps in the story. 'Do you know if he was here all that time?'

The manager flashed a grin at Shepherd. 'We do ask guests to return their keys when they leave for the day and collect them on their return.' She reached over for one on the other side. A rusted brass thing hanging off a lump of dark wood. 'Not everyone complies.'

'Right, so you're saying that he left?'

'Just saying that he didn't leave the key behind if he did.'

'I see.' Shepherd went back to the pages, trying to decipher some hidden meaning in the runes. 'Have you got CCTV here?'

'We do, but it's being used as part of the construction work to guard the building materials outside.'

'Fantastic.' Shepherd shook his head. 'So, we were—'

'Can I just stop you there?' The manager flashed a smile. 'One of Mr Mason's colleagues might be better placed to answer these questions?' Before Shepherd or Vicky could argue, she set off through the door to the Banks Suite. She waved a hand across the foyer. 'James!'

The attendees stood around, chatting and tucking into salmon and cheese. The two nearest men bellowed with laughter, their suit jackets bulging as they tossed their heads back. Looked like genuine laughter, too.

Behind them, two builder types talked at each other, barely making eye contact.

The manager rubbed a licked finger across her eyebrow. 'Mr Corey's just coming.'

'Thank you.' Shepherd gave her a warm smile. 'Mr Corey?'

A man stood on his own, staring into space. Guy could've worked in Silicon Valley. Sharp suit, tailored to his very un-Scottish physique. Shining shoes, shining teeth. Hair spiked in just-that-perfectly-messy way.

'DS Luke Shepherd.' He held out his warrant card. 'This is DI Vicky Dodds. We'd like to ask you some questions.'

'Pleasure to meet you both.' Corey picked up a plate completely covered in smoked salmon and lettuce. Nothing else. 'Let's do this over here, if you don't mind?' He marched through a side door into a large ballroom. Ten little boxes were dotted across the floor, each barely three metres square. He opened the nearest. Four chairs were rammed tight around a circular table. 'Sorry about this. The conference has some break-out sessions and these *things* are what the hotel pulled together.' He took a seat and spread his legs wide. 'Don't mind if I eat while we talk, do you? I'm doing OMAD.'

'OMAD?'

'One Meal A Day.'

'Not a problem, sir.' The smoky fishy reek was churning Vicky's stomach. 'We understand you work with a Doug Mason?'

Corey speared some on his fork, put it in his mouth. '*With*.' He smiled as he finished chewing. 'Been partners for the last five years. Green and Clear Ltd.'

Vicky almost groaned. 'Cute name.'

'Thanks, can't take credit.' Corey took a mouthful of lettuce and spoke around his chewing. 'Doug's the numbers guy, whereas I lead on the sales side. He keeps the trains running on time, while I open up more stations. If that makes sense.' More lettuce. He clamped his free hand around his kneecaps, tucked tight to his body. 'Heard his brother died yesterday.'

'That's right.' Vicky couldn't find a position where she could both write and not rub her knee against Shepherd's. 'That's what we're investigating.'

'Horrible business.' Corey wiped something from his chin. 'I was there when Doug got the call. Just... Can't imagine, can you?'

'Only too well.' Vicky smiled. 'Did you know Mr Mason's brother?'

'Gav, aye. Been out golfing with him a few times. Not for a while, mind. Cracking golfer, though.' Corey swallowed down some salmon. 'Doug and Gav were close. I never speak to my own brother, but those guys were tight. Can't believe what's happened.'

Vicky smoothed out the margin of her notebook. 'How has he been recently?'

'Busy. Focused on this event. We're co-sponsoring it.'

'Aside from that, has Douglas seemed preoccupied with anything recently?'

'What's this about?' Corey got to his feet, arms folded, his head almost reaching the ceiling of the tiny space. 'You don't think—'

Shepherd raised a hand. 'We need to get a bit of background colour on Mr Mason, that's all.'

'But you can't think he's got anything to do with his brother's death?'

Vicky held Corey's gaze for a few seconds before he looked away. 'We're paid to keep an open mind.'

'Of course.' Corey sat again and attacked the lettuce with his fork. 'The last few months have been hard on us. We're doing another round of funding from investors. Not easy in Scotland, so I pushed hard to get a keynote speech here, which cost us a big chunk in sponsorship. That was Saturday evening. Went down really well. Then I was down to do a panel yesterday with another three firms.'

'But?'

'Well, I had to pull out, so Doug did it. Had food poisoning and took so much Imodium I swear I'll never crap again.' He covered his mouth and burped. 'Sorry. Over a hundred people watching, though. Lots of businesspeople. The kind who can help us with our funding.'

Vicky's knee brushed against something.

Shepherd cleared his throat. 'This panel. What was it about?'

'Solar battery installations. Where that'll take us. How to grow the industry. How to influence government policy. Doug talked about the medium-term stuff, whereas I'd just talk about bamboozling people into spending money.'

Vicky couldn't quite square the mobster-in-hiding with the businessman talking to over a hundred people.

Corey speared some more lettuce. 'Like I say, Doug's a smart guy. Knows where to put resources to make our gambles pay off.'

Shepherd shifted back and got out his notebook. 'When was this panel?'

'Told you. Yesterday.'

'What time?'

Corey's tongue flapped around between his lips, his forehead creased. 'Noon. Hour of chat, hour of questions. Then we had some drinks in the bar. I was trying to work the room, spread my tale one-on-one, despite having to dash off to the crapper every five minutes.'

'And Doug was here all that time?'

Corey set his fork down on the plate. 'Not sure.'

Vicky checked her notebook. 'When did you last see him?'

'Well... Half nine last, when he got the call from Emma.'

'Before that?'

Corey exhaled slowly. 'Not after the panel, sorry. Like I say, I was on the porcelain throne a lot of the time.'

Vicky's jolt of excitement was matched in Shepherd's eyes. 'You didn't see him between two and half past nine?'

'Sorry, no. Look, I don't know. The business types I wanted Doug to chat to went to watch the rugby in the bar, so I presume they continued chatting in there over beer rather than wine.'

'But you didn't see him between two and nine?'

Corey's frown switched to a nod. 'Aye, that's when he got the call about Gav. He was broken. Upset. I sat him down and gave him a coffee. Tried to get him to take his time, not do anything rash. But he drove back to Dundee.' He yawned. 'I took some guys out to show them the sights of Edinburgh.'

Read: We went to a strip club and I paid with company money.

'Is it possible Doug slipped off after the panel?'

'Excuse me.' Corey burped into his hand again. 'Salmon keeps repeating on me. On a high-protein diet. Got to keep my shape, you know?' He patted his flat belly, then pushed his plate away. 'Listen, Doug mentioned something about meeting a friend.'

'Here?'

'No. Back in Dundee. He mentioned a name but I… I can't remember it. Sorry.'

'Male or female?'

'One of those which could be either. Ach, it'll come to me.' Corey clicked his fingers a few times. 'Would it be Morgan?'

Shepherd stared at Vicky. 'The girl he was running with this morning?'

19

He looks up and down the street again, his back starting to ache from sitting there so long. Dark houses on a dark day. Supposed to be noon, but it feels like dusk. Some lights on, but most wait in the gloom for the owners to return. Deadly quiet, except for the occasional gust of wind.

Easy to get carried away, thinking nobody can see him, that he's invisible, but there's always a curtain-twitcher watching. That's their trick – watching everything but never being seen themselves. Cross-referencing established movement patterns copiously annotated in their journals with what they see with their own two eyes.

Still, the house is mostly dark, just a side light on in the living room. Music tinkles out of the windows, the *Frozen* soundtrack.

She's such a little princess.

And alone in the building.

He eases the car door open, then steps out and scans the

houses. He pulls the coat down and the bulge is obvious, the big chunk of metal in his trousers. The known curtain-twitchers are all out or eating inside. Underneath the blanketing wind, there's the sound of cutlery hitting crockery.

The car door barely clicks as he nudges it to.

Time to strike.

An engine moans from the far end of the street. Headlights arc round. A car.

Just perfect...

He gets back in his car and slumps low behind the wheel. Just enough that he can watch it track past, slowing as it pulls into a drive. Then a couple get out, arguing with each other about school fees and something else he doesn't catch. Welcome to suburbia.

The house door slams behind the husband and the sound rattles around the street.

Curtains twitch to his left, then another pair further down on the right.

Thirty seconds after they're gone, the curtains go back to where they were.

He gives them another ten, then nudges the door open again. The street's silent, just the distant rumble of the main road.

So he gets out and crosses the road, stepping over the low wall and across the mossy slabs, avoiding the pebbles until he's at the house. One last check of the street – still quiet, the curtains in their place – and he slips down the side of the building.

Around the back, a pale glow comes from the conservatory, lighting up the lawn. Nobody's in there, though.

But he sees her inside the kitchen, absently staring out of

the window. Hair tied back, a deep frown on her forehead. Then clattering as she loads the dishwasher. It stops and she's gone.

Down low, he inches below the kitchen window, stepping across to the conservatory. Listens hard.

Nothing.

Then he opens the French door and steps inside. Lavender candles. Burnt toast. That music playing.

She's in the lounge now, staring out onto the street, her head jerking in sharp reptilian movements. That's how they start. No curtains, just twitches. Then they start hiding it.

He steps through the dining room, through the sliding doors, hanging open, and into the living room, knowing which floorboards to avoid and which to step on, into the light.

Cream walls, wooden flooring. A few pictures here and there, abstract art.

She's five metres away, still looking out of the window, *Frozen* blaring away.

Morgan swings around and her forehead twitches. 'Doug? What are—?'

'Shhh.' He grabs her by the throat and pushes her back, pressing her milky skin against the window, twisting her around so she's facing away from him.

'What—?'

He grabs her shoulder and pulls her away from the window, then twists her around and pushes her against the wall, pressing the knife into her hip, then against her spine. Just the right angle to pierce her heart. Enough to terrify her.

'No!' Her scream is muffled by his gloved hands.

He's got no choice here.

His throat is thick. He swallows down the saliva.

I'm sorry.

He wishes he could say the words, but he can't.

Take it slowly. Give yourself time. Her parents won't be back for hours.

Her head twists around, eyes full of fire. 'Why are you doing this to me?'

He's got no choice.

And he really, really doesn't want to.

He accidentally steps on her shoe and it comes off. He catches an elbow in the face and stumbles back.

Morgan bombs off into the house.

20

Vicky gripped her mobile as Dundee blurred past, cutting through the Victorian terraces on both sides of the road. She couldn't figure out how the hell to stop the music. 'Can you turn that off?'

Shepherd reached over and turned what passed for music down. 'Just have to ask.'

'Off, not down.'

'What can I say? Can't drive without Blind Bob.'

'Turn it off!'

'Jesus, keep your hair on.' Shepherd slammed a finger on the steering wheel and the music died.

Blissful silence.

'Right.' She put the phone to her ear. 'Sorry, Jenny, you were saying?'

'What the bar staff told you stacks up with the CCTV we just got through. Loads of rugger buggers watching the rugger. But none of them look like Doug Mason, according to that Summers clown you've sent here.'

'Excellent. Listen, thank you for doing this. I'm struggling to corral the horses a bit—'

'—and you need someone with management experience. It's cool.'

'Thanks. Got to go.' Vicky slumped back in her seat. 'Well, Doug wasn't there.'

'Bloody hell.' Shepherd's hand reached over to the stereo.

'Please, no more.'

'Seriously?'

'Seriously.' She folded her arms. 'So he could have driven up to Dundee to kill his brother?'

Shepherd was doing twenty over the forty limit. He slammed the brakes as he pulled up at the lights. 'You don't seem happy with that?'

'I just don't know what to make of it.'

'Cheer up, Vicky. We've dug a big hole in his alibi. Doug lied to us. Told us he was in the bar for drinks with these guys, but the truth is he wasn't seen until nine, when Emma called. That's more than enough time to get to Dundee and back to kill his brother. He's got a wide window of opportunity here.'

'True. And he got Emma to lie to us too.'

'Christ.' Shepherd hauled the car around a sharp left onto a road full of Seventies bungalows nestling in trees. He pulled up outside Doug Mason's house.

PC Dewar was limping around in the front garden, craning his neck to see in the living room window.

Vicky hauled open the door and crunched up the pebbles. 'Dewar, have you got him?'

'No sign of either of them. Mason was at his mother's, then left to get some air. Not been seen since.'

'And Morgan Miller?'

'She's not at school. Tried the neighbours as well. No sign of her, sorry.'

'That's not good.'

'Eh, sorry.'

'Not your fault.' Vicky looked over at Shepherd approaching. 'Both missing.'

'He's definitely not in?'

'Nope.' Dewar snorted, thumb over the other nostril. 'Well. Nobody's answering.' He thumbed the buzzer and shook himself down. 'Gilmour's gone round the back.'

Vicky stepped onto the small circular lawn wedged between some old paving slabs and peered through the window. 'No signs of life inside.'

'Right.' Shepherd thumped at the door. 'We got anything pointing to him sleeping with her?'

'Not yet.' Vicky huffed out a breath. Sweat prickled on her back. 'Jesus, Luke, she's *fifteen*.'

Dewar opened his eyes wide. 'Oh my god. He's a paedo?'

'Technically, he's a hebephile, but it's the same difference.' Vicky waved over at the grey Golf parked on the street. 'Doug's car's here.'

'Bloody hell.' Shepherd knelt and knocked on the door. 'Police! Open up!'

They'd hear that in Fife.

No response, though.

Shepherd twisted around to glare at Dewar. 'Have you tried the neighbours?'

'Not had the chance yet. Just got here ourselves.'

Vicky crunched back down the drive and turned left, heading for next door, the only house with a light on at that time. She stomped across the slabs just as the rain started spitting on the concrete, then jabbed at the doorbell.

The door opened a fraction, a lined face squinting out. 'Can I help?'

'Police.' Vicky held out her warrant card. 'Wondering if you've seen your neighbours this afternoon?'

The door creaked open. An old woman, almost as wide as she was tall. 'Which neighbours?'

'Mr and Mrs Mason?'

'Well, I got back from the Asda just after twelve. Thought I saw both cars in the drive.'

Vicky looked back at the Golf. 'You definitely saw both cars?'

'That one.' She pointed at the drive. 'And her one. It's blue. Wee thing. Thought it was strange how he was still at home. Of course, they've had that bereavement, haven't they?'

'You didn't see her drive off?'

She squinted down the street. 'Sorry. No, I didn't. I was out putting my fish in the freezer.'

Vicky smiled at her. 'Thanks for your help.'

'I'd ask at the Millers' house, if I was you.'

Vicky turned back. 'The Millers?'

'Well, I think Douglas has been helping young Morgan with her maths tutoring.'

And that wasn't all.

'Which one's that?'

She waved across the road. 'Number seventeen. Think I saw someone in earlier.'

'Thank you.' Vicky stormed off down the drive, rain thudding on her head, hoping Morgan's mum or dad were in. That they had an innocent explanation for all of this, because the truth was digging into her bones. 'Luke!'

Shepherd and Dewar both looked over.

Vicky pointed at the house she was closing in on. Didn't seem like anyone was in. No cars, no lights, no sounds.

No doorbell, so she rattled the letterbox.

Waited.

Nothing.

So she stepped across the pebbles at the front and peered in the living room window.

Dark in there on a gloomy day.

Wait.

Music played inside.

She groaned. The *Frozen* soundtrack. She'd only just weened Bella off it after *years* of enduring it.

Dewar was on the doorstep. 'Aye, nobody in.'

Vicky checked around the room again. A running shoe was lying in the middle of the wooden floor.

Seemed strange.

Vicky darted over to the door. 'We need in there.'

'Why?' Dewar stood up from the letterbox. 'Nobody in, ma'am.'

'No, there is. Or might be. And we've got probable cause.' She nodded at him. 'Want to do the Superman thing?'

'Watch out.' Dewar took a few steps back and flung himself at the door, shoulder first. It crunched open with a deep thud and he tumbled arse over tit. He lay on the floor, groaning. 'I've buggered my foot again!'

Vicky helped Dewar up. 'Call this in!' She entered the house. 'Stay there. Nobody gets past, okay?'

'You can rely on me, ma'am.'

Nothing, just silent cream walls and wooden floors.

'You hear that?' Shepherd inched across the flooring to a right-hand bend in the hall.

Vicky extended her baton and followed him in. 'Coming from through there.'

Shepherd opened the glass door at the far end of the hall. The music got louder. He stopped by the living room door, waiting on one side for Vicky to join him. Then counted to three on his fingers.

Vicky burst into the room at the same time as Shepherd.

Empty.

Just the stereo playing.

Shepherd snapped it off. The case for the *Frozen* soundtrack sat on top of the speakers. 'Who has CDs these days?'

'Me.' Vicky walked over to the discarded trainer and stopped dead.

Morgan lay on the floor, gasping for air, hands around her throat. It was like she was trying to speak, but she could only swallow the words.

An engine roared on the street.

Vicky shot over to the window.

Dewar lay on the pebbles, clutching his balls.

Doug's Golf sped off back to the main road.

'Bollocks.' Shepherd raced back to his car.

'Get inside and check on Morgan!' Vicky shot after Shepherd, feet slamming off the pebbles then thudding over the tarmac. She tore open the passenger side, got in and hit dial on her mobile.

The driver's door slammed. Shepherd got behind the wheel and fumbled with the ignition, struggling to get it to start. 'Come on, come on, come on.'

Jenny answered with a sigh. 'Hey, ANPR support line, doing cops' jobs because they can't be fu—'

'Need you to track a car.'

'What? Another one?'

Shepherd nudged Vicky's arm. 'Seatbelt!'

'What?'

'Put your bloody seatbelt on!'

She tugged it over and clicked it in.

The engine finally jolted and they shot off. A horn blared from behind as Shepherd barged into the traffic.

'Need you to track Doug Mason's Golf. Silver or grey.'

'Got it. This is the one—'

'Live pursuit, Jenny. End of his street, I think there's a camera.'

'There he is.' Shepherd waved a hand through the glass.

The Golf was stopped at the lights, in the left-hand filter.

Shepherd pulled up two cars behind.

Vicky opened her window and leaned out, trying to peer forward. 'Can't see the number plate.'

The lights changed and the Golf eased off.

Shepherd followed the car, keeping a two-car distance, then put his foot down as the road widened out, trees lining both sides, the murky Tay to the left. Heading into the town centre. 'Brace yourself.' He pulled out into oncoming traffic and undertook the white van hogging the fast lane.

'Steady on!' Vicky clung on. 'Jenny, we're heading to the gasworks down on East Dock Street.'

'Got you.'

Shepherd weaved out, a black Kia all that lay between him and his prey.

'Put the siren on, Luke.'

Shepherd rubbed at his ear and said something Vicky couldn't hear.

The Kia drifted to the left.

Shepherd floored it, swerving in and out at the sharp left bend in the road, just missing a lorry as it thundered their way. 'Where's he gone?'

Vicky darted her head around. She clocked the Golf as it turned past the modern hotels on either side. 'Over the bridge!'

Shepherd gunned the engine, shooting across the road right in front of a bus, but he skipped over the line onto the lane heading for the Tay Road Bridge. A long straight, cast under dark rainclouds.

The Golf was gaining speed as it thundered over the bridge.

Vicky put her phone to her ear again. 'Jenny, we're on the bridge now, heading towards Fife.'

'Okay, well I've got you some backup.'

'On the Fife side?'

Vicky didn't catch the reply.

Shepherd closed on the end of the bridge. The Golf was just in front, hugging the left lane.

Shepherd pulled out then tugged the wheel hard left, forcing the Golf to make a sharp left onto the slow road to Tayport. 'Got him.'

The Golf hurtled along the road, then took the right into the car park.

Shepherd waited for a bus to pass, then pulled in.

The Golf was easing into a space.

Shepherd skidded to a halt behind it, blocking it.

Vicky pocketed her mobile and got out first, extending her baton as she ran over to the Golf. She tugged at the handle. Locked. 'Police!'

A woman cowered in the driver's seat, arms curled over her head.

Shit. Where the hell was Doug?

'Madam, I need you to open the door.'

Shepherd tugged Vicky's sleeve. 'You need to—'

'Madam, please open the door.'

The woman looked around, eyes wide with terror.

'Vicky, will you listen to me?'

She tried the handle again. 'Please open the door.'

The woman had a mobile clamped to her ear and mouthed, 'I'm calling the police!'

Shepherd grabbed Vicky and pushed her away from the car. 'She's called 999 and reported us. You know that fake cop rapist urban legend? Unmarked police car with its sirens on forcing a car to pull over?'

Vicky pinched her nose. She tapped at the window, warrant card out. 'Madam, we are the police.'

The woman stared at her for a few seconds, then leaned over to wind the window down a crack. 'I don't have to open the door to you.'

'You need to get out of the car, otherwise I'll be forced to arrest you.'

'How do I know you're police?'

Vicky flattened her card against the glass. 'This is a genuine Police Scotland warrant card.'

The woman shook her head. 'How do I know it's real?'

'Are you still on with the emergency services?'

The woman frowned. Then nodded.

'There's an active pursuit of this car. Ask them if I'm genuine. They've just spoken to a colleague of mine; she can confirm my location.'

She wound the window up again and turned away, her jaw moving as she spoke into her phone.

A squad car appeared at the end of the road, flashing blues and twos.

Shepherd smiled at the woman, her hand still on the door. 'Madam, I'm very sorry.' He grabbed Vicky and dragged her away. 'This isn't Mason's car.'

'What?'

'That car.' He pointed at the plates. 'It's not Mason's.'

Vicky ran a hand down her face. 'Shit, shit, shit.' A yawn tore into her. 'God, I'm so stupid.'

Shepherd sucked deep. His exhale wisped away into the air. 'My mistake too, but we need to leave this in the hands of uniform.' He strolled away back to his car. 'Where did we lose him?'

'Luke, I don't know if we ever had him. Not since the house.' Vicky grabbed her mobile from the footwell. Still on the call. She stuck it on speaker. 'Jenny, we must've lost him on the bridge.'

'No, you lost him earlier. I've been going through the street footage and he turned left at the end of the street, not right.'

'Shite. You're kidding me.'

'No, but at least console yourself in the fact that a grey Golf is the second most common car in Scotland. Any ideas how we find him?'

Vicky raised her eyebrows. 'Well, left would've taken him to his mother's.'

21

Vicky knocked on the door and waited. She wanted to yawn but it wasn't even half past one. Helped if you got a full night's sleep. Helped if you could get a full night's sleep ever. Helped if you didn't get adrenalized in a stupid car chase that didn't catch anyone.

Shepherd joined her on Doreen Mason's doorstep, stomping his boots like he was on guard duty in mid-February. He pressed the bell.

The door clattered open and Emma Mason peered out. The din of TV news behind her, the earnest chat of a Family Liaison Officer. 'Has something happened?'

Vicky smiled at her, her best police officer's grin. 'Just need a word with your husband.'

'Oh?' Her gaze flashed between them. 'What about?'

Shepherd stepped forward. 'Just a few follow-up questions. Nothing to worry about.'

Other than your husband being a probable murderer, a definite attempted murderer and someone who fled from the police while attempting that murder. And whacked a cop in the balls.

Emma tugged her arms around her torso. 'Doug's at home. I'm heading there soon.'

'Okay, sorry to trouble you. But get him to call either myself or DI Dodds if you do speak to him.' Shepherd flashed her a beaming smile and stepped away, scowling at Vicky. He charged down the path, mobile out, then stuck it to his ear. 'Right, Considine, please make sure Dewar takes some time off. Good. Who have you got tracking Doug Mason?' He stopped by his car and rested his free hand on the roof. 'When?'

Vicky turned back around.

The door was still open and Emma leaned against the side, arms still folded. Tears streamed down her cheeks, snot bubbled in her nose.

'Emma, is everything okay?'

'Of course it's not okay.' Emma clambered down the steps and collapsed into Vicky's arms, bucking and racking. 'Gav's dead!'

Vicky held her there until she stopped. 'It's okay, Emma. Whatever's going on, you can talk to me.'

'Gav and me... We were...' Emma's tears caught the light, glistening. 'I didn't love him, but... We needed each other. We found each other and it was good.' She jerked forward and hugged Vicky like Bella would, even though there was at least fifteen years between them. 'You don't think Doug might've murdered Gav, do you?'

'You told us—'

'Please. Tell me the truth.'

Emma deserved it, so Vicky nodded. 'We've tracked a car from near to where he was staying. It travelled to and from

Dundee. The timeline fits and your husband doesn't have an alibi for the murder.'

'Jesus Christ.'

'Look, I know how tough this must be, Emma, so I'm not going to judge you. I'll help you change your statement. Get your friends to change theirs too. But I need you to be completely honest with me from now on, okay? Do you think Doug knew about you and Gavin?'

Emma wiped away the tears. 'We were discreet.'

'You visiting his home last night isn't discreet. You visiting his bar isn't discreet.'

'We just talked!'

'Okay, but you being there would start tongues wagging. Possibly make someone suspect something else.'

'I've no idea, then.'

'It's Gavin's baby, isn't it?'

Emma stared at her for a few seconds. 'What?'

'Is it?'

Emma gripped her arm even tighter. 'I'm only nine weeks.'

Vicky stood there, letting Emma burrow in and hold her tight. A million thoughts flashed through her brain.

Doug had killed because his wife was carrying his brother's child.

And he went to kill Morgan too. He was abusing her, so he needed to cover his tracks. The noose was tightening in a way he didn't expect.

Prick thought he was smarter than the cops, that his travel would go unnoticed. His time working for an Albanian mob in London had set him up well. Trained him in how to evade detection. Or so he thought.

'Did Doug know?'

'Just Gav.'

'Vicky?' Shepherd was right by them now, his face twisted up like a shelled pistachio.

She didn't let go of Emma. 'What is it?'

He leaned in to whisper, 'Doug's car's been found down near Broughty Ferry Castle. No leads on where he went afterwards.'

Vicky gestured for him to go inside, mouthing, 'Get the FLO out here.' She broke off from Emma. 'There's something else I need your help with, okay? Morgan Miller was attacked in her home about five minutes ago. She's been taken to hospital.'

Emma gasped, her breath misting in the air. 'Christ.'

'Talk to me about her.'

'I don't know her, really.'

'But your husband does.'

'Right. Doug runs with her mum and dad a few times a week. Morgan started going with them a few months ago.'

'You run, don't you? Don't you join them?'

'Not road running. Way safer in the gym.'

Was that all it was?

'Talk to me about Morgan, Emma.'

'I don't know anything.'

'Come on. What's really going on?'

She exhaled slowly. 'Doug hasn't touched me for over a year. Why I started talking to Gav.' She bit her bottom lip. 'Why it became more than that.'

'You think Doug's been having sex with Morgan?'

'She's *fifteen*.'

'Even so.' Vicky's heart was hammering. 'If there's—'

'Aye.' Emma looked up at the sky. 'I've been fucking terrified that my fucking husband has been sleeping with a fucking *child* while I'm fucking pregnant with his fucking *brother's* kid!'

Vicky stood there, stroking her arm. 'Emma, we need to get all this down in a statement, okay?'

'You really think Doug attacked her?'

'It's likely, yes. Possible. We really need to speak to him.'

'I've no idea where he is.'

'What about where he could go?'

'If it was me? I'd say London. He used to live there. Before me, before this.'

Vicky gave her a kind smile. That was going to be an absolute nightmare.

Shepherd returned with the kind-looking FLO and let her take over hugging duties.

22

Vicky pushed through the door into the ward. Tried to ignore the cloying smell of the disinfectant. She smiled at Dr Rankine. 'Hey.'

'Vicky Dodds, as I live and breathe.' She was doing something with a blood sample, pumping it into a bottle. Hard to see her involved with Considine, but stranger things had happened. 'You here about DS MacDonald?'

'Why, what's happened?'

'Oh, nothing. He's been asleep since his procedure. Way out of my jurisdiction, so I'd have to redirect you to another ward.'

'We're here about Morgan.' Vicky glanced inside the ward. 'How's she doing?'

Rankine exhaled like Forrester with a cigarette. 'You know I can't grant access to her. Right?'

Vicky folded her arms. 'See, the thing is, we really need to find her attacker.'

'So find him.'

'We've run out of leads.'

'Vicky, her health has to take priority.' Rankine pointed inside the room. 'See?'

Morgan lay on a bed. Groans and shouts came from behind the screen. That disinfectant smell stung her nose worse than Rob's aftershave in the morning. 'Morgan's in a significant amount of pain.'

'She's awake?'

'Like that screaming isn't enough of a clue? As it stands, I'm going to have to sedate her.'

'Listen, I *really* need to speak to her.' Vicky gave a smile. 'She's the only lead we've got in this case. Other lives are at stake here.'

Rankine clicked her tongue a few times. 'You're not going to let this go, are you?'

'Much as I hate putting a friend under pressure, we think Morgan's attacker has killed before. And we need to find him before—'

'—he does it again?' Rankine rolled her eyes. 'Aye, I've heard that before. Is she really your only lead?'

'Absolutely.' Vicky patted her on the arm. 'Sure I can't have a quick word?'

'I just can't—'

'Please.'

Rankine rubbed at her forehead, looking Vicky up and down. 'Two minutes at the very most. Okay?' She stepped out of the way and let Vicky through.

Morgan stared at the ceiling, moaning low, fingers tightly gripping the blanket. Sweat darkening her hair until it was almost brown. A ring of red marks around her throat, not even bruises yet.

Vicky crouched next to her and smiled at the girl. 'Morgan,

my name's Vicky. I'm a police officer.'

Morgan was staring right through her, like Gavin Mason's corpse. She screwed up her eyes and growled. 'My throat's on fire. I can't cope with this.'

Vicky nodded in sympathy. 'Morgan, did you see who did this to you?'

Morgan took a deep breath. 'It happened so fast.'

Vicky tried to make eye contact with her. 'What's the last thing you remember?'

'I didn't go to school today. Felt rubbish. Not covid. Well, my LFT was negative but I had a PCR booked for tomorrow, so... Mum didn't want to risk it. I was so bored and... Someone was in the house.'

'Did you recognise them?'

Morgan pressed her fingers into her neck, then screamed again, her eyes screwed up. 'He had a knife! It all happened so fast!'

'He?'

'A knife!'

Rankine grabbed at Vicky's arm. 'That's enough...'

'I don't remember what happened next. Wait, you were there. Did you save me?'

'I did.' Vicky glanced over at Rankine. 'Was it Doug Mason?'

A leading question, sure, but Vicky didn't really have a choice here.

Morgan shut her eyes, her breath coming even faster. 'Yes.'

Jesus. The whole thing was true. All that high-level assassin bullshit.

Vicky stayed crouched for a few seconds. She reached for

her hand. Instantly regretted it – Morgan snapped on a vice grip. 'Morgan, has he been abusing you?'

She glared at Vicky. 'I love him.'

'Morgan... You know it's wrong, don't you?'

'He loves me too. He's said.'

'So why was he trying to kill you?'

'I think he just... He's into stuff like tying me up. He was going to marry me; we were going to have babies together. And he's helping my pals to—'

'Come on.' Rankine thumbed outside the room. 'Time's up.'

'Wait.' Vicky kept her focus on Morgan. 'Helping them do what?'

But Morgan was gone, eyes shut, breathing deeply.

Vicky knew she wasn't getting anything else out of her now, so she followed Rankine out, her gut churning.

Rankine pulled the door shut. 'That get you what you need?'

Vicky doubted she'd gained anything, but she smiled. 'Thanks for this. I owe you.'

'You owe me at least sixty, I reckon.' Rankine walked off.

Something crawled up Vicky's windpipe, felt like it was going to eat her brain. She sucked in a deep breath, stale hospital air.

It was all slotting into place.

Doug killed his brother because he was sleeping with his wife.

Doug tried to kill Morgan because he was abusing her and didn't want her to talk.

The only reason Morgan was alive was because she'd stopped him.

But if he was helping her friends... Shite, Doug Mason was

some kind of Jeffrey Epstein? Was he using Morgan to recruit others?

She rubbed at her temples.

The monster crawled up the back of her throat now.

What the hell would Doug do to *them*?

Her mobile rang. Unknown caller. She hit answer. 'Hello?'

'Vicky?' A man's voice. Like a demon, whispering.

Vicky felt like someone had stuck a spear through her brain. Left it poking out of the right eye. 'Doug?'

'I'm glad you answered.'

She swallowed but had no idea how to play this now. 'I need to speak to you.'

'You do, do you?'

Vicky swallowed harder. Like a golf ball was stuck down there. 'We need to talk about what you did to Morgan.'

A long pause. 'What's happened to her?'

'Someone attacked her at her home.'

'Christ.' Doug paused. Sounded like he was outside, wind battering against the mic. 'It wasn't me.'

She'd seen this so many times before. 'Doug, she identified you. Where are you?'

'I...'

'Please, turn yourself in to the nearest station.'

'That's not going to happen.'

'Please. You say you didn't kill your brother, didn't try to kill Morgan. Prove it to me. If it's not you, it'll help us find who it was.'

He paused, like her gambit was working.

'The V&A. Two o'clock. Don't be late. And don't bring any friends.'

'You're threatening me. Okay. I'll see you there with all of my friends.'

'You want me to turn myself in? Tell you the truth about what's going on? Just you, Vicky. I see anyone, I'm out of there.' Click.

Vicky stared at the phone. Dead. Only ten minutes until the meeting. Fifteen-minute drive, at least.

Vicky ran down the corridor, hit another number and put it to her ear. 'Jenny, can you get me a trace on a mobile?'

23

Vicky could barely walk now, let alone run.

A car was double-parked ahead of her, just outside the hospital. Shepherd tore out of the driver side and jogged over to Vicky. She pushed away from him. 'Out of my way.'

'You're not going!' He grabbed her by the arm. 'It's way too dangerous!'

'I don't really like the idea either, but there's not a lot of choice.' Vicky tried to push past, but Shepherd was a foot too tall and five stone too heavy for her to get past. 'Besides, this is the perfect opportunity.'

'For what? To get yourself killed? Remember what happened to Doug Mason's brother? What he did to Morgan Miller?'

She didn't have an answer for that.

'You want to join Gavin in the grave, do you?'

Vicky tried to dodge past him.

Shepherd grabbed her arm again. 'Vicky, I need to keep you safe.'

'Luke, he doesn't want to kill me. It's in a public place. Broad daylight. It's a more than acceptable risk.'

'That's not your choice to make.'

'No? But I'm a DI and you told me I get to make my rules. Right? But if I don't meet him, who knows how many more people he'll go on to kill? I don't want that on my conscience. Do you?'

'A moral conundrum. Well done.' Shepherd groaned. 'Right, we need to brief Forrester and—'

'We don't have time for that.' Vicky stopped. 'I need to be there by two.'

'I'll drive you.' Shepherd set off back towards his car, sticking his mobile to his cauliflower ear. 'But I'm not letting you out until I've cleared this with your DCI.'

Seemed like a team of pathologists were carrying out a post-mortem on the street. Everywhere Vicky looked, road surfaces were peeled back, insides exposed. The cars crawled past a fenced-off section of road, an entire lane where a long dirty-white pipe angled out of a sixty-foot trench. Workmen stood around in hard hats and steel-toe-capped boots and padded jackets and shouted at each other over the noise of a pneumatic drill. A digger pecked at the road.

The skeletal roof of the new Victoria & Albert Museum loomed over her as she walked past.

Vicky sat on the bench and scanned the passing pedestrians again, but there was no sign of Doug Mason.

Just after two.

Looked like rain. Felt like it too.

Doug was thirty-five going on forty-five. Athletic physique, though. She had his height at five eleven. Certainly wouldn't be a pushover, physically.

She had this.

Really, she did.

Another glance around. Couple of mothers with prams, chatting, faces red with the cold. Scabby bloke standing outside the doughnut stand, sucking on a roll-up, hands cupped around it to keep the smoke in.

Vicky checked her watch again. Ten minutes late.

Between her bench and the next, a teenage girl sat on the pavement, blanket over her legs, cardboard sign propped on her lap:

Fuck you
I don't want your charity

Seemed to be working, though. Her flat cap was running over.

Vicky dug into her pocket and dropped a fifty-pence piece in.

The girl scowled at her.

The smell of hot chestnuts wafted from a nearby stand. Christmas was starting even earlier this year. Probably still had the red-nosed reindeer over in the square in front of the Caird Hall.

When Bella first saw them…

'They're real, Mum!'

Aye, it wasn't all a big lie. Just Santa sprinkling his magic.

Bella was disappointed they couldn't fly. And when the red nose fell off...

Vicky got up and started walking around. The anticipation alone would be enough to make her pace about even if it wasn't freezing and she had a pounding headache coming on.

A guy in a huge, padded overcoat walked past. Dressed for the Arctic. Vicky could do with a coat like that. Should just stop him and buy it off him.

But it might send the wrong signal to the marksmen on top of the nearby buildings. They'd see her approaching someone and assume it was Doug Mason.

That's if they'd even been deployed by now.

She didn't much like the idea of guns pointing at her. A slip of the finger and it'd be her head exploding. All it took was a firearms officer with a hangover he hadn't told anyone about.

Still, if they were out there, they were well hidden. Not that she could afford to take a proper look. If Doug was watching and saw her scouring the rooftops for snipers, it'd give the game away.

She hit the crossing towards the train station and turned around again, started heading back towards the V&A.

Of all places in Dundee, why here?

Doug couldn't know. Could he?

Her mobile rang. She took it out and checked the display, hoping Jenny was getting somewhere with tracing it. 'Hello?'

'I told you to meet outside the museum.'

Vicky's mouth was dry. 'I'm there.'

'You were late.'

'Please, I—'

'Take a seat on the bench next to the bus stop. See it?'

Vicky looked along the street. The bench was empty. God,

that was where she'd tackled… him. Her mouth was dry. 'What do you want?'

Doug paused. Like he was chewing something over. 'I want you to sit down on that bench and stay sat. Think you can manage that?'

'No problem.'

'Glad to hear it.' Doug hung up.

Vicky walked along the pavement.

A child yelling. Came from HMS Discovery, hundreds of feet away. Then it was drowned out by a blast of jackhammer drilling into the ground. God knows what they were doing, but this stretch of road had changed around at least twenty times in the decade since the V&A was announced. A bus passed, making a noise like an electric razor. The poles supporting a canopy in front of the deserted café swayed in the wind, squealing like rats.

A taxi whirred past, followed by a bus, the brakes hissing as it stopped, the sound knifing through the dead air.

A young couple were waiting in the bus shelter, keeping each other warm. They looked alike. Same pointy chins and cat-like eyes. Her musky perfume overcame his citrusy aftershave.

Vicky checked the bench was dry and sat down.

Then waited.

24

He gets out and locks the van. His bloody back's absolutely brutal today. Checks his face in the wing mirror. Hood up, cap tugged low, shades on.

Nobody was recognising him.

He sets off through Dundee. Shithole of a town, barely a city. The street's clear, just a few taxis lurking around, some out-of-season tourists mooching about. He walks along the side of the road, hands in pockets, listening to the drone of traffic. Eyes alert, logging license plates. Just a man, out walking. Nothing to see here. Move along.

Buildings across the street are three stories tall. No sign of anyone up there. No snipers or even idiots with binoculars.

Got a clear run at this.

He stops in the wee park that looks over to the new museum. Place is completely empty. Still, last thing he wants to do is to sit. Not with his back.

Instead, he gets out his mobile and checks through the call log and messages.

Well, good riddance to this.

He powers it down, snaps out the battery and dumps it in the bin. Another burner burnt. He walks across the park towards the museum and drops the handset in another.

Why on Earth they put that thing here is anyone's guess.

Brown envelopes, no doubt.

And there she is, sitting on a bench in the pissing rain. No umbrella.

Detective Inspector Victoria Dodds of Police Scotland.

He reaches into his coat pocket. The revolver feels really cold today.

Must be this bloody city.

25

'Don't get up.' A hand clamped Vicky's shoulder.

Her gut lurched. She tried to keep her breathing level but wasn't making a very good job of it.

Doug Mason stood over her. Must've approached from behind, through the gardens. A ginger growth speckled his chin and upper lip. He indicated the bench. 'Please. May I?'

Not a 'Can I?' but 'May I?'

Mum always said it cost nothing to be polite. She'd approve of Doug's manners.

'Of course.' Vicky shuffled along an inch or two.

Doug sat down next to her, leaning forward, head in hands.

Let him know you're familiar with his situation.

'Morgan's going to be okay, Doug. After what you did to her.'

Doug nodded. Exaggerated. Kept nodding. Like he couldn't stop. 'A real shame.'

'What is, Doug? You strangling her?'

'Thanks for coming.' Doug turned to face Vicky. 'You're not going to try anything daft, are you? Like arrest me or something?'

Vicky raised her palms. 'I'm just here to talk, Doug. Find out why you wanted to meet.'

'That's good.' Back to the nodding. 'You know what's at stake, don't you?'

'I do, Doug. I do.' Keep using his name. Build rapport. 'Doug, why did you kill your brother?'

He sat back and chuckled.

Vicky got up and stuffed her hands in her pockets. 'Nice seeing you.'

'Stay there.'

'Why?'

'I have a gun.' Doug slid his hand inside his pocket. 'And I'm sure you'll believe me if I tell you I'm not afraid to use it on you.'

Bad enough having a sniper pointing a gun at her, but when a crazed psycho who wasn't weapons-trained was sitting right next to you with a shaky hand on the gun in his pocket, Vicky really did begin to wish she was somewhere else.

Wind whistled through the trees just over in the park. A bus pulled up and the smooching couple got on. A family walked past. Mum, dad, two kids. They all looked angry with each other.

Vicky scanned Doug's coat for any proof he was armed. Saw nothing either way. 'You going to use it on anyone who gets in your way?'

'Not decided.'

Vicky stayed standing. Couldn't spot any police marksmen. 'What do you want, Doug?'

'What do I want?' Doug chuckled. 'That's a good question. I want an end to it.'

'To what?'

'You'll see.' Doug got up, hand still in his pocket. His coat bunched up around an object. Long. Very definitely a gun. Not worth taking a risk over. 'Come on, we're going for a little trip.' He nodded at the bus. 'Get on.'

'Doug, I'm staying here.'

'Then you'll never find out the truth.' Doug raised the gun in his pocket and walked over to the bus. 'Come on.'

Vicky chanced a glance at the nearby rooftops. The museum was the most likely spot, but the only figures up there were reindeer. They weren't going to be shooting anyone.

The driver leaned over. 'You getting on, son?'

'Just a sec.' Doug looked over at Vicky. 'You first.'

'I need to get a ticket, don't I?'

'So pay for both of us.'

Vicky stepped onboard. 'Two singles, please.'

'Short hop or a max single?'

Vicky tried to make eye contact with Doug, but he wasn't paying attention. 'Two max singles.'

'Four sixty.'

Vicky pressed her card against the reader and collected the tickets.

The doors hissed shut and the bus set off.

Vicky had no idea where they were going.

So bloody stupid. Rushing here, just to fall into a trap. Becoming his hostage.

Focus.

Keep calm.

She walked up the bus and found an empty pair of seats,

side on. Could see outside. No sign of any marksmen. Someone ran past outside, heading for the front of the bus. Nobody she recognised.

Doug settled down next to her, giving a little flash of the gun, still pocketed. But she saw it. The cold steel. 'How are you doing, Vicky?'

She swallowed. 'I'm doing just fine, Doug. What's this about?'

'You think much about your death?'

'No, Doug. Can't say I do.' But her voice was a croak.

'You do believe you're going to die, don't you?' He smiled at her. 'God, you don't. You think you're an exception, that you're going to cheat death. Right?'

'I don't want to die, Doug. Not today.'

'Who does? But that's not the point. You ever heard of anybody who didn't die? It's stupid to say you don't want to die. You got a degree?'

The bus rattled past the train station, dark through the misted windows. 'Sure you don't already know the answer, Doug?'

'I don't.'

'A degree in law.'

'Wow. So, you're smarter than the average person. Don't bullshit yourself, Vicky. You're going to die. I'm going to die.' Doug waved out of the window with his free hand. 'That girl dressing the display in that bookshop across the road. The bus driver. Everybody's going to die. The important question is when.'

'I know that, Doug.'

'Do you? Or do you just pretend you know. Most of us go

through life believing that death only happens to other people. Until it's too late. Cancer, heart attack—'

'—some idiot pointing a gun at you.'

He laughed, but it didn't reach his eyes.

'If you think about death too much, Doug, it makes you stop thinking about life.'

'Ah, that's an easy thing to say. But what's life without death? Death is what gives life its meaning. Have you seen it up close?'

He grabbed her arm, barely enough strength to hold on to her, to hold on to life.

Vicky looked away, rubbing at her eyes. 'Most cops have, Doug.'

'And you, Vicky, have you seen it?'

'Yes, Doug. Several times.'

'Well, a universe dies with each of us. A whole universe, Vicky. Gone.' Doug snapped his fingers. 'In an instant. You've seen death, haven't you? Stared it right in the eye. Watched it snuff out.'

He couldn't know. He just couldn't.

She needed to turn this around on him. 'Did you see death in your brother's eyes when you killed him? Are you disappointed Morgan's still alive, Doug, that you didn't get to witness her death?'

'You don't know anything.'

The bus started slowing, the Perth Road blurring in Vicky's eyes. 'You want to control death, Doug? Is that what this is about?'

'Oh, don't try to psychoanalyse me. It's a waste of your time.' Doug stood up as if to leave. He took his hand out of his pocket and pointed the gun at Vicky, right between the eyes.

A revolver, the hammer cocked, ready to fire.

Cold against her skin.

Someone screamed.

The bus stopped. 'Shite!'

'Put the gun down, Doug.' Vicky clenched her fists. Tried to keep her voice level. Felt like she was going to have a heart attack, like someone was hitting her chest. 'Please, Doug. Put the gun down.'

He smirked, aiming the gun at Vicky's thudding heart. 'It's time.'

Shouting came from both ends of the bus.

A woman nearby hammered her thumb on the door buzzer.

Vicky reached towards the gun. 'Come on, just—'

He swiped, clattering her knuckles. 'Keep your hands down.'

Vicky held them out like she was balancing. Leaned as far back as she could on the seat, her neck muscles burning. The muzzle dug into her skin. 'Why are you doing this?'

'Does it matter?'

'Come on, Doug.' Vicky tried to stare into his eyes but it was so hard with a fucking gun pointed at her. 'I'm here because you promised me the truth. We know about you. About your history, Doug. The nasty people you worked with down in London.'

'I worked *for* them.'

'Still, they were trafficking people. That where you got the taste for young girls from?'

'What?'

'Morgan.'

He looked away. Then back again. 'I did what I had to do.'

'Trying to kill her, Doug. Like you killed your brother. Because you knew he was sleeping with your wife, didn't you?'

'Would you kill someone to have an extra day?' Doug grimaced. 'For one more day on this Earth, would you kill someone?'

'Why did you kill Gavin, Doug? Why?'

'I didn't. What about for a week? A life, in exchange for an extra week?' Doug stepped back, away from Vicky. Like he was ready to shoot and run when the doors opened. 'But that's... We're nearly out of time.' His eyes blazed. 'Forty seconds left. It's a lifetime, really. If you want it to be. How do you feel, Vicky?' Spit flecked the sides of his mouth.

'Don't do this.' Vicky's breaths came in sharp stabs. 'For God's sake, don't. I've got kids.'

'Thirty seconds. You thought your friends up on the rooftops were going to shoot me, didn't you? They'd never risk it. My trigger finger's liable to twitch. And *boom.* No more Vicky Dodds. Fifteen seconds. It's not long. Would you like to say anything?'

'Why are you doing this, Doug?'

'That's not very creative. I'm disappointed.'

'You're a sick man, Doug. Abusing girls. Morgan Miller's *fifteen*. You had her recruiting her friends. Tell me it all now.'

'We're all just sacks of water and hatred, Vicky. We all deserve to die. Five, four, three.'

Vicky shut her eyes.

'Two.'

Thud.

She opened them again.

A blur of a suit pushed Doug over.

Bang.

The window behind Vicky smashed.

White noise screamed in her ears.

Crack.

Shepherd got a punch in on Doug.

What the hell? When did he get inside?

Stupid bastard.

Doug rolled away, past the door, and pushed himself up. He waved the gun at Vicky.

She couldn't move. Couldn't find anywhere to move to. Nowhere the shot was blocked.

This was it.

The end.

Doug grabbed Vicky, holding her from behind. Gun to her temple.

Shepherd held Doug's gaze, his cheek twitching. Pure terror on his face.

This is it, how it ends.

The mechanism of the revolver rumbled in her ear. Doug pulled back the trigger, spinning the cylinder.

She tried to spin free to face her killer. Look him in the eye as he killed her.

A loud bang in her ears.

Something smashed against the back of her head.

This is how it ends.

This is how I die.

26

The ceiling of the bus was covered in blood, bone and brain.

Blood covered her. On her back, pooling on the floor.

She closed her eyes and waited for the end to come, lying in the aisle of a bus, sucking in her last breaths. Her chest was so heavy. Every breath hurt.

She wished it didn't have to end this way.

She wanted to grow old. Have grandchildren. Great-grandchildren. Retire and travel.

She was getting married next summer.

She wanted to see Rob. To see Bella and Jamie.

She wanted to have another baby.

The veins in her neck felt like the ropes on a boat's sails, tight and straining against strong winds. Felt like someone had replaced her skin with broken glass.

Feet stomped towards her. No gunshots. Nothing.

The light levels dimmed then lightened. Felt like a weight had been lifted off, like she was climbing out of her body.

'You okay there, Vicky?'

Could barely hear the voice. Sounded like he was underwater.

Vicky opened her eyes again.

Shepherd loomed over her. 'Are you okay?' She had to lip read.

She ran her hand down her face, damp and lumpy, like she could scrub the last few minutes. Wipe it all clean. Start again. She stopped. Clawed at her shoulder, like something was eating her flesh. Vicky pinched her nose. Tickling inside, like there was thick fur all the way up. Like she was going to cry.

Her skin itched with a thousand tiny ants crawling over it.

'What the hell happened?' Vicky crawled to the side and gripped the seat. She staggered up to standing, heart pounding, adrenaline spiking in her veins.

Still the ringing in her ears, like a million smoke alarms going off at the same time.

Something wet on her face, in her mouth. She tasted it. Iron. Blood.

Death.

Splinters of bone on her jacket.

Vicky touched the back of her head. Intact. Dry, even. Well, damp with sweat.

Doug Mason lay on the floor, his body contorted, his long coat lying open, his white shirt covered in blood. His limp hands by his side. The gun had scattered into the footwell. Looked like someone had used a tin opener on the top of his skull.

Vicky clamped her eyes shut, her hands shaking. Couldn't

stop them trembling. Her jaw locked tight, tongue secure behind the wall of teeth. Couldn't even swallow.

She tasted blood again, smelled piss and shit.

Not hers.

Doug's.

Shit. Shit. Shit.

Armed police officers started filling the junction with the Perth Road. Silent movement like they were soldiers in a film. One of them was at the bus door, pressing the controls. The door slid open and they let the passengers off, then stormed the vehicle.

'Come on, Vicky.' A hand on her shoulder. Shepherd. 'We need to get you away from here.'

Vicky couldn't walk. Her feet weren't listening to her legs, legs weren't listening to her brain.

Shepherd helped her up and said something.

'What?' Vicky pointed at her ears. 'My hearing's fucked.' She gripped the pole, the only thing keeping her upright, the cold metal cooling her hands. 'Fuck.'

Shepherd helped her over to the door. 'When did you know he had the gun?'

'On the bench. He got it out on the bus.' She stepped off the bus. A whisper of rain blasted her face, washing some of the blood away. 'Does that mean it's over?'

Shepherd nodded. 'It's over.'

'He didn't shoot me, Luke. Why didn't he kill us?'

'He shot himself, Vicky. Right in front of us.'

27

Vicky hauled the blanket around her shoulders. Good to be sitting down, even if it was in the back of an ambulance. Her legs were shaking and she felt lightheaded.

A crowd of gawkers stood outside the Rep, frowning at the bus. The buses would be diverted. It'd be all over the news.

CSIs were already dusting and cataloguing inside. The occasional camera flash seemed too bright in the November chill.

Red spray caked the window.

All over her clothes. Her face had been cleaned but she still felt the stickiness of dried blood.

Doug Mason's blood.

Vicky closed her eyes, trying to clamp them shut. She kept hearing the gunshot. Over and over again. She kept hearing a whistling on the left side.

The ambulance darkened. Forrester stood in the open door,

looming into the ambulance. Could just about make out what he was saying above the white noise. 'How you doing, Doddsy?'

Vicky couldn't speak. Even if she could, she didn't know what to say.

She could still feel the hard metal of the gun digging into her skin.

Blood spray all over her clothes.

'Vicky?'

'DI Dodds is experiencing shock.' The paramedic smiled at Forrester, cool and confident and capable. Like she'd seen it all. Even this. Vicky envied her. Wanted to be her, wanted to be able to cope like she did. 'Perfectly normal under the circumstances. Might take a little while for her to come round.'

Forrester climbed into the van. 'But she's okay otherwise, right?'

The medic shrugged. 'Headache. Touch of nausea. Is there someone who can take her home?'

'I'll deal with it.' Forrester smiled at her. 'Can you give us a minute?'

'Sure thing.' She walked away, snapping off her green gloves splattered with crimson.

Water clicked in Vicky's ear, then it was like someone switched a light on, a blast of buzzing from outside. Voices. Police vehicles. A helicopter droning in the sky. Then it was all gone, back underwater. Then it came back again.

She tried to get up, but it felt like she'd been shot. Pain in both shoulders, down her arms. Couldn't feel her feet.

'Vicky.' Forrester put a hand on her shoulder. 'Sit down.'

She looked up. 'I couldn't stop him. Couldn't get any answers from him.'

Forrester stuck his thumbs in his belt buckles. 'Focus on the result, okay?'

'It all happened so quickly. And he could've killed us. Killed me.' She swallowed the word.

'He didn't. Main thing, Vicky, is that you're safe.' Forrester paused. 'One mad bastard is dead thanks to you.'

'Thanks to me?' Vicky blew air up her face. Then swallowed, a thick lump catching in her throat. 'Shepherd saved me.'

Forrester's brow creased. Seemed to go all the way around his head as he glanced outside. 'All's right with the world, Vicky.'

'Wouldn't go that far.'

'But it's better than it was an hour ago. One less murdering scumbag in it.' Forrester rested his bulk against the gurney. The wheels squeaked against him. 'Still there's a lot of work to do in closing off the case. Bring all of the evidence together. Tie his movements to Gavin and Morgan. Guarantee there'll be a Fatal Accident Inquiry.' He waved at the bus. 'It's already all over the news. DCS Soutar's being swallowed up by the press and politicians.' He clenched his jaw, his teeth grinding. 'Anyway, that sort of malarkey isn't for us to worry about. Superintendents from all over Scotland are probably manoeuvring for a piece of the action. Probably Glasgow or Edinburgh.'

Vicky swallowed hard. 'I should be out there helping instead of sitting on my arse feeling sorry for myself.'

'Hardly.' Forrester gripped her shoulder again. 'Right, once the CSIs turn up to take your clothes, you're going back to the station for the mother of all showers. And then home. Okay?'

'I don't think I'll ever forget someone sticking a gun at me.'

'In time, it'll all be fine. But you need someone to give you a lift home. Once you're out of the shower, I'll take you.'

'What about tomorrow morning? How do I get in?'

'You could get the bu— Right. Aye. I'll drive your car. Okay?'

'Maybe.'

Forrester gripped her shoulder. 'It's over, okay? Doug Mason's dead. He won't be killing anyone else.'

28

These back roads just go on and on, with nothing to differentiate yet another mile. No cars, not even the faint trace of headlights in the distance, just the occasional farm lit up in the cold night. A sign for Big Stevie's Woodworking Grotto. Getting dark now. Bloody November. What he wouldn't give for some winter sun. Argentina or South Africa. Hell, New Zealand would be lush. Australia'd be a bit too hot, but preferable to this blast of sleet drumming off the car roof.

Brazil. Now that was the ticket. The World Cup there was a blast, one crazy summer of drinking and carousing. Not that he saw a single game. Tickets were crazy prices.

His headlights catch the road sign:

TORPHICHEN 1
BATHGATE 4
EDINBURGH 23

Another yawn and he blinks hard, trying to keep his eyes focused. Such a long drive and the adrenaline ran out a long time ago.

There. The turning. Blink and you'd miss it. A break in the feral beech and birch guarded by two wheelie bins. He slows down and eases the car into the bay opposite. A yellow grit box almost glows in the darkness. Must be pretty empty just now, given how cold it's been recently.

The engine purrs then dies. The headlight glow fades to nothing, just pitch black and the lowland wind battering the glass. Trees rustle on both sides, barely any leaves left. Pricks of frost glint in his headlights.

He reaches over for some paracetamol and dry swallows two.

They catch in his throat and his gag reflex kicks in.

Christ!

One final glug from the WakeyWakey can and they go down.

Stupid. Choking to death on painkillers would be a very silly way to go.

He pats his pockets. The left has a syringe, double the dose he needs. The right has a cable tie and a plastic bag, airtight.

Another look ahead, then in the rear-view, both black emptiness. He opens the door and gets out.

Frail lights shine on the house, white and grand. Crow-step gables buffet a small cottage, extended to three times the size out the back, with hulking big outbuildings looming behind, barely catching any light. Place is way too big for one man.

Dark inside. Just like he'd expected. Just like it'd been for the last six Sundays he'd visited.

His phone blasts out.

Christ.

He fumbles with it, dropping it into the pine needles and rotting beech leaves. He picks it up and stabs a gloved thumb on the red button and the sound dies. He holds the button down until it switches off.

He stands there. Waiting, listening. The lane is deadly still.

Nobody around.

Nobody heard that.

Right?

He teases the car door open and gets back in. Careful to leave it ajar. The cold has already got inside.

The low rumble of a 4x4 comes from behind, car headlights penetrating the back window.

Orange flashes join the blue headlight din and the brute of a car turns down the lane, grinding up the pebbled driveway.

Just like the last six Sundays.

Every week, without fail.

Thomas Riley is such a mummy's boy. Sitting with the old dear in that nursing home. Listening to the same story every week, sometimes twice. Her confusion, thinking he was her brother and not her son. Must be heart-breaking, but Thomas Riley doesn't have a heart, does he?

He just has to nudge the door for it to open this time, then he lets it bounce against the lock, still open. He sets off, across the road and over the wall, through the undergrowth, tracing the path he's tested out six times previously. Over the fence into the garden now, slower, stepping across the steps on the lawn towards the side of the house.

Riley's Porsche Cayenne thrums in the parking bay by the house, Metallica bleeding out through the windows. *Enter Sandman*. The tipping point between their speed metal and cock rock phases. The Goldilocks zone. Not too metal, not too bland. The sound dies and the driver's door opens.

He holds the syringe in his right hand like a jazz drummer would a stick – resting loose under the thumb, the ring finger and middle providing the control, ready to hit the snare drum – and sucks all the juice into the syringe and pockets the empty plastic tub.

Riley gets out of his SUV, too focused on his mobile to notice anything. Whistling that infernal guitar riff, wildly out of tune, as he walks over to the door. He over-yawns, stretching out. The clink of keys missing the lock, then the thump of them hitting, then rattling as the door opens.

And he pounces. Left arm around Riley's throat. His phone cracks off the step. His keys clatter onto the slabs.

His right hand jabs the needle into Riley's neck, just over the vein. And he pushes it all in.

Riley wriggles, twists, trying to elbow him.

He just has to hold on, hold him there.

Riley collapses, tottering forward like a drunken uncle and tumbles onto the parquet floor, brief flickers of light catching the varnish. Chest barely moving. Eyes flickering. Riley is a big guy. He thought it'd be harder taking him down, but it was almost too easy.

He nudges the door behind him so it rests on the lock, just like his car, then grabs his ankles and hauls him over the smooth surface. Barely a sound as he drags Riley through the house. Like he's stepped through every week, breaking in and planning the route through this garish monstrosity. Even in the darkness, the statues and paintings leer out, vulgar expressions of material wealth.

The door to his den lies open, the 'Man Cave' sign above it.

Switching him from the parquet to the thick hair-cord carpet takes a shove, but he can't get Riley up into the office chair like he planned, so he just leaves him there, propped up against the wall.

He flicks on the overhead lights.

The walls are filled with posters and news articles. Like some jaded private investigator in a cheap film, covering the walls of a motel with paperwork. All about *him*.

Bloody hell.

He stares at Riley, heart thundering.

Riley is still out of it, but still awake, paralysed.

He gets out the wire and the bag, then rests them on the carpet. Then sucks in deep breaths.

His veins fill with ice.

Just do it. Get it over with.

He pulls the bag over Riley's head, getting it almost air-tight, then ties the wire round and pulls it, locking it in place.

No matter how bad they are, ending a life is difficult...

He hasn't expected this to be so hard.

Riley kicks out. Then again.

He almost topples over.

Christ, he should've used more. Or knocked him out.

Riley is rocking, scratching at his jacket. Kicking the desk. Something clatters to the floor, the carpet dulling the thud.

A little metal box.

Riley is staring at him but doesn't understand what's happening or why. Doesn't know who it is. Wouldn't. Couldn't.

They've never met. The beef with Riley isn't his.

And he can't do this.

He lets the tension go and Riley starts breathing again, puffing the bag.

It was supposed to be easy.

But it was anything but.

He reaches for the blue box, the kind you'd store drill bits in or a sandwich on a construction site, and eases off the lid.

Ten little objects, like little mice.

Fire burns through his veins now.

His hands start shaking. Legs struggling to support him.

Riley's breath is misting the bag. Still alive. Just.

He puts the box on the desk in front of him and snaps the lid as tight as his fingers allow. Then sucks in a deeper breath, his lungs filling up with the house smell. Furniture polish, stale garlic, pungent air freshener.

Strangling isn't enough. Thomas Riley needs to truly suffer. To learn true pain before the end.

But he doesn't want to delay anything, to risk Riley being saved by someone, so he tightens his grip on the wire, holding it until the thrashing stops.

He watches the flickering behind Riley's eyes fade to nothing.

Eyes staring at him now stare right through him.

29

The wind cut through Vicky as it howled across the damp car park. Just about dark now. She had to lean against Forrester's car. Her own was just a few metres away, the space next to it empty.

Where Euan MacDonald's car would be.

Christ, it was so close to being two empty spaces today.

The tracksuit she wore was a size too small and thin as hell. She was freezing. At least that's why she thought she was shivering.

Forrester finished sucking on a cigarette, his hand cupped around it, the dank smell crawling all over Vicky, then dropped it and stamped on it. 'Let's get you inside, eh?'

Vicky followed him across the tarmac, feeling like she had tight bands around her knees and ankles. And someone had filled her shoes with glass. Each step was like walking with bad pins and needles. She tried stamping her feet to get rid of it.

Forrester scowled at her. 'Are you okay there—'

Vicky slipped on the pavement and went down in a heap.

Cracked her arse off the ground. She yelped.

'Watch yourself.' Forrester stretched out a hand.

'Bit late for the warning.' Vicky brushed away the offer of help and picked herself up. A rash of red on her left palm. Felt like she'd dislocated her bum. And bruised her ego.

'What happened?'

'Just slipped. It is icy, you know.'

'Right, you really do need to get home.'

Vicky wasn't going to argue, but she couldn't help herself. 'I can work through it.'

'Doddsy, a murderer's just shot himself in front of you after threatening you with a gun. You need a shower. And now you're falling over? You definitely need to get home.'

'I didn't get much sleep last night, sir. That's all it is.'

'Insomnia usually makes you slip up like that, though.' The way Forrester was looking at her, she wanted to punch him. 'Shower, now.' He ran a thumb down the length of his nose as if he was smearing war paint down it. 'Come on, let's get you inside.'

Vicky set off ahead of him, splashing through the car park, the biting wind digging its claws across her face. She trudged up the stairs, so tired she could sleep standing up, then stopped in the corridor. The usual bedlam came from the incident room.

Shouting, swearing, stapling, slurping, farting.

Forrester clumped up alongside her, mobile stuck to his ear. 'Right, sure. Later, then.' He killed the call and sighed. 'Considine's managing the crime scene. Told him to get Shepherd to head back here, but he's even more stubborn than you.'

'Sure he is.'

'You don't rate the kid, do you?'

'No, but he's not that bad.'

'Christ, you really are in a bad way.' Forrester laughed. 'Okay, you shower and I'll try and get my arms around the rabble in there.'

'Don't know what I'll do when I get home.'

'Fill a hot water bottle and climb into bed. Try to get some sleep.'

'I'll just lie there until I see...' She trailed off with a gasp.

Forrester set off towards the incident room. 'Shower, then I'll drive you home in your car. Okay?'

THE HOT WATER hit her head like bullets.

Bullets, like the one that went through Doug Mason's skull.

Why?

Why the hell had he done that?

They knew he was the killer. Murdering his brother, then trying to kill Morgan.

But why did he have to torment Vicky?

Why?

What the hell had she done that warranted someone shooting himself in front of her?

Shepherd flew in like a superhero, but the gun wasn't trained on her when he fired. A suicide. Sending her a message.

And she just didn't know why.

She wanted to sleep. Right now, if she closed her eyes, she'd probably drift off.

She'd get five minutes at most before her brain woke her up. But they'd be blissful.

Doug Mason's suicide would keep rattling around inside

her head.

She ran a hand through her hair and it felt clear of blood. Bone. Brains.

She reached over to the tap and—

Gun against her temple.

BANG.

Doug Mason's skull, like an open tin.

VICKY OPENED the door to their office space. Shivering. Hair damp, but at least in her own clothes, though they were for the office party in a few weeks. Assuming there wasn't a new wave.

While the incident room sounded like an office party in a TV show, the office space was quiet and almost empty. Just Jenny rattling away at a laptop in the window. She clocked Vicky's approach. 'Heard what happened. You okay?'

Vicky didn't have anything to say about it. She just saw Doug Mason's opened-up skull. And still had so many questions. 'Why are you up here, Jenny?'

'Eye of the storm.' She stretched out and her top rode up to reveal pale skin. 'When there's a big murder on, my place is like Tannadice or Dens on any given Saturday. Same with the incident room. But this is nice and quiet, meaning I can get on with the work.'

'You're in charge of them. You should be there with them.' Vicky sat down at her desk. Photos of Rob, her and the kids on holiday three years ago. All seemed so different to a world where someone could point a gun at you. Could shoot themselves in front of you.

Vicky closed her eyes and tried to clear her mind.

BANG.

Skull.

Shell casing.

Dead eyes.

Doug's skull, open and empty, dead eyes looking up at her.

She opened them again and dug her knuckles into her eyes, trying to scratch away the image of Doug's empty skull.

BANG.

She leaned forward in the desk chair, stomach spinning. Head like a thousand junkies were shooting up in it.

The taste of bile was about gone now. Finally.

'Forgot to say.' Jenny pointed towards Forrester's office. 'Someone wanted a word with you.'

'Who?'

'Search me. Old bloke.'

'Great. Forrester was right. I need to get home.' Vicky took a couple of goes to get up. 'I'll see you tomorrow.' She set off across the carpet tiles towards his office. She opened the door and peered inside.

A man stood by the window, talking on the phone, his shrivelled face screwed tight. Vicky recognised him but couldn't quite place him. Thick winter coat, a heavy scarf tight around his throat. Thin silver hair scraped across a pink forehead. He spotted her. 'Need to go, bye.' He ended the call and grinned at Vicky. 'DI Dodds, I presume?' London accent, clipped Cockney rather than drawn-out Essex.

She stepped into room. 'And who might you be?'

'Detective Superintendent Derek Broadfoot.' He tilted his head to the side, his hair barely shifting. He carried himself like he'd just fought a war all by himself. And won. 'Professional Standards in the Met.'

Another internal affairs cop turning up just like that? After Shepherd?

Vicky knew how to act, though. Doing that was the hard part. She sat in Forrester's chair like it was her own office. The room was spinning. 'Where's David?'

'I heard about what happened, Vicky.'

'You've got good ears for a Met cop.'

Broadfoot unbuttoned his coat and draped it over the chair. He scraped it back across the wooden floor, the sharp squeal stinging Vicky's ears, then sat down. He undid his scarf and placed it on his lap in a perfect square.

And Vicky got it. He was the arrogant prick she'd seen at Gavin Mason's crime scene. Forrester's liaison. 'So what brings you up here?'

'Nothing I particularly enjoy. Like I say, I work for the Met's Complaints, as you'd call it. But I'm working part of a specialist investigation. A few years back, we took down a nasty Albanian gang. Huge case, all over the news. Drug smuggling, people trafficking. You name it, they had their fingers in that pie. I worked it from the drugs angle, DCI Howard Savage from the people trafficking side. Intersected with a murder investigation. Several, actually. And we took them down.' His nostrils flared. 'But they had officers from several police forces on the payroll.'

'Guys on the inside covering it up?'

'Correct. Not just cops. Everywhere. How they managed to get that many people and that much drugs into the country without being caught. I led the team that took the whole thing down.' His smile had no warmth in it. 'Now, you'll notice I'm not getting any younger, so as part of my last couple of years on the force, I was given the remit of investigating and catching said bent cops across Britain.'

'Gavin Mason was involved?'

'Both brothers were. Why I drove myself up here at the crack of sparrow fart to see for myself. I was down in Grimsby, interviewing some local officers about a shipment they'd conveniently lost a few years back. Got me a few leads on who might know a thing or two about it.' Broadfoot cleared his throat. 'But yeah, Gavin Mason was involved. Just low-level stuff. Intimidating people, driving lorries around. That kind of thing. But the lorries he drove were full of people. Desperate souls escaping war or famine. Others being brought here against their will to walk the streets, or inside certain private clubs.'

'Nasty business.'

'Douglas, on the other hand, he was helping them launder the proceeds of their profits. When my colleagues caught him, he flipped and we won. We got a trove of evidence from him. Helped us put away seventeen of the worst people I've ever even heard about. Gave me leads on who was helping them. You could say they're even worse, but let's settle for just as bad.'

Vicky was struggling to focus. 'There a point to this?'

'Okay, I imagine you want to get home, so I'll be brief. Both Mason brothers should've called in at six o'clock yesterday. It was for their own safety, you understand. When Gavin didn't and you found him, well that set hares running.' He raised a finger. 'But the conclusion myself and your gaffer have come to is that this is only tangentially to do with my case. Douglas happened to discover his wife was sleeping with his brother.' He smiled at her. 'But he hadn't counted on you being so tenacious. Destroying his alibis. Finding out that he'd been grooming a young woman. Just a girl, really.' He sighed deeply. 'And it's hard to get away from the fact that Doug Mason lost his mind. He might've been an accountant for the mob, but he'd spent so much time with these people, their solutions rubbed off on him. And when all you've got is a hammer, everything looks like a nail. So Douglas took their lives, thinking he could get away with it.'

'Thing is...' Vicky's head was thumping so hard she could barely focus. 'There's just something I can't shake. He'd killed his brother in cold blood. Tried to do the same with Morgan. When he got me on the bus, Doug... He just wanted to talk. He admitted to trying to kill Morgan. He said, "I did what I had to." Something like that. But when I asked him about Gavin, he said he didn't kill him.'

'Come on. You're a detective inspector. I'm sure you must've come across criminals who deny their actions even to themselves?'

Vicky smiled. 'One or two.'

'These people cope by dissociating themselves from their actions. Douglas was the same. Sure, his work was one step removed from what was going on. Just numbers on a spreadsheet to him. Easy to convince yourself what you're doing doesn't impact the lives of real people.'

'I know, but—'

'David Forrester said you got the inkling that he was using Morgan to groom others?'

'Right. Possibly. Someone needs to speak to Morgan about that.'

'Forrester's asked a DI McNeill about taking that side of things over from your team.'

'I know Sharon. She's one of the best.'

'Good.' Broadfoot held her gaze for a few seconds. He reached into his boot to scratch some itch. 'What I want to know is why didn't Doug kill you?'

'Because of Luke Shepherd. It all happened so fast. I….'

'So why not kill Shepherd?'

Vicky didn't have an answer. Didn't have a lot of anything. 'Listen, can we—'

'I think Douglas wanted us to know this was nothing to do with the gang stuff. It was only about him and his brother.' Broadfoot seemed to wince. 'I'm going to let you in on a little secret here. The stuff Douglas did down in London wasn't good. At all.' His eyes twitched. 'He was abusing young victims himself.'

'Girls like Morgan?'

'That kind of age, yeah.'

'You didn't think to get him put on the register?'

'All charges were dropped. You of all people know how hard it is to prosecute these crimes, right? Victims don't want to testify. Defence lawyers are *animals*.'

'You're saying a leopard never changes his spots?'

'A child molester never stops. Believe me, I know.' Broadfoot got to his feet and hauled his jacket over his shoulder. 'What I think is, Doug couldn't face prison. Every time we spoke to him, that's what he focused on. What could he do to avoid jail time? Child abusers are not popular in there, as I'm sure you know. So, given you'd stopped him killing Morgan, he'd be going away for that. At least. Hence him killing himself.'

'Why didn't he change his name? Why didn't Gavin?'

'Don't know why he'd have wanted to.' Broadfoot shrugged. 'We deemed him low risk. The six o'clock phone calls were all we needed from them.'

'Why did he put me through that?'

'Because he's a sadistic bastard, that's why. He didn't intend to kill you. Listen, I wish we could've put him away.' His jaw clenched hard. 'I wish he was the eighteenth scumbag inside and his brother the nineteenth. But he's not. Both of them are dead. I'm trying to take some solace from the fact he won't be able to abuse any more girls.'

'Morgan's going to need a lot of help.'

'And that's on me.' Broadfoot dragged his thin hair over again. 'I've got a decent budget to help the victims of these crimes cope with what's happened to them.'

'I wish it hadn't happened. I wish I hadn't been taken on a bus at gunpoint, hadn't had that gun stuck right here.' She pointed at her forehead. 'I'll never stop hearing the gunshot. Never stop seeing his skull, opened up like that. The taste of his blood.' She had to shut her eyes.

'I'm sorry, Inspector. I truly am. Might want to get some counselling.'

She stared hard at him. 'Are you serious?'

'Deadly. You've just witnessed a traumatic event. Counselling is the number one treatment for complex PTSD.'

'I've not got that.'

'You will probably develop it.' Broadfoot checked his watch. 'Listen, I've got to set off home. Well, back to Grimsby to see how my guys are doing interviewing people.' He put a card down on the table. 'If you need anyone to talk to, please call me.'

And with that he marched out of the office.

Vicky leaned back, watching him go. Seen his type before.

Maybe Broadfoot was right, that this was just a simple case of a man pushed to the brink by his evil actions. Who saw everything as a means to his own ends.

And she really needed to get home and get to sleep.

30

'I've arranged for someone to pick you up tomorrow morning, okay?' Forrester was leaning across the passenger seat. 'If you need anything, give me a call. Okay?' He held out her keys. 'I'm meeting a boy from Carnoustie who's giving me a lift back.'

'Thanks, sir.' Vicky slammed the door and got out. She waved him off, his footsteps slicing through the icy darkness.

The street was quiet, but at least there were lights on in her home.

Not many times in the last few years she'd been home this early. Usually a lot later.

Vicky traipsed up to the house. Almost went over again. She stopped on the top step and blew air up her face.

Why did she feel so tired?

Her mobile thrummed in her pocket.

Sharon:

In Dundee. Fancy a coffee or some wine?

Vicky replied:

Sorry. Had a day of it. Tomorrow?

Tomorrow I'll be back home. I heard about incident. You okay?

I'm a survivor. I'll be fine

Call me if you're not.

Deal. Safe drive home.

Vicky opened the door and crept into the long hall and kicked off her shoes, then hung up her coat. The noise came from the living room, so she paced through.

Rob sat on an armchair reading a book, the dogs at his feet. 'Hey.' He put his book on the side table and yawned. 'The wanderer returns.'

'Sorry.' She walked over and cuddled him. 'I've missed you.'

'Me too.' He wasn't letting go of her, holding her there. 'Busy day?'

She shrugged.

'Have you eaten?'

'Had something earlier, aye.' Not that she'd eaten much of it. 'How are you?'

'I'm fine, Vicky. Kids are in their rooms, doing their homework. Come on, what's going on?'

'I'm good.'

'You're not and you haven't eaten, have you?' He got up and led her by the hand through to the kitchen. 'Let's get you some soup.'

'Hopefully not celeriac and watermelon.'

He laughed. 'Just stilton and liquorice.' He stuck a tub into the microwave, then hit the button. 'It's lentil.'

'Thanks.'

They stood there, silent, just the machine droning until it pinged.

'How's Jamie been today?'

Rob served up the soup into a bowl. 'He's being strong.'

Vicky leaned against the kitchen counter and took a spoonful of soup. 'I'm so sorry it happened.'

'It's okay.' Rob perched against the counter next to her and wrapped his arm around her. 'It's not like we haven't discussed this kind of thing before, is it? What'd happen if your world collided with theirs. He'll be fine.' He kissed her on the forehead. 'You do a very important job, Vicky. Okay?'

Vicky took another spoonful then pushed the bowl away on the breakfast bar. 'He's a good kid. Shame about his stepmother.'

'Still the eternal joker.' Rob gave a slight shake of the head. 'Listen, it's okay. What happened, it's okay.'

'I'm not.'

Rob wrapped his arms around her. 'Okay, so what happened?'

Vicky shut her eyes. For once, she didn't see Doug Mason's skull. 'Someone shot themselves in front of me.'

'Seriously?'

'I'm okay, but—' A metal rod spiked Vicky's throat, stopping her breathing. 'Jesus Christ.'

She'd tried to deny it. Tried to push it out of her mind. Tried to avoid coming home, because here meant time where she might think about it.

But she was here. Now. With the love of her life.

So she let herself think of Doug Mason's head, opened up.

The tears streamed down her cheeks. Rob's big arms enveloped her.

Why?

Why did he do that? Why did he do that to her?

'The guy who shot himself, Doug Mason, called me and got me to meet him, then I saw that he had a gun and it's Scotland, for fuck's sake, there aren't a lot of guns outside of hunting collections, so we just don't think that way in Dundee, that someone might be armed and he killed himself right in front of me and I don't know why.'

She swallowed. The words came out so fast it felt like she was running down the stairs, out of control.

Rob raised his eyebrows. 'Wow, that's a lot.'

'I know. I can't piece it all together.'

He sniffed. 'How about you get in the shower and then get all nice and cosy. We can sit down, the four of us, watch a film. Hopefully you can switch off that giant brain of yours and get some sleep?'

It sounded impossibly perfect.

'You've got a whole day off tomorrow with the kids.'

Vicky let her head go. 'I can't get the time off.'

'What?'

'Seriously. This case...'

'Someone shoots themselves in front of you and you can't call in sick?'

'Rob, I'm sorry.'

'Vicky. It's an in-service day. The kids are off all day.'

'I'll get Mum to cover.'

'You know she's in Glasgow.'

'Dad, then.'

Rob laughed. 'Seriously?'

'He was a cop for umpteen years. He can handle those two. Besides, they're both on their phones all the time.'

'I'm worried about you. Something like this happens, you need time to process it.'

'I need to get stuff out of my head. That's all. Okay, I hear you. How about I go in and empty my head, type up my statement and then I'll come home and look after the kids?'

'Well, I'm not happy, Vicky, but I know you.'

DAY 3

Tuesday

31

Vicky slumped behind her desk. Not even Jenny was here this early. Just her, her computer and a traumatic event to document.

Where do you start?

She had no idea.

'Penny for them.'

She turned around.

Shepherd stuffed his hands into his pockets and shuffled over to Vicky's desk. 'How are you doing, Vicky?'

'Shite.' She slumped back in her chair. 'Not great.'

'You can talk to me about it. I hope you know that.'

She looked at him and saw two men.

One, the cop who put himself between her and a bullet.

Two, the cop who was lying about not being Professional Standards and Ethics.

'Thanks, Luke. I'm just going to type up my statement, then get home. Kids are off school today, so...' She leaned forward.

'Listen, before I left last night, I spoke to Forrester's Met liaison. Broadfoot. Well, he spoke at me.'

Shepherd narrowed his eyes at her. 'Broadfoot?'

She nodded. 'Know him?'

Shepherd grimaced. 'From my old Complaints days, aye. Worked a few cases with his lot. What was he asking?'

'Well, he's investigating a lot of gang stuff, but his focus is on bent cops. Still, his take is Doug Mason killed his brother because he was sleeping with his wife.'

'Don't you think that?'

'Right.' She looked up at the ceiling. The tiles had a dark patch of water damage. 'Open and shut.'

'Not your assessment?'

'It stacks up, sure. Kill his brother, try to kill Morgan to shut her up. But... Maybe it's because of... What we saw.' She swallowed down the image of Doug's open skull. Two glasses of wine had blocked that out overnight, but still... Her previous dream had returned with a vengeance. 'Have I thanked you for saving me?'

'Fifteen times, so far.'

'Right.' She laughed, but it caught in her throat. 'I still don't get what he was doing. Why take me? Why bring the gun? Why shoot himself?'

'Thing is, you're always going to have questions. And he'd almost got away with it. Could be he believed he needed to kill you first.'

'In public? With a warning? Surely his plan would be to flee. Probably still knew people in that racket who could get him a fake passport. Even get to Albania or as far away as possible. He's an accountant, surely he's got money squirrelled away somewhere hot, exotic and with no corporate governance.'

'Not always. Possible he just didn't know what to do. He was talking to you a lot. What did he say?'

'He was asking me lots of weird shit. If I got an extra day by killing someone, would I do it? Weird stuff like that.'

'What did Broadfoot say about that?'

'Well, not much. That Doug couldn't face prison, basically. His mind imploded from the stress.'

'Believe it?'

'Can buy it. He'd cracked. Not being able to kill Morgan tipped him over the edge. Maybe you're right, Luke, maybe he thought he needed to kill me. Still, if it was like that, the thing I don't get is that Emma was at Gavin's flat just before he was killed. Why didn't Doug kill her at the same time?'

'Could be he believed there was a possibility of patching things up with her?' Shepherd shrugged. 'And I suspect Doug thought he was smarter than us cops, thought he could execute that plan and get away with it.'

'It just seems a bit... out of his reach. Don't you think?'

'I think he's picked up some tricks and techniques from his old associates. He's got a gun too. Where the hell from, we don't know. But if he was using Morgan to groom other girls?'

'Did we get anywhere on that?'

'Sharon McNeill was asking after you.'

The office door opened and Jenny walked in, blanketed by bedlam. Shouting and typing. The incident room was getting worse. Then it stopped as the door closed again. 'You two could clear off and give me some peace, if you want.' She sat at her desk and reached for her headphones. 'Swear I'd much rather be at the crime scene than doing this.'

'Doing what?'

'Reviewing the DNA reports. But the crime scene's taking

up more than all of my resources, so I'm having to do the job myself.'

'You got anything?'

'Not yet. But while it runs I've got hold of stuff from the car hire company for you. Sure you've got cops for this kind of donkey work?'

'Have you?'

'Have I what? Got cops for donkey work?'

'No! Jenny, have you got anything?'

'What do you wish to know, O master?'

'Well, where the car is now?'

Shepherd leaned forward. 'Listen, when you went home yesterday, I had a trip down to Fife. We found what we think is the hire car, burnt out in a wood near Cupar.'

'Crap.'

'And that's the MO of a pro, Vicky. Proof that Doug picked up some tricks from them.'

'Hang on.' Jenny opened her machine, the screen showing the route between Dundee and Edinburgh, all timestamped. 'The hire company kept a log of its movements. Hard to tell, but before it was burnt out in Fife, it went back to Edinburgh.'

'Where about?'

'Erm.' She pulled up a map. Showing a location about six miles west of Edinburgh.

Shepherd grunted.

Vicky gave him a pause, but he didn't fill it. 'What's up, Luke?'

'Well, that's like Bathgate, Livingston way. Not really Edinburgh, is it?'

'Near that hotel? Neshinton whatever?'

'Not walking distance, but it's not a million miles away. And I'd assumed Doug walked between the car and the hotel.'

'But?'

'But the timeline doesn't fit. Unless he caught a cab...' Shepherd stared at Vicky. 'After the new bridge, you join the M9 until the M8. But he turned off way before. Backroads around there... Absolute nightmare.'

Vicky yawned into her fist. 'Listen, I'll let you two puzzle this out. I've got to get this statement done and head home to manage my kids.'

Shepherd raised his giant bear paw. 'Vicky, I think you're right to doubt it.'

Ah shite. Vicky sucked in a deep breath. 'Go on?'

'Well, there's just something not sitting right with me. While it was all holding together in our heads, Doug shuttling between Edinburgh and Dundee so many times without detection is pretty fanciful.'

'Luke...'

'That's what you're saying, right?'

'Well, aye, but... Our whole thing's based on that. How he managed to kill his brother.' Vicky glanced at Jenny, but she seemed distracted. 'Do you agree with this?'

'Mm?' But she didn't look over.

'That Doug travelling between Dundee and Edinburgh to kill his brother is too much?'

'Mm.'

'Jenny.'

'Mm?'

'Jenny, are you even listening?'

'Aye, sure, I'm listening.' But she was leaning forward and staring into her screen.

Vicky craned her neck to see what was so important and distracting. 'What's that?'

'The crime scene DNA stuff.' Jenny twirled her hair around a finger. 'It's *weird*.'

Vicky exchanged a look with Shepherd. 'Weird how?'

'Well. Gavin's DNA is everywhere. Like you'd expect. And I've got Emma Mason there too. And you, Vicky, left a couple of hairs behind. And Jamie, obviously. And that Broadfoot twat.'

Shepherd frowned. 'Broadfoot?'

'Didn't you see the stramash at the crime scene? He walked in with a crime scene suit, like he was Batman or something.'

'That's Derek Broadfoot for you.' Shepherd winced. 'Okay, so you've got three traces to exclude. What's weird about that?'

'Well, the weird bit is... There are loads more DNA samples there. A few of which I can identify because they've been arrested previously.'

'Meaning Gavin associated with criminals?'

'Not a surprise given he's been a member of a people trafficking gang. But there's no DNA from Doug.'

'What?'

'He's on the system. We've got his body. But I don't think he was there.' Jenny cleared her throat. 'Now, unless your guy is the best hitman the world's ever seen and cleaned up behind him, there's no way an amateur like him isn't leaving DNA at his brother's house when he kills him.'

Vicky knew she wasn't going to get away.

32

'Feels like we should just move in here.' Vicky pressed the bell and looked back along Doreen Mason's street. A squad car sat next to a brutish Subaru. 'Well, at least one of my lot's here.'

Shepherd was checking his mobile. 'I know you keep dissing him, but Considine seems like a good lad.'

'Really?' Vicky laughed. 'What do you see in him?'

'He's honest.' Shepherd held her gaze. 'I worked the Complaints beat for a couple of years. Saw some stuff that just shouldn't be allowed to happen. Bent cops are one thing, but when their superiors lie? That's ten times worse.'

'You really think Considine's honest?'

'As the day is long. Might be a bit thick and a bit arrogant, but I get a good read on him.'

Vicky tried the bell again. She'd never considered that before. Her only metric around the quality of a police officer was whether they did the job how she wanted it done. And she'd dealt with superiors who lied and helped people get away with things.

Still, she wasn't honest herself. Lying about what she'd done. Covering it up. Sure, people could begin to understand, but she was a cop. And cops were supposed to do the right thing.

The door opened and Considine stepped out, chest puffed up, trying to stand up as tall as Vicky or Shepherd. 'Boss. Sarge.' Weird how quickly Shepherd had acquired that familiarity with him.

Vicky felt a stinging up her back.

What if Shepherd knows him? What if Considine is undercover too?

Jesus. Paranoid, much?

She smiled at Considine. 'How is she?'

'Not great.' Considine dipped his head. 'Just delivered the death message about Doug.' He glanced back into the house. 'Never easy, but two in as many days?' He grimaced. 'And one killing the other…'

All questions Vicky had asked herself. 'We need a word with Emma. Gather she's here?'

'In you come.'

Doreen Mason was in the living room, sitting with the FLO and a neighbour, presumably Mrs Houston.

Vicky nodded at Considine to go back with her.

Emma was in the kitchen, staring out of the back window as the kettle rumbled to an anti-climactic click. She turned around to them, her makeup streaked down her cheeks. She rubbed at her face. 'Sorry, I'm such a mess.'

'It's totally understandable.' Shepherd walked in and took control of the tea situation, pouring the kettle into the world's biggest teapot, a rainbow of hoops. 'Wow, I'll need to fill this up again.'

Emma laughed through tears. 'I keep telling her to get a bigger kettle but she's had that one since nineteen oatcake and won't get rid. Probably need a separate power station just to generate enough electricity for that teapot. Still, she's one for tradition.'

Shepherd moved over to the sink to refill it.

Vicky walked over to Emma, standing far enough away to give her space, but close enough for Emma to reach out for a hug if she needed it. 'How are you feeling?'

'In truth?' Emma stopped rubbing at her face. Her makeup had mostly smeared off and she seemed a lot younger. Barely out of her teens, sure, but she could also pass for someone who hadn't even started them. 'I'm torn, is the honest truth. Between upset that he's done this and… and fury. Fury that he's killed himself. What kind of man kills his own brother and his teenage lover?'

Vicky nodded. 'I'm sorry for what's happened to you.'

'Please, don't. I'm not the victim here. Morgan's in the hospital, Gav's in the morgue and…'

'You're *a* victim, Emma. You've suffered. His lies, his deceit. All of it. What you told me yesterday, for instance.'

Emma smoothed a hand down her face and went back to staring out of the window. 'Thank you.'

Aye, she was a woman who hadn't experienced a lot of love or sympathy in her life. Someone who judged herself way too harshly.

Vicky gave her some space. 'I was there when it happened.'

'My god.'

'Emma, we can come back later, but we've got a few questions that might help shed some light on what's happened.'

'Please. I want to help. I'm going out of my mind listening to Doreen. I love her like my own mother, God rest her soul, but...'

'Okay.' Vicky pulled out her notebook and the print-out Jenny had been very reluctant to do. 'Did your husband talk much about his time in London?'

Emma winced. 'Not much.'

'Not to you, or not at all?'

'Not to me. And not to his mother, that's for sure.'

'To Gavin?'

Emma swallowed. 'I think so. Listen, the one time Doug talked to me about it, he was pissed. Took half a bottle of whisky to get him to start, a whole one to get him to finish. He said he had PTSD from what he did.'

'Do you know what he meant by that?'

'Not sure. But he got Gav into that whole thing. Said he helped him get out. This lawyer they had, he was sharp. On it. Got them a deal.'

'What do you know about this lawyer?'

'Nothing.' Emma brushed away a tear. 'Was Doug abusing girls back then?'

'We don't—'

'Come on. I know what was happening under my nose. Him and Morgan.' She shook her head. 'My husband was having sex with an underage girl. I want to know if there were others. I want the truth.'

The kettle came to a boil for a second time and Shepherd topped up the monster teapot, then started pouring out cups. 'This should be more than strong enough already.'

'When did he start seeing you?'

'Oh, I was twenty. Met him in a club. He's a lot older, but he seemed young-ish and into cool music. And had his own place. Swept me off my feet, really. But I wasn't a victim of his. Barely touched me after the first few months.'

'And yet you got married?'

'Please don't judge me.'

'I'm not, Emma. Plenty of reasons someone would get into this kind of situation. Like I said, you're the victim as much as Morgan. We're just building up a picture of your relationship.'

'Well, it's not a Da Vinci, more a Picasso. All wonky.' Emma laughed at her own joke. 'Jesus Christ.' She collapsed into a seat at the kitchen table. 'I was Doug's *beard*, wasn't I? I was his cover?'

'It's okay, Emma. Please. However wonky it was, just let us know.'

'What is it you're after from me?'

'Who says we're after anything?'

'Two senior cops come around and come to me first, instead of his mum. Of course there's something.'

God, she was sharp. 'Okay, Emma, there's something strange about the crime scene at Gavin's flat. There are a few DNA samples we know about, including yours.'

'How do you know?'

'Remember when you got arrested for smashing someone's head off a pavement?'

Emma screwed her face up tight. 'But I got off with that.'

'Still, your DNA's on file. But that's not important. It's what's missing that's interesting. Doug's DNA.'

'What?' Emma scowled at Vicky. 'But he killed Gav, didn't he?'

'Exactly. That was our assumption.' Shepherd handed them

both cups of tea. 'Question we're asking ourselves is how does someone kill someone without leaving a trace?' He took a sip of his own. 'I mean, it's vaguely possible that some world-class hitman could attempt it, but you'd need advanced cleaning equipment and so on. Besides, there were a lot of other samples so that's not what happened. And, as far as we know, your husband was an accountant, not a hitman.'

Emma put her teacup down on the table. 'What do you want me to say?'

Vicky took the chair next to her and set down the sheet of paper. 'Okay, so a basic assumption is that whoever killed Gavin was at his flat.'

'Well, duh.'

Vicky unfolded the page. 'Should we find Doug's DNA there?'

'What do you mean?'

'Did Doug ever go round there?'

'Never. Hated that part of Dundee. Reminded him of where he grew up. Always got Gav to come here. Or meet in town.'

Vicky pushed the page over the table. 'Did he ever mention any of these names?'

Emma took the page and scanned down it. 'Who's Jamie Hamilton?'

'That's a long story. Do you recognise him?'

'Nope. Why are some of these just Sample 16, Sample 23?'

'Because we don't know whose DNA the trace belongs to. Named people are either police officers, their associates or they're from the DNA database.'

'So you mean criminals?'

'Not just that. Anyone who's been arrested and had a swab taken. Like you.'

Emma tapped the page. 'Thomas Riley.'

'You know him?'

'Gav mentioned him being around on Saturday. Old pals.'

'Back in a sec.' Shepherd left the room, phone out by the time he even got to the door.

Saturday would be fresh enough to give a DNA trace. But he could've returned. Definitely someone they needed to speak to.

Vicky looked back at Emma. 'Gavin say how he knew him?'

'Not to me. Just that they had a drink and a smoke.'

'Did he know him from his time in London?'

'Gav was never in London.'

'He was. Stayed with his brother. Six years, the pair of them.'

'Lying bastard.' Her hand ran across her belly.

Carrying the child of a lying bastard...

Aye, join the club.

'Were they friends?'

'Well. I think Gav might've owed him some money or something. Trouble with Gav is he owes everyone, but I got the impression it was a lot.'

'Thank you. Is there anyone else on the list?'

'Not that I recognise.' She handed it back. 'Sorry.'

'No need to apologise. That's very helpful.'

Shepherd popped his head back into the kitchen and beckoned Vicky over.

'Thanks, Emma.' She got up and walked over to the door. 'What's up?'

'Okay, so Thomas Riley's address is a country pile just outside Torphichen in West Lothian. Near Bathgate. Near where the hire car was.'

33

First time in a while Vicky had been across the Forth. Still took a while to get used to the new bridge, one of three spanning the firth now. 'Nice to be able to sit back and not drive.'

Shepherd looked over at her. 'Even if the cost of that was listening to Blind Bob Bollocks?'

'Even if.'

The giant tablet lit up with an incoming call. Babycakes.

Shepherd bounced it. Blushing already.

Vicky grinned at him. 'Luke, who's "Babycakes"?'

'Nobody.'

'Aye, sure.'

Vicky's mobile rang:

Dad calling...

'Better take this.' She answered it, heart thumping. 'Hey, Dad. You okay?'

'Can't get your Disney+ to work. Bella and Jamie are nipping my head about watching Hawkguy.'

'He's called Hawkeye, Dad.' Vicky checked the clock. 09:06. 'Listen, Rob's in-service thing won't have started. Can you call him?'

'Not really. These two are eating me alive here.'

'Get Jamie to—'

'Already done that.'

'Stick on YouTube. That one where the guy eats old army rations from the Second World War. They love it.'

'Well, you assume that app will work. Or I can get it to.'

'It will. It'll be ready to play.'

'Okay.' Dad mouth breathed into the phone. 'Where are you, if you don't mind me asking?'

'I do, but we're near Bathgate.'

'Christ. Worked with a guy who lived there. Absolute arsehole. Thought he was God's gift to policing. Brian Bain. If the guy's dead, then there's another grave I need to go and piss on.'

'Dad!'

'I'm serious.' He laughed. 'You any idea when you'll be home?'

'I hoped I'd be home early, but something's come up. Rob'll be home at the back of four.'

'Right, right. Still. I wish your mother hadn't picked this week to go and see her sister.' Dad sighed down the line. 'Take care and don't do anything I wouldn't do.'

'Doesn't leave much. Thanks for doing this, Dad.' She ended the call and put her mobile away. One day, she'd not be able to rely on them to bail her out with the kids.

Shit, that was a bleak thought.

'Everything okay?'

She couldn't look at him. 'Just my dad losing his shit with the kids.'

'Sounds like fun.'

Vicky's phone rang again. 'Christ, it's like I'm working for the call centre.'

Sharon calling...

She answered it. 'Bit busy just now, Sharon, can I—'

'Why is Luke Shepherd searching for Thomas Riley?'

Vicky glanced over at him. 'How do you know?'

'Got a silent alarm on it. Spoke to Scott Cullen about it, who told me Luke's working for you now.'

'Right. He is.'

'And? That's it?'

'No, his name came up in our investigation. We're heading around to his house to speak to him.'

'Please don't go in without me, okay? I'll meet you outside.'

34

Shepherd slowed and hit the indicator, then pulled off the main road onto a small lane lined with old trees. He took the turning, the gatepost etched with GLEN-FIRTH, whatever that meant. Matched the address Jenny had texted. A grit box was toppled over, probably nowhere near full enough to last a winter like last year. Some recycling bins on both sides of the road, like that was the done thing. He killed the engine. 'No sign of Sharon.'

Vicky got out into the wind and rain.

Shepherd checked back down the drive.

Headlights rumbled towards them, stopping just short.

Vicky had to shield her eyes until the engine growled off, then shone her torch over.

A figure stormed towards them. DI Sharon McNeill. Hair cut short, with a sweeping fringe just below her ears. 'Sorry I'm late. Got a lad working down in London who is causing me no end of grief with the expense system. Anyway. Nice to see you,

Vicky.' She launched into a big hug, then stepped back and smiled at Shepherd. 'Luke, you too.'

'DI McNeill.' One hand in his pocket, the other shaking her hand.

'So.' Sharon looked between them. 'What's the plan here?'

Vicky smiled at her. 'I told you the link we found, so how about you share what you know?'

'Okay, so when I spoke to Morgan Miller in Dundee yesterday, she didn't stop talking. It wasn't Doug who was grooming the kids, but Gavin.'

'Shit.' Vicky could only think about Emma.

'Now, finding someone with Thomas Riley's history, well, that adds in a whole world of complexity.'

'What have you got on him?'

Sharon smiled. 'You show me yours first.'

'Just a vanilla police record. But he's on your database, so he's either been a naughty boy or a very nasty fucker. Which is it?'

'The latter. He was involved with a gang down in Southend-on-Sea. Arrested, charged, but provided details on a massive money laundering operation.'

'This gang Doug and Gavin were involved with?'

'I think so.' Sharon trained her torch over the path that lead up to a house, a low hawthorn hedge on both sides hiding it. An old shepherd's cottage, extended out the back so it was four times the size. Flat roof and white stone harling.

No lights on inside, no fumes from a central heating outlet, assuming there was one.

A Porsche Cayenne sat on the drive, the driver's door open.

Vicky's skin prickled. She walked over to the car, shining the sun-like light into the vehicle. Fast food wrappers and empty chewing gum tubs. 'I don't like the door being left like that.'

'No.' Sharon walked over the pebbles and knocked on the front door.

Shepherd joined her, folding his arms. 'What if he's not in?'

'Then you've driven down here for no reason. At least you're close to home. And I can buy you lunch.' She checked her watch. 'Well, breakfast.'

'Then we head back to Dundee.' Shepherd smiled. 'Tail between our legs.' He snapped on a glove and tried the handle.

The door opened, the curtains rustling as it juddered to its full width.

'The car's not the only one with an open door.' He held out a hand. 'Ladies first.'

Sharon stepped inside.

Vicky snapped on a pair of evidence gloves of her own, bright blue with a garlic-rubber tang, and entered. She tried the lights – nothing. Cross-hatched parquet surrounded by bare stone walls on either side, inset with a couple of internal windows. 'This place is an architect's nightmare.'

'Or dream.' Sharon opened the first door on the right. A kitchen. 'Bloody hell. You smell that?'

Vicky sniffed the bitter tang of death.

On the oak table, a Cornish bowl lay at the head of the table, empty.

Shepherd took a sniff. 'Don't think it's from that.'

'Come on.' Sharon walked back into the hall. The internal windows showed a living room and a dining room, both empty. It split out into a T at the end. 'I'll try this side.' She headed left.

Vicky stepped across the carpet, careful not to make a sound, and tried the first door. A bedroom or a study. Sofa bed, desk, office chair. The smell was even worse – Jenny would need a whole box of cigars. Yellow walls, covered in posters. Looked like newsprint too but it was too dark to read much of it. She scanned over the desk. Expensive-looking computer. A wallet sat in front of it.

She reached down and opened the wallet, then flashed her torch onto it. Driver's license for a man in his twenties with a pencil-thin beard lining his chin, coiling round his lips. Thomas Riley. Next to the wallet was a metal box, like you'd keep drill bits in. But bigger. Vicky reached over for it.

A shoe on the floor.

And another. And a pair of jeans.

She stepped across the carpet, careful not to make a sound, then crouched down.

A pair of dead eyes looked back at her.

35

The country lane in front of Thomas Riley's house was swarming with detectives and CSIs. Squad cars filled the parking bays in front of the cottage, bathed in blinding light. Someone was already dusting down the Porsche 4x4.

Nice to see Police Scotland's East division were on it, unlike the chaos of Vicky's North area.

No, it was soul-destroying.

Vicky walked off towards the house again, running a hand through her hair, twirling it, kneading the kinks. Still felt there might be bits of Doug Mason's brains in there.

A giant cop stood over her, almost blocking out the low sun. 'You can't come in here.'

Vicky held out her warrant card. 'DI Vicky Dodds.'

He stepped back. 'Sorry, ma'am.'

'It's okay. You're just doing your job'

Sharon was standing there, fists on hips. 'Craig, can you make a nuisance of yourself somewhere else?'

He narrowed his eyes at Vicky, then charged off.

Sharon joined her. 'You okay?'

'Just yet another dead body. What else is new?'

'Craig shouldn't have been so hard on you.'

'You know him?'

'Used to work for me. He's the one with PTSD. DC Craig Hunter.'

'Oh.' Before Vicky could feel much sympathy for the bully, her mobile rang. 'God, this thing's going to melt soon.'

Rob calling...

'Better take this.' She clutched the phone tight and stepped away. 'Rob, what's up?'

'Where are you?'

'Down near Edinburgh. Why?'

The lot of a police officer's spouse was a hard one. 'Okay, well, your dad's been on the mobile. Said he nipped to the toilet and came back to find them watching some Flat Earth videos on YouTube.'

Vicky shut her eyes. 'That's a long toilet break. Probably playing that stupid game on his phone.'

'It just came up, he said.' Rob laughed. 'I'll have to spend a couple of hours deprogramming them when I get home.'

Vicky felt herself smile. 'Are you okay?'

'I'm fine. Don't worry about me.'

'Thanks, Rob.' She stood there, letting the rain wash over her. 'I love you.'

'I love you too.'

She killed the call, pocketed her mobile and tried to get her bearings.

Sharon had slipped off somewhere, but Shepherd wandered over, hands in pockets. One thing about him was he was never sneaking phone calls to anyone. Just did them blatantly and they all seemed to be about work. No apologetic calls about running late. No wife – or husband – missing him. Guy was an enigma. Probably how you got ahead being in the Complaints, especially doing the undercover work he did. 'You okay, Vicky?'

She shrugged. 'What's one more dead body?'

'Know what you mean.'

'I'm fine. Too fine, maybe. Wonder how many dead bodies I've seen in my career. Wonder what that does to a brain.'

'Nothing good.' Over at the house, arc lights making it seem like Christmas over a month early. CSIs working away inside. 'Riley, Gavin and Doug... Surely this is too much of a coincidence?'

'You think Doug Mason might have done this?'

Shepherd gave a shrug. He pointed in the direction of their cars. 'He was staying near here for a couple of nights. Say he came out to meet this Thomas Riley. He was a contact of his brother's. Someone from their old world.'

'Why kill him, though?'

'You heard what Sharon said. He was in the same gang as Gavin and Douglas. Had to leave a trace, though. Some way of communicating. Some trail of IP addresses and God knows what else.'

'Good luck with that.'

He gave her a glower. 'Are you saying we shouldn't try?'

'Sorry. I'm tired, hungry and two hours from home.'

'I'll forgive your grumpiness, then. But let's pull in at the services next time, aye?'

'Thanks, Luke.'

A car pulled into the drive and rumbled towards them.

Vicky stepped back and let it through.

It stopped and the driver got out in a fog of super-strong cologne. 'First you steal my best officer, then you stomp all over my territory.'

Vicky squinted and tried to make him out. 'Scott Cullen?'

'As I live and breathe.' He walked forward and hugged her, cloaking her in his aftershave.

Shepherd stepped away from them.

She broke off and got a better look at him. 'You look well, Scott.'

Not her worst lie, but close to it. Seemed like he hadn't slept in the six months since she'd last seen him and had existed on a diet of ice cream and pizza. In that order too.

'Lying cow.'

'Okay, so you look like a bag of dirt. Is it because of what you went through in the summer?'

He snorted. 'When someone like Brian Bain has a vendetta against you... It's a nightmare. It's no wonder I feel like shite, Vicky.'

'What you went through at his hands, nobody should have to go through that. Digging up all that stuff on your private life, Scott. It's really, really shit.'

'Still, it's game over for him. Luke and I went to the funeral.'

'The urine must've dried on his grave.' The same joke her dad had used. Shit, maybe she wasn't that different from him, after all...

Cullen laughed. 'No, I keep driving up there to put down a fresh pee.' He winced. 'Seriously, though, I don't wish he'd died. He was a total cock, but still.' He sighed, just like he did at school. Like he'd always done. 'Have you lost a lot of weight?'

'You trying to flatter me?'

'No, it makes you look older.'

'Charming bastard.'

'You doing okay yourself, Vicky?'

She shrugged. 'Just keeping on keeping on, you know how it is.'

'Don't I just.' Cullen clapped Shepherd's arm. 'How's this one doing? Keeping out of trouble?'

Shepherd rolled his eyes. 'Day one, our suspect shot themselves in front of us. Day two, we find a body on your patch.'

'Sounds like the kind of work I expected when they took you away from me.' The light caught a vertical strip of hair lurking on Cullen's chin, a soul patch a Mexican cartel member would be proud of. 'Sounds like the sort of crap I have to deal with all the time.' He tugged at his micro-beard. 'So, I've caught this case, but there's a whole load of complications attached to it. Not least because your PNC check set off a silent alarm.' He waved over at another car, just pulling up. A sporty Focus. 'My boss isn't too happy about that.'

'Sharon's already here, Scott.'

'Is she?' Cullen looked like someone had burst in on his masturbating. 'Anyway.'

Vicky spotted Sharon berating a cop. Bald guy, overweight. Head bowed.

Cullen squinted. 'Jesus, is that Damian McCrea?'

Shepherd glowered. 'Got a transfer to the Sexual Offences Unit last year. Sharon called me, asked how good he was.'

Cullen laughed. 'And you lied, saying he was anything but useless?'

Shepherd shrugged. 'He was close to Brian Bain.'

'Right. My point exactly. Well, if anyone can make a cop of him, it's her.'

'True enough.' Shepherd let out a deep sigh, misting in the air. He waved over the hedge to the house, glowing white. 'How's it going with the body?'

'Jimmy Deeley called me on the drive over.' Cullen looked at Vicky. 'He's our pathologist. In there now. Early for once. Struggling to pin down a time of death on account of the temperature. Open doors and windows tend to make it hard.'

'As do showers.' Vicky pointed over at the Porsche, now surrounded by CSIs. 'The car door was open when we got here. That doesn't strike you as odd?'

'A wee bit, aye.' Cullen scratched the back of his neck. 'One of our guys plugged into the car's computer. Last trip was eighteen miles yesterday, down to Livingston and back. His mother's in a nursing home there. Engine shut off at 15:32.'

'Seriously?'

'No, Vicky, I'm making whatever shit up I want as I go along.' Cullen shook his head. 'Why is that significant?'

'Because our suspect shot himself about an hour before that.'

'Oh.'

'Aye, oh. And the worst part is, our suspect's DNA wasn't even at the crime scene.'

'So you don't have a suspect now?'

'Correct. Thomas Riley was suspect number two.'

Cullen stood there, arms folded, forehead twitching. 'There's something inside I need to show you two.'

36

Vicky's crime scene suit was two sizes too small.

Ahead of her, Shepherd ambled through the house, whistling a Vegas show tune, his crime scene suit crinkling. He idly stepped out of the way of a passing gurney as it trundled through the garden gate. The black body bag on top shoogled as they rattled over the pebbles.

Vicky tightened her mask over her face and followed Shepherd inside.

The local SOCOs were out in force, dusting and cataloguing the parquet hall.

Even through his booties, Shepherd's brogues clattered off the wooden floor. He stopped outside the office door.

Vicky started to sweat in the suit.

Inside the room, Cullen walked over to the desk. A pair of SOCOs were doing a limbo dance underneath, dusting and photographing God knows what. Cullen reached over for something in an evidence bag, then walked back. He held it out.

Shepherd snatched it off him and opened it through the plastic. Took a couple of goes and the metal case clunked open. He checked inside and grimaced. 'What the hell is this?'

Vicky peered in.

Looked like dead mice inside, ten of them, stuck down with something, like you'd mount butterflies or moths.

'Keepsakes.' Cullen's eyebrows flashed up and a sigh escaped through the mask. 'They're human ears.'

Vicky blew out air. 'Seriously?'

'Damn right.' Cullen took the box back. 'See the way they seem to be getting older? That's because they are.' He ran a finger over an ear. 'Reason I'm here is we've got a potential serial killer case going back to when I was barely a DC. MO is he stabs his victims through the heart, then cuts off their ears. Kept it out of the press to a large extent, treating it as three separate stabbings.'

'Three?' Vicky's skin crawled again. 'Scott, there are five pairs in there.'

'Exactly.' Cullen pointed at the two pairs on the right. 'While you've caught our killer, we're missing two victims.'

Vicky stared at the empty office chair. 'You think Thomas Riley's a serial killer?'

'Not quite.' Cullen shifted his gaze across the wall. 'Guy was a huge Mark Torrance fan.' He pointed at the walls.

In the middle, Robert Carlyle glared into a camera, the perfect blend of menacing hardman and family guy. Gaudy yellow text for the actor's name, red for the film title.

THE MARKSMAN

The rest of the walls weren't covered in posters, but press

clippings – newspaper stories, magazine articles. Going back to the late Eighties, early Nineties. Over to the right, some more recent articles.

'Scottish hitman who got caught in the Nineties.' Shepherd walked over and started reading the clippings. 'And you think this Thomas Riley is, what, copying Torrance?'

'Could be. You've seen the film?'

'Many, many times.'

'Robert Carlyle was brilliant.' Cullen chuckled, like they weren't talking about serial killings. 'Helen Mirren played the cop, Margaret something or other, but it was a bloke who put him away. Must've changed his gender to cash in on the *Silence of the Lambs*.' He walked over to the wall and stared at the poster. 'Thing is, they were just in time. Torrance had killed the last victim, a cop, and was about to kill the guy's wife. Their son was upstairs, locked in his room. Just a kid. Cops burst in and caught him. They asked Torrance his name and he said he was nobody. Pure Hollywood.'

'I remember that bit.' Vicky glanced over. 'Let me get this straight. Our victim, Gavin Mason, was meeting your serial killer, Thomas Riley, who seems to be a massive fan of Mark Torrance, a hitman. That film poster. All those news clippings. It's got to be connected. But I don't see how.'

'Everything's connected, Vicky. Just most of those connections are gibberish.'

'Do you have anything on Riley?'

'Nope.' Cullen sniffed. 'Only reason I happen to be here is the Livingston MIT are flat out with another case. My fiancée works for them.'

'Congratulations on that, Scott.'

Cullen looked away. 'Thanks.'

Shepherd folded his arms. 'So Riley's killed these people to copy Torrance?'

Cullen shrugged. 'Stranger things have happened.'

'But Torrance was a hitman.' Vicky picked up the box but didn't dare open it. 'Riley seems more like a serial killer. Why keep the ears if it's just a murder?'

'A serial killer might make the best hitman.' Cullen took the box off her and opened it again. 'Gets his kicks as well as money from it. You see this place. Must've made a fair amount of dosh.'

'Still don't buy it.'

'Torrance was one of the best hitmen in the world in his day. He's been rotting in a cell for twenty-five years. Seven consecutive life sentences for the murders they could do him for. Suppose he gets the itch again? Thomas Riley could be a proxy.' Cullen crouched in front of a row of boxes running along the bottom. 'Holy crap.'

A pile of storage boxes were stacked up alongside the desk with what looked like police case files spread out over the top.

Vicky picked one up. The files from the Marksman case back in the early Nineties. 'These are supposed to be confidential.'

'Supposed to be, aye.'

'And why does Riley have them?'

'Exactly. Documentation nobody should have.'

'I need to get these to our forensics lab. Hopefully Anderson can pin it down to which photocopier, which scanner, which printer.'

'Big if.' Shepherd had one open, flicking through it. 'Nothing unusual about Torrance's background. Only child. Parents were both teachers. He worked mainly as a labourer, before joining the army. Lasted a couple of years. He was a pretty good boxer, apparently. No previous convictions. Got a job as a labourer after, back where he started.'

'You know a lot about him?'

'Looked into the case a few years back when I was doing a course at Tulliallan.'

'And one day he just started killing people?'

'Well, he'd been killing people in the army. Marksman. Tried to join the police, but he was refused on mental health grounds. Began killing when he was thirty-four. Kept it up until he was forty-six.' Shepherd turned the page. 'It was the press who called him the Marksman, by the way, ahead of his trial. Trying to find the other victims. Probably people who wouldn't be missed.'

'That's a bit harsh.'

'I mean the victims were gangland hits, Vicky. People who died as soon as they signed up.'

Vicky felt dizzy. Cullen didn't say anything. Just chewed his cheek. 'Scott, are—'

'Sorry, just thinking. If Riley was copying Torrance, fair enough. Why would someone kill *him*?'

Vicky frowned. 'Because he's a serial killer?'

'That's a bit of a stretch, though.'

Shepherd thumped his file down on the desk. 'Listen, our victims – Gavin and Doug Mason – were involved with a people trafficking organisation down in London. Gavin and Riley were mates, which is how we found out about this.'

'And you think someone's bumping them all off?'

'We thought it was Doug, but he killed himself.' Shepherd stopped rifling through the box. 'Bugger me.' He held it out.

Vicky looked at it. A notebook, the last pages scribbled in blue ink. Headline:

Interview with Mark Torrance

Cullen swallowed. 'Doesn't take a lot of imagination to think he was more than copying his work, does it?'

37

Cullen put his foot down and pulled out into the fast lane, hurtling past the lorry. Dirty water sprayed across the windscreen, the wipers struggling to cope with it. Dark even at lunchtime, just the lights from the other cars and the varying colours of cat's eyes at the side for company. The headlights picked out tiny dots of frost lining the motorway in quiet stretches.

Vicky reached over and pushed the heating up again. She knew the road well so she could almost see the sheer cliff face on the right climbing up, the tower on the top, looking out across Perthshire and northern Fife.

They were wandering into the wrong lane.

Cullen adjusted the wheel just as he overtook a grit lorry, sending tiny shards skittering off the car's bodywork. Not the best driving conditions to get distracted. He stretched back in the driver seat, stroking his beard in time with the wipers.

'You okay there, Scott?'

'Been a hell of a time, Vicky. Hell of a time.'

'You know you can talk to me, right?'

'About what?'

'About what you went through.'

'Thanks, Vicky. I appreciate it.'

'But you're not going to, are you?'

Cullen gave a shrug. 'Sorry.' He got a flash from behind, some posy git in a Merc, and pulled back into the slow lane way too slowly.

Vicky stared down a lane traced out by yellow lights, casting a glow over snow-covered fields, blinking tears out of her eyes. She sucked in a deep breath through her nostrils. 'Next turning.'

Cullen had to swerve across both lanes to make the Perth slip road at seventy-four miles an hour. 'Thanks for the warning.'

'Sorry; you didn't say you didn't know the road.'

'Just thinking about who's here.'

'Mark Torrance?'

'No. A serial killer. The case that made me, I suppose you could say. I keep asking to speak to him, but... I don't know why. But the arsehole never lets me. Can't figure it out. Why would someone kill?'

Something made an attempt to climb up from Vicky's gut. Slithering. Sliding up.

Lots of reasons, Scott. Lots of reasons.

She sat back in the chair, arms folded, her whole body fizzing with electricity.

Cullen pulled up in front of the prison, gripping the steering wheel tight. His seatbelt plopped into his lap, lying like a pack of sausages. 'Okay.'

She let her seatbelt go, whirring up to the holder.

The door clicked open and a heavy bulk entered, rocking the car.

Vicky leaned around to check. Shepherd was in the back seat. He rested a hand on Vicky's shoulder and whispered, rancid coffee breath stinging her ear. 'Well, what's the plan here?'

Shepherd looked at Cullen, then at Vicky. 'Look, I don't think it's a good idea you speaking to Mark Torrance.'

'You don't, do you?'

'Me and Scott will speak to him.'

'Why?'

'Because he doesn't like women. Won't speak to them.'

'Seriously?'

'Seriously. Absolute arsehole, by all accounts. But the reason we've got an audience with him is they're doing a deep clean of his cell right now.'

Vicky opened her door and let the cold air in. 'Come on, then.'

Cullen grabbed her arm. 'Vicky, I told you, he—'

'I know.' She focused on the prison. Dark and desolate in the grey afternoon rain. 'Let's use his misogyny against him.'

38

'Your grave, then.' Senior Prison Officer Paul Jobson held open the door with his pudgy hands. Stumpy fingers, nails bitten unevenly, one or two not bitten at all. He seemed in his early thirties but might have been younger. The receding hairline probably added a few years. Overweight, but his uniform still managed to be a couple of sizes too big for him, the material hanging off his rounded shoulders. Fifty-fifty chance the handlebar moustache was for Movember or for life but, either way, the ginger conflicted with his raven hair. 'Wait in the secure interview room, please. You're lucky he's agreed to this. Usually it's a flat no, but he's eager to help. I'll just fetch Mark.'

The room was small and cramped, the whitewashed walls feeling a metre too close.

Vicky gave him a smile. 'Thank you.' She tossed her notebook and pen on the table, then took a seat. One of the knots in the table's wood looked like a shotgun. The door clicked shut. 'First name terms.'

'I noticed that, too.' Cullen sat alongside her, the metal chair crunching against the concrete. 'This chair's knackered. Can we swap?'

'I'm settled here.' Vicky wrote the time and date next to Mark Torrance, HMP Perth. 'Reminds me of sitting next to you in maths.'

'Remedial class.' Cullen smirked. 'Takes me back.'

The door opened and Jobson entered, leading Mark Torrance into the room.

Hard to imagine this frail figure had caused so much damage. No longer a boxer's physique, but that of an old man whose appetite had vanished. Spindly legs, the only bulk on his torso was his rib cage. Still, his eyes were dark, almost black. The Marksman stared back at Vicky and eased his skinny frame into the chair opposite, without saying a word, hands cuffed behind his back.

Jobson retreated towards his observation position by the door, thumbs in belt loops, trying to appear like a hard prison guard in front of the cops.

Vicky had met rapists, paedophiles, murderers. She ought to have been prepared for the Marksman. A man who had murdered for a living. But it wasn't just that thought which threatened to turn Vicky's stomach inside out. She wasn't particularly squeamish, and yet the nausea was acute enough for her to be worried she might throw up. She managed to hide it for now, though, and stared at the Marksman until the Marksman became Mark Torrance, an old man grinning at something. Still had his own teeth, the colour of milky coffee.

No, it was the fact she was face-to-face with another killer. Someone else who'd taken a life. But Torrance could justify his actions too. Maybe his family was threatened.

'I'm DI Vicky Dodds.' She smiled at him. 'This is DI Scott Cullen. We work for Police Scotland.'

'Very pleased for you both.'

'Mr Torrance, we're here to ask you about Thomas Riley.'

Torrance sniffed. 'Name supposed to mean something to me?'

'You've never heard of him?'

'A piece of advice.' Torrance looked at Vicky, dark eyes drilling into her skull. 'Life's way too short to ask stupid questions.'

Vicky broke off eye contact, her heart pounding. She stared at an empty page of notebook until it slowed back down to something approaching normal. 'We have notes he'd written from an interview with you.'

'And you believe him?'

'Why wouldn't I?'

'Some people have rich internal lives. Think things have happened that actually haven't.'

'So you don't recognise the name?'

'See what I said about stupid questions?'

'Mark.' Cullen returned the smile, even looked like a serial killer himself. 'Mind if I call you that?'

No change. Just that smile.

'Right. Mark it is, then. You finding something amusing there?'

Nothing from Torrance, just that inane grin.

Cullen rocked his chair to the side. 'Seriously. I'm not in the mood here. Be great if you shared it with us. We might be cops, but we have a sense of humour.' He nudged Vicky. 'Don't we?'

She felt like she'd had the blood drained out of her. The

lights in the room were too bright. What the hell was wrong with her?

'I'm saying we have a sense of humour.' Cullen's eyebrows were doing an Irish jig. He was giving her a *look*. They hadn't planned a good cop/bad cop routine, and this was a bloody awful one.

'Sometimes.' Vicky sat back, couldn't bring herself to face Torrance. Felt like she was going to throw up. Some bad cop she was. 'But not right now, though. Not when face to face with this evil bastard.'

'Just thinking to myself how she's the first woman I've seen in a very long time.' The normal voice of a 73-year-old Scotsman. That was the thing about killers: they were all so normal. Boring, even. Boring and lethal. And normal. Normal people. So many normal people were killers.

'I see. Word is you don't like women.'

'Oh, I like women.' The grin returned. 'Couldn't eat a whole one, mind.'

A stifled laugh came from the doorway.

Torrance leaned forward, twisting his whole body, and motioned with his head for Vicky to come towards him.

She ignored him.

His gestures grew more exaggerated. Bird-like.

Vicky cleared her throat. 'You want to whisper something to me?'

Torrance nodded.

'Go ahead. But I think I'll stay here. I like my ears where they are. Attached to my head.'

Still that grin. Then his lips moved. 'You're just like me.'

Vicky stared at Torrance, trying to see the old man, not the

Marksman. He wasn't going to win. 'What do you mean I'm just like you?'

'You and me, love, why are we both so angry?'

'Mark, we're the ones asking the questions.' Cullen's smile didn't distract him.

'Who says?'

'Will you just answer a few questions? Then you can go back to your bed.'

Torrance shrugged. 'Bedroom's being tossed, so I'm out of there for two hours whether I like it or not.'

Cullen faced Torrance again. 'This murderer we told you about, he's got posters on his wall of you. Even got hold of some of your case files. Doesn't that bother you?'

'Should bother you a whole lot more.' Torrance stood up, hitched up his trackie bottoms. 'I'm bored. Time to go.'

'The name Thomas Riley doesn't mean anything to you?'

'Son, you should listen to a man when he's talking to you.'

Cullen showed him a photo of the wall from Riley's house. 'What about this?'

Torrance stared at it for a few seconds. 'He's this fan I'm supposed to be all twisted up about?'

'We discovered Riley's body this evening. Turns out he's been killing people near Edinburgh. Keeping their ears as a souvenir.'

Torrance looked at Vicky. 'Sorry to disappoint you, love, but I've never been into ears. And no, I don't know this bloke. I don't get out much these days, in case you hadn't noticed.'

Vicky got to her feet. 'Mr Torrance, Thomas Riley visited you in September.'

Torrance puckered his lips, like he was thinking through his calendar. 'Tell me something. Do you have a son?'

Vicky held Torrance's gaze. This was part of it. His whole thing. Surviving in a place like this, surrounded by your peers in murder until you either get stabbed in the showers or they leave you alone and you die of old age. Cancer, heart attack, stroke. Get inside their heads and you only have to worry about your health.

And the likelihood was it was a scattergun approach. Trying it on with both of them. Asking questions, throwing around accusations. Seeing what got a reaction. How psychics and horoscopes got away with it. Pickup artists. Be vague, get the marks to offer up information. Like detectives were trained to do. Get a reaction.

Torrance knew Vicky was the weak link here, so he was drilling into her.

She struggled to keep looking at him. 'Doesn't inspiring someone else to murder upset you? Even a little bit? Or does it arouse you?'

'Answer me. Do you have a son?'

Vicky peered into those dark eyes, avoiding the urge to look away. 'Being a cop's a lonely job. Don't get time to have a personal life. Do you have a son?'

Torrance nibbled his bottom lip. 'Nine. He's nine years old.'

He'd been inside for close to thirty, with minimal contact.

'Do you think you're a good dad, Mark?'

'I...' Torrance swallowed. 'I try to be, but you know what kids are like. Still, it's important to have people looking up to you. Respecting you. I'm a good father. That's my only pride.' He looked over at Jobson. 'I want to go now.'

Jobson opened the door. 'On you come then, Mark.'

39

Vicky leaned back in her seat, shivering from the exchange.

Face to face with Mark Torrance.

Cullen glanced over. 'Why was he asking if you had a son?'

'He didn't know about what happened. Gavin's death. Doug stringing us along. Riley's death. But he thought he knew how to play us. Right?'

'Mm.'

'Maybe I should've told him about Jamie. Kept him talking.'

Cullen raised his eyebrows. 'Didn't know you had another baby?'

'I haven't. He's adopted. Same age as Bella.'

'Adopted, eh?'

'I'm getting married, Scott. To his father.'

'Congratulations.' He looked her up and down. 'Listen, I heard on the grapevine about your brush with death last year. And taking a life. Must've been hard.'

'Scott, you of all people must know what it's like to be attacked by someone.'

'Touché.'

Shepherd stepped into the room. 'Right, we definitely shouldn't have come here. That was a waste of time'

Cullen slumped back in his chair and waved him away. 'Luke, we got something out of that.'

Shepherd was leaning against the wall, the lining paper frayed all along the top. 'Didn't seem like that to me.'

Cullen winced. 'Torrance's just messing with us. Messing with Vicky.'

'Why did he ask about Jamie?' Vicky stabbed a finger towards the door. 'I just don't get it.'

'He's trying to get inside your head. That's all.'

'I know that, but...'

'Sorry, officers.' Jobson came back in, resting his hand against the doorframe and looking back at them, chest heaving. 'Now, if you'll just follow me?'

Vicky stayed sitting. 'We weren't finished with him.'

'He's finished with you, though.'

'He often like that?'

'Sometimes.' Jobson's fingers twitched. 'Nothing we can do about it.' He ran a tongue over his teeth. 'My job is to keep order in here. If Mark gets upset, word'll get around. We had a full lockdown last time. Complete nightmare.'

'Are you saying he's running things here?'

'Hardly.' Jobson smoothed down his moustache. 'It's just... The other inmates kind of live in fear of Mark. Bit of awe as well, I suppose.'

'Have a seat.' Vicky reached over and pulled out the chair Torrance had been in. 'Need to ask you a few questions.'

'Nice one. Don't mind if I do.' Jobson perched on the seat. 'How can I help?'

Cullen leaned back in his chair. 'Vicky's Clarice Starling trick didn't exactly work there, did it?'

'Come on, Mark's hardly Hannibal Lecter, is he? He didn't *eat* anyone.'

'No, he just shot and killed them.' Vicky raised an eyebrow. 'We've just been at a crime scene where the victim seemed to be a big fan of Mr Torrance.' She smiled at him. 'The name Thomas Riley doesn't ring any bells with you?'

Jobson clicked his tongue a few times. 'Should it?'

'We have notes from an interview the victim had with him. Back in September. Here.'

'Right. There was a bloke came in. Couple of months back. Said he was writing a book about him, but Mark just sat there, didn't say anything. Smiling.'

'Was that Thomas Riley?'

'Would have to check the name, sorry.'

'Torrance claimed he'd never heard of him.'

'There's a surprise.'

Vicky splayed her hands on the table. Her mouth was dry. 'You overheard our interview. Why didn't you mention that someone had visited Torrance when we asked?'

'Sorry, I just know better than to interrupt a detective... No matter how wrong you are, you lot know everything.'

Cullen glared at him, mouth twitching. 'What sort of questions was Riley asking?'

'About the killings, you know. How much Mark got out of it. Who it was for. Like I said, he didn't respond to a single one.'

'That was it?'

'Well. He asked what it was like murdering someone. Seeing them die.'

Jesus Christ. Vicky pinched her nose. 'He ever come back?'

'Not on my watch. We had a wee chat about it, me and the other lads. They'd have mentioned him if he'd visited again. You can't think... No... Mark didn't *say* anything to him.'

'Right, I need you to check through your visitor logs.' Shepherd looked ready to swing for him. Pin him to the walls and stick the head on. 'Every time this Thomas Riley's visited. And I want interview transcripts of each visit.'

'We don't keep—'

'Shut up, I know you do.'

'Right, aye. I'll see what I can get you. Aye. Might be a few days, mind.'

'Tomorrow. First thing.'

'But that's—'

'No buts. Tomorrow, nine o'clock.'

Vicky raised a hand to get Shepherd to back off. 'Did Mr Torrance have any other visitors at all?'

'Some. Volunteers came in now and then. Woke wankers checking on his human rights.' Spat out like a swearword. 'But nobody else for a long time. And he doesn't say much, if anything, which makes it pretty dull for them. Thing is, Mark gets a lot of letters, as you can imagine. Some of them make your stomach churn and that's just the nice ones.' He laughed, stopping when they didn't join in.

'We need copies of them.' Vicky noted it down. 'He ever send anything out?'

'Nope. Banned from it.'

'He said he was proud of being a good father.' Shepherd frowned at Jobson. 'I wasn't aware he had any family.'

Jobson nodded. 'He doesn't.'

'So why say it?'

'No idea.'

'Strange he should think of himself as a father.' Vicky tried to swallow down the horror of having Torrance in the same room as her. 'Told us he was proud of it.'

Jobson grinned. 'But you try telling him that. I mean, he really believes it. I'm a good father. I'm a good father. It's like a... whatchamacallit? A mantra.'

'Does he have any family at all?'

'Not that I know of. Parents are long dead. No siblings. Not aware of any cousins or that.'

Vicky held Jobson's glare. 'Anyone else spring to mind?'

'Nope. I mean, he was in the army. Think he was a bit of a shagger back then, but he's not mentioned anything about having any bairns. Said the kid was ten, eh?'

'Nine. What about other prisoners?'

'Eh? Has he had any kids with them?'

'No. Is he a troublemaker?'

'Never. Not once in all the time I've been here. But he says if he's returned to gen pop, he'll kill somebody.'

'What do you mean?'

'Like, he'll murder someone.'

'No, about being returned to general population.'

Jobson leaned in. 'You do know his cell's in the seg unit, right?'

'Segregated?' Shepherd looked up from his notes. 'What did he do?'

Jobson shook his head. 'He's not been sent there as punishment. That's just where he lives. All the time.'

'For how long?'

'Since he was moved here from the Bar-L in...' His eyes rolled upwards while he thought, then back. 'Way before my time, like. '99? Autumn, I think it was.'

'He's been in solitary all that time?'

'No. Segregation. Christ, are you sure you're a cop? Don't even know the basics about prisons.'

'I know the difference.' Shepherd narrowed his eyes. 'And it's his own choice?'

'Totally. He really doesn't like company.'

Vicky felt the burn of Torrance's glare again. Couldn't get those eyes out of her mind. 'Either that or he's punishing himself.'

'You've met him. He's not the type. Just sits there, grinning.'

'What does he do all day?'

'He reads mostly.'

'What kind of thing?'

'A bit of everything, really. Probably read everything in the library at least once. But he's very fond of romance novels.'

'Romance?'

'Billionaires were his big thing for a while, but reverse harems are where it's at now.'

Shepherd scowled. 'What the hell is a reverse harem?'

'Instead of the Sultan of Forfar having a harem of lassies, it's a lassie having a harem of blokes. But only one's been set in Forfar, that I remember.'

'Seem to be an expert on it?'

Jobson gave a flash of eyebrows. 'Have to read them before he does, make sure the author isn't sending him subliminal messages. Or whether he's likely to read something into any of it.'

'That ever happen?'

'Not yet.'

'You're kidding us, right? Because it feels like the first of April.'

'Cross my heart. You don't need to read horror novels when you've caused enough of the real thing. Just want to know that Sandie from Missouri or Jeanette from Forfar finds the love of a good billionaire. Or exploits a bad one and traps him in her reverse harem.'

'Who looks after him?'

'Three of us manage him around the clock. Couple of others provide holiday cover and weekends.'

'Think there's any way he could be communicating with the outside world? Mobile hidden somewhere?'

'Absolutely no chance.' Jobson shook his head from side to side again, but his jowls were shaking this time. 'He gets an intimate search after each and every visit. One a week, at a random time. Like now, which is why it's convenient for your mob to come in.'

'How intimate are we talking?'

'Put it this way, I know he's not got prostate cancer.' Jobson fidgeted in the seat, shifting slightly to the side. 'Different officer every time. Could be anyone on the staff. Besides, the high-security wing is a Faraday cage. Electrically insulated. No chance he'll get a phone signal, even if he had a mobile in there. Bit of a nightmare when there's a Rangers game on and I want to follow the score. Not allowed to have the radio on in case he hears the news and it triggers him.'

'So he has no contact with anyone?'

'None. Listen, I'm no shrink, but here's what I think. He's created a fantasy world for himself. All that time on his own, he's made up a family for himself to keep him company. Hence asking about them. Makes it real in his head.'

'You said he didn't like people.'

'He doesn't. Family's different, though. Especially imaginary family. Don't argue with you. Don't let you down. Do what they're told.' Jobson shrugged. 'And they survive, don't they? If he's got a daughter, she'll likely have kids. They'll have kids. His legacy will live on.'

Aye, don't give up the day job.

But it built a picture it was hard to argue with. A man in solitary, his only human contact three guards. Reading books all day. Aye, he had a rich fantasy life.

But what was the connection to Thomas Riley?

'No other visitors that stand out?'

'Not really.' Jobson tilted his head from side to side then snorted. 'Apart from Margaret.'

'Margaret?'

'Margaret Fields. Visits Mark every month come rain or shine. Makes the old guy cry. Been doing it for years.'

'And you didn't think to mention that until now?'

40

The road sign read:

INCHTURE 1

Vicky pointed at the sign. 'Margaret Fields lives there.'

Shepherd winced. 'Don't you think we should get back to base?'

'I want to speak to her.'

'Why? It's probably nothing to do with our case, Vicky.'

'I still want to rule it out.'

'Fine.' He took the turning and slipped over the A90, heading into the village, a hamlet stuck between Dundee and Perth, slap bang in the arse end of nowhere. Then through it. A lonely row of streetlights led out of the village.

Vicky's phone flashed up in the fading winter light. A text from Cullen:

Good seeing you, Vicky. We should do it again sometime.

Every word with him dripped with smut. He was engaged – and so was she – but it just took her back to her schooldays, flirting with him in French and Biology.

Aye, she didn't want to repeat any of that.

'Here we go.' Shepherd pulled into a parking bay, a gust of wind rustling the branches. He switched off the growling engine, cutting Blind Bob Bollocks off mid-holler. 'Torrance got to you, didn't he?'

Vicky tried to peer through the thick evergreen hedge. Where the Marksman's endgame happened – the last victim's death, where he was captured.

The guy deserved to rot away in prison.

'He's just a man.' Vicky shrugged, trying to hide the shiver running down her spine. 'It's good to see him wasting away in there.'

Shepherd undid his seatbelt and shoved it away. 'He deserves it.'

'I've been thinking. All that "I'm a good father" stuff. While he tried to kill the cop, there was a kid upstairs when he was captured, remember? That could've confused him.'

'Mm.' He opened his door and got out.

Vicky did the same, then opened the gate, a screech tearing out. The concrete slabs were covered in moss and lichen, stray grass colonising the cracks. She knocked on the door and waited, trying to spy through the drawn curtains.

'No sign of anybody. No car.' Shepherd stepped off the path, tramping across the grass to peer through the windows.

Vicky knocked again. 'Mrs Fields? It's the police.'

A bell chimed as the door juddered open, catching on the

plastic sheeting protecting the wood flooring. A thin woman squinted out. Silver hair, lined face. Smashing Pumpkins T-shirt on long-faded black cotton. Designer jeans, barefoot. One of those broken noses that hadn't healed properly, always off at an angle. 'Can I help you?'

'I'm DI Vicky Dodds.' She showed her warrant card. 'We need to speak with a Margaret Fields.'

'That's me.' She stepped in front of the door. 'What's this about?'

'Wouldn't mind asking you a few questions about Mark Torrance.'

Margaret clamped her jaw tight. 'Are you serious?'

'I'm afraid so.'

Margaret looked away. 'I'd rather not, if it's all the same.' She stepped back into the house and pushed the door.

Shepherd stuck his foot in the way. 'Excuse me?'

'I've said enough about him.' Margaret kept her focus away from their faces. 'Now, good day.'

Shepherd put a hand on the door. 'We know you've been visiting him.'

Her head hung low. She rubbed her eyes for a few seconds, then pushed the door fully open and stepped to the side, gesturing into the house. 'Come in, then.'

Vicky felt a tightening in her gut as she followed Margaret down the dark hall, her shoes clicking on the scarred parquet flooring. Where it happened... Still living here, after it all.

Place hadn't been painted in years. The lining paper was torn, dust rectangles outlined where two pictures had once been. The smell of baking scones came from somewhere deep in the house, like that could exorcise what had happened here.

Margaret stood by a dark oak door, waving into a room. 'Can I get you a cup of tea?'

'Bit late for me.' Vicky sat on a dark green sofa. Heavy shelving units lined the magnolia walls, most of them covered in Indian elephants and African masks, tiger figurines. The sort of exotic trinkets Vicky's ancient aunts and uncles had brought back from post-war travels, industrialising the Third World. On the tiled fireplace, a series of photos snaked around a carriage clock, ticking away in the silent house. A younger Margaret Fields standing with a man, both of them smiling to the camera.

She staggered over to a settee and collapsed into it. Sounded like a spring snapped. She shut her eyes. Didn't say anything.

Shepherd stayed standing by the door, but Margaret Fields wasn't a flight risk. 'Gather you visit Mark Torrance every month in prison, Mrs Fields.'

'It's Ms Fields. Never married. Call me Margaret.' She shut her eyes for a few seconds, rubbing a hand across her forehead. Every movement seemed to hurt. 'Is Torrance dead?'

'We believe he's connected to a murder. Two, maybe.'

Margaret reopened her eyes, fire burning. 'But he's been in prison for almost thirty years?'

Shepherd nodded. 'Do you know a Gavin Mason?'

She shook her head.

'What about Thomas Riley?'

Her brow creased. 'Never heard of either of them.'

'Well, Mr Mason was murdered on Sunday night. Mr Riley probably yesterday, but we haven't confirmed it yet.'

Margaret bit a fingernail. 'I've been here all weekend.'

Didn't even have to be asked.

She slowly licked her lips. 'My son can confirm I was here all weekend. He'll be back from his work soon.'

'He live with you?'

'No, just comes in for his tea.'

'Mark Torrance never mentioned either name to you?'

'He'll burn in hell for what he did to us. Just a shame he won't suffer in this life.'

Vicky cleared her throat. 'We've just been to Perth prison and had an interesting chat with him. Makes me wonder why the wife of the Marksman's last victim visits him every month.'

Margaret was staring at the photos on the mantelpiece again, forefingers clicking against her thumbs, like a crab or a lobster. Didn't say anything.

'Why do you visit, Margaret?'

The bell by the front door tinkled.

Margaret rose to her feet. 'Back in a second.' She went out into the hall, then the door clunked. The smell of cigarette smoke wafted in. Heavy footsteps and the rustling of carrier bags, then clattering around in the kitchen.

Vicky left the room and followed the noise through.

No sign of Margaret Fields, just a tall man standing by the open fridge, facing away, lips slapping together. He turned around, a full wedge of brie sticking out of his mouth.

PC Billy Dewar.

His face twisted up and he removed the cheese, setting it down on the counter, the end cut off with a bite mark. 'Ma'am? What are you doing here?'

'Here to speak to Ms Fields.'

Dewar shut his eyes. 'She's my mum.'

'What?'

'She's my mum.'

'You're the... Christ.'

'We need to ask her a few questions about Mark Torrance.'

'What? Why?'

'She's been visiting Mark Torrance in prison and—'

'I'm sorry? Mark Torrance?'

'Every month, she's been—'

'My God.' Dewar covered his eyes with his hands. 'There's no chance Mum would even give him the time of day. Absolutely none.'

Vicky glanced at Shepherd and got a shrug. 'Then why has she been visiting?'

Dewar opened his eyes, glaring at Vicky. 'She's not!'

Shepherd got between them. 'Son, she's been there. Every month. It's on the visitor logs.'

Seemed like Dewar was going to say something, but he looked away. Sniffed. 'I was just a laddie when it happened... When... Mark Torrance killed my father.'

Shepherd scowled at him. 'David Dewar was your father?'

He nodded.

Vicky could see the finale of the film, Helen Mirren rushing home to catch Robert Carlyle in the act of killing her police officer husband while her son was locked in a room upstairs. 'I'm so sorry, I didn't realise.'

'Not exactly something I want to shout about, eh? Lads at the station take the piss enough as it is.'

Vicky waved around the room. 'Wasn't this cottage where it happened?'

The front door clanked shut. Margaret stood in the doorway, silent, staring at the floor. 'This was our home. Been in my family for decades.' She was carrying two bags of shopping from Ashworth's, a bunch of lime-green bananas sticking out. 'I wanted to move into a flat in Perth or Dundee, but Billy wanted to stay here. Only home he's known.'

How could they stay here, knowing what'd happened?

Dewar scowled at her. 'Mum, why the hell have you been visiting Mark Torrance in jail?'

'Getting closure on what happened to your father.'

'He died twenty-seven years ago!'

'And I've been seeing Torrance for the last seven.'

'*Seven*?' Dewar dragged a hand down his face. 'Jesus Christ, Mum. Why?' The word was a hollow gasp.

'Why?' Margaret went over to the framed photos on the mantelpiece, her shoulders collapsing. 'I wanted to get some closure on what happened. Just after I got laid off from my job, I finally got some therapy for what happened. My therapist suggested I visit him. See him for who he really is. The first time, when he finally showed up, Torrance just sat there, grinning. Like he was goading me. Didn't answer any of my questions. Then I told him my name. My husband's name. Your father... And... And he broke down in tears.' She gnawed at her bottom lip. 'Next time, the same thing happened. So I kept going back, to punish him. Every month. Seeing him break down like that. It... I don't know, could be it makes him realise what he's done. Makes me feel like he's paying for what he did to your father. Properly. Not sitting in luxury in that jail, but really paying for all those crimes.'

'He ever open up to you?'

'Never even said a single word. Just sat there and cried.' Margaret tugged her arms around herself and sank back against the wall. 'Tears streaming down his face.'

Vicky flashed her eyebrows at Shepherd. *We're done here.*

She gave an official smile to Margaret Fields. 'We'll leave you to it. Thank you for your time.'

Dewar wrapped his mum in a desperate hug, the inverse of the reluctant one Doreen Mason had inflicted on him.

The letterbox rattled as Vicky shut the front door.

'I can't believe they still live here.' Shepherd marched down the path. 'You ever see anything like this?'

'Something mildly similar a few years back.' Vicky opened her car door and eyed the house. 'She's just trying to twist the knife. You saw the mind games Torrance was trying to play with me. Nice to know that someone played them back.'

'What do you think about Dewar?'

'What about him? He's a daft wee laddie.'

'But daft wee laddies can kill.'

'Aye, but he was on duty when at least one of the murders happened.'

'He can still kill on duty.'

'True.' She opened the passenger door. 'Right, Luke, let's get you back to Dundee before you turn into a pumpkin.'

'Hopefully not a smashing one.'

41

The rain smeared the windscreen, sending another chill up Vicky's arms. A flash of the wipers revealed people walking along West Bell Street, mostly students heading home or to the pub after lectures. A homeless guy slept in a shop window, ignoring the teeming rain.

'Weird to see people out and about again.' Vicky craned her neck around to look at Shepherd. 'Back to doing normal stuff.'

'As normal as it gets, I suppose.' Shepherd trundled across the car park, staggering like a drunk. 'Man alive. I could sleep for a thousand years.'

Vicky got out into the rain. Forrester's office light was on. She squinted and was sure she could see him peering out at her.

Shepherd was already out of his car, yawning into his fist. 'All I can see is the bloody A90. Even when I close my eyes.'

'Shouldn't do that while you're driving.'

He smiled. 'Right, I need some coffee and some food, then

get back to it. Maybe at some point I can sleep the sleep of the dead.'

The yawn caught hold of Vicky now. 'Not sure the coffee will help with that.' Her mobile blared out.

Forrester calling...

She answered, rolling her eyes at Shepherd. 'Boss?'

'Doddsy, meet me in the café.'

VICKY SAT in the window of the Auld Cludgie café, looking out onto the Marketgait, the inner-city dual carriageway slicing through the town centre. Time was, this would've been old tenements, properties with character to staff the mills. Now the mills were all empty relics and their homes paved over. The sign swayed in the wind just outside. Office drones buzzed past, brollies catching in the strong wind.

Vicky and Shepherd were at a table. A glass of water in front of her. She sucked in the bitter coffee smell.

Forrester stopped outside the door, painted mid-blue, inset with glass. Gave a wave, but he was still on the phone.

The place was pretty busy for a late afternoon, though most of the punters might as well not have been here. Headphones on, staring deep into their laptops. Pale blue walls, yellow tables matching the chairs. Very tasteful.

A couple perched on a settee, arguing about something, arms windmilling, their voices quiet. He seemed to be giving more than he got.

The chalkboard on the wall above them had a list of

specials, but either Vicky's eyesight was going or they didn't know how to write with chalk.

The door clattered open and Forrester barrelled through, his silver hair catching the spotlights. 'Doddsy. Luke.' He grinned at Shepherd. 'The little lady's just making up the spare room for you.'

Vicky frowned at him. 'Thought you were in a hotel, Luke?'

'So did I.' Shepherd stirred his coffee. 'But David insisted I stay at the Chateau Forrester.'

Forrester plonked himself on the chair opposite. 'Not exactly five stars, but it'll be good to catch up.'

'Remember I don't drink, so no trying to foist whisky on me.'

'Aye, aye.' Forrester winked at him. 'Anyway. Thanks for seeing me.'

Vicky didn't know what to think of that. That Forrester and Shepherd were friends... He couldn't know, could he?

'You look like you need a coffee, David.' Shepherd waved at the waitress. 'I'm buying.'

Forrester smiled at the waitress. 'Americano. And I'll have the chilli.'

Shepherd smiled. 'I'll have the Mexican cauliflower cheese.'

The waitress winced. 'Brave man.'

'It's not good?'

'No, Fergus goes a bit heavy on the spices, that's all.'

'I like it a bit heavy.'

'Good luck.' She scribbled. 'And you, madam?'

'What's the soup?'

She thumbed over to the board. 'It's up there, doll.'

'Right. I can't make it out.'

'Should've gone to Specsavers...' Muttered under her breath. 'Fennel and stilton or broccoli and Guinness.'

Not much of a choice. 'I'll have a chilli.'

'Coming right up.' She charged off like she was powered by very strong batteries.

'So.' Forrester ran a hand through his hair. 'Gather you two have visited half of Scotland today?'

'Feels like it.' Shepherd smiled. 'Hate to think what my fuel expenses are going to be like.'

'Careful. Don't want the Complaints investigating you.'

Shepherd laughed. 'Been there, done that.'

'Seriously?'

'In a manner of speaking, aye.' Shepherd snorted. 'Anyway. What's this about?'

'Thank you.' Forrester took his coffee and wrapped his hands around the mug. He shrugged off his jacket and reached inside for a sheet of paper. 'I tell you, the only time I've spent more hours on the phone is when I last moved house.'

Shepherd raised his monobrow. 'What's the latest?'

'This is a sensitive business, Luke.' Forrester sat back in his chair and took out his mobile. 'Just off the blower with DCI Davenport down in Edinburgh. Gather you two and the golden god paid Mark Torrance a visit in Perth prison?'

Vicky winced. 'I take it the golden god is Scott Cullen?'

'Aye, wee nickname Ally has for him. Anyway. You get much out of him?'

Vicky huffed out a sigh. 'For starters, I didn't know the Marksman killed one of the team who investigated him.'

Forrester slurped his coffee. 'Davie Dewar, aye. Good man, he was. His boy's not up to much as a copper, mind.'

'You know Billy's on this case, right?'

'Shite. Well, that's him off it as of now.' Forrester tore at a brown sugar sachet and tipped it in the mug. 'I've tried to mentor the laddie, but he's thick as mince. Hate to say it, but I think he'll get the heave-ho soon.' He stirred. 'How did you get on with him?'

'Hard to say. Things seem pretty weird. The wife of the last victim's been tormenting the Marksman in prison.'

'Margaret?'

'Every month.'

'Christ. What the hell's that about?'

'Search me.' Vicky sipped her water. 'Luke and I have been discussing it. All we can think is she liked getting him to suffer for what he did in some small way.'

'Well, good luck to her.' Forrester took another slurp of his coffee. 'Okay, so Thomas Riley has been the subject of much discussion and conjecture between us all. Now it's not just us and the Met. Thanks to your discovery, the old Lothian and Borders mob are getting in on the act too. Trouble is, we can't see how Riley fits in.'

'Had a lot of time to think about this with all the driving we've done today.' Shepherd stirred some brown sugar into his own coffee, disturbing the perfect feathering, the granules fizzing as they dissolved. 'Whoever killed Gavin Mason was good. We thought it was Doug Mason, but it can't be him because his DNA wasn't there.' He took a sip of coffee. 'So we have a few known people on there. Vicky here. Her son. Gavin himself. Emma Mason. And Thomas Riley.'

'You think he did it?'

Shepherd leaned back. 'Hard to say, really. But DI McNeill had him flagged on the PNC. He was involved in the same gang as Gavin and Doug.'

'Wasn't he just money laundering, though?'

'He was, but it's possible he wasn't just doing that. One theory we're working on—' Shepherd gestured between himself and Vicky. '—is he might've been an assassin himself. He was obsessed with Mark Torrance. Visited him in prison. Somehow Riley had the police files for the Marksman case back in the Nineties. He'd been to see him. Sounds like he'd been studying him.'

'You don't commit a hammer attack from two streets away. Someone got up close and personal. Doesn't sound like Torrance's MO, does it? If that's what you're thinking. That this Riley boy copied him.'

Shepherd took a big drink of coffee, his moustache soaking up the foam. 'Edinburgh think Riley's killed five people.'

'What?' Forrester's eyes jolted up. 'He's a serial killer?'

'Five victims that we know of. He's kept the ears from them.'

'Christ.' Forrester seemed to shiver. 'You're sure?'

'They are, aye.'

'Bloody Davenport didn't tell me.'

'Well, Scott Cullen is.'

'The golden god... Okay, so let me get this straight. We've got a copycat hitman who was also a serial killer. Jesus Christ, this is a mess. The shite he was saying to Vicky about if he killed, he'd get another day.' Forrester ran his hand through his hair, slicked with rain.

They sat in silence for a few seconds.

Vicky was first to speak. 'But we know Thomas Riley was killed.'

'Indeed.'

She stared at Forrester. 'What aren't you telling us?'

'Feels like nobody has the full picture.' Forrester passed her his mobile. 'Have a look at this.'

Vicky held it up. The screen was filled with a photo of a card. Handwritten, but no easier to read than the chalkboard:

JOHN LITHGOW
SUSAN INGLIS
IAIN SLAVIN
HAMISH MURDOCH
DAVID DEWAR
GEORGE DODDS

Vicky's heart thumped in her chest. 'Dad?' She could barely get the words out. 'What is this?'

'Well, as far as I can tell, it's a list of officers in Tayside Police, God rest its soul, who worked on the Marksman cases in this area. See, Davie Dewar's on there.'

'What does it mean?' The words caught in her throat.

'No idea, Vicky. Edinburgh found it amongst all the stuff in Thomas Riley's flat. He's got files on every one. Seems like the guy was very interested in them.'

'You think their lives are at risk?'

Forrester shrugged.

Vicky got up. 'I need to speak to Dad.'

42

Vicky pulled up, the engine still running, then let her seatbelt go. She killed the engine and slumped back in the seat.

So tired.

So bloody tired.

She opened the door and ice-cold air leaked in. Woke her up a bit, at least. She got out of the car and walked over to the gateposts at the end of the drive. The salty sea tang frozen in the air. Distant swishing of traffic and a train heading south. She stepped up to the house, knocked on the door and waited, checking her phone.

No messages or missed calls from either parent.

Back the way, headlights turned around the far end of Bruce Drive, a bulky SUV rumbling over the tarmac and turning down North Burnside Street.

'Just a minute!' The door flew open and her dad peered out. Looked a state. Tracksuit bottoms, moccasins, faded running t-shirt over his pot belly, skinny arms dangling at the side. 'Vicky? What's happened?'

'Need a word, Dad.'

'Are the kids okay? I left them with Rob when—'

'They're fine.'

'In you come, in you come.' Dad let her into the hall. 'Tough day?'

Vicky scowled. 'Like you wouldn't believe.'

'Come on through.' Dad led inside, then into the living room. Heavy wood panelling. Black leather settee. A small TV rested on dark oak furniture. The evening news played, showing a cut of DCI Forrester at a press conference, overlaid with a photograph of Doug Mason.

Dad collapsed into his recliner, rocking the mechanism as he shuffled forward. An open can of Old School's Old London Grapefruit Porter sat on the table next to him, but the glass was empty, just foam. 'You want a drink?'

'I need to get home. Early start tomorrow too. Like every day.' Vicky sat on the armchair across from him. 'Where's Mum?'

'Glasgow, remember?'

'Right. Sure. Sorry, I forgot.' Vicky pinched her nose. 'Sure you should be drinking, Dad?'

'Just a wee treat.'

'You're on those heart drugs for a reason.'

He tilted his forehead forward. 'What's going on, Vicky?'

'How do you know something's up?'

'Because you're here at this time and you're having a go at me.'

Vicky let out a breath. She shivered, noticing the window

was open a crack. 'You hear about what happened at the Rep yesterday?'

'Saw something on the news, aye.' He narrowed his eyes. 'I heard from a few old lads that it was a suicide. You working it?'

'Aye...' She swallowed hard. 'Dad, I was there when it happened.'

'Bloody hell. I hope the poor bugger who was with that loonie on the bus is getting counselling.'

'I was that poor bugger.'

'Jesus Christ, Vicky!' Spit flecked from Dad's mouth, a white blob against his grey skin. 'Vicky! Why didn't you tell me?'

She shrugged.

'You've got to watch for that PTSD. Few of the lads I worked with ended up suffering from it. Don't hide it.'

'I'm fine, Dad. Doubt I'll ever be able to go to the panto at the Rep, mind.'

'That's my girl!' Dad punched Vicky's shoulder, making her wince. 'Never lose your sense of humour.'

'I didn't have a choice, Dad. He forced me onto the bus at gunpoint.'

'Really? Like when that guy stabbed you?'

Vicky ran a hand over her stomach, where the wound still throbbed. 'I'm still not recovered from that.'

'No. Don't expect you are.'

And I'm still lying to you about what actually happened.

'Dad... Thing is, that incident... When I got stabbed... It didn't happen like I told everyone.'

He narrowed his eyes further. 'Go on?'

'Dad, you don't understand...'

'Let me guess. He threatened Bella?'

'And Jamie.'

Dad crushed his can. 'And you believed him?'

'This isn't the kind of—'

'Know how many times some wee shite threatened you or Andrew?' Dad was red, like he was going to have another heart attack, one no number of bypasses would save him from. 'Because it was always bullshit.'

'Aye, I've had those kinds of empty threats. Some wee prick just mouthing off. But this was different. That guy was connected. Part of a child abuse network. Bent cops on the payroll. Like Raven.'

'Shit.'

'Aye. If I didn't do what I did, he'd have... I don't know what he would've done, Dad, but if he was still alive, he'd be able get a message out to people. Something would've happened to us. I know it. So I... I did what I did and, almost two years later, nothing's happened to them.'

'I asked you, Vicky.'

'I know.'

'And you lied to me?'

'I did. I'm sorry. But I did what I did to protect my children.'

'Well, confession's good for the soul.'

Because he knew. Of course he knew. They'd made it look like self-defence, but someone like old Dodie Dodds had seen through anything.

And maybe he'd done similar in his day. Maybe that's what kept him awake at night.

'Did you—'

Dad got to his feet and cracked his spine. 'Cup of tea?'

'That's it?'

'Listen, I did my thirty and got out. Did a lot of things I wasn't proud of. Not a day goes by when I don't hear the phone ringing or a car outside and think the past's caught up with me. Some of the hooky shite we did—' He did rabbit ears. '—to "secure a conviction", well... I live in constant fear it's caught up with me. Either the news that Pretty Boy Dave has got out because of me or that Pretty Boy Dave's wee laddie has got my address and is here to take revenge.'

'Who's Pretty Boy Dave?'

'Never you mind.' Dad picked up his can and glass. 'Point is, people think policing is black and white. Goodies and baddies. Heroes and villains. A lot of the time it's all grey, hard to figure out what's black and what's white. Good men doing bad things for the right reasons. Bad men doing good things for the wrong reasons. Sometimes bad cop isn't just an act. And sometimes you need to blur the lines.'

'That's it?'

Dad shrugged. 'That's all there is to it. We raised you to do the right thing, Vicky.' He set off through to the kitchen.

'Have you ever—'

'No, but at least two people never walked again because of me.'

'Seriously?'

'Nothing malicious, just got into a few scrapes.' Dad raised the kettle. 'It'll be decaf at this time.'

'If you're making one, then.' Vicky leaned against the counter. 'Thank you.'

'What for?'

'Listening.'

'It's what I'm here for, my girl. Being a cop's a lonely game at times.'

'Dad, I fucking killed someone.'

He raced over and wrapped her in a hug. 'Hey, hey.'

'I stabbed him and he died and it's all because of me.'

'Listen, you did what you did. Think about what would've—'

'That's all I can do, Dad. Think about how right I was to do it. If I *hadn't* done that, blah blah blah. But I still killed someone.'

'You did what you had to, Vicky. Anyone would understand.'

'Hardly.'

'Of course they would. That scumbag would've got the word out. You, Rob, Bella and Jamie would be living under assumed names in Milton Keynes or Inverarsehole. You'd be looking over your shoulder all the time.'

'But I—'

'Vicky. As a police officer you know you may have to use force to defend yourself. That includes lethal force. Listen, I'd much rather be judged by fifteen than carried by six.'

'Dad, I—'

'Shh. I don't want to know the details. I don't want you to put voice to them. Now, does anyone else know?'

'That's the thing. Yes.'

He shut his eyes. 'Forrester?'

'God no. It's a DI who works the Sexual Offences beat down in Bathgate.'

'Can you trust him?'

'Her. And I think so. We're friends. It was her idea to stab myself.'

'So she's up to her oxters in it too?' Dad nodded, answering his own question. 'I forgot if you still take milk?'

'Oat milk, please.'

'Your mother stocked up before she went away.' He reached into the fridge. 'Nobody else knows?'

'Nobody *knows*.' Vicky reached into the cupboard for two mugs. Fifty years with Mr Right. Fifty years with Mrs Always Right. Bella had picked them out... 'Thing is, Dad, it's about who can deduce it all... There's this cop I've got seconded to me from Edinburgh just now. Luke Shepherd. He's... I know his boss. Helped him out a few months ago. Turns out Shepherd's not who he says he is.'

'He's bent?'

'Worse. Professional Standards and Ethics.'

'Oh. And you think he's investigating you?'

'Seems a bit coincidental that when I lose a sergeant, I get him of all people.'

Dad poured water into their mugs, though the kettle had clicked off ages ago. 'Thing is, when you're keeping a secret like you have, you start to get paranoid. Start to see connections that aren't there. Coincidences that seem too unbelievable.'

'Dad, I—'

'Listen, Vicky, you said you know this Shepherd lad's boss, right?'

'Right. It's Scott Cullen.'

'God, there was a kid who fancied himself.' Dad laughed. 'You still got a thing for him?'

'No.' Vicky was blushing. 'We're just friends.'

'Right. That's what you said every time your mother told you to keep your bedroom door open when he was in there. Does *he* know about this guy's double life?'

'It's how I know he's working for the Complaints. We did a case together earlier in the year.'

'And you found out he's Complaints?'

'Right, so you're saying I need to ask him.'

'No, Vicky, you don't. They investigate you in one of two ways. Overtly, by sitting you down with someone a grade above. Or covertly, by getting someone to investigate you on the down low. You knowing he's Complaints means he's not investigating you.'

It made sense, but the fact it did meant she didn't take any reassurance from it. Relying on logic to dictate safety... Aye, that wasn't going to work.

'Thanks, Dad.' Vicky sat at the kitchen table, the same scuffed one she'd eaten at every day for eighteen years. Most of the rest of the place had changed and been redecorated but that was still the same. 'Thank you for listening.'

'I'm always here for you, Vicky. Whatever happens.'

'Thanks.' Vicky took her cup of tea but didn't trust it to be decaf. 'As part of the investigation, we... We've found a list of names, Dad. Police officers.' She got out her mobile and showed him it. 'You're on it.'

Dad had to pop on his specs. 'Christ, this takes me back.' He hauled himself to his feet. 'Mark bloody Torrance... They're all still alive, apart from David Dewar, as far as I know. Hamish and Iain I think are still serving. Well, they're both down at Tulliallan. Hamish was implementing legislation changes last I heard. Iain was a Super up in Grampian but now he's teaching. Know what they say: those that can't do, teach.' Dad laughed. 'Still see them every so often for a catch-up.'

'And several whiskies, no doubt.'

'No comment.'

'Dad, this list was found in a serial killer's home.'

He took a slug of tea and grimaced. 'And?'

'The guy was obsessed with the Marksman. We visited him

in Perth. I sat there, staring into his eyes. Just like looking into a mirror.'

'What?' But Dad wasn't really listening. 'You're nothing like him, Vicky.'

'I've killed, Dad.'

'You're absolutely nothing like him.'

'I am. I've spent so long trying to get into the skulls of monsters that my brain's turned itself inside out. I'm a monster myself.'

'Vicky. What you did was self-defence. Anybody would understand that.'

'Still murder.'

'Come on, it's not even manslaughter.'

He had a point, but it wasn't getting her anywhere.

'So you did work the case?'

'I did, aye. But this was before I was a detective. Just a daft wee laddie. Wife and two kids already. In it for the Saturday policing. Why I joined in the first place, if you must know. Get to go to every United home game at Tannadice, then see the other lot at Dens the next week.' He pushed his tea away. 'And someone got shot and killed at a United match.'

'Seriously?'

'Seriously. Of course, they pretended it was a heart attack to cover it over. Prevent mass panic and all that. It would've come out in the case when they finally caught him, except Torrance pleaded guilty. Case closed. End of story.'

'So you were there. I don't get why your name would be on the list of people who worked it.'

'Because they seconded me to the case. We knew the names and faces of all the regulars. Thousands of people every week, but I could pick them all out. Being on that case, I saw there was something more to being a cop than cadging free football matches.' He pursed his lips. 'Who's this serial killer guy?'

'Thomas Riley.'

Dad looked up at the ceiling like he was searching for cobwebs. 'Means nothing to me.'

'You know Margaret Fields?'

'Davie Dewar's wife. Well, they weren't married. Quite uncommon in those days. She managed the call centre up here before it all got shoved down to Bilston. Think she got a very nice redundancy payment out of it.'

'She's been visiting Torrance in prison. Every month for seven years. She goes in and torments him.'

'Torments him? How?'

'Says he just sits there, crying.'

'And he still meets her?'

'Every month.'

'Christ.'

'You ever meet him?'

'Nope. Haven't even thought of that scumbag in years. Actually, tell a lie. Caught the last twenty minutes of the film a few months ago while I was surfing.' Dad finished his tea in a long mouthful. 'Thing with Davie's death is he was a personal target. Torrance knew Davie was closing in on him. Boy was tenacious. Knew he was the Marksman. But the rest of his kills were paid for. Like the boy at Tannadice. Antonio Bottone. This Italian guy on the run from the Sicilians, so he moved over here to hide away. Only he couldn't help himself. Six chip shops later and he's buying his way onto the board at United. And this was when they were in European finals, mind. Club was a big deal. The profile he gained meant he became a target again. But he was secretive, only time out in public was to watch the Terrors.

So Mark Torrance just had to sit and wait. Rented a flat overlooking where he parked, then shot and killed him for the Cosa Nostra. Two hundred grand he got.'

Vicky tried to play it all through. It made some kind of twisted sense. 'The fact he'd let it get personal was what got him caught?'

'Right.'

'Dad, we found the case files in this guy's house.'

His eyes went wide. 'Seriously?'

Vicky sat back. Something wasn't clicking here. Like there was a missing piece of the jigsaw that had fallen under the sofa. 'What did you do?'

'Nothing… It's just… That stuff being in the public domain. It was the Nineties, Vicky. There's bound to be some stuff in there that could help an appeal.'

'Torrance pleaded guilty.'

'Even so.' Dad shook his head. 'I wasn't even central to the investigation. Far from it. Just helped a bit. Drove people around. Asked questions.'

'Even so, Forrester wants you in a safe house.'

Dad laughed. 'Am I hell going in a safe house.'

'Dad, think about it. Please? For me?'

'I have. Anybody who wants to kill me? They're welcome to give it a shot.'

DAY 4

Wednesday

43

Vicky wrapped herself up tight in the quilt, shivering. House was an ice box.

She shouldn't have told Dad everything.

She was that little bit more exposed, like Sharon said. One more person who knew what she'd done. Who knew how she'd lied.

But he'd understood. All too easily. Saw what she did as acceptable.

Taking a life.

Jesus.

Roasting. She peeled the quilt back off her and poked her feet out of the side of the bed.

Too cold, too hot, she wished her body would make up its mind.

It wasn't as simple as wishing she could take it back. To undo a death. Dad was right. Because of what she did, they were able to live here. If not, they'd be on the run or in a safe house. Always looking over their shoulder.

Could Jamie or Bella go on that play date with a pal from school? Could they go to that sleepover?

That new school mum, was she really that kid's mum?

And the coach on Bella's football team?

It would be endless.

She was just as bad as Mark Torrance.

The sweat cooled on her skin and before long, she'd cocooned herself once again in the quilt.

Why had Doug Mason done that to her? Why put her through that just to kill himself?

Rob was snoring, worse than her mum's rendition back when she lived with them.

Vicky pulled back the covers, turned on the light and tried reading. Some book on Ancient Rome. She'd never had the slightest interest in history, but Rob got her it for Christmas and she was enjoying it. Even wanted to visit Pompeii, but the kids would be bored.

She'd read the same paragraph for the third time now. Nothing was going in. She flicked through the pages, looked at a few of the photos. Couldn't concentrate, tried the same paragraph a fourth time, still none the wiser. She turned off the light and lay back, stretching out.

Even tried some relaxation techniques Rob had taught her.

But they made no difference.

She lay there in the dark, listening to a bird warbling random patterns of notes.

What kind of bird was doing that in November?

She must've drifted off because the bird told her its name was Doug Mason and it was going to eat her soul.

The heating cranked into life.

Almost four o'clock.

Aye. Sleep wasn't happening tonight.

Vicky got up and padded through to the hall, then into the kitchen. She switched on the light again and let her eyes adjust to the dazzle.

Peralta lifted his head up from his dog bed, but Holt was out for the count. Smelled like they'd both been burning tyres all night. Or breaking wind. Too cold to crack the window, so she'd just have to stomach it.

She set the kettle on to boil, yawning. A meow, then Tinkle started swishing around her feet. She lifted the fat wee cat up and put some biscuits in her bowl, out of reach of the dogs.

Last couple of camomile bags, not that they'd helped with sleep any.

Was it worth trying to get another hour or so? Even a little sleep was better than none. Right?

That bird was at it again. Trilling away. Trying to tell her its name again. What it was going to do to her.

Her phone blasted out, gave her the sensation of a hundred hands rolling the nerves in her forearms between fingers and thumbs.

She picked up her mobile, still charging. A few texts, but nothing pressing.

Forrester calling...

What did he want?

'Doddsy, thank God. Need you to get to Edinburgh airport. First flight down to London.'

'Why?'

'Luke's coming to pick you up. He'll fill you in.'

44

Vicky stood on the frosty street, right in the middle of the streetlight's cone. As much to see the slipperiest parts when Shepherd arrived as for him to spot her. Her home was dark and silent, five sleeping bodies inside, though the two dogs slept so much they were probably closer to mineral than animal. And Tinkle was out prowling in the cold.

Her home, her life.

And she hated being away from it.

London.

Why the hell was she going to London?

Her phone rang. Unknown mobile number. She put her bag between her feet and answered it. 'Have you got lost, Luke?'

'I'm nowhere near that sexy.' Not Shepherd's voice and Vicky was too sleep-deprived to figure out who it actually was.

'Who's this?'

'Christ, you need to start writing numbers down or something. It's Scott. Scott Cullen.'

'Right. Right.' Vicky stepped down onto the street and walked around to the main road. 'You're up early?'

'Haven't gone to bed yet, Vicky. Been working all night. Didn't expect you to answer. Too tired to type out a message, so I thought I'd leave a voicemail, but you answered. So you can hear my dulcet tones.'

'Sure, that's a rare treat. Well, as it happens I'm waiting on Shepherd to take me to the airport.'

'There's an airport in Dundee?'

'A tiny one. But we're flying from Edinburgh.'

'The way Luke drives, you'll get there quicker in his motor.'

Vicky laughed, her breath like smoke in the air. 'Never flown with BuchanAir, but they're the only one with seats on the first flight to London. Sounds like the kind of single-prop jalopy that'll fall out of the sky around Leicester.'

'Why there?'

'Search me. It's in the Midlands and I thought it'd fly down the east—'

'No, London.'

'Oh, right. Well, I don't know. Luke hasn't turned up yet and he's been briefed. Staying in the boss's spare room. Won't answer his phone, either. Keeping me in suspense.'

'That's Luke. Mysterious to the end.'

'Scott, what's happened?'

'Happened?'

'Why are you still up? You know anything about this?'

'Nope.'

'Nothing's happened?'

'Not that I'm aware of. Other than Aberdeen losing yet again.'

She checked her watch. Christ, they'd be pushing it to get to the airport in time. 'Sorry, if this is about football I'm—'

'It's not.' Cullen sighed. 'Listen, I've been up most of the night, trying to tie things together. Both of our cases, really. Gavin Mason and Thomas Riley.'

'Have you found anything?'

'Possibly. I've managed to get approval to speak to the doctors treating Morgan Miller. Your Dr Rankine? She's something else. Anyway. Took me a lot of effort to get her to tell me Morgan wasn't knocked out.'

'I could've told you that, Scott. Why were you asking?'

'Well, Riley's bloods came back. He was injected with suxamethonium chloride and—'

Felt like two giant hands clamped Vicky's head. 'Sux?'

'That's the kind of reaction I enjoy. You know it?'

'It's a paralytic. Use it in hospital for intubation, right? With sux you're conscious but you can't move.'

'Right, aye. Upshot is, Riley would've been conscious when he was killed.'

Her sigh froze in the air. 'That's... brutal.' She looked along the old road to Barry. Still no sign of Shepherd.

'Vicky, Davenport and Forrester have been sitting in their offices having these chats about stuff with some guys in the Met. Meanwhile it's up to you and I to do the work to catch the bastards, right?'

Vicky was walking past the old school now, towards the roundabout. 'Right.'

'You stopped him before he could kill Morgan, but aye.'

Vicky stopped and dropped her bag at her feet. 'So why London?'

'Who can say. They don't let the likes of you or I onto their calls, do they?'

'No, they don't. Listen, remember back in May or whenever, when I was down your way?'

'Right?'

'How we found that Shepherd was still working for the Complaints?'

'Aye?'

'Well, is he still?'

'What, you think Shepherd could be investigating someone in Dundee?'

'That's what I'm wondering, aye.'

He laughed. 'What did you do, Vicky?'

She tried to laugh it off, but it sounded hollow to her. 'It's just that... We've got a history of bent cops here. If Luke's looking into someone, I'd rather know who.'

'Well, Luke's not doing that shite anymore. He got himself into a bit of hot water.'

'Oh, really?'

A car was shooting towards her along the new road. A Tesla. Shepherd.

Perfect...

'Scott, I better go. But let me know if I should be worried.'

'Oh, always be worried, Vicky. That way when the buggers fuck you over, you're at least bracing your bum cheeks.'

She smiled. 'Catch you later, Scott.' She hung up and waved at the car.

Shepherd slowed to a halt, then reached over to open the door. 'Sorry I'm late, should've got you to meet me somewhere.'

'It's okay. I'm too tired to drive.' Vicky got in the passenger seat and shut the door. An M&S bag was stuffed into the footwell. Fresh pants and socks. New shirt. No sign of the dirty ones.

'Sorry.' Shepherd grabbed it and shoved it on the back seat. 'At least they're clean, eh?'

'Small mercies.' Vicky buckled up and, holy crap, the seat was comfortable at this time. 'So, what's this about?'

Shepherd floored it and it felt like Vicky was taking off already. 'Forrester didn't tell you?'

'Nope.'

'Right. Well. A DNA sample from Gavin's flat matches a sample taken from four rapes in London.'

'So we're heading down to Belmarsh or whatever to interview this guy?'

'That's the thing. Never caught. But the Met have a suspect. Never arrested or charged. Alibis and all that.'

'So?'

'So the DNA from Gavin's flat matches the rapist's. Could just be a friend of Gavin's.' Shepherd shot through the chicane outside the horse-riding place Vicky used to go to. Tried to take Bella and Jamie there, but neither were interested. 'But if we can pin down this suspect's movements, we can arrest and charge him. And get his DNA. Prove it was him. At least solve four rapes, one way or the other.'

'How likely is it?'

'Not sure, but we've got to try.'

'Long way to travel for just a try, Luke.'

Shepherd shrugged. 'How'd you get on with your father?'

'Spoke with him. He confirmed it.'

'Oh. You okay?'

'I'm fine.'

'Sure?'

'Dad doesn't think there's anything in it. No serial killer hunting them down. Barely worked the case.'

'No, I don't think there's anything in that either.' Shepherd pulled up at the lights. 'But I've been thinking. Thomas Riley. Scott's team have been hunting him for years. I worked one of the victims. We think he's a serial killer because we found the ears at his house, right?' Shrivelled-up ears, like dead mice. 'Five victims. And now he's someone else's victim. But that's not proof he was the one killing those people.'

Vicky dared another glance at Shepherd. 'Who do you think did it?'

'It could be him, don't get me wrong. But our problem is he's dead and can't answer our questions.'

'You think it's Doug?'

'Do you?'

'I don't know. The only attack we know he did was Morgan Miller.'

'Right, but he could still have killed Gavin.'

'Thing you're forgetting is Doug couldn't have killed Riley. Time of death was pretty much when we were on that bus.'

Shepherd pulled away from the lights. 'Don't know what to believe, Vicky.'

'How about someone framed Riley? Stuck all those posters on the wall. Whoever found the body – Edinburgh cops or Dundee – didn't matter. What mattered was the misdirection.'

'How's that tinfoil hat fit, Vicky?'

'Look, it's entirely possible Riley was just researching a book, hence all the case files. Us interviewing Mark Torrance was a diversion, pushing us in the wrong direction. Away from Doug. And you're assuming this list was Riley's. Same with the ears. The killer could've planted them there.'

'And maybe he was actually an assassin. He was money laundering for the Albanians.'

Vicky's head was thumping now. She checked the clock. 'It's half four. Are you sure we're going to make this flight on time?'

'Relax. The way I drive, we'll be there with ages to spare.'

She shut her eyes. 'Well, wake me up when we get there.'

45

He double-parks on the street and leaves the engine running. Seems the same as last night, the November daylight not any brighter than its night. Overlooked on all sides by—

What do they call the owners of these? Young professionals? Accountants, actuaries, doctors, coders. First rung of a tall, tall ladder. Twenty-somethings full of WakeyWakey and lattes, tapered off at night with an unhealthy dose of alcohol with their takeaway in front of Netflix.

No. Not lattes. Flat whites.

Either way, they'll all be out in their wage-slave jobs already. Too many windows pointing down at me. Too many people passing the van, their voices slicing through the sheet metal.

He needs to be smart here.

A quick check in the mirrors. Just a post van, the rain and gloom turning the red to a bloody maroon swirling around the shower plug hole.

The sort of driver who will notice things. Any deviation

from the established pattern they see every day. He waits till it's gone.

It drones past, the engine's sub-bass thud like some boy racer's pimped-up Corsa.

He leans over and opens the glovebox, which is crammed full of absolute shit, but he finds it right at the back. A police warrant card.

DI Alex Moffett.

He gives it another scan – looks authentic enough. Should do, given he stole it from a serving officer, dribbling into a pint of lager as he rifled through his wallet. A few tweaks here and there – change the name, change the photo – and it's good, really good. Probably won't get him into any police stations, but it'll get him everywhere else. And that spelling's odd enough to make it distinct enough to pass for real.

He pockets it and now it's a waiting game.

The light above his door is broken, blinking in one of those patterns that doesn't quite resolve. Just when you think it's—

The door rattles open and a man appears.

Keith Dawson. A handsome face, hair cropped short, jagged lines on his forehead like he's in a state of constant worry. Dressed for a run.

All three mirrors are clear, so he nudges the door and gets out. The syringe is in his left pocket, already filled up with sux. The warrant card's in his right, just in case.

Street's quiet, just the soft shuffle of Keith's feet on the steps down from the flat.

'Keith!' A woman steps out of the door behind him. Frosty eyes, hatred seeping out of her pores. Little dog yapping at her heels. She grabs Keith in an embrace and kisses him deeply. All those windows, all those flats. Watching them.

They don't care who sees them.

He gets back in the van. His twitchy fingers can't start the engine, so he just sits there.

Keith kisses her on the cheek, then runs off down the street, the little dog following.

He gets the engine to fire, then pulls off, way faster than Keith's running.

Got somewhere to be.

46

Even though it was called London City, it felt like it was one of those airports certain airlines flew to which were named after a city but were at least twenty miles away from even the outskirts. Cops armed with rifles. Planes zooming in overhead. Kids shouting and screaming somewhere nearby.

Vicky stepped outside and tugged off her mask. Had been on for the last three hours, pretty much. Reminded her of that first trip to the supermarket with one on, almost having a panic attack at the tills. Then hating it. Then catching the bastard bug from the kids and feeling like shit for ten days. And vowing to wear a mask forever to stop anyone else catching that horrible, horrible virus.

She couldn't stop yawning. It was a lot warmer down here, but just as windy. She could cope with a warmer wind, but not the heavy rain.

Shepherd trundled through behind her, sighing as he tore off his own mask, scanning the taxi rank. 'No sign of him, then?'

'Who are we meeting again?'

'Forgot to say. While you were in the toilet, I got a call from Jobson. He gave me a timely update on Thomas Riley's visits to Mark Torrance. Turns out Riley had been in a few times, but somehow it was another guard on duty each time. Riley kept asking him what it felt like to kill someone. Torrance never spoke.'

'You think that means something?'

'I think Riley had a hero. But— Ah, there he is.' Shepherd grabbed his bag and set off towards a blue Mondeo.

A tall, muscular guy was writing on a sheet of cardboard. Silver hair, just a few strands of colour in there. Piercing blue eyes trained on them. Massive bags under his eyes, like he'd never slept a wink in his life. He squinted at them. 'Luke Shepherd?'

'That's me.' He thumbed to the side. 'This is DI Vicky Dodds.'

The guy tossed a sheet of cardboard in the car. 'Saves me writing my name like I'm some kind of limo driver.' He held out a hand. 'DCI Simon Fenchurch.'

47

He parks the van at the side of the road and gets out. Still dark. Cars thundering past, swooshing the rainwater. White noise everywhere.

He checks his watch – still plenty of time – and powers on through the downpour, along the path. Rain splashes against his face. His trousers are soaked through, right down to his socks and his hood isn't protecting his hair any.

The path's still empty. Too late for the serious morning joggers and dog walkers, too early for the casual ones. Goldilocks Zone of quiet. The weather's keeping them away, too. Poor dogs, sitting inside all day without releasing their energy in even a walk. Not getting to sniff others.

Another glance at his watch, then behind him, scanning for anyone walking along the glowing path.

Where is he?

A tall man jogs along, a husky padding along behind, dutiful, eyes scanning for threats. Just like he is. He waves as he passes. 'Morning, mate.'

Not good – means he's laying down tracks, establishing his own pattern. People could recognise him. But it's not Keith, so he settles back on the bench.

The jogger and his husky splash along the path, clearing the area.

Movement to the left, behind. 'Come on, Yoda.'

That voice. The purposeful stride.

It's him this time.

Keith Dawson. AirPods deep in his ears, just the white tips sticking out, means he doesn't know about the distinct sound his dog makes. The collar rattles against the lead, clattering in a rhythm. Little West Highland terrier, fur on its face like it's grinning, hair hanging down like a valance on a hotel bed.

Twenty-five metres away, by his reckoning.

He runs his thumb down the blade of the knife, cutting into the glove's leather. He gets up from the bench and steps towards Keith, head low, shrouded by his collar. And his back gives him a spasm of pain, almost makes him shriek. He dips his head towards Keith, same as most days. 'Morning.'

Keith replies with a nod, powering on, hood hanging back, face soaked in rain, and jogs past.

And he moves, stepping onto the path and wrapping his arm around Keith's throat. Like a cuddle, the kindest caress. He spikes the syringe into Keith's vein. Keith moans and staggers. He holds him until it's all sprayed into his bloodstream.

The dog yaps at him like machine-gun fire.

He helps Keith away from the path, over towards the wall. Keith's swinging his arms, trying to catch him. But each swing is that little bit less furious, less energetic.

The dog bites his leg. Easiest thing in the world just to kick out and send it flying. But he holds back. The little sod bites again, breaking the skin.

Keith's legs press against the low wall. His eyes plead, just one earbud in now. The other's missing. He can't speak, so he just grunts. Language is gone.

He has to die.

Keith's awake, watching this happen. Maybe he should knock him out, but Keith needs to know what he did. Why he has no choice but to kill him.

Tears trickle down his face, mixing with the heavy rain, washing away. He holds the knife over Keith's throat, panting. Heart thudding.

The dog nips his ankle, then bites his shoe.

Keith's eyes plead with him. A grunt, like he's saying no.

Like he let anyone say no.

Like he listened if they did.

It has to be this way.

No choice.

The blade digs into Keith's throat, tearing at his skin, biting into soft flesh like the dog gnaws into his. Blood splashes down his neck, spreads out on his pale jacket, patted away by the rain. His eyes show bitter disgust.

He stamps on the dog's lead, trapping it in place, and holds Keith until he's gone, just a hollow skull.

Dead.

He pushes Keith over the wall. He tumbles, rolling and rolling, until he can't see him. The perfect spot, exactly where he wants him. The knife and syringe go back into his coat.

He snatches up the dog's lead and tugs it away from its master, powering along, just another dog walker. It has to be this way. The only way.

Keep telling yourself that.

The little sod tries for his legs again. Yapping away.

He grabs the dog's lead. Keeps it tight as he picks up little Yoda. He bites at the gloves, almost piercing the leather. He crosses the path and ties the lead around the bench, then tests it for strength.

That'll do.

Handsomely.

Little sod will bark his head off until someone comes.

So much risk in this, but there's no way he can let an innocent dog suffer like that. Just the guilty. Minimise the collateral damage of their loved ones.

And he's gone, jogging back to the van. He gets in, sticks it in first and hoofs it before he can even grab for the seatbelt.

His back's an *abomination*. He really needs to get back to doing the Pilates.

48

Vicky jerked awake and blinked in the morning sunshine. She was in the back of a car and her head felt like it'd been stuffed full of ripe brie.

Brie, like Billy Dewar had been munching whole from the packet.

Shepherd was in the front with that guy... Fenchurch, was it?

God, she really needed to snap her brain into focus.

They were parked outside a white-harled Sixties box, the red-tiled roof pockmarked with Velux windows. A dark-blue Peugeot in the drive, 57 plates.

Fenchurch turned around to look at her. 'You okay there, sleeping beauty?'

She yawned into her fist. 'Didn't get much sleep last night.'

'Me and sleep aren't the best of friends either.' Fenchurch smiled and handed over a bottle of water. 'Have a drink of this. It'll wake you up.'

She took it. 'And I can trust a Met DCI?'

He laughed.

Vicky took a glug. 'So, is that his address?'

Fenchurch nodded. 'Now, let's be clear here. This is my operation. I'm not particularly happy having two Scottish cops being on my patch, but if you can help get a collar on Keith Dawson, then I'm all for it.' He paused. 'And if we can prove it's not him, same result.'

'Okay. Luke and I are just here to help.' Vicky got out and followed them over to the address, powering across the pavement.

Fenchurch scraped open the gate then led up the short path, peering into the front window. 'Somebody's home.' He thumbed the buzzer and waited. Just stared right at Vicky. No shame in it, either.

The door opened and a middle-aged man stood there, hands on hips. Salt-and-pepper hair, fake tan, tight shirt, navy jeans with scuffed knees. 'Don't want any, sorry.' He moved to shut the door.

'Detective Chief Inspector Simon Fenchurch.' He showed him his warrant card. 'We're looking for a Keith Dawson.'

The man folded his arms and tilted his head to the side. 'He ain't here.' He blinked hard a few times, then sneezed, a spray of snot hitting Vicky in the face.

Her stomach lurched, coffee and bacon roll gurgling in the pit.

Jesus, if he's got covid?

She wiped her hand across her face, thick gloop sticking to her skin. 'Can I ask your name, sir?'

'That's none of your business.' Another sneeze, this time into his hand.

Vicky stepped back off the step. 'Does Mr Dawson live here or not?'

The sneezer glanced away, sniffing hard and fast like he was going to sneeze again. 'I told you, he ain't here.'

'We need to speak to him in connection with a murder inquiry. He does live here, right?'

Shifty eyes darted between them, nostrils twitching. 'You've got a bloody cheek.' He made to shut the door.

It bounced off Vicky's shoe. Felt like she'd cracked a nail. 'Where is he, sir?'

'I told you – leave me alone!' He pushed the door again.

Vicky's shoe crumpled up – the toenail must've cracked. 'Can I take your name, sir?'

'Hugh Dawson.' He reached into his pocket for a handkerchief and blew his nose. 'This bloody cold. Swear it'll be the death of me.'

'It's not covid?'

'Been testing all week. Still negative.'

Vicky could smell burnt toast. 'Your toast's—'

'I know! There's nothing wrong with my sense of smell! I ain't got bloody covid!'

Fenchurch flicked up his eyebrows at Vicky, then smiled at Dawson. 'Sir, we need to speak to your son. This is the only address we've got for him.'

'Bloody hell.' Dawson shut his eyes. 'You said a murder case. What's he done?'

'It's just a routine part of an inquiry.'

'These two are Scottish.'

'Scottish people are still allowed in London.' Fenchurch left a gap, filling it with a smile. 'Come on, mate. Where is Keith?'

Hugh's lips started quivering. Then another sneeze. He rubbed his hands together. 'This is about those girls, isn't it?'

'Afraid so.'

'You mob trying to fit him, thinking my son's a serial rapist.' Dawson shook his head, eyes narrow. 'That's a load of bollocks and you know it.'

'Mr Dawson.' Fenchurch thrust his hands into his pockets. 'My colleagues here have travelled down from Dundee to speak to your son.'

'Dundee?' Dawson seemed to fight off another sneeze attack. 'Should've got you to check he was here before they travelled, shouldn't they?'

'We found DNA traces at a crime scene which match the sample in the crimes your son's wanted for.'

Vicky shared a look with Shepherd – that was way more than either of them would share.

'Now.' Fenchurch stepped closer to him. 'I'd love to be able to clear his name. Must be hell for the both of you having that hanging over your heads. Wouldn't that be nice?'

Dawson looked up at the sky and let his breath go. 'That would be lovely.'

'So, where is he?'

Dawson put his hands on his hips and glared at Vicky. 'I don't know, do I?'

'So, let's wind it back a bit, Mr Dawson.' Fenchurch was grinning at him. 'When was the last time you saw him?'

'About six weeks ago.'

'Do you mind telling us what happened?'

'It's a long one.'

Aren't they all? Vicky smiled. 'We've got time.'

'Keith went to university. Smart boy, my son. Not like me. Got in to Southwark. I was so proud of him.'

Fenchurch winced. 'My daughter studied there. It's a good university.'

'Right. Well, straight out of university, Keith married this lovely girl, Annabel. Then all of a sudden, he turns up here and I'm expecting him to tell me I've got a grandchild on the way, but no – he says they're getting divorced. Saying he'd lost his job. Worked as a lawyer for Ogden and Makepeace in the City.'

'I know the firm.' Fenchurch left him some space, to see if he'd elaborate.

Dawson's lips twitched. 'She caught my boy in bed with another woman.' He balled his fists. 'I tried to get him to go back and save his marriage, but no. Not for Keith. So he moved back in here, said he'd easily get another job.' He exhaled slowly. 'Can you imagine? Going from expecting to have a grandson dancing on my lap, to having a thirty-five-year-old teenager back in the house?'

Fenchurch narrowed his eyes. Clearly couldn't find any sympathy for him. 'So where is he now?'

'Well, he told me this tale. How he bumped into a pal from school in Tesco. Kind of went their separate ways at uni, you know? Next thing I know, Keith's telling me he's in love with this girl called Sara. Moved in with her six weeks ago. Ain't heard from him since.' Teary eyes stared at Fenchurch. 'Tell me straight, one father to another, do you think he raped these girls?'

Fenchurch stood there, arms folded. 'It's possible, sir. Have you got an address for this Sara?'

49

Vicky dabbed a hand to her cheek as she checked her face in her make-up mirror. Got it all off, just about. But she was still a panda who hadn't slept in days. She put her mask back in place.

Fenchurch killed the engine and snapped the keys out of the ignition. 'Before we do this, I don't want any more of that.'

Shepherd frowned. 'Any more of what?'

'I told you I'm in charge. This is my case. You're here as guests. I lead, okay?'

'Fine, sorry.'

'Sorry for what?'

'Talking to a suspect's father.' Vicky stepped out onto the street instead and tore off her mask.

Prick.

One of those grotty London tenement streets full of one-bedroom flats, at least two on sale at any one time. And nowhere near gentrified. And people said Dundee was a dump...

'Inspector.' The noise of Fenchurch's slammed car door ricocheted off the buildings. He stood between the car and a communal bin, blocking the pavement. 'I don't have to do this, you know? You can get on the first plane back to Scotland. Or Newcastle, come to it, and you can get a taxi the rest of the way.'

Vicky huffed out air. No getting past him. 'Listen. Your rapist was at our crime scene, so let's just agree to play ball, aye?'

Fenchurch stared at her for a few seconds. 'Play ball. Right.' He twisted around and stared up at the block. 'It's this one, yeah?'

'Think so.' Vicky used the diversion to barge past and thumbed the buzzer. Probably the only flat on the street with a working intercom system. She hit the buzzer again. Pulse racing, skin crawling. Just Fenchurch's breathing washing over like waves breaking on pebbles.

'Hello?'

Vicky gestured at the buzzer.

Fenchurch leaned down to its level. 'Police. Need a word with a Keith Dawson?'

A long pause. Then the door clunked open. 'You'd better come up.'

Fenchurch gestured for Vicky to go.

Shepherd slipped between them.

Fenchurch smiled, then set off up after him. He walked with a limp.

Vicky followed them.

At the top, a young woman tugged at her baggy grey jumper. Dark skirt, too much make-up. Late twenties and had one of those faces that was pretty enough to seem familiar. Pacing around like she'd drunk a whole jar of coffee. 'I'm running *so* late for work.' Gravelly voice, at least forty-a-day. The sort of English accent Vicky struggled to place. She ushered them in. 'Christ, you can take your bloody masks off.'

Vicky kept hers on.

A tiny living room with a kitchen area tucked in the corner. A dog bed sat next to a scabby settee. The place smelled freshly painted, but the air was thick with cigarette smoke. Not that Vicky had been to London much, but she got the impression this was how most of them lived. In tiny boxes. And the rent would be about ten times the mortgage on a Broughty Ferry jute baron's old mansion.

Vicky stepped over to the window. Cracking view across a canal and some lower rooftops on the other side. She had little idea which part of London they were in, having slept a lot of the way, but she assumed it was north and east.

Fenchurch gave her a smile. 'Like I said outside, we just need to speak to Keith Dawson.'

'Okay.'

'Keith does live here, right?'

'Yeah. I'm his partner. Zara Corrigan.'

Not Sara, then.

She stopped pacing and shifted her gaze between them. 'He's out.' She nibbled at her knuckle. 'Walking Yoda. Well, running.' She scrubbed her hair with a hand, left it all frizzy. 'Keith left at seven. Takes Yoda for a run every morning.' She checked her watch again. 'He's usually back by now. I need to go and find him. He's... Why do you want to speak to him?'

'It's part of a routine enquiry.' Shepherd looked up from his notebook. 'Where—'

'You're Scottish?'

'It's not a crime.' Shepherd crunched forward on the sofa. 'Where does he run?'

Zara frowned. 'Do you think something could've happened to him?'

'We just need to find him, Ms Corrigan.' Fenchurch smiled. 'Now, where would he run?'

'Along the canal. Usually heads towards Islington then on to King's Cross and Camden.'

Fenchurch smiled. 'Okay, we'll get out of your hair and see if we can find him.'

Shepherd pushed himself up. Took a couple of goes.

Zara nibbled at her lip, the lipstick cracking, and ran a hand through her hair. Her eyes filled with tears. 'Just find him for me.'

'It'll help if you give us his mobile number.'

50

Vicky leaned forward in the car seat, listening to the ringing tone switch to office noise.

Fenchurch drove, swerving out into the oncoming traffic. Guy was even worse than Shepherd.

'Morning, Vicky.' Jenny sounded distracted, like she was reading while she spoke.

'Hey, Jenny. Can you do a trace on a mobile for me?'

'What did your last slave die of?'

'Come on, Jenny...'

She groaned. 'What's the number?'

Vicky glanced into the wing mirror, a queue of traffic behind them trying to turn right towards somewhere. Could be into the City, could be heading out of London. Or anywhere in it. The whole place seemed to be city centre. 'I texted you it.'

'Just a sec.' A pause, some loud clicking in the background.

Fenchurch braked.

Vicky jolted forward.

The row of cars in front screeching to a halt as an old man drove his mobility scooter off the kerb.

Fenchurch looked over at her. 'I don't like the fact he's gone missing.'

'Me neither.' Vicky clutched her phone to her ear. 'Jenny, you got anything?'

'Hold your horses.' Fingers clattered keys. 'Here we go. Last ping is at seven o'clock this morning.'

Vicky swallowed hard. 'Where?'

'Just checking the GPS logs.' Jenny clicked what sounded like a pen against her teeth. 'Says *London*?'

'Right.'

'You're in London?'

'Flew down this morning.'

'Christ. Well. One of the cell towers is on top of the Happy Yorkshireman pub, the other just off a canal towpath.'

'Cheers for that. Speak soon.' Vicky ended the call and glanced over at Fenchurch. 'You know the Happy Yorkshireman?'

'Just down from my dad's house.' Fenchurch pulled out into the oncoming lane, squeezing past a slow-moving Vectra. The road bent to the left, a car showroom on the corner. 'Sounds like Keith's taken the dog the other direction, though.' He ploughed past the traffic, then took a hard right.

Vicky spotted it – a whitewashed pub just behind a pedestrian crossing, fancy chalk-written board out front. Over the road, an old path climbed down into some trees. 'There!'

Fenchurch braked hard, mounting the pavement and knocked over the pub's chalkboard. 'You two go down to the canal. I'll catch you up. Got a dodgy knee.'

Vicky got out of the car and bolted down the lane, following the sign for Regent's Canal, blood pumping hard as she followed the path snaking to the left, the water deep below them.

Shepherd's heavy footsteps slapped behind her.

She looked around, just houses and bridges. School kids screamed from the playground on the opposite bank. The trees on either side were half bare, the leaves turning to mulch. She continued towards the steps up.

Shepherd was jogging behind her, wheezing. 'Anything?'

'Nothing I can see.' Vicky powered on up, stopping at a railing.

Police tape flapped in the breeze, covering a length of the banister. Suited figures tramped around in the undergrowth. A tent sat in shadow of the bridge by the towering old trees, the arc lights at risk of outshining the weak sun.

Fenchurch clattered to a halt behind her. 'We're too late.'

51

Vicky crouched down, her Tyvek SOCO suit crinkling. Someone's knee clicked, but not hers. She sighed into the face mask and her goggles misted up. These things needed windscreen wipers. On the inside.

Through the mist, a young man lay on the thick grass, head lolling to the side, eyes dead. His clothes were soaked, his damp hair shaved at the sides, but longer on the right. A red line circled his throat, splitting the skin.

Keith Dawson.

A blue-suited man walked over and crouched next to the body, prodding a syringe into the body's abdomen. Sounded like he was humming something from an opera.

Fenchurch shook his head as he stood, the suit swooshing, and glanced at the suited figure next to him. 'We're sure it's him?'

The other figure nodded, suit twisted around his jaw, with a grimace.

'We'll leave you to work in peace, William.' Fenchurch

opened the tent flap and held it for Vicky, his head hanging low. 'Let's get out of here.'

Vicky walked out into the downpour, tearing off her face mask and dumping it in the discard pile. The bitter morning air attacked her face, clawing at the sweat. The sickening burn in her gut was back.

Hard to believe Keith had been alive so recently.

Breathing, running with his dog.

Shit, shit, shit.

'Where's the dog?' Vicky looked over at Fenchurch. 'What did Zara call him?'

'Yoda.' He was doing something with his knee. Made it pop.

Vicky felt it down in her own knee. 'You okay there?'

'Got an op coming up. Been a bloody nightmare for a few years now.' Fenchurch got an almighty crack. 'Reason the body was found. Someone had tied Yoda to the bench just up there.'

A bag clattered to the ground near Fenchurch's feet, skidding into his leg.

Then the other figure – William – crawled out of the tent and stood, tugging at his mask. A thick beard burst free.

'Dr Pratt.' Fenchurch kicked at the bag. 'Watch what you're doing with that.'

Pratt held out a hand and muttered some arcane incantation.

Vicky could barely make out a word. 'Can you please speak up?'

If anything, he got quieter.

'Right, William.' Fenchurch nodded at the tent, breath thick in the air. 'What's happened here?'

Pratt smoothed down his beard, like someone gutting a fish. 'Male, mid-thirties, throat cut with a serrated blade. From my investigations, I'd say he died not long before discovery and as a result of his injuries.'

Vicky tried to add it to the timeline, but it slotted in just fine. 'What time?'

'Dog walker found a pooch tied to the bench.' Pratt waved up the hill towards the path. 'Then searched around for its owner, thinking they'd got caught short. Spotted them down here in the bushes. Around about quarter to eight, I believe. Death would've been quick. Probably rolled down here, given the bruising.' He scratched behind his ear and coughed away. 'Sorry, but I do need to get back to my lab.'

Fenchurch smiled at him. 'We'll bring the next of kin down to ID the body.'

'Better get my skates on then.' Pratt started on the rest of his suit. He undid the zip on his suit but stopped, blushing. 'There was a needle mark on his skin. Seems to have been incapacitated before he was murdered.' He hefted up his bag, then glimpsed back at the tent. 'I'll fast track the blood toxicology, naturally. Don't hold your breath.' He picked up his bag and waddled towards the barrier.

Vicky watched him go, hardly getting his skates on. 'Who's in charge of this investigation?'

'It's my lot, sadly. Yet another death to add to the books.' Fenchurch got out his mobile and checked the screen. 'One of my DIs has been calling me, must be what this is about.' He checked his watch. 'You heard what I said about the boy's father IDing the body?'

52

Vicky kept her distance from them, just observing. Shouldn't even be doing this. But Fenchurch seemed to be stretched beyond breaking. And if it got any answers for her case, then all the better.

The room was clean and modern, even if it was tiny. The floor was maybe emerald-green marble, but closer inspection revealed it to be just fancy linoleum. A couple of two-seater couches, a little table with a jug of water. A few small modern landscapes – fields, mountains, a burn with crofters toiling on either bank. Chintzy tartan shortbread tin rubbish.

'What happens now?' Hugh Dawson's voice was thick with 'flu. Proper 'flu, not man 'flu. Didn't have the energy to boil an egg, or even pick one up. 'Is it my boy in there?' His boots clicked on the polished floor as he took a couple of shaky steps towards the doors. He stopped, and his hand went to his mouth, adjusting his mask. It was keeping it all in, though.

'Can we get on with it?' Zara wedged her hands in the pockets of a short black jacket. Slip-on shoes, olive-green trousers made of some thin material that barely came down to her ankles. Just looking at her made Vicky shiver. Dry eyes, whereas Hugh Dawson was like someone had squirted lemon juice in his. 'I've got to get back to Yoda.'

Dr Pratt cleared his throat. 'We can go through to the viewing room whenever you're ready, Mr Dawson.' Steady gaze and a sincere smile. 'The deceased is resting on a table, but I should warn you he's going to appear pale. Pale, but at peace.'

Hugh stumbled.

Zara lurched towards him, propping him up.

'He was special!' He looked around, wanting everybody to hear. 'My Keith was a special boy!'

Shepherd nodded and Vicky found herself nodding too. Of course your child was special. Everyone's was.

Pratt waited until Hugh was upright. 'Are you ready?'

'I… I don't want to do this. I can't…'

'You can wait here if you prefer.' Pratt smiled. 'No need for everyone to go in. The viewing room *is* quite small, after all.'

'I need to see him.' Zara stepped forward and placed her arm round Hugh's shoulders. 'You can come in with me or wait here.'

Hugh reached up and linked fingers with her. He rubbed a hand across his face. 'You don't need to.'

'Yes. I do.'

'Then I'll go too.'

'Sure?'

'I've made my mind up.' Hugh wrapped his hand around Zara's. 'I'm ready.'

Vicky stayed back as they entered the viewing room.

A body lay in the middle, a sheet tucked over his head.

Pratt stood next to it, and everyone was watching him. He raised his eyebrows at Hugh Dawson. 'Here we go.'

Hugh stood there, eyes closed, his jaw all steely. The slightest tilt of his head.

Pratt pulled back the sheet covering Keith's face, a scarf placed over the wound. And he was pale, like all of his blood had been sucked out by a vampire.

Zara's hand went to her mouth.

Hugh sank his head into Zara's neck and wailed. He put his arms around her, hugging her tight. Eyes still closed.

'I have to ask you. Do you recognise him?'

Hugh cried even louder, sinking to his knees, wrapping his arms around Zara's leg, his body spasming against her.

Zara's face was wet. She blinked through the tears. 'That's him. That's Keith.'

'Okay. Thank you.' Pratt covered the body over again and led them back into the family area.

Vicky stayed by the window. 'I'm sorry for your loss.'

Hugh sat at the table in the middle. 'My boy's gone. That's just a lump of carbon and other minerals. What used to be a man, where he used to live. Gone now, to wherever people go. Hard to think of it as Keith.'

'Mr Dawson, I know you've just suffered a great loss but—'

'Get on with it.' Hugh scowled at the tabletop. Blood red eyes, narrowed. 'I've got things to do.'

'We need to find out everything we can about Keith. Don't hold anything back, no matter how small it seems. It might be the difference in catching your son's killer.'

'Right.' Didn't seem it.

'Earlier, you told us he was divorced. Is it possible his ex-wife would hold a grudge against him?'

'No idea. Never talked to me about her.'

'And you, Zara?'

She shook her head. 'Not to me, either.'

'We just want to eliminate the possibility it's just a coincidence. Did his ex make any attempt to contact him since he moved back home or in with you?'

Hugh was frowning. 'If she had, Keith didn't... No. Well. Not that Keith told me.'

'If she had, I would've throttled her.' Zara ran a hand through her hair. 'She put Keith through hell.'

'No other partners?'

'There was one back at uni, but she moved back to Germany. It was fairly amicable, from what he told me.'

'Has he got many friends?'

'Most of his pals from the school've moved away at uni. Zara here's the only one he's in touch with that I know of.' His lips were quivering.

'Keith didn't exactly maintain relationships, put it that way.'

'What about friends at work?'

'He's not got a job. Well, he's been temping at this human rights law firm and...' Zara broke off, tears staining her face. 'Liberal Justice.'

'Right.' Fenchurch rolled his eyes. 'Does the name Gavin Mason mean anything to either of you?'

Zara shook her head.

Hugh rubbed his hand under his nose and sniffed. 'Should it?'

'Traces of your son's DNA was found at his flat in Dundee.'

'Dundee?'

'Mr Mason was murdered on Sunday night. Possibly by the same person as your son.'

'Christ.' Hugh let out a deep breath and collapsed back into the chair.

Not going to get anything else out of him. Too much for him to process and he'd been out of his son's life for so long.

Let him connect with Zara and share their loss.

And besides, Vicky's headache felt like it was going to start drilling down her neck.

53

Vicky and Shepherd stood at the back of the incident room. Heaving, at least double the number of officers as in Dundee. Showed the difference between the Met and Police Scotland. They could throw more bodies at a murder than was useful.

Her sore head hadn't shifted, still lingering on like thick haar blocking out the sun on a Scottish summer's day. Pressure building up inside her skull, like thunder and lightning was on its way. Being in a stuffy room in East London didn't exactly help.

Fenchurch was at the front, resting against a desk, arms folded. 'Again, one of the victims in Scotland was injected with suxamethonium chloride so we're checking that as a priority. He was injected, so it appears to be a connection.' He checked a notepad and winced. There was someone behind the pillar but Vicky couldn't see who. 'Now, the Commissioner has asked Detective Superintendent Derek Broadfoot to consult on this case.'

'Thank you, Simon.' Broadfoot walked over and smiled. 'Well, as you all know, I was on the team who apprehended Mark Torrance back in the day. Worked across Britain but ended up catching him up in Scotland. Place called Inchture. If anyone knows Perth or Dundee, it's between them. Assuming you don't, settle for it being up in chilly jockland. Anyway, they made a film about it and cast Helen Mirren as me.'

His pause was filled with laughter.

'Anyway. I bring with me considerable experience, both in this country and in the States. Your DCI and I both trained at Quantico, though at separate times. Obviously, it's Simon's case, so I'll avoid damaging anyone's ego. Just here in an executive consultation role in light of my unique expertise. But I've worked all over the Met. Murder squad like you lot in the main, but drugs and even Professional Standards and Ethics. I've been asked to review progress and cast another pair of eyes over the evidence.'

'Thanks, Derek.' Fenchurch scanned around the room. 'You've all been given actions on HOLMES. Let's get to it, people. Dismissed.'

Vicky slumped back against the wall.

Fenchurch split Vicky and Shepherd. 'You guys needing something to eat? Usually go for a burrito at lunchtime.'

Vicky frowned. 'As in, Mexican food?'

'Don't knock it.'

'I wasn't. You don't really get them in Dundee.' She smiled at him. 'Don't get a lot of things in Dundee.'

'So.' Broadfoot walked over, hands in pockets. He had this amazing effect of clearing the incident room – the place was empty now, just them. 'Victoria Dodds, we meet again?'

'It's Vicky.'

'Of course. Sorry.' Broadfoot was sipping from an unlabelled coffee carton. He took a long look at Vicky, tilting his head to the side, his hair barely shifting. 'How are you doing?'

Vicky took a seat and rested her hands on the table, palms facing down. 'I'm okay.'

'Someone shot themselves in front of you and you're okay?'

Vicky smiled now. In no mood to deal with this prick. 'It's going to go with me to the grave, that's for sure.'

'Been there, done that.' Broadfoot's gaze shifted between the three of them. 'Gather you spoke to Mark Torrance yesterday?'

Shepherd raised his eyebrows. 'How did you know that?'

'I have an understanding with the guards at Perth prison. Any unauthorised interviews with Mr Torrance should be approved by myself. You two blundered in along with that clown from Edinburgh and pressured them to let you talk. Not a smart move.'

'You can relax.' Shepherd leaned back in the seat. 'We're not reopening the investigation, if that's what you're worried about.'

'Hardly. I expect you didn't get much out of Torrance?'

'Wasn't exactly communicative, no.'

'And what were you after?'

Shepherd scowled at him. 'That's our business.'

Broadfoot's face tightened. 'You heard Simon.' He waved a hand at Fenchurch. 'I'm consulting on this case. That's your case too. So you need to talk.'

'To Sherlock Holmes, Consulting Detective? Brilliant.' Shepherd grinned. 'Until we're told otherwise, our cases aren't the same.'

'Listen, nobody knows the Marksman better than me.'

'And I'm very pleased for you. But this is nothing to do with Mark Torrance, so you can leave us be.'

'Why were you there, Sergeant?'

'Didn't your friendly guards tell you?'

'Listen to me, Sergeant, your chief constable and the Met's Commissioner have asked me, given my vast and varied experience, to help close out this case. I'm a superintendent. I outrank you. So you're going to tell me precisely why you were there.'

Shepherd clicked his tongue a few times. Then smiled. 'We needed to speak to Mr Torrance as part of an ongoing enquiry.'

'Come on. Don't give me that.'

'It's true. We spoke to him and excluded him from our inquiries.' Shepherd blew air up his face. 'Mark Torrance is an old man who killed a lot of people a long time ago but has lost his marbles since. He's got nothing to do with this case other than a slight tangent. Just an unfortunate coincidence that a murder victim happened to be a Mark Torrance fanboy.'

Broadfoot flashed up his eyebrows. 'And you're absolutely certain of that?'

'Absolutely certain, *sir*.'

'You thought you had a copycat hitman on your hands, didn't you? Someone copying Mark Torrance.'

'Not exactly.' Shepherd slouched back against the wall. 'Thomas Riley was obsessed with him. His home office walls are covered with news stories about the Marksman. Posters from the film. A bookshelf full of books on him. Stolen case files. But he's dead and we don't know who killed him.'

'Well. Nobody knows Torrance like I do.' Broadfoot clenched his jaw, his teeth pushing the lined skin outwards. 'I caught him. Helped prosecute him. Sat in on all the interviews. In any case, Torrance can't be involved in anything other than playing with his own imagination. He's had minimal contact with the outside world for over twenty-five years.'

'We don't think he was involved.'

Broadfoot slurped coffee through the lid and grimaced.

Shepherd smiled. 'Can you trust his guards?'

The entire left side of Broadfoot's smug porcelain face twisted up. 'The prison staff are under twenty-four-hour surveillance. Calls, movements, bank records, family members too. Mark Torrance isn't killing anybody with *their* assistance. Besides, Torrance was a sole operator. He didn't collaborate. He doesn't speak to anyone. He's not involved in your case.' He patted his hair, flattening the quiff slightly. 'You believe Mr Riley was a serial killer, don't you?'

Shepherd shook his head. 'We don't. The police in Edinburgh do.'

'Ah yes. But you're an Edinburgh cop, aren't you?'

'You've done your homework.'

'Know thy enemy.' Broadfoot stuffed his hands in his pockets. 'Let me tell you a story. Have you ever heard of Quantico?'

'FBI Academy in Virginia.'

'Top of the class, Victoria. The Behavioral Sciences Unit is based there. I was seconded for a few months at a time over a four-year period. Same as Fenchurch here. Very interesting work, but of course I had very little to do in the evenings and at weekends. Once you've eaten, it's going through more casework or maybe going to the movies, as they'd say. Some went to bars, others the gym. But I started doing homework. Poring through boxes and boxes of paperwork, day in, day out, searching for serial killers and hitmen who operated in the same way as Torrance did.'

Vicky couldn't follow where he was going with this. If he

was going anywhere. Broadfoot was just a pompous old man who needed to feel important. Put himself front and centre of any investigation.

Shepherd and Fenchurch clearly thought the same from the glazed expressions on their faces.

'Mark Torrance thought he could get away with what he was doing.' Broadfoot seemed to shiver. 'The things I've seen...'

'Even after all your time in Quantico, working with the FBI, they still get to you?'

Broadfoot locked eyes with Shepherd, tilting his head to the side. 'The day they stop scaring the bejesus out of me is the day I give up.'

Vicky was close to rolling her eyes. Anything keeping her away from painkillers was getting worse by the second. 'This going somewhere?'

Broadfoot shot Vicky a warning glare and gave a flash of teeth. 'We have hitmen this side of the Pond. The Cosa Nostra in Sicily, for instance. But the United States of America is a melting pot. They've got gangs from all nations working over there. Russians, Italians, Albanians, Chinese, Japanese and, of course, Mexican. The cartels alone have three operatives who had a similar MO to Mark Torrance. But a hitman is just a serial killer who does it for money rather than because the voices in his head tell him to or whatever. They both hunt their targets with the sole intention of murdering them and usually have no relationship with their victims.' He paused, licking his lips. 'Virtually all serial killers prey on strangers, killing them for reasons unknown to anyone but themselves. Some set of rules being transgressed. Lifestyle choices they don't approve of – prostitutes, rent boys. Colour, gender. Even age. But whatever the MO, most serial killers prefer to kill strangers. Why? For one, it makes you harder to catch. Also, it's easier to torture and kill someone you don't know.'

'Sounds like you spent your time in America very wisely.' Shepherd folded his arms. 'What's your point, caller?'

'The thing with Mark Torrance is, like I say, he never talked. Except to admit his crimes. Just sat there, stony silent. We read out a charge, he said guilty or not guilty. Because of that, we could never trace his crimes back to a client. The paper trail was very clean. Makes it frustrating as whoever it was must've been using other people since. Probably coming from abroad. Just one hit and they leave the country before we know what's happened.'

'But?'

'When it got personal for him, that's when it ended. He stopped it being about cold, measured kills and took down one of the team chasing him. Not one of my guys, but still... When it gets personal, that's when they slip up.'

Shepherd gave a polite smile. 'Is this your way of saying our guy has slipped up?'

Broadfoot leaned forward. 'We might have a way of finding your killer. Follow me.'

Vicky walked lockstep alongside Fenchurch, behind Shepherd and Broadfoot.

Broadfoot opened a meeting room door and gestured for them to go first.

A small man was perched on the edge of the desk, his trousers bunched together round his crotch. Staring at his phone.

Broadfoot sat at the head of the table. 'I've recently been working with DCI Howard Savage of the Trafficking & Prostitution Unit. They have a UK-wide remit, as I'm sure you know. Mr

Savage has been called to Scotland Yard today, so he won't be able to meet with us. But we've also been working with Police Scotland's Sexual Offences unit.'

Vicky narrowed her eyes. 'Sharon McNeill's team?'

Broadfoot waved a hand over to the guy at the side. 'DS Damian McCrea from her unit is down here on secondment.'

'Three days a week.' McCrea stood up and waved. Glasgow accent. 'Used to be in the Glasgow MIT but had a bit of a change of heart after my mentor popped his clogs earlier this year. Wanted to do something with my life. So I'm working for DI McNeill. Sharon's sent me down here to investigate the gang Gavin and Doug Mason worked for.'

Vicky looked around at Shepherd and saw him raising his eyebrow. 'You got a name for them?'

'No.' McCrea sniffed. 'They don't have one. Or nothing that we've heard of.' He sighed. 'But we believe Keith Dawson was a lawyer for the group.'

'Really? Well done. We didn't know that a few hours ago.'

'Sarky bugger.' McCrea sniffed again. 'Boy defended a few of the bozos who stood trial in this group. But he turned to our side. Acted for Doug and Gavin to help get their deal but passed over evidence.'

'We know this.'

'Thing is, the gang are still operating. We've heard whispers of some small pockets repeating what happened before. Coming from different parts of Europe, through different routes than before. And Thomas Riley has been back working for them. Mostly money laundering, but he's done some "wet work".' He did the rabbit ears. 'It means killing people.'

'I know what it means.' Shepherd frowned. 'So Riley *was* an assassin?'

'Right. We think we know six hits carried out by him in the last two years. People who used to be in that organisation, who aren't anymore. People who gave us evidence.'

'So you've got a leak?'

'Maybe, aye.' McCrea put his mobile away. 'I was at the crime scene yesterday. You found some trinkets in his house. Ears of his victims. So, while he wasn't killing, he'd extended his work into the personal domain. Satisfied his bloodlust that way. Until he started killing again.'

Vicky was close to snapping here. 'Do you know who killed him?'

'Well. We thought we knew *why*. Obviously bumping off former members of this organisation. Gavin, Douglas, Thomas, Keith. While we don't have a suspect, this might help find one.'

Fenchurch sat back, arms folded. 'William Dewar.'

'Excuse me?'

'You heard me. William Dewar. Son of the last victim of the Ma—'

'Billy Dewar?' Vicky laughed. 'No. It's not him.'

Fenchurch eyed her. 'Go on?'

'Well, he works in Dundee as a cop. He's... He's useless.'

'So you think.' Fenchurch refolded his arms. 'Been going through the file and the fact his old man was killed by Mark Torrance stood out to me.'

Broadfoot gestured at him, like he was on some kind of gameshow. 'You think Dewar's blaming these people for what happened to his father?'

'Not quite, but his father being killed by the Marksman got me thinking.' Fenchurch leaned across the table. 'His mother had been visiting Torrance for the last seven years, tormenting him. Right? But according to the file, Billy Dewar applied several times to see Torrance.'

Broadfoot nodded. 'I let the first few go through, but Torrance refused.'

'Then he didn't.'

'And I made sure I was there to witness it. He was furious. Shouting and screaming. Torrance just sat there and took it. Smiling. Dewar never went back.'

Vicky wasn't buying any of it. 'It's a grieving kid angry with his dad's killer. How does this connect with anything?'

'Thinking about it, might have something.' McCrea got to his feet and started prowling the room. 'Dewar worked as part of a case near Dundee. Van I'd been chasing from Glasgow. Four trafficked Vietnamese women were found dead in the back.'

'Jesus Christ.'

'Aye.' McCrea winced in a way that only a man who'd seen true suffering would. 'DI McNeill's unit took over the case, but William Dewar was the first-attending officer. He got there as the last one died. It's possible they named names. And there's some evidence the Marksman worked for a predecessor to this group.'

Broadfoot clapped Fenchurch on the arm. 'Your father called them the Machine.'

Fenchurch glowered at him but didn't say anything. 'So it stands to reason that Dewar has confused or conflated both groups and is taking them out, one by one.'

Vicky didn't know whether to buy it. 'Assuming he killed them, it took a lot of chicanery. A lot of travel. Trying to throw us off the scent.'

Shepherd laughed. 'You think he's pulled a Clark Kent?

Trying to appear bumbling and inept, but really he's a vicious cold-blooded killer.'

'It all hangs together.' Fenchurch counted on his fingers, starting with his thumb. 'He was in Dundee when Gavin Mason was killed. Copper working the case too, so his DNA is excluded. Off-duty when Thomas Riley was murdered. There was a burner phone on Douglas. Lots of calls from Dundee.' He narrowed his eyes at her. 'Someone talked Doug into killing himself in front of you to throw you off the scent. Throw us all off the scent.'

Broadfoot raised a hand. 'Could be that Dewar and Doug were working together, which is why Dewar let Doug go at Morgan Miller's home.'

'Shit.' Vicky tried to lay it all out in her head, end-to-end. It all stacked up. All of it. Dewar was close to every murder. Except... 'But he was in Dundee when Keith was killed this morning.'

'Nope, he was down here.' Fenchurch folded his arms again. 'He's driving home now, actually. According to my team, he's just passed Wetherby Services.'

'Shit.'

'Told his sergeant he's getting some parts for his girlfriend's dad's Capri from a garage in North London.' McCrea smirked. 'Drove himself down, even with his dodgy foot, which I don't believe is actually injured.'

Broadfoot got up. 'Well, I'm heading back up to Scotland to interview him. You're welcome to join me.'

54

'Flight's in forty mins, so we'd better head to security.' Broadfoot and McCrea jogged off into the bowels of the airport.

No way were they missing the flight up to Scotland.

'I'll get our tickets.' Shepherd shuffled over to the desk.

The airport entrance wasn't exactly teeming with people. Still had its armed guards. Possible that a politician used it, but the cabinet wasn't exactly stuffed with Scottish Tories.

Vicky sighed.

Fenchurch glanced at her. 'You okay there?'

'I'm going to get such a doing for this. A same day return flight from Edinburgh to London is really expensive. To pull it forward and return three hours earlier?'

'Your boss told you to come down, right?'

'Right, but I haven't cleared this.'

'I'll square it off with him. Forrester seems like a decent guy.'

'Decent enough, aye. Listen, I met Broadfoot in Dundee the

other day. Might even be yesterday, I'm losing track of time.' She rubbed at her aching forehead. 'I need some paracetamol. Or a new head.'

Fenchurch winced. 'He's a slippery bugger, so watch your step.'

'Slippery, how?'

'The perils of being a DCI is you stop attending crime scenes and start having to do admin and sit on telephone calls with other cops all day. Your Forrester. Some guy called Davenport. And bloody Broadfoot, lording it over us. Worked with him in the past. A good mate of mine reported him in one of our many drugs squads. He got burnt badly by it.'

'Ouch. By Broadfoot specifically?'

'Nah, he was a daft sod.' Fenchurch craned his necked to look over at the queues. 'So. You get everything you need?'

'I don't know. We came down to find a suspect, but we've got yet another victim. And another suspect.'

'Sounds familiar. You don't believe what they're saying about Dewar, do you?'

'Believe anything's possible but him? No, to be honest.' Shepherd was at the front of the queue, at least. 'What did he mean when he said the Machine?'

Fenchurch grimaced. 'My old man's a cop.'

'Mine too.'

Fenchurch smiled. 'Then you know where I'm coming from. After he retired, he was working in the archives in Lewisham. Using it to search for what happened…' His nose twitched and he shut his eyes. 'Anyway, he stumbled over this operation. Called it "the Machine". I won't bore you with the details, but Broadfoot pretty much did…'

'People trafficking?'

'Child abduction. A few other things. Nasty, nasty pricks.'

'What happened?'

'That law firm Keith Dawson was working for, Ogden & Makepeace. *Private Eye* called them Slowdown & Makecash. Had their fingers in lots of pies. Including the Machine. They were…' Fenchurch looked away, jaw clenched. 'Nasty bastards. Suffice it to say, the firm's no longer trading under that name on account of one of the names above the door serving forty years for various offences, not least child molestation and people trafficking.'

'*You* okay?'

'Not really. Just… This whole thing brings up a lot of memories.' Fenchurch flared his nostrils. 'He kidnapped my wife. And… Put it this way, he's not got any front teeth left.'

'Jesus Christ.'

Fenchurch swallowed hard. 'He was involved in my daughter's abduction.'

Vicky felt it deep in her gut. 'What?'

'Happened seventeen years ago.'

'I'm sorry to hear that. Are you okay?'

'Fine now.' A long, slow breath. 'I stopped short of killing him, but I kind of regret it. Knowing he's still alive. If anything happens to my girl or to my boy, I won't hesitate next time.'

Something stuck in Vicky's throat. Was this a setup? Had Shepherd got him to do this, get her into his confidence, then bang, arrest her? 'Must be tough living with that.'

'You've no idea.' But he was narrowing his eyes at her. 'You've done something similar, haven't you?'

She raised her hands. 'Woah, where's this come from?'

'The bags under your eyes, being so exhausted you slept in a stranger's car. I can tell the signs.'

She couldn't look at him. 'You're hardly a stranger.'

He gripped her by the shoulder. 'Are you planning it?'

'God no. Listen, I was forced to defend myself in an attempt on my life and the suspect died.'

'Been there, done that. Got T-shirts in any size you want, male or female cuts.'

His mobile blasted out. Fenchurch checked it. 'It's my wife, so I better take this.' But instead of that, he looked right at her. 'Don't tell me what it is, Vicky. But learn to live with yourself and your decisions. Whatever it is. From the little I've seen, I can tell you're a good cop. I'd hate to see you go down for something I could've easily done myself.'

Shepherd was walking towards them.

55

The cold air hit Vicky like a splash of icy water. 'Oof, I hadn't packed for Edinburgh.'

A bus pulled in with a slow hiss. Over the way was a giant parking complex. People headed for the trams.

'Relax, we'll be heading north soon enough.' Shepherd laughed. 'I take it uniform have got Billy Dewar?'

'Nope.' Broadfoot shook his head. 'Dundee plod went around to his flat. No answer at the door. Spoke to a few neighbours. Haven't seen him since yesterday morning, which matches the story we've got. Drove down to London after his shift yesterday.'

Vicky had seen him at his mother's. Long drive after that, through the night, but then she knew a thing or two about not sleeping. Her gut was burning.

Shepherd led her across the walkway over to the parking tower, following McCrea and Broadfoot into the open-sided parking area, where cars pulled in and buggered off even quicker.

A giant man helped his wife with some luggage. She pecked him on the cheek and walked off into the terminal. She stopped twice to look back at him. He was standing there, smiling and watching her go.

McCrea and Broadfoot walked over to the lift, presumably heading for McCrea's car.

Shepherd walked over to his Tesla and opened the door.

The door almost slammed with the wind. Then it did.

Vicky wrestled it open and got in, riding shotgun. She wished she had one on her. She got out her phone and hit dial.

Shepherd squealed off, racing towards the barrier, behind a black Focus. McCrea was reaching out to pay.

Sharon answered the call. 'Hey, Vicky, you okay?'

'Finally, you've deigned to take my call.'

'Been in meetings all afternoon.' Her yawn buffeted against the speaker. 'What's up?'

'Talk to me about Damian McCrea?'

'Damian? Why?'

'Flew up with us.'

'What? Christ, I *told* him to stay in bloody London until Friday.'

Shepherd hammered the horn, but the barrier rose and he sped off. 'Bloody useless bastard.'

'Do you mind?' Vicky elbowed him. 'Okay, forget about that. How long has he been working down there?'

'A few months now. At first it was remote, then I had to get him down pretty much full-time.'

Shepherd pulled forward and tapped his debit card against the machine, then the barrier rose up and he drove off.

'The powers that be up here want to treat Scotland as an island, but we've got so much interaction with the rest of the

UK. So of course I need to engage with the Met. Trouble with that lot is they think they can still run national policing initiatives from the southeast. Not much use when they're bringing in women from ferries at Troon or Aberdeen, is it? Wasn't easy running that kind of investigation during a pandemic. Hardly any flights. Moaned about taking the train down. His hotel rooms kept getting cancelled because of travel isolation. You name it. When I sent him down there, it was to dot the Is and cross the Ts.'

Aye, that was a woman under a huge amount of stress.

'Sharon, I'm sure it'll all come out in the wash. I'm guessing the meeting was—'

'—the world's most-boring conference call with Messrs Forrester, Davenport and Fenchurch. Aye. Bloody twat of a boss told me to attend, but I'll be buggered if I'm dialling back in.'

'What do you think of the theory they've cooked up?'

'What, Billy Dewar? Solid motive, sadly. I think it holds water.'

'I've met this Dewar kid a few times. He's wetter than water.'

'Come on, Vicky. Killers come in all shapes and sizes. Just takes one thing for good men to crack.' Sharon paused. 'And I saw those poor women in the back of that van, Vicky. It was barbaric. It's enough to make anyone flip over. Especially after what he'd been through as a kid.'

56

The whole street is dark, the streetlights flickering. Spaced so far apart. The van's on the street, ready to take them away from this godforsaken town, engine pluming.

He takes a look around the street. This is far from the perfect house. Plenty of curtain twitchers overlooking it. Still, it's between school home time and work home time, so they might be okay.

Inside the house, he's sitting by the window, whisky glass in hand. Throws it back and tops it up, splashing Grouse all over the table. The clock on the mantelpiece reads 16:24. Very early to be getting tanked up.

He stares at the door, at the cracked paint. Shivering. The cold bites at his fatigue, though, giving him a bit of energy.

Just the syringe in his left pocket. Already loaded. Ready. Running low on this shit, but he needs to shut him up. Different task for him. End game now, so spicing things up a bit is what it's all about.

He gives the door a knock and sucks in a deep breath.

'Just a minute!' The voice comes from inside the house. Harsh. Like a drill. The door opens. A fat man with Teddy Boy hair stands in the doorway. Big guy. Huge gut.

He gives a smile and flashes his ID. 'DI Alex Moffett, sir. Looking for George Dodds?'

'Aye?'

'Mind if I come inside?'

'I do, actually. The wife's away and I'm trying to catch up on my telly.'

'It won't take a minute. It's important.'

'Let me see that ID.' George reaches out a hand.

He hands it over and stands there smiling. 'I'm based in Dundee, sir.'

'With that accent?'

He smiles. 'Know how many times a day I get that?'

George grins. 'Can imagine.' But he doesn't hand back the ID just yet. 'Hard to tell with your mask on.'

He flips it down to show the rest of his face. Would rather avoid that, but hey ho.

Seems to satisfy George, but only partially. 'Never seen that name spelled that way.'

'Mine's the original. Much rarer.'

'Imagine it is.' Now George hands it back then steps back into the house. 'In you come, pal.'

He follows him inside. So risky, but this is pure improvisation. No plan tonight, just see how it goes. Feels the electricity pulsing through him. The place is cold, like there's a window open. Heating off to save all those pennies. George must have a thick whisky coat on today.

'So, what's this—'

He's on George before he can finish the sentence. Jabbing into his neck, in just the right spot, and George tumbles down to the floor. Wriggling and kicking, furious eyes staring up at him. Then he's just a sack of potatoes, empty and lifeless, eyes open wide. And he can carry a sack of spuds. George is nowhere near as heavy as he expected, so he walks him back out, down to the van. Engine still pluming in the cold air. Taste the metallic clouds.

He slides the back door open and the light flicks on. The sodden mattress lies there. God knows what the previous owner used it for, but it's perfect for this.

He grabs George by the armpits and hauls him up to standing, then nudges him inside. Takes a while to get the belt strapped on. No chance George is wriggling his way out of it. Not tonight, not tomorrow.

He slides the door shut and gets in.

The fresh can of WakeyWakey in the door is the best thing he's ever seen in his life. Going to need it to get through tonight.

He guns the engine and eases off along the street, sipping peppermint and pear drink.

57

Vicky hadn't experienced driving like this since her dad rage-drove home a couple of times. Terrifying, but he always claimed he was in control. Never felt it.

Shepherd pulled in off the roundabout at the start of Dundee. 'Siri, call Damian McCrea.' He put it on speaker and the ringtone drilled into Vicky's skull.

Shrill, harsh and a million other things. This headache wasn't clearing. It better not be bloody covid again.

The call was answered. 'Luke, my man!'

'Damian, thank you for finally answering.'

'Eh, mobile hasn't rang all the way back from Edinburgh?'

Shepherd scowled at it. 'Where are you?'

'Hang on a sec.' His voice went all muffled. 'Derek thinks we're just passing Perth.'

'*Perth*?' Shepherd looked like he was going to smash the phone. 'We're already in Dundee.'

'Stopped at Kinross services for a bite to eat.'

'Well, can you tell him to stop driving like my mum and put his foot down.'

'Won't take a telling from me.'

'Right.' Another sigh. 'We're going to head around to Dewar's flat. See you there.'

'Cheers, man.' And he was gone.

Shepherd put the mobile away. 'Honestly. I bet Sharon thought she was getting a police officer when she hired him, but instead she got a useless sod.'

Vicky glanced over at him. 'You know her?'

'Aye, quite well.' His eyes were tracking the road. 'Sharon asked me if I knew him. Spoke to his previous boss in Glasgow for her. Guy I'd, well, worked with.'

'You mean investigated?'

Shepherd grinned. 'Anyway. He told me McCrea was a "killer". Said he'd be sad to lose him. Never believe a previous line manager's glowing praise.'

'Considine is a great officer. You're welcome to him.'

Shepherd didn't laugh. 'What's your beef with the lad?'

Vicky got out her phone and started dialling. 'Just a brown-noser, that's all.'

Shepherd drove on, heading into Dundee. Yet another sigh. 'Gives that vibe, that's for sure. Still, he seems like a good cop.'

'There you go. Sharon was mad to ask you if anyone was any use.'

The call was answered. Howling wind buffeted the phone. 'Evening, PC Johnny Gilmour—'

The rest was snatched away by the wind.

'Johnny, it's DI Vicky Dodds. Need an update on the address in Dens Road you're monitoring.'

'Aye, nobody was there.'

'Was?'

'Well, we got called away. They're shutting the bridge because of the wind, so we need to—'

'Get back around there!'

'Sorry, but those are orders from my boss—'

'Right, I get it.' Now Vicky was the one sighing. 'I'll be in touch.' She killed the call and dialled Forrester's number.

Answered straight away.

'Sir, it's Vicky. I need you to get some of our uniform resource redeployed.'

'What the bloody hell's going on? I thought you were in London?'

'We were, but we—'

'Why am I finding out from Simon bloody Fenchurch that you've flown back to Edinburgh?'

'Sorry, sir, I tried calling but—'

'Didn't try hard enough.' Forrester paused, the background drone of the office swelling up around him. 'My office, now.'

58

'It's more that I'm disappointed.' Forrester sat in his office chair, shifting his gaze between them, jaw clenched tight, nostrils flaring. 'Whatever it is you pair are cooking up here, you've kept me out of the loop. Vicky, I'm your boss.' He was staring hard at her. She knew when he used her name, he meant business. 'I'm your *friend*. You're supposed to keep me updated.'

Shepherd raised his hand. 'Can I inter—'

'No, Luke. You can't.' Forrester glowered at him. 'I'm most disappointed with you. You're a pal. Or supposed to be. You didn't think to text me? Give me a bell? Sitting on that plane, waiting to take off? You can have your mobile on the whole bloody flight nowadays, pretty much.'

Shepherd refolded his arms, keeping his eyes narrow. 'David, you mind if we have a minute to ourselves? Just you and me?'

Forrester sat back, laughing. 'This just gets better and better.'

'I'm serious.'

Forrester waved her off. 'Go on, then. Let's see what the golden boy here has to say for himself.'

Vicky got up and left the room as quickly as she could, slamming the door behind her. Felt like being back at school.

She got out her phone and glanced back at the door before hitting dial. Whatever they were talking about in there, they were doing it quietly.

'Hey, Vicky, you okay?'

Hearing Sharon's voice should've reassured her but it didn't. 'Why wouldn't I be?'

'Well, I heard what happened. And you keep calling me.'

'Right, right.' Vicky stepped away from the door and kept her voice low. 'Luke and I were in with Forrester and he's pushed me out.'

'Seriously?'

Vicky shoved her free hand in her pocket. 'I hope it's because those two are pals. Trying to appeal to Forrester's better nature.'

'Has he got one?'

Vicky laughed. 'Not sure.'

'But you're still worried it's because Shepherd is a Complaints DCI, right?'

Vicky couldn't speak.

'Well, I was worried too, but I called my ex. Scott bloody Cullen. He insists Luke's all above board now. Something went down, I don't know what, but as far as Scott's concerned, Luke's definitely not working for Professional Standards and Ethics. And he's not investigating you.'

'You can't be sure of that.'

'I can. You know he's ex-Complaints. He knows you know.

That means he can't be investigating you. If he's actually there to investigate someone, it's not you.'

'I've heard it all before, Sharon, but I don't believe it.'

'You are in the clear.' Sharon gave a pause for the words to sink in. 'Nobody knows, Vicky. Nobody can know. I'm the only one who was there and I'd never tell. Besides, you did what you had to. You acted in self-defence. We just finessed things a bit.'

Vicky let her breath go, but her chest felt so tight. 'I can't sleep, Sharon. Every night, I just lie awake thinking about what I did. If I could take it back, I would.'

'Listen, you made the right choice. He had crooked cops working for him. He would've got away with it. Or if he hadn't, what would've happened to you or your kids is... Well.'

Vicky swallowed. Couldn't speak.

'You did it at the only time you could. None of his colleagues knew about you or what you knew about them. We made it seem like he was the aggressor and you were the innocent.'

'But I worry it could still happen.'

'It won't, Vicky. It can't. Your family's safe. Your name was kept out of the press for that reason.'

The door clattered open and Forrester stepped out first, head hanging low. He rubbed his hands together. 'Right, you pair get on over to Dewar's now, okay? Don't want Broadfoot catching him first.'

'Thanks.' Vicky walked off, but the last thing she wanted was to thank him, especially when their uniform cover had been taken from them.

Shepherd was keeping pace with her through the empty office. 'You okay?'

'Just wondering how you persuaded Forrester.'

'Told him how good an officer you are, Vicky. And how we caught a murder down there that Fenchurch won't be able to solve.'

'He's not that petty.'

'No, but he's still petty enough to want to get one over another cop on those conference calls.'

59

He sits back in the bus shelter, hiding from the street. Pretty dark now, the sun now set but still giving off a glow. Not that he could see it behind the clouds in this place. The floodlights at both Dens Park and Tannadice are on tonight. He has no idea who'd be playing. Possibly just a maintenance thing.

Still.

No sign of Billy Dewar.

A gang of kids in black T-shirts are outside the block of flats, sucking on vape sticks. One of their mobiles blasts out heavy metal, the kind of shite he'd have listened to as a kid – all those CDs were now boxed away in his loft – but it sounds all tinny and shrill instead of like the gates of Hell have opened.

Lights on inside the flats, but Dewar's is dark. Least, he thinks it's Dewar's.

A couple face each other either side of a car parked across the road, whisper-shouting an argument. Neither of them notices him.

A loud rattling comes from over by the football stadiums and, sure enough, Dewar's car rumbles over. Low-slung Japanese thing from at least twenty years ago. Surprisingly, it still drives, even got the div from here to London and back.

How the hell is he going to get over there, knock him out and steal his car with him in it with all these people around?

Sod it. Fortune favours the brave.

He crosses the road and waves at Dewar as the car comes in to park. 'Police!' He holds out the shonky warrant car. 'Need a word.'

The engine rattles and dies. Dewar reaches over and opens the passenger door. 'What's up?'

He gets in. 'Easier if you drive, sir.'

'Eh? Get out of my car!'

'William Dewar, I've been sent to bring you back in to help the murder investigation.' He pushes the warrant card in his face, but the wee guy's gripping the wheel tight. 'I work with Luke Shepherd.'

That seems to ease Dewar. 'Big Luke?'

'Right. You've met him?'

'Aye, seems like a good lad.' His hands grab the key, but he doesn't twist. 'What did you say your name was?'

'DI Alex Moffett. With an E and two T's.'

'Right. Odd.' He twists the ignition. 'Better put your belt on, sir.'

Good boy.

He complies and sits back, hands in his pockets, cradling the syringe, then leans forward to check the wing mirror.

A van's headlights light up and starts following them.

He leans back in the seat and waves to the left. 'Pull in down there.'

'Eh? That's not the way to the station.'

'Someone's following us.'

Dewar glances at the rear-view. 'Shite and onions.' He takes the turning, his car bumping the pavement.

One of those post-industrial streets you only really seem to get in this town. Not in Edinburgh, Aberdeen or even Glasgow. The lock-up garages sit in darkness.

'Pull in.'

'What? Here?'

'Please. It's important.'

'Wait a second, I'm not—'

He jabs the needle into Dewar's vein. Covers his hand over his mouth, raises Dewar's foot off the pedal, then he steers the car towards the garages, and jerks on the handbrake.

The car stalls.

He gives Dewar a minute or two to settle.

Aye, he's gone. Just wild eyes looking at him.

He opens the passenger door and gets out. No sounds, just distant traffic swooshing against the rain up on Dens Road.

Headlights follow down and the van pulls in behind.

He walks around the car, opens the driver's door and eases Dewar out. He hauls him over to the van and is almost out of breath. All that running, all that boot camp fitness shite, it isn't enough to carry a skinny wee bugger five metres.

Still, the door slides open and Broadfoot's there. Crouching, hat on, collar up. He hops down to help him get Dewar into the back. Sticks the lump on a mattress, next to where an old man's lying. Eyes open, but paralysed.

'Now, you grab his car and follow. It'll be over soon.' Broadfoot gives him a pat on the arm. 'Good work, Damo.'

Perfect time for his phone to ring with the boss's number on the screen.

60

Vicky got out and walked along the quiet street beside Shepherd. Still no sign of any uniform support, but the pair of them could handle the kids lurking around. Skateboards and heavy metal T-shirts... Like the Nineties hadn't happened. Or they were destined to keep repeating them.

She still didn't know what to believe about Shepherd. Until this was over, the jury was out on him. If he was investigating her, well, she knew she deserved what was coming to her.

Bella, Jamie and Rob didn't, though. And she'd done it for them. To protect them.

Fenchurch, though, he seemed to know what it was like. She'd only just met the guy, but she could see the darkness in his eyes. How lost he was. How damaged he'd been by what he'd gone through.

She'd killed a man, sure, but those kinds of men would stop at nothing to make people pay for trying to bring them to justice.

Sitting on the plane, waiting to take off, she'd googled Fenchurch and found out what he'd been through. Losing his daughter for ten years. While he'd found her, it had cost him greatly. And her too.

Vicky had to reconcile herself with the fact she'd spared Bella or Jamie that ordeal.

Her mobile rang:

Mum calling...

She answered it, keeping on walking. 'Hey, Mum, you okay?'

'Victoria, have you heard from your father?'

'No, why?'

'Well, I'm down seeing your auntie Pam in Milngavie and he's not answering the phone. I told him to stick a pasta bake in the oven for his tea. There's a *Pointless* special on tonight and I wanted him to tape it.'

'Sorry, Mum. I'll let you know if he gets in touch.'

'Okay. Thank you. I'm worried he's not taken his pills.'

There it was. The real reason, hidden behind the excuse. 'I'll make sure of it, Mum.'

'How are you?'

'Busy, Mum. Got to go.'

'Okay, Victoria.' And she was gone.

Shepherd stopped, mobile to his ear. 'I'll keep an eye out for him. Thanks.' He ended the call and put the phone away. 'Well, sounds like Damian McCrea is going to be the death of Sharon McNeill after all.'

'Hopefully not literally.' Vicky hit the flat buzzer. 'What's up?'

'She's just spoken to him. Sent him here.' Shepherd was

searching around the street. 'This where the football grounds are?'

'Right. Dens Park's on this street. Tannadice is up on Sandeman Street. Closest two grounds in Britain.'

'Well, I never. More of a rugby guy myself.' Shepherd looked over her shoulder.

Damian McCrea was sidling up to them, hands in pockets. 'Hey, the boss called me. Luckily I was around the corner.'

Shepherd scowled at him. 'Where's Broadfoot?'

'Dropped me off. Said he's going to see Forrester. Got a few bridges to mend, judging by the dog's abuse he got down the phone.'

'From Forrester?'

'Aye, lad said he's feeling kept out of the loop.'

Shepherd loomed over him. 'Well, DI McNeill is disappointed in you for not being in London. Your role is to liaise with the Met, not to come up here with the Met.'

McCrea looked at Vicky like she could get him out of it. 'Isn't that the same thing?'

'No.' Shepherd pointed at the football stadium. 'She said she's been trying to call you. Wants you to get back to Bathgate and report on what you found down in London.'

'But my car's at Edinburgh airport.'

'There's a reason they built Edinburgh Gateway station. There's a station here in Dundee. Sure you can swap at Perth or Cupar or some mountain village in Fife to get back to base.'

'Right. Supposed to take orders from you, am I?'

'You hung up on her before she could give you an order.'

'You're the same rank as me so I'll be buggered if I'm taking—'

'Call her back.' Spoken with the air of an energised DCI,

not a jaded DS. 'Jesus Christ, I shouldn't be the one telling you that.'

'Right.' McCrea took one last look at them, then strode off into the night.

'Absolute clown.' Shepherd spat out the words, loud enough that McCrea must've heard. He jabbed the intercom button, then held it down. 'Where the hell is he?'

'Don't you think you might've been a bit hard on him, Luke?'

He lifted a shoulder. 'Just following orders.'

'Mind not doing that?' The entrycom had a video screen. A tired-looking young woman yawning into her fist. 'Trying to get some sleep here.'

'Police.' Shepherd shoved his warrant card up against the tiny camera dot above. 'Looking for Billy Dewar.'

'He's not back yet.'

Vicky tilted her head to the side. 'He lives here?'

'Aye.'

'With you?'

'Are you stupid or something?'

'You're his girlfriend?'

'Aye.' She seemed to shiver. 'And I tested positive for covid yesterday, so I can't come out and you lot can't come in. Eighteen months I've avoided it and I test positive this morning when he's away. Then I start to feel like someone's standing on my chest.'

'Do you know where he is?'

'Billy's getting a battery housing for my dad's old Capri. Told him not to bother, but it's Dad's fiftieth and Billy wanted to treat him, so we've been doing up that old banger, good as new. Dropped a battery on his foot on Sunday.'

What the hell? It was all true?

'Thank you for your time.' Vicky stepped back, over to Shepherd, who had his mobile to his ear. 'It's all checking out. But… where the hell is he?'

'Elvis.' Shepherd smiled at Vicky. 'Need an updated trace on those plates.' He paused. 'Okay. Cheers.' He put the phone away. 'Last sighting of Dewar's car was two minutes ago, just getting on the Kingsway and heading towards Perth.'

'He's heading away from Dundee?' Vicky grimaced. 'Dewar's heading to his mother's.'

61

McCrea pulled up at the lights. And just sits there. Keeping quiet. So close to the end of their little plan.

His old boss was right. Sharon McNeill is an arsehole. So far up herself. Thinks she's God's gift to policing. And who is she? Just some—

Ah, sod it. Not worth thinking about.

McCrea drums his thumbs on the steering wheel.

A young mother walks past the car, pushing her double buggy, two horrible little brats inside, screaming their heads off. In the depths of a sugar rush. Way too late for them to be out.

McCrea pulls away, the engine grumbling, like it was in too high a gear. Dewar fancies himself an amateur mechanic, but this thing needed a professional service, or scrapping.

Up ahead, the van pulls into a back road in a village he doesn't know. Near the Tay, according to the crappy old satnav stuck to the dashboard, but there's no sign of the river. Just lots of semi-detached bungalows up ahead.

The van stops outside a house standing on its own, set back from the road.

He pulls in a few car lengths away, outside a drive. No other cars nearby, so he pushes the car door wide. The air chills him, makes him start to shake and shiver.

He gets out and walks over, hood up.

Broadfoot leans against the van. 'She's in.'

'Sure?'

'Car in the drive. Radio on. Cooking smells. God, you are a cop, aren't you?'

'Of course, it's just...' McCrea's mouth is dry. 'I'm nervous.'

'Damo, mate, this ain't your first rodeo. Sure, I got Gavin and Keith, but you were the one who tipped Doug over the edge. I'd never have thought about doing it that way, but you got him to kill himself in exchange for protecting Emma and his mother. Excellent work.'

'Eh, thanks.'

'And you killed Thomas Riley. On your own. You did all the prep work, knew his movements, knew when to strike. And boy did you strike.'

McCrea knows Broadfoot's right, but still. It's taking someone's life. 'You want me to walk into her home and shoot her?'

'Our objective here is to kill her and make it look like her son did it. Straight in the head when she opens the door. Chase her down the garden path and shoot her in the middle of the road if you like. But she has to die. And we should really get a move on. There's a short window to exploit here; I suggest we get on with it.'

'What if nobody's home?'

'Don't be so pessimistic, Damo. She's home.'

'What if she's home, but doesn't answer the door?'

'Who wouldn't answer the door to a couple of police officers?' Broadfoot flashes a card at him. DI Alex Moffett. Has his photo on it.

'Why would she let us inside?'

'Both DI Moffetts can be quite persuasive. And if that doesn't work, we pull her teeth out.'

'I can't just—'

'I'm joking. Damian, just take the gun. You know this is the right thing to do.'

'Now?'

'Good a time as any.'

He picks it up. Just a lump of metal, but it feels so heavy.

Broadfoot sticks his hand in his other pocket and takes out a handful of bullets. 'Take two. I'd advise you to aim for her head, close up. Should be enough to kill her. If not, fire again.'

They feel so light compared to what they could do. Barely any weight at all when you think about it. He searches for the latch to release the cylinder so he can load it, then slots in the first bullet. The second needs a bit of a shove but it goes in okay. He opens it again just to make sure, then pushes the cylinder back in place. 'So, do we get them out now? Or later?'

'Later. Always focus on control, Damo. Always. Let's get her sorted first.' Broadfoot tilts his head towards the house. 'Do it. Now.'

'Okay.' The gate creaks open, tearing out onto the quiet street. He pads up the short path towards the house. Tiny, just two front windows and a door. Old. Really old. One of those houses that'd be easy to get lost in, too. Slabs and steps lead up to the door, two box plants either side. Can smell them from here, stinking things. No flowerbeds in the front garden, just pebbles and bushes. Probably a kitchen area out the back.

Next door is on the market. Possibly empty. The other side seems pretty far off, far enough they won't hear a gun going off. He walks past a garden gnome. The fat little bastard is laughing at him. Up the steps and he stands at the door.

Blue paint flaking. Wide letterbox. Another stretched mouth. Everybody is laughing. Everything is laughing at him. He can hear the sound of it in his head, feel it in his shoulder blades, in his knees, in his toes.

A deep rumble, car engine, traffic accident, factory roar, bomb blast. Noise. All noise at once. Everywhere. Overpowering. The touch of it. In his hair, on his neck, on his cheek like a hostile kiss. In these clothes. He isn't a killer.

No, he is.

He breathes in the smell of frying onions and shivers.

Broadfoot leans over his shoulder, coffee breath on his face. 'Ring the bell, Damian.'

No choice, so he presses it, hard like DI Alex Moffett would, if he existed.

Even the bell sounds old, clanking in the wall behind his hand.

Broadfoot joins him on the top step. 'Need me to do the talking or are you okay?'

He isn't sure he *could* speak. His mouth is dry, lips frozen.

He can't shoot her.

Can he?

Killing Riley was different. He knew precisely what he'd done. He'd seen the files. Seen how he'd got away with it all. Seen *what* he'd got away with. Providing evidence against a criminal gang was one thing, but he'd been a beneficiary of their work. That house was because of them. The car. Never having to work, not having to get up and work for an arsehole like Sharon McNeill every day.

No, but he knew what Riley had also done. Those ears. Gave him no choice, really.

This isn't his fight, really, but killing her is key to them getting away with what they've done so far.

Get behind her, shoot her in the head, make sure she doesn't notice.

Footsteps inside. An eye at the spyglass. The door clunks a couple of times and a shaggy-haired old woman scowls out, frowning, looking between them. The metallic tang of lentil soup shrouding her, drowning out the onion smell. Sounds like Alice in Chains playing somewhere inside. Some sort of recognition flares in her eyes. 'Aye?'

'Police. Need a word with William Dewar.'

'What's he done?'

'Look, is he here?'

'Not to my knowledge.' She huffs out a deep sigh. Starts coiling wiry hair round her finger. 'Just shows up, does what he fancies, then leaves. Got his flat in town now.'

He flashes up his eyebrows, friendly, like DI Alex Moffett would. 'Can I take your name, madam?'

'Margaret Fields.' She stares at him, like she's daring him to just shoot her there and then. The woman he's going to kill tonight. Jesus Christ. 'Can I see some ID, lads?'

He steps forward, hands in pockets. Left was the gun. Right was a syringe. Fresh. Ready. The last one, but he hopes it won't be needed.

Also his credentials. He flashes them at her. 'DI Alex Moffett. Glasgow MIT. We need a word with William Dewar.'

She inspects the warrant card. Goes over it a few times.

Every line. Every dot of ink. Then she hands it back. 'What's he done?'

'Mind if we do this inside? Don't want to let the heat out.'

Her lips twitch. 'Okay, but get your masks on.' She opens the door wide and steps back. 'After you, gents.'

He blinks a few times, then puts his mask on and follows her inside. The door clicks behind them, the echo rattling around his head. The hall is dark. Heavy oak floor, green paint. Old oil pictures, like royalty lived here or something.

She paces along the hallway, then stops in a doorway and clears her throat. A rapid bark. 'Through here.'

He follows her into the long galley kitchen overlooking a dark garden. Looks like someone had just installed it. Smells like it, too.

'Cup of tea?' She goes over to a kettle on the worktop and fills it at the sink. 'You going to tell me what this is about?'

He reaches into his pocket for the syringe and uncaps the lid. He has to do it this way. The last wee tub of it.

She switches off the tap and thunks the kettle down on the base.

Another step across the laminate and he's just behind her.

She glances around. 'What the—?'

He smothers her mouth with his left and jabs the needle into her neck with his right.

Her hands reach up, fingernails clawing at his skin. Her teeth bite at his fingers.

He hammers down the plunger and she becomes like a doll, slumping in his arms. He shuffles her down onto the floor.

Margaret Fields lies there, spasms shivering across her body, the cold light almost making her glow. Staring up at him. Paralysed, but awake.

He pulls his mask off and sucks in a deep breath. Takes a step back to allow himself a look at the prone figure. Six hours and she'd be right as rain, give or take. But it'd all be over by then.

'Right, now, let's get the other two inside.' Broadfoot claps his arm. 'You're a natural at this.'

The last thing Damian McCrea wants to be was a natural born killer.

62

Vicky could barely hear the car sounds, just white noise from the road, the tyres swooshing through puddles. The wind buffeted the windows, rocking the car enough that she needed to compensate with the steering.

The dark night lit up with Shepherd's indicator, pulsing with its own Morse code. She shifted down and sped past a lorry, using the long straight to catch up with him, then followed him off the dual carriageway, winding up and over the slip road, then into Inchture. One of those blink-and-you'll-miss-it wee towns between Dundee and Perth. A reasonably fancy hotel opposite big housing estates, hidden behind trees.

Shepherd powered on through, at least twenty over the thirty limit. He squealed to a halt and parked up amongst the last houses.

Vicky pulled up at the side of the road between two cars and got out. The wind cut through the thick hedge in front of the house. Snow floated down, soft and pure, but not lying, just melting as soon as it kissed the pavement. The yellow street lighting was dyeing the snow like smoked haddock.

The house looked quiet inside. Nothing from the front, anyway, but a glow from the back.

Shepherd was staring at the car in front, mobile to his ear. 'This is Dewar's car. Thanks, Elvis. I owe you.' He pocketed the phone and stared at Vicky. 'No sign of him, though.'

Vicky nudged her door shut, then walked towards him. She slipped, tumbling to the stone slabs. Cracked her wrist off the ground. Grazed her knuckle. Tore her trousers at the knee.

Shepherd reached down to haul her up. 'Jesus, are you okay?'

'I'm fine.' Vicky staggered to her feet but felt dizzy.

The scraping gate sounded like someone was pulling her teeth out.

She followed him down the short path.

Lights on inside the house.

Vicky stopped dead.

In the sitting room, her dad was sitting on the settee, hands between his legs. Head rolled back. Eyes open.

What the hell?

What the hell was he doing there?

A big hand grabbed her jacket. 'Vicky, come on.' Shepherd hauled her back to the street.

'I need to get inside.'

'No, you don't. Vicky, we've called this in. Units are heading here now. This is their job.'

'I've got to go in!' Her wrist was throbbing, worse than her head. She tried to free her hand again and stumbled. Dropped to one knee. Pain shot through her kneecap. She shook free of Shepherd's grip finally and stepped out onto the road. A lorry boomed past, the clanking of its cargo driving like a nail gun right through her skull. She kneaded her temples, then looked back down the side lane. A long stretch, beech hedges on both sides. Easy enough to sneak into the back garden. 'Cover for me.'

'What?'

'I'll sneak around and break in.'

'No way.' Shepherd grabbed her arm again. 'That's a stupid plan. You'll get caught.'

'I've got to go in!'

'That's not a good idea.'

'It's a fucking shite idea. But Dewar's going to kill my dad! Do we have a choice? Dewar is going to murder my dad. He's going to murder—'

'It's way too dangerous, Vicky.' Shepherd was scowling at her.

'Of course it's dangerous. But I don't care. We're fucked any way I think about it.'

Shepherd shrugged. 'Nothing's going to persuade you, is it?'

'Nope.' Vicky staggered up the path, then crept through a side gate and eased across the damp lawn. She crouched as she neared the living room window and let herself peer in.

Dad was in the exact same position.

Wait. Dewar was next to him. Seemed out of it too.

What the hell was going on?

Both had their eyes open.

Shit.

Sux?

Margaret Fields was slumped on the armchair next to the fireplace.

Margaret and her son. But Vicky's dad? Why?

She crept to the opposite end of the window.

Damian McCrea was there, running a thumb over one of his eyebrows. He was talking, but the windows sucked in the sound.

Jesus Christ.

Him. He was behind it.

He'd killed them. Gavin, Thomas, Keith. Shit. He'd been in London for Keith.

Framing Dewar.

Vicky looked back at Shepherd, on the phone as per bloody usual. Lost in an argument. Sod it, she had to get in there.

She tried the door and it opened, so she stepped inside and nudged it to.

The voices were muffled. She inched down the hallway, bracing herself against the wall. Almost knocked a painting off. She stopped by the living room door and peeked inside the room.

McCrea was leaning back against the window now. Curtains bunched up behind him. Shoulders hunched over, forehead creased. The occasional nod.

BANG.

Ears ringing again. White noise screeching.

McCrea went down in front of the sofa.

Vicky ran into the room, over to McCrea.

He was dead, his chest a bloody mess.

'Victoria?'

She glanced back into the corner and narrowed her eyes, trying to resolve the gloom into a human being. Broadfoot stood there. Pale skin, almost blue. Dark rings round his red, red eyes. Sweat soaking his hair. He had a revolver in his hand, aimed at her head. 'Thank God you're here.'

Just looking at him made Vicky's head throb. 'What happened? What the hell's going on?'

Broadfoot lowered the gun. Sweat trickled down his forehead. Splashed on the floor. 'I thought he was a good guy, but... McCrea's been killing everyone. Tried to set up poor Dewar for this. I just got here. You see what he was doing?'

Her dad and Dewar looked like they'd had a few too many whiskies on Hogmanay. Same with Margaret Fields. But the trail of blood on the parquet in the corner...

Vicky pointed over to McCrea's corpse. 'Damian was sent home.'

'I offered to give him a lift. He was stuck in Dundee after his boss ordered him back to Bathgate. We heard your request on the radio as we were driving past, so we came here. We got around here only to find Margaret and your dad were both out of it.'

'Why did you shoot him?'

'Can't you see? Because he was going to kill them. He's been working with Dewar.'

It all slotted together.

'This is bullshit. *You* killed them, didn't you? Keith, Gavin, Doug, Thomas. You did it.'

Broadfoot's mouth hung open. 'What are you talking about?'

'You shot Damian. You were going to kill the rest of them, make it look like Damian killed them all.'

'Vicky. I know you had a traumatic—'

'This is nothing to do with me! You were going to torch the place, weren't you?'

Broadfoot stared down at the gun in his hand. 'Well, it's way too late for you.' He raised it and pointed it at her.

Vicky felt her heart pounding in her throat. 'I'm not alone. You know we've got backup.'

'You've just signed your own death certificate, I'm afraid. If it'd just been you, well, we could've let you go. Nobody would believe you, Victoria. Your word against mine. But if you've got friends outside? That's just too bad.' Broadfoot pointed the gun at Vicky's father. 'Might as well get this over with and start killing the guilty.'

Keep him talking. 'Why? Why him?'

'Your dad looked the other way to allow a good man to be taken out.'

'What?'

'Bottone. He was a mafioso, wanted by the Sicilians. He'd come over here, invested money in the club, hoping his public face kept him safe. Invested a lot in the community. Jobs. Charities. Your dad worked the football match. He was supposed to guard his post, but he was distracted, watching the game instead, while Mark Torrance killed him.'

'That's bullshit.'

'You can think that, but I've got CCTV that shows otherwise. Rangers had just equalised and he didn't seem too pleased.' Broadfoot walked over to her dad and put the gun against her dad's heart. His dodgy heart.

'Please, I just want to know why.'

Broadfoot smirked. 'Some people get away from justice. Gavin and Douglas Mason both worked for an organisation I helped take down, but they got a deal thanks to Keith Dawson. Thomas Riley was involved too, laundering money for them.'

'Why now?'

'Because they were conspiring. Getting the band back

together. Abusing girls again. Bringing them into the country again. I had to act now.'

'You and Damian were working on it as an official case. Why did you—'

'We didn't have the power to do anything, Victoria. Doug's involvement in the gang was more than just being a money guy; he was abusing kids. He was still doing it. Gavin and Doug had procured girls in the past, down in London, but they were doing it again up in Dundee. Doug killed himself because he was having sex with underage girls and he knew we knew. Persuaded him to kill himself. But Morgan Miller... She was just the tip of the iceberg.'

'Sharon McNeill's team are on to it now.'

'And they dropped the ball on it. Damian reported a lead a year ago. It went nowhere.'

'That why you killed him?'

He sighed. 'I've no faith in anyone up here. Any investigation will take time. Meanwhile, girls are being trafficked. I hoped Doug killing himself would make you think he was the killer, but sadly not. Too smart, aren't you?'

'You shouldn't have killed Thomas Riley. At least, not then.'

'Hard not to. Riley laundered money for them but kept a financial trail. He was a hitman for them, how he got started, but he progressed into being a serial killer in Edinburgh. Nobody could pin the crimes on him. We had no choice but kill him, don't you see? It's the natural thing to do.'

'Why are you doing this?'

'Because I've not got long left.'

'You're dying?'

'God no. That's such a cliché. No, I'm retiring. Building a

house down in Devon. Want to get all my ducks in a row before I have no influence left. Before people stop listening to me.'

Vicky had to keep him talking. Just had to. Dad could wake up. Take him out. 'These people escaped justice for what they did. I can sympathise with how you feel.'

'Can you?'

'Of course I can. You don't think I'd wished I'd taken the law into my own hands sometimes? Some guy threatens your kids or a lawyer gets him off? Every cop has regrets. Just ask my dad here.'

'Well, that's going to be impossible in a few minutes.'

'Please. Don't.'

'No, Victoria, this has to happen.'

'Why do you want to make Dewar take the fall for it?'

'Easy. He's gone insane. Killed his mum and your dad.'

'No, why him?'

'For me to get off with this, I need a patsy. It was going to be McCrea, but I saw a chance to take out both of them. He makes perfect sense. Father killed by the Marksman. Driven insane by seeing the girls in that van. Besides, she screwed up the old Marksman case.'

'What are you talking about?'

'She stopped Torrance getting caught before we took him down. Dropped a call from a neighbour. Someone overlooking the stadium. We would've caught Torrance if she hadn't done that.'

'But Torrance killed her husband!'

'Still doesn't make it right what she did.'

'But you still caught him?'

'I did. But there were two other hits after that. Then he was interviewed by David fucking Dewar and HE LET HIM GO!'

Jesus. He'd really lost his mind.

Vicky stepped forward. 'Because Torrance made it personal, you caught him.'

'Right, you're starting to catch up.' He grabbed Vicky's ponytail and aimed his gun at her. Sweat was dripping down his face.

Vicky was trying to shake free. 'Please, don't!'

'I've got to.' Broadfoot wiped a hand across his mouth. 'This is our only way out of it. Don't worry, it won't hurt.'

'Please, I've got children.'

'So? Do you think I care?' Broadfoot pressed the barrel against her forehead. 'Do you think I give a shit about you?'

She wanted to bite off the fucker's nose. Finish what it looked like somebody else had started. 'And me and Billy Dewar? What have we ever done to you?'

'I'm sure there'll be something.'

'I can follow your logic to a point, but—'

'Join me.'

'What?'

'Join me, Vicky. You took a life.'

'What, I—'

'You killed someone in self-defence. Sure, he was going to kill you. But you know what it's like when a bad man dies. Someone who would escape justice.'

Broadfoot tumbled forward and took Vicky down with him. Her knee hit the fireplace with a crunch. Then she was horizontal. Something clattered to the ground.

Broadfoot was lying on her, a dead weight. He shuffled around and choked her from behind.

She scrabbled and tried to snatch his gun.

Shepherd was standing over them, holding his baton.

Broadfoot trained his gun on her, grabbed her ponytail. 'Don't you move! I'll kill her!'

Something battered off her nose, tore into her temple. She couldn't see. Everything was black. Then stars, then she was back in the room. Her nose was on fire.

Broadfoot hauled her up to standing, then aimed the gun at Shepherd now.

Vicky reached for it, patting at his hand.

He pushed her hand away.

She slapped at it.

The gun fired.

The window smashed.

Shepherd went down.

Vicky tried to move but Broadfoot grabbed her arm, his grip squeezing until she yelped. 'Let us go.'

'It's okay. It's all going to be okay.' Broadfoot stepped away and aimed at her father. 'Needs to look real, right?'

She timed it so she took out his leg just as he pulled the trigger.

His hand swayed but the bullet drove into Dad's chest.

'You shouldn't have done that.' Broadfoot grabbed her by the throat and pressed her against the wall, pressed the gun to her forehead again.

The barrel was still hot, searing her skin like a sirloin on a griddle.

'I asked you if you wanted to join me. But I'm going to kill you now.'

'You won't.' Vicky breathed in, swallowing back her emotions, keeping the words inside this time. A wave of nausea hit her. She tried to push herself away. No strength left. He was going to shoot her, shoot her father again and that was it.

Shepherd was on his feet, wheezing hard but primed like a sprinter. He was rocking on his heels, like he was ready to drive off, try to smack into Broadfoot. Like he didn't care he had a gun trained on him.

'Okay! I'll do it!'

Broadfoot locked his piercing blue eyes on Vicky. 'What?'

'Put the gun down. I'll join you.'

'He needs to die.'

'We both will. Luke, right?'

Shepherd nodded. 'Right.'

Broadfoot lowered the gun a touch.

Vicky shot forward and crashed into Broadfoot, pushing him over the armchair.

The gun scattered across the floor.

Shepherd picked it up and trained it on Broadfoot. 'This is where you tell me you've got friends in high places. How you'll get off with it all. How it was McCrea framing Dewar. Not you.'

'Listen, those guys worked for the Machine. They'll come after all of us.'

'Bullshit.'

'I'm serious. I don't care who you are, Shepherd, but they'll kill your sister and—'

Shepherd fired.

The sound tore into Vicky's ears.

Broadfoot screamed but Vicky couldn't hear anything. He slumped back onto the settee, then rolled off onto the floor. He lay there like a drunk, one foot twitching. Three times. Four times. And then it stopped. No sign of movement. Just a thick pool of blood coming from the wide tear in his stomach.

Vicky heard a voice from somewhere. Quiet, tiny, shrill, like a man trapped in a box:

'You okay?'

A wave of dull pain clanged at her temples. Different pain to the shit that'd been tormenting her all day. She touched it.

Blood, halfway to caking.

A hand grabbed her shoulder, pressing the flesh tight. 'Vicky?' Shepherd held out his hand.

'I'm fine.' Vicky blinked hard. Felt like she'd sliced a few layers off her eyeballs. 'What happened?'

Shepherd stood in the middle of the room, staring at the gun in his hand. He stared at Vicky, swallowed, then at Broadfoot's body. 'Well.'

Vicky got up and walked over. 'Drop it, Luke. Drop the gun.'

'I…'

'We need to make this look like McCrea turned on Broadfoot and they did a *Reservoir Dogs* on each other.'

Shepherd stared at her. 'No. I need to take the fall for this.'

'Luke. You're a good cop. I won't let you lose your career over two bad ones.' She snatched the gun from his hand, wiped it on her blouse, then put it in Broadfoot's hand. 'Okay?'

Shepherd was shaking his head. 'It's not right. I've spent my career taking down people like him.'

'I know. And you like things to be black and white. But sometimes they're shades of grey. I killed someone, Luke. Someone who'd get away with things. Who'd come after my children. I know what I'm doing. We need to act fast here.'

Shepherd glanced at her. 'This doesn't feel right, but I don't see any other way.'

63

Vicky opened her eyes. Felt like they were still shut. So dark in here. Can barely see anything. Felt as if she had a couple of old pennies stuck to her eyelids. Drenched in sweat. Odd. She felt cold and her hands were bone dry. She sat bolt upright. 'Dad?!'

She felt a hand on her arm. 'He's okay.'

Vicky looked around. Hospital corridor. The smell of hospital. Bleach. Arms aching. She glanced over. 'What?'

'Evening, you.' Shepherd sat in the next chair, almost tilted diagonally under his bulk. Mask on. 'Your dad's okay.'

Vicky tried to get up, but just collapsed back onto the chair. Panting. No energy. She stared up at the ceiling as it swirled above her.

The doctor appeared, then entered her dad's room.

'You fell asleep.' Shepherd got to his feet. 'I need to update Forrester, okay?'

'No. We need a chat.'

'No.'

'Come on, Luke.'

'Later, then.' He set off away.

She gave a fleeting smile and walked over to Dad's room. Every step ached. Vicky stopped, bracing herself against the wall.

Dad lay on the bed, tucked into his sheet, a drip coming out of his arm, piped into a machine, blood pouring in and out. He stared at the wall, like he could see the paint drying and it was more exciting than the truth. Barely breathing. Mouth twitching. Eyebrows lifting and falling. Fists clenched. He slumped back in the bed, the crisp sheets rustling and jagging his neck. He ran a hand through his hair. 'What happened?'

Vicky sat on a chair and leaned forward, rocking the chair. 'You got shot.'

'Jesus Christ.' Dad bared his teeth. 'Was that about the Marksman?'

'Sort of.'

'So what's it got to do with me?'

'Dad, he said you were watching the football when Antonio Bottone was killed in Tannadice.'

'I don't understand.'

Vicky bit her lip. 'You missed Torrance. You were right next to him.'

'Nobody blamed me.' Dad shook his head. 'I've had a lot of time to think about this stuff, Vicky. All of your life. Most of it, anyway. It happened, but I was just a wee laddie.'

'Still, Derek Broadfoot held a grudge against you.'

'Well, I'm glad he's dead. He can rot in hell.' Dad grabbed Vicky's hand and sandwiched it between his. 'Thank you. You saved me.'

'Dad, I was just in the right place at the right time.'

'Aye, but you could've stayed outside, waited for support. You came inside the house. That takes guts.'

'You saw it?'

'I did. Bastard drug. Kept my eyes open.'

'See what we discussed—'

'Shhh.' He put a finger to her lips. 'That didn't happen. Okay?'

'But I'm just like Broadfoot or McCrea.'

'Are you hell. You were backed into a corner. Your boss's boss had been covering it all up. He threatened your kids. What else were you going to do?'

She didn't have an answer.

'That wasn't some wee ned you've arrested coming to your house, okay? You'd never sleep if you didn't do what you did.'

'But I am just as bad. You can't argue with that.'

'I can. Broadfoot's mind rotted away. So much stress. He... Just killed people because he thought he could get away with it.'

SHEPHERD WAS SITTING in the Ninewells café.

Forrester stood up and left through the other door.

Vicky didn't know if that was to avoid her or what.

She needed to speak to Shepherd. Right now. She walked over and stood by his table. 'Hey, you okay?'

He held a coffee mug in his big bear hands. 'I've had better.'

'Mind if I sit?'

He frowned. 'Of course not.'

Vicky took the seat. 'How are you? I mean, really?'

Shepherd sat back and sighed. 'Well, now I know what it's

like to... kill somebody.' He whispered the last two words. 'We watched him go, Vicky. He died at my hand.'

'If you hadn't shot him, he'd have killed my dad. He'd have killed me next. Billy Dewar would be going down for a series of murders.'

'Doesn't make it right.'

'Doesn't make it wrong, either. You worked in the Complaints, right?'

That got a nod.

'It's all black and white there. But the world is shades of grey. You have to examine each shade and decide which it is. Black or white. And if it's black, you have to come down on them like a ton of feathers. Squash them, but by the rules.'

'Where's this going?'

'The world isn't black and white, Luke. The real world is grey. Broadfoot saw it that way. The resentment had festered away at him for years, until he saw that – even if we caught them – no conviction could ever be good enough. We didn't prosecute three members of a gang. They gave us information. That's the kind of stuff big cases have to deal with every day. Because of them, they put away over twenty men, six women. They recovered millions. Impounded drugs and other assets. Freed over a hundred. But Broadfoot couldn't see it that way. And he persuaded McCrea it was that way. The two of them cooked up this whole thing because he couldn't see it was all just shades of grey.'

'But how do I look at myself in the mirror when I shave in the morning?'

'Grow a beard.'

Shepherd glared at her. Then laughed. 'Jesus.' He ran a hand down his face. 'I'm serious. How do you deal with it?'

'Deal with what?'

'Knowing you killed someone.'

'It was an accident, Luke. Self-defence. He came at me with a knife. We tussled. He fell down.'

'You stabbed him in the cock and he bled out.'

'Right.' She stared up at the ceiling fan, still flapping around in November. 'I'm not sleeping, Luke. That's the truth. But the more I talk about it to people I trust – Sharon, Dad, you – the easier it gets and the less I beat myself up about it. I had a choice, just like you had a choice back there. But there's no "do nothing" option in situations like that. It's all or nothing. You had to kill him or watch him kill my dad, then kill me. I had to choose whether he killed me and came after my kids or... That's the decision I had to make in a split second. Sharon persuaded me to stab myself with the murder weapon to get me off.' She touched the scar on her abdomen. 'But I'd do it again to save my kids.'

'I'd do it again to save you. To save your dad.' Shepherd smiled. 'Funnily enough, when I told him, David persuaded me to make my statement match what you said.'

'You told him?'

'I'm an honest man. Except for one thing.' Shepherd shrugged. 'I am still working for the Complaints. Undercover, to root out corruption in Serious Crimes. And wider.'

'Jesus. You were investigating Scott Cullen?'

'Not quite. But that's in the past. Just so happened you lost a DS on Sunday, but I was to provide maternity cover for DS Woods.'

'What are you investigating?'

'Nasty shit. We think there's a network of twenty-odd ex-cops. It's bad, Vicky. Very bad. All across Britain. But we've got two of them now.' His fingernails drummed the tabletop. 'And Forrester raised suspicions about you.'

'Jesus. About—'

'I'll clear you.'

'What? But how could he know?'

'He didn't. But he had suspicions. That's all.' Shepherd smiled at her. 'Like I said, Vicky, you're a good cop. You did what anyone would do. Hell, I did what you did.'

'Doesn't make it right.'

'No, Vicky. It doesn't make it wrong. I'm starting to see the world is shades of grey.'

AFTERWORD

Hey,

I hope you enjoyed that book.

It was good fun to write, actually. In the end. This book has been burning away for a long time, since 2014, after I wrote the first of Vicky's books (now the second). It was a collaboration with Allan Guthrie and it took us until 2019 and several hours of work to realise it didn't work.

But I had a lot of investigative stuff I liked in those drafts. Stuff that ate away at my brain. And I decided to turn it into more Vicky Dodds books. Took a lot more effort to change things than I anticipated, but I'm really pleased with the outcome. There's a lot of stuff I discovered as I was editing it, like the connection Vicky and Fenchurch shared over stuff they'd done. How the villains mirrored what she'd done.

And I hope you liked seeing my other three series leads appearing in this book. Cullen was obvious as the case originally took them north but I thought it'd be nice to have Vicky and Shepherd team up here, and he "works for" Cullen.

Fenchurch, though, that was something I improvised. I had an idea that it was a dog handler in Fife who was doing it, but things started to slot into place. Derek Broadfoot featured in the sixth Fenchurch book, KILL THE MESSENGER, as a bit of a dickhead. And Damian McCrea has been in a few Cullen books, starting with the fifth, COPS AND ROBBERS. I do like cross-pollinating my books like that, kind of what Marvel Comics used to do and what they're doing now in the Marvel Cinematic Universe. It connects all the stories together now and puts a nice, neat bow on.

If you haven't read any of the others, I suggest you start at the start with Cullen's first book, GHOST IN THE MACHINE, which came out almost ten years ago, or Fenchurch's first, THE HOPE THAT KILLS. Either way, let me know how you get on.

Huge thanks to James Mackay for the brutal edits, Allan Guthrie for help with the story, John Rickards for copy editing and Mare Bate for proofing.

What's next?

Well, a series starring Luke Shepherd is kind of itching at me. Feels like there's something in it. Sign up to my newsletter to see if I do anything with it!

And I've got to make Fenchurch's life a misery in December, so be there for THE LAST THING TO DIE.

And if there's more Vicky? Well, hopefully enough of you will buy this to make it worth the pain.

I did the bulk of the work on this after a recurrence of my atrial fibrillation, so it was nice having something to focus on. I had a procedure at the end of April to zap it back to normal and six weeks on, it's rock solid and I'm feeling the fittest I ever have. The cause was downing frozen smoothies, so I feel a bit daft. Thank you for all the well wishes I've had over the time.

And if you could leave a review for this title wherever you find it, that'd really help me.

Thanks,

Ed James

Scottish Borders, June 2022

ABOUT THE AUTHOR

Ed James writes crime-fiction novels, primarily the DI Simon Fenchurch series, set on the gritty streets of East London featuring a detective with little to lose. His Scott Cullen series features a young Edinburgh detective constable investigating crimes from the bottom rung of the career ladder he's desperate to climb.

Formerly an IT project manager, Ed began writing on planes, trains and automobiles to fill his weekly commute to London. He now writes full-time and lives in the Scottish Borders, with his girlfriend and a menagerie of rescued animals.

If you would like to be kept up to date with new releases from Ed James, please join the Ed James Readers Club.

OTHER BOOKS BY ED JAMES

SCOTT CULLEN MYSTERIES SERIES

Eight novels featuring a detective eager to climb the career ladder, covering Edinburgh and its surrounding counties, and further across Scotland.

1. GHOST IN THE MACHINE
2. DEVIL IN THE DETAIL
3. FIRE IN THE BLOOD
4. STAB IN THE DARK
5. COPS & ROBBERS
6. LIARS & THIEVES
7. COWBOYS & INDIANS
8. HEROES & VILLAINS

CULLEN & BAIN SERIES

Six novellas spinning off from the main Cullen series covering the events of the global pandemic in 2020.

1. CITY OF THE DEAD
2. WORLD'S END
3. HELL'S KITCHEN
4. GORE GLEN
5. DEAD IN THE WATER
6. THE LAST DROP

CRAIG HUNTER SERIES

A spin-off series from the Cullen series, with Hunter first featuring in the fifth book, starring an ex-squaddie cop struggling with PTSD, investigating crimes in Scotland and further afield.

1. MISSING
2. HUNTED
3. THE BLACK ISLE

DS VICKY DODDS SERIES

Gritty crime novels set in Dundee and Tayside, featuring a DS juggling being a cop and a single mother.

1. BLOOD & GUTS
2. TOOTH & CLAW
3. FLESH & BLOOD
4. SKIN & BONE
5. GUILT TRIP

DI SIMON FENCHURCH SERIES

Set in East London, will Fenchurch ever find what happened to his daughter, missing for the last ten years?

1. THE HOPE THAT KILLS
2. WORTH KILLING FOR
3. WHAT DOESN'T KILL YOU
4. IN FOR THE KILL
5. KILL WITH KINDNESS
6. KILL THE MESSENGER

7. DEAD MAN'S SHOES
8. A HILL TO DIE ON
9. THE LAST THING TO DIE

Other Books

Other crime novels, with Lost Cause set in Scotland and Senseless set in southern England, and the other three set in Seattle, Washington.

- LOST CAUSE
- SENSELESS
- TELL ME LIES
- GONE IN SECONDS
- BEFORE SHE WAKES

Manufactured by Amazon.ca
Acheson, AB